THE
HIGHWAY OF DEATH

JS MACEACHERN

THE HIGHWAY OF DEATH

PILWILLA PUBLISHING

The Highway of Death © 2021 by JS MacEachern.

www.jsmaceachern.com

Cover Design by LMH and DJR @ *www.djr.com*

Cover Photo by Krivosheev Vitaly

ISBN: 978-1-7378115-1-0

To Mom, *for instilling a love of stories.*

To Dad, *for living some of these.*

Gloria,

Enjoy the ride down the Highway of Death!

[signature]

AUTHOR'S NOTE: In the 1980's and early 1990's, Route 101 in New Hampshire — a two lane highway running from Manchester to the seacoast — had one of the highest rates of fatalities per mile of roadway in the United States. Locals called it the Highway of Death. The following is a lie about that truth.

PART I
JUNE

CHAPTER ONE

A phone call at 2 AM meant two things to Will Boucher: misfortune for others and money for him.

Will threw the single sheet covering him aside, slid out of bed, and picked up the phone on the fifth ring.

"Will?"came the voice through the line.

"Yeah?" he answered, rubbing the stubble on his face with one hand and cradling the phone with the other.

"It's Lonnie in dispatch. You up for a tow?"

"Yeah," Will replied, doing his best to stifle a yawn, "sure, what is it?"

"Another up on 101 westbound side, almost into Epping, but still in Derryfield." Lonnie spoke quickly, his tongue flicking off the words, driven by caffeine and memory and imagination. "Single vehicle, passenger car, off the roadway," he continued. "Fatal."

"Another?" Will sighed before suppressing another yawn.

"Yeah, another. I called Skip's last time, you're not getting them all."

"I know, I know."

"Responders including the Troopers should only be at the scene another hour or so cleaning up, if you can make your way over now," Lonnie added.

"Yeah," Will said, "I'll head over now. Thanks."

Will hung up the phone, stretched his arms over his head, and craned his head from side to side, relishing the crack as his neck popped. He turned on the bedside lamp and stared at the green floral print on the walls. A print his mother had picked out years ago, a print he had hated then and didn't care enough about one way or the other now. He remembered putting up the wallpaper with his father over ten years ago, before he had left for college. Felt strange, he thought, sleeping in his father and mother's bedroom. But his old room didn't have a phone line, and he needed to be near the phone for calls like this.

Will stepped into yesterday's jeans, still on the floor beside the bed, pulled a shirt on over his head, and stopped before the mirror across the room. His brown hair erupted from his scalp like an overgrown hedge, and he grabbed the battered Red Sox cap — frayed on the brim — to cover up his unruly cut. He pocketed his keys and wallet on the nightstand, and left his parents' bedroom. He passed his bedroom down the hall, the door closed. He hadn't stepped inside in over a year, not since his mother had left for the nursing home. Daisy's room — his only sibling and older sister — was similarly unused, though hers was mostly empty after she had taken her effects with her on the move to California.

His stomach growled so Will stopped before the avocado green GE refrigerator. He realized that this too was unchanged from his parent's time, and it was the only refrigerator he had known in this house. The light from the fridge spilled out across his feet and illuminated the kitchen behind him, revealing the table still piled high with half-read *Derryfield Gazette* newspapers and never-read mail.

The refrigerator shelves held little: a carton of milk, orange juice, a half-eaten package of hotdogs, a loaf of bread missing a third of its slices, and a jar of pickles. The milk was past its date, so Will grabbed the carton of orange juice and downed a few swallows as he moved towards the kitchen light and snapped it on. After slipping into his boots, Will grabbed the keys and headed for the door. He paused on his way out and glanced back into the front hall and kitchen and imagined Mom and Dad sitting at the table in the shadows, one of their old dogs underfoot — Kacie or perhaps Pudge, named after Red Sox catcher Carlton Fisk.

As Will expected, the white 1990 F-350 diesel in the driveway burped for a moment, as if trying to dislodge a lingering unpleasant taste, before roaring to life. The engine hiccuped and chattered along, and Will cranked the radio up. U2's newest single, *Hold Me, Thrill Me, Kiss Me, Kill Me*, filled the cab. The closest neighbors were about a half-mile away; he knew the noise wouldn't bother them at this level. The air was still heavy and wet, even at this hour. Will rolled down the window and hooked his left elbow on the edge of the door as he drove, letting the air from driving work up his sleeve and into his shirt, hoping that it would draw some of the moisture and heat off his chest.

Derryfield was quiet this late at night. Within five minutes Will had approached the circle at the eastern edge of town and rounded it, passing his father's — well now his — shop. He slowed as he did so and leaned slightly out the window, confirming that all was as he had left it yesterday. No amount of locks or security systems or guarantees of insurance could replace the comfort of putting eyes on the family's livelihood and ensuring that everything was as it should be.

The few traffic lights near the center of town all blinked yellow in unison and cast a lemon strobe across the barren parking spots, empty storefronts, and crumbling mills. It made Will think of *Escape from New York*, like a post-apocalyptic landscape, devoid of life but still bearing its touch. The heavy air changed as he drew closer to the center of town and closer to the Pilwilla River: the atmosphere became thick with the scent of decaying vegetation that lined its banks, as well as a sharp odor that lingered with every breath like a metallic aftertaste.

Will didn't see another soul until he entered the on ramp and merged onto Route 101. Even this late on a Thursday, or rather at this point, early on a Friday, the traffic on Route 101 was heavy. Some act was playing the venue down on the boardwalk in Hampton, Will remembered, but he couldn't remember who it was. Some small time comedian or journeyman band most likely, managing to make a living in entertainment but struggling, popular enough to fill a small venue in a small city in a small state. Will drove, enjoying the weather and trying not to dwell on the white crosses every few miles that stood silent testament to those who had previously died on this stretch of road.

After a few miles traffic began to slow on the highway and Will knew he was close. This was the second fatal accident he was responding to that week, and though the tows helped fill the time and his wallet, responding was never easy. The only part of the job he really liked was helping people: getting their cars off the road, fixing what was wrong, and getting it back to them. He couldn't do much for the dead.

The Ford rounded a corner, and Will spied a collection of Crown Vics ahead, pulled to the opposite shoulder. The flashing lights of the cruisers illuminated the passing cars with a dim blue glow reminiscent of a bar near closing time. Two officers stood by the road, directing traffic. The eastbound lane was closed. The officers slowed and stopped one lane, letting it pass, and then alternated, slowing and stopping the other to let that lane pass. From his vantage point high in the cab of the Ford, Will could see over the line of cars in the lane before him. The man in front of him, sitting in a green Mercury Sable, rubbed his head with his left hand while his right sat atop the steering wheel. Someone sounded a horn in the traffic ahead, a mechanically assisted cry of frustration. The next car ahead — a blue Chevrolet Malibu, speckled with rust — held a woman with her head tilted back, staring into the cloth roof of her car.

In a minute the cars in front of him began moving, and as Will approached the scene he pulled the Ford over onto the shoulder behind the closest Crown Vic.

One of the officers — Officer Dougherty — walked over towards the wrecker. Will stepped out of the truck and waved to him.

"Hey Will," Dougherty said. At 26, Dougherty was a few years younger than Will, though much taller and considerably broader. He carried his cap under one arm, and with the other ran his hand through his short brown hair. "Fucking hot," Dougherty said.

"Yeah, one of those nights," Will said.

"I wish they'd let us wear shorts, you know?" A ring of sweat ran under his arms, staining his dark blue uniform a shade darker.

"Yeah, I know." Will pointed to his jeans and added: "I've got to wear these things, crawling around on the ground, gravel and glass and all."

"You too then." Dougherty began walking towards the wreck and Will fell in beside him. "At least the Chief's OK with us not wearing our vests on these kinds of days. Just too damn hot for them."

"Yeah, at least you got that." Will looked to the vehicle and back to Dougherty. "Fatal, Lonnie said on the phone. Single vehicle."

"Yeah, fatal," Dougherty responded, nodding along, "The LT will tell you more. I've got to get back," he added, motioning with his thumb back to the line of cars.

"Well good to see you," Will said.

"You too." Dougherty turned and walked back towards the line of cars waiting for direction.

"Billy!" Lieutenant Hebert said, waving to Will. "Over here!" Lieutenant Hebert was an old Frenchman, due to retire two years ago. His years on the force were slowing him down, and it showed in his waistline and jowls, as they continued to expand each year in step with his paycheck. The shock of black hair atop his head was peppered with grey, and his eyes were clear blue, slightly hidden now by his drooping eyelids.

"Lieutenant Hebert." Will walked over and raised a hand in return. "Hey, how are you?"

"Good Billy, all things considered. Damn hot night though. You?"

"Will please, Lieutenant. Billy was fine as a kid, but..."

"Ah sorry, I know, I know. You told me last time too. Didn't mean anything of it. I'm an old man you know," he said, "forget things like this." He seemed to enjoy reminding those around him of his age, as if it provided some immunity from the criticisms or corrections and added some additional luster to his accomplishments as a Lieutenant.

"It's fine," Will said, "Anyways, Jesus, hot night. The humidity is killing me."

"Killing him too." Hebert nodded over to the wreck. He laughed once, a short guffaw expressing his pleasure at thinking of the joke.

"What happened?" Will asked. From where he stood he could see the rear end of the vehicle, a late '80s model Toyota from the look of it. The front end of the vehicle met an oak tree down off the embankment. The tree had come out the better party to the collision. Will could smell the gas and fluids bleeding from the ruined Toyota.

"No other vehicles involved," Hebert began, turning his attention away from Will and towards the wreck. "Went right off the road, down the embankment and hit that tree." He pointed towards the vehicle. "Operator was thrown through the windshield. Not wearing a seatbelt, you know, and likely drunk. They usually are."

"Yeah," Will said, thinking of all the other wrecks caused by drunks he had pulled in the last few years.

"Well, don't call it the Highway of Death for nothing, eh?"

"Yeah, guess not."

Hebert shook his head. "Damn shame, but that's what you get with a road like this. Too many people driving too fast, liquored up from a night out. Road's too small for it all. They've got to finish the damn expansion. It's taking them long enough."

"You surprised by that?" Will said and laughed.

"No, not at all. Honestly, can't half blame 'em. Could go for a cold beer on a night like tonight myself. Always enjoyed sharing one with your old man."

"Yeah, I'm not surprised," Will said, his tone even. His memory of his father's drinking was not one of enjoyment. The old man had liked his lager, liked it often, and when he liked it, his temper came out, usually at his family. Will could only guess at what Hebert knew of his father as a drinker; from what Will had been told by many — most of it at his father's wake — the memories were probably fond, alcohol sweetened remembrances of drinks shared at the Hilltop.

After a few moments, Hebert added, "Well, the State Troopers already finished up. The DOT guys are looking it over, but this seems pretty straight forward and I think they're about finished up with the scene too. You bring it over to the lot once you have it on the truck."

"Will do," Will replied before walking back to the Ford.

Will raised his hand and nodded to the officers directing traffic. They nodded back to him, waved a few more vehicles by, then stopped both lanes and motioned for Will to drive over. Will pulled into the road and backed down the shoulder towards the wreck, preparing to get it up on his truck. First he lowered the flat bed, bringing it level to the road. Then he unhooked the winch and grabbed the cable with its thick metal hook at the end, pulling it behind him down the embankment and towards the vehicle.

The Tercel had crumpled on impact. The hood was curled up like the top of a bean can and the fender below it was caved in, the liquids of the engine and transmission wetting the ground below. As he drew closer and the sounds of the people and vehicles behind him grew quieter, Will could make out the steady drip of the fluids into the puddles below the Tercel. The smell of the accident grew stronger: gas and brake fluid and an earthy smell that Will figured was the burst bark and sap seeping from the battered tree.

A jagged hole looking like the maw of some beast lay dead center of the windshield, blood ringing its edges. One wheel, tire still intact, lay thirty feet ahead, having broken free from the axle and after, apparently carried forward to its current resting place by the force of the impact.

Will checked the area behind the vehicle for glass or debris. Finding none, he knelt down, the metal hook heavy in his hand. He snagged the hook on the rear frame near the center of the vehicle and pulled it tight. As he stood he heard something, a noise to his right off into the darkness, beyond the cone of light shed by the F-350 and the swirling blue atop the police cruisers. The rustling sounded like something large moving in the darkness. Will stood still, the hairs on his arms rising in the humid air, and stared into the darkness. His focus deafened the sounds of the traffic. He scanned the area behind the Tercel but saw nothing aside from a handful of white cedar trees. After a few moments he took in a deep breath and shrugged; likely just something out in the wetlands that ran alongside Route 101.

Will climbed the embankment back to the F-350 and engaged the winch. It whined as it withdrew the cable onto its spool, and slowly dragged the Tercel back towards the road. The whining of the winch increased in pitch as it pulled the Tercel to the embankment. Rather than force it up the embankment, Will locked the cable and eased the F-350 forward. It pulled the Tercel back onto the side of the road, where Will winched the vehicle onto the flatbed and hopped back into the cab.

Will craned his head out of the window and asked: "Lieutenant, where you want it?"

"Just take it over to the lot. Troopers'll be by later in the week if they want it. Drop it in the back corner, away from the station. Thanks Billy," Hebert said.

"Yeah," Will answered, not bothering to correct Hebert again. He activated his emergency lights, maneuvered around the police cruiser blocking traffic, and set off for Derryfield.

Towing and repairing vehicles didn't normally lend itself to introspection, but Will always found these rides the most disquieting, knowing that behind him lay a man or woman's final ride. He found nothing inherently wrong about dying in — or in this case, just outside of — a car. After all, motor vehicles were his life, and his father's before him. But dying alone thrown out of a Toyota Tercel against a tree off of Route 101 in Derryfield, New Hampshire? No dignity in that death.

The hour picking up the Toyota hadn't changed Derryfield. The town still slept as Will worked his way back through the quiet streets. The houses were dark, the mills by the Pilwilla River empty. Will slowed and looked longingly at the shuttered remains of King's Chicken. A favorite hangout of his during high school, the place had closed sometime after Will had left for college. The owner, Jacob Reilly, had moved down south to Florida to enjoy his retirement years. Will had heard the management who had purchased the property ran the place into the ground and it had closed within 10 months of the transfer. He wasn't sure what disappointed him more: that the place had shut down after Jacob left, or that someone else had run it so incompetently that it had closed.

As Will neared the police station he saw its lights shining bright in the early morning air, the yellowed boxes of the windows glowing like an oasis in the darkness. While most of Derryfield slept, Will knew that a few still stood watch, mainly police, firefighters, some EMTs and perhaps a single taxicab driver. Will pulled into the parking lot and up to the back gate and honked. Lonnie's face appeared in the nearest window, his eyes scrunched together as he peered out to identify the source of the honking, his long white mustache plainly identifiable even at this distance.

Still not wearing his glasses, Will thought, and raised his hand to wave. Lonnie waved back and moved away from the window. A moment later the gate mechanism of the lot clanked to life and moved the fencing out of his way. Will dropped the vehicle in the far corner as Hebert had directed. He avoided looking at the bloody ring of broken glass in the windshield, hoping to forget the ragged hole and remains of human tissue.

The drive home was similarly quiet, Derryfield yet to wake. By the time Will was pulling into his driveway it was nearly four in the morning; too late to get back in bed but too early to enjoy the time, the dead space between night and morning. Figuring he had nothing better to do, Will started a cup of coffee, grabbed yesterday's *Derryfield Gazette*, and waited for dawn.

CHAPTER TWO

Erica thought the walk from her car to the office would be easy. She thought it would be a return to a routine, like a record player needle falling into the groove or the familiar feeling of slipping into a favorite pair of jeans. But a part of her was gone from this world and the bulk of humanity didn't care. The world spun on and no one recognized what had changed and what was lost.

She stopped in the parking lot and stared at the Franklin Building. It was one of the older buildings in downtown Derryfield, a red brick three story structure built in the last century and plodding towards the next. It's survival was not perhaps one of engineering marvel but instead that of fortuitous location and material: far enough from the Pilwilla to avoid the major flooding that occurred every generation or so in Derryfield, and a structure of brick resistant to the fire that had swept through downtown in 1936 and destroyed many of the stick built structures. A survivor, like herself.

Erica tried to push the thoughts away and to smile as she entered the building. She nodded briefly towards a man standing just inside the doorway but dropped her head and started quickly for the stairs. She went up, avoiding the basement which housed the enormous presses that printed the bulk of the *Derryfield Gazette* that would be couriered across much of southern New Hampshire. She climbed the steps towards past the first floor and towards the second floor, both of which held a collection of cafes and offices including the paper's bull-pen. The third floor contained the administration and billing offices of the paper as well as a few legal services offices.

While attractive from the exterior — even sporting a few areas of verdant green vines along its brick — in contrast the interior of the building was worn down, the carpets thin, the stairs themselves eroded with visible valleys on the sides of each step by hundreds of footsteps over a hundred years. Erica looked down at those valleys as she climbed to the second floor. Upon entering the second floor she glanced up once at the white painted exposed pipes that ran along the ceiling, their twins evident in every room in the building, later additions that modernized the heating and plumbing systems but which also left further imperfections in nearly every space.

"Good to see you back Erica," Katie, the second floor receptionist said over the wall of her cubicle as Erica entered the office, Katie's hair a flash of red over the beige of her cubicle wall. Katie dropped back into her seat and by the time Erica was alongside her station and could peek over the wall Katie was back on the telephone, likely speaking to a reporter out of the office on assignment or directing a call to someone still here.

"Good to see you, too, Katie," Erica replied. She was certain that Katie could not hear her over the general din of the newsroom and the sounds of whatever conversation she was now involved in, but the response itself felt a bit cathartic, once again an attempt at a return to the normal. The air was filled with the clacking of keyboards and typewriters and the hushed tones of muffled telephone conversations. It sounded familiar and comforting.

It had been a week and a half since Erica Couture had last been at work. In her last seven years as a reporter for the *Derryfield Gazette* she had never been absent for so long: even her vacations were usually under a week. Vacations did not sit well with her. Time sitting idle only brought to mind what she wasn't doing, and what work was waiting for her when she returned, a never ending pile-up of assignments like a car crash on a foggy road, new traffic hurtling in to make an even larger mess. The same restlessness had carried her through four years of college at UNH in Dover, a stint with an advertising firm in Manchester, and now continued at the Gazette, reinforced with the looming deadlines and occasional praise when those same deadlines were met.

Erica glanced around the office and was relieved to sense the growing feeling of familiarity and comfort in being back where she felt she belonged. No matter the loss she felt, there was work to be done. Most in the cubicles were ignorant of her passing presence, engrossed in a phone call call or computer screen or typewriter, but Erica didn't mind. Being back in the office was return enough. As hard as the last two weeks had been, being out of work had only compounded it, had given her the time to ruminate on her loss. Work would at worst prove a distraction.

"Hi," Erica said to Sarah, the receptionist for the local reporters. Sarah was a few years older than Erica and the two had shared drinks after work on a few occasions, but their differences were too great to form a solid friendship. Sarah was married, a son in elementary school, and more interested in discussing the struggling Celtics or hapless Red Sox than anything else. They didn't even look as if they should be friends: Erica short and slim, her hair a dark auburn and cut to the shoulders, Sarah tall and with wide hips, her blonde hair running halfway down her back in a tight ponytail.

"Hi!" Sarah smiled. "Good to see you. How are you holding up hun?"

Erica knew she would be asked this, but still was not ready for its asking. She had thought about it, thought about what she might say to properly describe herself — she was distraught, depressed, yet relieved the service was over, the extended family gone from Derryfield, and herself back to work. Instead, she said: "I'm fine, thanks." The silence between them that followed lasted a moment too long and Erica asked: "Any messages for me?"

"Let me see," Sarah said and tapped her left index finger on her cheek. With the other hand she flipped through a stack of paper on her desk and said: "No, no, nothing here. There may be some on your desk though, I think a few calls did come in. Might be something there, worth checking."

"I will, thanks."

As was usual for the late morning, the floor was teeming with activity as reporters finished up drafts and editors reviewed those drafts and prepared tomorrow's paper to print. Phil Lewindowski, another reporter who mostly covered sports, raised a hand as Erica walked past but said nothing, and it took Erica a moment to spot the phone cradled against Phil's left shoulder. A few other staff members caught her eye and raised a hand in greeting, but none interrupted their work or made their way over to Erica. Erica smiled and raised a hand up quickly before dropping it back to her side.

Erica slipped her messenger bag off her shoulder and pulled out her chair. Frank Harris, the managing editor of the paper, emerged from his den of an office and stomped over to Erica's desk. "Glad to have you back," he said. "Most of the assholes around here," Frank continued, taking an exaggerated look over his left, then right shoulder, "couldn't report a story if it took a shit on their desk and wrote them the lede."

Erica smiled at the remark, but didn't laugh. She'd heard the same refrain from Frank nearly every week for the last five years, and knew others heard the same when he walked them into his office. Frank was quick to point out that other than ten years in his father's taxidermy studio from the ages of 12 to 22, he had never done anything else but work at the paper. He had never married, and was thin to the point that others in the office, often similarly single women, would offer him pasta or cookies or soup, which he would always initially decline but finally relent and accept. He appeared to eat it all, but never gained the weight others expected, though most realized that his constant pacing and brooding and yelling 12 or more hours a day, five (or even six) days a week certainly worked to counter the calories he consumed.

"How are things going?" Erica asked.

Frank ignored the question and provided the answer he always would: what news he was working on covering.

"We've got OJ stuff coming in off the wire. I've got Richard up in the Lakes on Motorcycle Weekend, Beth is covering the graduations, and Dave's still in Concord on the legislature before they adjourn for the year."

"Who's on crime?"

"Jeff and Peter of course," he answered. "Susan's also working. She's up at the AG's as we speak."

"I want back on crime," Erica said. Susan had not been working crime two weeks ago; Jeff and Peter and Erica had all worked that beat, each covering different parts of the state. Erica knew what Susan's assignment to the AG's meant.

"I understand." Frank pursed his lips. "I want Susan to have a little time doing it, OK?"

"Frank, I don't want business, I don't want sports, I don't want

Concord. I gave those a shot. I want to be back on district, back on crime."

Frank rubbed his forehead. "I said I understand, but I've got to give Susan a chance. See if she likes it. It's good she gets a taste of it." Erica started as if to speak, but Frank held up his hand and continued: "Plus, you've been through quite a bit lately, you should get a break from that shit. I want you assisting Karen on some local interest, follow up on some leads. Assist her with the drafting, some editing before it hits someone else's desk."

Erica felt her emotions rising, a swirl of anger seeped with something deeper, a fury and sadness she had carried for the last two weeks. "What the hell Frank," Erica said, "you want me to babysit Karen for you? I'm here to report and write."

"I get it," Frank responded. "I do, I do. I've got the word from up above and they want some more local stories, the flavor of New Hampshire, tales of granite and maple syrup. Karen's working on some of that. You're on it now too, give you a chance to pen some of your own."

When she said nothing he continued: "Something for the locals and something for the tourists here for the season. Educate them about the finer points of New Hampshire living."

"Christ." Erica sighed and pinched the bridge of her nose between her right thumb and index finger. "So what, Old Man of the Mountain? Mount Washington? The Presidential Primary? What's it going to be?"

"Something like that." Frank smiled again. Occasionally, on occasions such as this, his smile unnerved Erica. She had no reason to be unnerved around Frank — he had treated her fairly for years, critiqued and edited her writing and provided professional advice — but his smile always struck her as predatory, the kind of grin one would imagine a fox made when cornering a hen.

"Fill the back pages with feel good stories of Yankee ingenuity?" Erica shook her head.

"I knew I kept you around here for something," Frank replied, smiling again. "Today Karen's working on a story about the recent graduates in Derryfield, what the class is planning on next, and she has another slated to go about the new supermarket opening in

Manchester. She has a list of other ideas that came through at the weekly meeting. Will have another next week for a fresh batch."

"And for me?"

"Work off her list, and get creative. I'm giving you a bit of latitude here. Put something interesting on my desk. But to get you started: heard there's some issue staffing the city park and pool."

Erica grabbed a notebook off her desk and asked: "Anything else?" As the words left her mouth she realized she had done a poor job of masking her annoyance.

"Don't cop an attitude with me," Frank said. His voice was stern although the corners of his mouth were beginning to pull back into another smile. "You just told me you want back on crime, some better assignments, right?"

"Yes, you know I do."

Frank nodded and continued walking into his office. He looked over his shoulder as he spoke. "A while back you said you wanted something with more... how did you put it?" He asked and laughed, his laugh inviting no answer. "More long form. You wanted to write some prose." He dragged out the word prose as he maintained eye contact with her.

"Yes," Erica said, holding in a sigh.

"Well this is your chance. Write me some prose about the fine state of this State. Tell the readers something they don't know about New Hampshire."

When she didn't say anything he continued: "Like I said, I'm giving you some latitude here. Karen will run point, help her when she asks, but give me some of your own. I need at least one a day in addition to whatever you help Karen with. Impress me and the fellows upstairs. You got it?"

"Yes."

Erica only looked at his retreating back for a moment, his shoulder blades prominent through the thin fabric of his shirt, before turning to her desk and collapsing into her chair and checking her pager out of habit. In contrast to nearly every other cubicle in the office, Erica's was neat, the little paper on her desk stacked in two columns. Someone must have gone through her desk while she was on leave, making sure to confirm that all her articles were in, and had left the desk even cleaner for the act. Probably Frank, ensuring the paper was filled with as many stories as could be fit between the advertisements on every page. Erica shifted forward and grabbed the sweater off the back of her chair and slipped it on; though the temperature outside was set to crest 80, the office temperature was at least 15 degrees cooler than that. She leafed through the documents that remained, as much to bring herself up to speed as to avoid — for a few minutes at least — the work with Karen that would follow.

Erica's distraction didn't last long. She had only made it through half of one stack when Karen lumbered past Erica's cubicle and said, "Hey!", her tone a mixture of surprise and delight. Karen was only a few years older than Erica, but the years showed. Her hair already streaked with gray, and her normal attire — a blouse and ankle length skirt — added even more years to the total. Erica didn't like the assignment, but she had to admit that she did — for the most part — like Karen. Karen enjoyed the work, enjoyed speaking with people, enjoyed the writing; she enjoyed being a reporter. And she did so with good cheer and a straight forward manner which Erica knew to be genuine. Karen was always pleasant, but didn't much care what others thought of her. She didn't color her graying hair; she didn't wear make-up, or heels; she didn't jockey for new assignments or push other reporters off a story. She just did the jobs assigned to her and did them well.

"So I hear you're with me," Karen said, her mouth breaking into a wide grin. She didn't wait for a response from Erica. "Glad to have you on board. Actually, glad to have you back." The nearly constant smile vanished for a moment. "I'm a, I'm very sorry for your loss."

"Thanks," Erica said, eyes downcast. Desperately searching for a transition away from this topic, she asked: "What are you working on?"

"Well," Karen said, her smile assuming its normal place, "I've got a telephone call set up early this afternoon with the Superintendent of the Derryfield SAU to discuss the graduating seniors and all of their plans, and I'm waiting for a call back from the recreation department about the staffing issues at the pool and park — Frank keyed me into that one. I have been told that they are still having issues filling those positions, and that the town might have to limit the schedule for both if not enough people are available to staff. I've got a list of other topics as well, all signed off on from *above*." She emphasized the last word with a raise of her eyebrows. "It's not the most exciting stuff, but much of it's good news, good things to print." She smiled and cocked her head and awaited a response from Erica.

Erica grunted affirmatively.

"What do you want?" Karen asked. "I'll let you have the pick of the litter."

"Can I see the list?" Karen handed her the list and Erica glanced over it. She saw nothing that particularly interested her until she spied a line two-thirds down the page reading *Summer Construction/ Route 101 Expansion??*. That damn road had taken many lives over the last ten years. It had claimed one of its latest victims, her brother Nate, only two weeks ago. Erica knew that there was no sense in his death, no reason for it, but perhaps a story about the construction and the deaths on 101 could do something, spark some change, whether in the road or herself she wasn't sure. It just seemed to be the right thing to do: focus on the story and get it out there, work it until she somehow made sense of it all.

"I'll..." Erica started, then hesitated, her mind on 101, "I'll cover the staffing issues at the Rec. You talk to them already?"

"I've got a call in, but no call back yet," Karen said.

"I'll follow up." Erica nodded and stared at the list. "I'll follow up with them. I'll look into this one too," she added quickly, pointing to the summer construction listing. "Can get out on the road with it, visit some of the sites, talk to the DOT or Road Agents involved."

If Karen recognized the import of that listing and the reason for Erica's sudden interest, she said nothing of it. Instead she said: "Sounds wonderful, provided the AC in your vehicle is running well. It is, I presume?"

Erica laughed once, amused and thankful for Karen's concern.

"It is, it is. What's the time frame on these? As long as we get one in, Frank's not being a hard ass about the content each day, is he?"

"No, he's not thankfully. Get him one a day and he's happy."

"Great. Well, don't let me keep you," Erica said. "Once I speak to Rec and get what I need from them, I'll get a draft to you, and vice versa on the graduation article, right?"

"Just what I was thinking," Karen said, smiling again. "Great minds think alike, right?" Karen laughed; others might think it was forced — too loud and too long — but Erica knew it to be genuine, just the way Karen enjoyed her harmless wit. Erica laughed back and turned to her desk as Karen returned to hers.

Erica picked up the phone and thinking still of Nate and 101, dialed the Derryfield Parks and Recreation Department, wondering at the same time how long this would be her future at the paper.

CHAPTER THREE

The first day of summer is always the sweetest. For Corey Barrington, twelve years old, the ten or so weeks of summer before him were limitless with possibility.

He stretched his legs and arms but remained in bed, staring for a moment at the poster of Jurassic Park he had pinned to the ceiling last year. The radio or television was on in the kitchen, and Corey could hear the voice of a newscaster from down the hallway. He couldn't quite make out the words, but from the cadence of the speech he was certain it was news his father was listening to. They all spoke the same way, a sort of animated declaration that reminded Corey of the way his classmates spoke in the play they put on last year, a way of speaking that seemed so phony.

The floorboards in the hallway creaked as his dad shuffled down to his bedroom.

"Corey, time to get up," Ted, his father said, tapping his wristwatch. "The bus will be here in 25 minutes."

"Dad, I don't have school today."

"What?" he asked, turning back around to face Corey, as he had already started to return to the kitchen.

"School's out Dad. For the summer."

"Oh really," Ted said, nodding. He backed away slowly, his eyes cast down, like a man retreating from a cornered primate. "Too much to keep track of these days. Well, I've got to go in, work the 1st shift today. Stay out of trouble. There's peanut butter and jelly, bread, make yourself a sandwich for lunch, OK?" By the time he finished this string of instructions, Ted was back in the kitchen and moving towards his seat at the table.

Corey threw the covers off and stepped out of bed, stretching again. "Sure, OK Dad." He quickly changed into a t-shirt and shorts and joined his father in the kitchen. It was a small room, big enough for a short counter and cupboards, a cream colored refrigerator and matching oven and range pushed against the far wall, as well as a squat wooden table with four chairs, one mismatched and bought at a yard sale years ago. Ted was hunched over the kitchen table, a paper laid out under his left hand while his right periodically raised a piece of toast to his mouth, where he would take a bite without looking and swallow after a few exaggerated chews.

Corey didn't know why people said he looked like his father; Ted was a little overweight, a height Corey would describe as "medium", and his brown hair was thinning atop his head. Corey had his mother's blonde hair and — until last year — had been the kind of thin that made everyone's' mother and grandmother want to give him a second helping whenever he ate at a friend's house. Corey guessed it was his nose that reminded others of his father, as both had short, broad noses that always ran a little redder than their faces, no matter the weather.

"Toast on the counter," Ted said, his eyes still on the paper. Corey took a slice and sat with his father. He glanced over at the two empty chairs across the table.

"What are you going to do at work today?"

"Make sure no one kills themselves," Ted said, his eyes never leaving the paper. The radio droned in the background and the newscaster mentioned something about another fatal accident up on Route 101.

"Since I can't be here to make certain you won't," Ted continued, eyes still on his paper, "don't do anything stupid. Check in with Mimi, OK?"

"Do I have to?" Corey asked. Mimi Gagnon lived across the street from them in an increasingly dilapidated house. Corey figured Mimi was at least 70 years old, and had never gotten the hang of exterior maintenance; the paint on the side of the house was flaking, the grass this late into June well past the ankles. The interior of the house, though overfilled with knick-knacks, handmade quilts, and plastic covers for the furniture, was spotless. Whenever Corey visited, she was always in some state of cleaning, either dusting, vacuuming, washing, or mopping, the television always on in the background to some daytime soap opera.

"Yes, you have to," Ted responded. He dropped his piece of toast and his eyes finally left the paper to zero in on Corey. "I'll be at work all day, and someone has to keep an eye on you. Go over there for lunch. We already talked with Mimi about this, her keeping an eye on you once school was out."

"But Dad-" Corey began.

"I don't want lip about it," Ted said, his voice rising, "you'll do as I say."

"Yes, sir," Corey said. He looked down, his shoulders hunched in. Ted turned the page of the newspaper, retrieved his toast, and returned to the news.

In a few quick chomps Corey finished the toast and after a glass of orange juice, called Alex, and wasn't surprised when Alex's mother picked up the phone.

"Marino residence," she said. Corey could picture her in their kitchen, probably making breakfast for Alex and Alex's sister.

"Hi Mrs. Marino, it's Corey. Is Alex there?"

"Hi Corey," she answered. There was a momentary pause, which Corey imagined to be her shifting the phone to her shoulder, before she continued: "I think he's in his room, one moment." Corey kept the phone pressed tight against his ear and heard Mrs. Marino walk away and yell out "Alex! Telephone!" Her voice distant and somehow stripped of enunciation, the syllables running together to make it across the telephone line. He heard the patter of footsteps and a rustling before Alex yelled: "Hello!"

"Alex, it's me, Corey."

"Yo, Corey, what's up?" Corey could hear the smile in Alex's voice and imagine it easily. Alex lived two streets over — about a quarter of a mile away — and the two had been friends ever since they met in second grade.

"What are you doing today?" Corey asked,

"I don't know. Let me ask my Mom," Alex answered, and following up with "Mom! What are we doing today?" Corey couldn't hear her answer, but a moment later Alex responded. "Nothing, I guess. Meet you at the corner in ten?"

"Awesome." Corey hung up and quickly cleared the table, then piled the dishes in the sink atop last night's plates.

"Where you off to?" Ted asked, eyes still on the paper.

"Off to play with Alex."

"Check in with Mrs. Marino, and check in with Mimi later, OK?"

"Yes, sir."

"And make sure to clean those dishes in the sink and take out the trash while you're at it. I don't want to come home to a house stinking like garbage."

"Yes, sir," Corey said. He looked away and tried to hide his frustration.

Corey cleaned the dishes and took out the trash while Ted finished his breakfast. As soon as he was done with these chores Corey was out the door and headed to Alex's. The air was already hot and combined with the humidity was enough to create a haze that seemed to hover above the pavement. Corey stuck towards the far right edge of the sidewalk, trying to avoid the sun under the occasional shade cast by trees or bushes in the yards he passed.

The road Corey followed was flat and straight and the houses were small and close to one another. Most were relatively recent developments, built in the last twenty or thirty years as Derryfield grew and families moved to the outskirts of the city, away from the mills and businesses of downtown. The ranch he and his father lived in was a faded pale brown he had heard one of his aunts describe as eggshell. The bushes hugging the front of their house — in years past trimmed into rectangular shapes — now grew haphazardly, nearly reaching the bottom of the bedroom windows.

The other houses on Morrill Street were similar in size and age. The yards were all small, most well maintained and a vibrant green this early in the summer, before the sun had a chance to bake away any life that took root and leave behind a browned turf.

When Corey rounded the corner at the end of Morrill Street, he saw that Alex was already waiting under the massive oak that stood further down the street, at the corner of Morrill and Pine by the Robertson's and the Smith's houses. As he drew nearer, Corey recognized for the first time the incongruity between the name of the street and the landmark. When he was a few feet from Alex he asked: "Why do you think they named it Pine? It's just oak trees here, right?"

Alex shrugged his shoulders and answered. "I dunno. I think maybe it used to be lots of pine trees here. Maybe there was logging or something that came through and cut em all down."

"Yeah, maybe," Corey said as he shrugged.

Alex wore a Jurassic Park t-shirt with the fossilized skeleton of the Tyrannosaurus Rex roaring in the logo, the shirt matching the poster in Corey's room. Corey looked down at his own t-shirt: it hung a little too loosely on his frame and he didn't particularly care for the green and blue stripes. Another buy from the Salvation Army. Alex didn't notice or didn't care that Corey's shirt wasn't as cool as his. The two had met in second grade when Alex's parents had moved into town. They took the same bus into school, Corey getting on the bus at the stop after Alex. This alone would have likely been enough to start a friendship, but their mutual appreciation for Ripley's Believe It or Not and all cryptids — those creatures long lost to science, such as Bigfoot, the Loch Ness monster, and the Yeti — ensured that their friendship had a solid foundation.

Physically though, they were a study in contrasts. Even at 12, Corey was beginning to fill out like his father and carried enough extra weight that his gym teacher had told him he should think about trying out for football. Alex, on the other hand, was tall and lanky and was never seen without a pair of glasses, either the pair he wore to school with the band around the back to always keep it on his head, or, like when Corey stayed the night, his other pair that just rested on his ears like every other set of glasses Corey had seen.

"Do you have the plans for the fort?" Corey asked.

"Yeah." Alex pulled a folded piece of paper out of his back pocket and slowly unfolded it, careful not to put too much pressure on the creases of the folds where the paper could easily rip. Corey and Alex had worked together to draw up plans for a fort they would build this summer. They had scouted locations in the woods along Pine Street, behind the houses and Mark's Convenience, deep in the forest and far — the two hoped — from some of the other kids in the neighborhood. Construction had started at the beginning of June, and now with their days free of school, they each hoped the fort would be ready before July.

"So I was talking to Jeff about it-" Alex began.

"About the fort?" Corey interjected.

"Yeah, and he said, well he said we should check with the dump, see if there is any wood we can take to build with."

"What the hell man. Why'd you tell Jeff about it?" Corey asked, throwing his hands up in the air.

"Well, I wasn't gonna, but he was asking what I was up to, and I didn't know what else to tell him. Plus, his dad works at the hardware store anyways, so maybe he can help us get some stuff to build with."

"Yeah, I guess," Corey said, drawing out the word guess. "Is he gonna hang out with us out there?"

"Yeah, why not? I mean, he doesn't have to be a Chief like us, like own the fort like we do, but maybe he can be a Sergeant or something."

"Fine, OK, I guess. Is he gonna help us with building it at least?"

"Yeah, I think so."

"Is he gonna help today?"

"Nah, not today. Plus, it should be us anyways, right? Like, we should be the ones getting the big stuff done, 'cause it ours."

"Yeah, sure," Corey said. He walked with Alex back to his house. The construction of the fort was going slowly. Between the two of them they could only carry a few boards at a time and each trip there and back took at least half an hour. Alex's dad had offered them the pile of scrap lumber behind their shed, and in the last few weeks of school, in the afternoons and weekends, Alex and Corey had carried much of that wood out to the tree and built most of a floor and one wall of the tree house.

After reaching the pile of scrap wood behind the shed, the two deliberated which lumber should move next. Corey shrugged into their backpack filled with tools and nails. After deciding on the two by fours, Corey grabbed the far end of three stacked boards and lifted. Alex grabbed the other end of the same three boards and the two boys began to walk together in time through the backyard and into the green space behind it, walking slowly to ensure neither dropped their end, less concerned about personal injury and more so with potential damage to the boards.

The forest stretched as far as each could see before them, a portrait of green. As they stepped deeper into the forest, the green swallowed them, working to block out the blue sky above and all traces of civilization behind them. Their journey was not direct — they began by following a path between ferns and fallen trees that lead them over the sudden hills and valleys and alongside a small stream, its waters low but still enough to burble along and provide an accompaniment to the wind and wildlife. But the path petered out, the dark brown of the packed earth giving way again to the green of the forest, making travel more difficult.

The two had played out in these woods for the last few years but it was not until this spring that they had found the perfect place for a tree fort. Behind a copse of trees a little more than 10 minutes walking from Alex's house, beyond the stream but still a ways from the highway, the two had found a massive wolf pine. It almost looked like some giant arboreal hand, as about seven feet off the ground its one enormous trunk split into what appeared to be at least five separate trees, each growth the diameter of a normally sized pine. The boys had begun building a tree house at this point, the "palm", and were using each of the distinct offshoot trees as an anchor point for their platform.

After much deliberation they had decided upon a name for the endeavor: Fort Barren. The land wasn't barren and was in fact lush and green at this time of the year, but they had both read tales of the Jersey Devil from the Pine Barrens of New Jersey. They imagined this forest as the Barrens, the fort a safe harbor from the Jersey Devil.

Though they only carried three boards back with them they still felt the need to deliberate where these particular boards would go. Corey wanted to continue building the back wall while Alex wanted to shore up the floorboards with more bracing. They finally decided to use two for bracing and one to heighten the back wall. Neither boy was very confident with the hammer and each had suffered some injured thumbs and fingers due to their own clumsiness. But they were gaining confidence and once they had decided upon where to install the boards it only took them a few minutes to do so, one boy holding the board in place while the other nailed it in.

Corey laid down on the floor after they had finished nailing in the three boards. The several trunks and countless branches off those trunks spiraled out above him. Most of the sunlight was blocked by the pine needles above, though he could still make out a few flashes of the brilliant blue sky above. It was a few degrees cooler in the shade. The slight breeze rustled the limbs and caused the specs of sky to disappear and reappear in flashes of dark green and light blue. He could occasionally hear the passing of a large truck some distance off on the highway. The forest was otherwise quiet beyond the rustling of nearby leaves and the chirping of some birds.

"What ya looking at?" Alex asked.

"Nothing. Just the sky," Corey answered.

"This'll be wicked awesome once it's finished." Alex grinned and surveyed the tree and construction.

Corey sat up and smiled. "Yeah. Fort Barren will be the best tree fort this land has ever seen."

As Corey spoke Alex took a step to the side and looked past Fort Barren and deeper into the woods.

"Did you hear that?" Alex asked. Corey rolled over onto his knees and propped his head over the half-built rear wall of the fort and listened. He slightly closed his eyes. Under the sound of the shifting foliage Corey again heard distant traffic off to the right. The birds had quieted. He turned back to Alex and began to shake his head when he heard a disturbance in the nearby underbrush that was growing louder.

To the surprise of both, a brown squirrel came bounding out of the underbrush, its fluffy tail twitching in time as it ran along the ground. Behind it more followed. Each was darting along low to the ground as they scurried past Fort Barren before they disappeared into the brush. Corey and Alex watched quietly, their eyes wide and mouths agape as more than a dozen squirrels appeared in the clearing around the fort and disappeared into the brush just as quickly. The sound of the squirrels' passage lessened as they put more distance between themselves and the fort.

Alex turned to Corey and pushed his glasses up the bridge of his nose. "What the hell?" It was as much a question as a statement. His voice felt weak, as if the sound couldn't carry the meaning of the words.

Corey didn't know what to say or how to answer so he shrugged his shoulders.

Alex coughed, feeling as if he needed to clear his throat, and asked again, "What the hell was that?"

"I... I don't know," Corey replied. "Maybe like... a migration or something? Like birds. Do squirrels migrate?" Corey remained on his knees with his chin over the half-complete wall of the fort to watch the area from which the squirrels came. The trees rustled in the wind but nothing else moved. Slowly, one by one, the birds nearby began to sing again.

"Let's get going," Alex said in a hushed tone.

"Yeah, I have to get to Mimi's anyways." Corey needed no more encouragement and he leapt down from the fort and moved forward with the momentum. As he jogged away from the fort Alex followed. Both glanced over their shoulders as they walked, and continued to do so until the fort and the clearing were no longer in sight.

CHAPTER FOUR

Will opened the bay door, stepped in, and immediately regretted it. The air inside was at least 15 degrees warmer than the air outside, and it smelled of sweat and oil and fuel. He hustled over to the fan in the corner and turned it on, hoping the once cream-colored blades, long stained black from the soot of the garage, would blow some of the still muggy air out the door.

The building was small, one story and gray brick, and clung to the side of the traffic circle at the eastern edge of the center of town. Besides Derryfield Auto, the circle held a small seasonal restaurant named the Snack Shack, the local Legion Hall, and a small dirt parking lot that people often used if they were hiking or fishing along the Pilwilla River. At Derryfield Auto, a single pump dispensed regular gasoline, its red paint flaking away with rust, its sole hose littered with fine cracks. The office contained three chairs, their cushions stained and long since worn flat from the weight of years of customers. A single wooden desk, painted the same slate gray as the interior walls, stood near the entrance to the garage. An old gum ball machine stood guard next to the desk. The gum balls inside never enticed a sale and were now covered in a thin layer of dust that matched the color of the walls and desk. Only 1,200 square feet, the garage had enough space for three lifts for vehicles as well as assorted chemicals, tools, parts, and supplies.

Two bays were currently empty. The third held a Mercury Sable faded the blue of an old man's veins. A bright green puddle lay beneath it, remnants of a radiator pulled from the vehicle the day before. Will switched on the air compressor and walked away from it as it chugged on, filling the tank with air. He went into the office and checked the schedule: one oil change for 9:00 AM, and a 30,000 mile service for the afternoon.

The roar of a motorcycle's engine heralded Robert's arrival. He pulled up with a smile on his face which transformed to his signature scowl the moment he stepped off his ride. The bike was old, a 1975 Harley Davidson, and (as Robert was quick to tell anyone who would listen) since his second divorce, the only thing besides a good steak he still loved in the world. It was pristine, the chrome gleaming, the paint bright.

Robert the rider did not match the bike. While the Harley was clean, sleek, and quick, Robert was dirty, rough, and tended to move pretty slowly. His beard was tattered and uneven, the gray hair speckled with bits of brown hair and additional spots of brown which Will could only surmise was oil. His shirt — the left breast adorned with his name, the right with the name of the shop, Derryfield Auto — displayed an assortment of stains of unknown origin that turned the navy blue shirt into a blue-collar imitation of modern art. Robert moved slowly, each step a calculated act to keep his considerable bulk upright and minimize the energy he need expend.

"Morning Robert," Will said.

"Yep," Robert responded.

"Fucking hot."

"Yep. What we got coming in today, boss?"

"Not much," Will answered as he again looked over his notes scribbled on the mat calendar placed on the desk. "An oil change and 30 thousand mile service in the afternoon. We've got to try and get this Sable out today as well."

"Got it. I'll get on the Sable."

Though he moved slowly, Robert did so carefully, as if he planned each movement a few seconds beforehand. This patience was displayed in the way he repaired automobiles. Robert never wasted a movement, never hurried, but almost never backtracked or had to redo a repair. Robert did it slowly, but right, and Will had quickly learned to appreciate that and to learn from it, to always take his time when working in the shop.

Robert flipped the switch on the dirt encrusted boom box sitting behind his toolbox and cracked a smile when Led Zeppelin's *Kashmir* filled the garage. He pushed his tool cart up to the Sable and opened the top tray before raising his hands over his head and twisting his head to the side to produce a satisfying crack. As with his motorcycle, Robert's toolbox was nearly spotless. The tools inside sat in small ordered trays, the sockets laid out from smallest to largest. The silver of the metal tools reflected the fluorescent lights overhead. The box, a dark green, was also wiped clean of dirt and oil.

The Sable's front and rear strut and spring lay on the ground below it, as if Robert was a hunter dressing his fallen prey. Robert pushed the the old parts away with his boot and set out the new springs and struts. It took him a few hours to compress the shocks over the struts and install the new assemblies. While Robert worked on the Sable, Will pulled around a Chevrolet 1500 and worked on a front brake job, oil change, and tire rotation.

The work was dirty, frustrating, and often unpleasant. But it was honest. When he left for college, Will had never expected to be running his father's shop. He had dreams of being an architect, of drafting and creating buildings that fused utility with beauty. But only a few months after graduating, his father had passed, and Will returned home to assist his mother with all that entailed. Will didn't know it at the time — the diagnosis of Alzheimer's would not come for another few years — but his father's death knocked his mother a blow that she did not recover from. She was forgetful, confused, and at times argumentative, all traits that were foreign to Will's memory of her prior to his time away from New Hampshire. So he remained back in Derryfield after the funeral once he recognized that his mother would not be able to remain independent without the support her late husband had been providing.

Will began taking stock of the fluids in the shop when the phone rang. He left the garage to answer the telephone in the office.

"Good morning," Will said after picking up the phone, "Derryfield Auto."

"Will, where's my money?" a voiced hissed through the line.

"John?"

"Yes — who else you owe that you've gotta ask?" John said. John Schmidt owned one of the local parts store, Price Right Auto Parts. The man loved to talk about two things, business and politics, usually of a similar theme: how running a business cost too much these days, and how the government took too much. He was the type of man that wasn't happy unless he was complaining.

"I'll get it to you, soon John," Will said. He rubbed his eyes, the attitude from John mixing with his exhaustion to create a cocktail that was quickly bringing on a headache. Yet another tow up on Route 101 last night had stolen hours of sleep; another fatal, the third this month.

"You told me that last week," John continued, "and the week before that. You still owe me half of April, and all of May. I'm not running a charity here; I've got bills too ya know."

"I know John, I know. Cash is tight right now. I'll have a bit more coming in this week, and should be able to clear out the rest of April's bills and most of May's."

"You keep telling me that. But I ain't operating a charity, I've said it before and I'll say it again. You don't square up, you aren't getting anymore from me. I can't be giving away parts for free now, you understand, right?"

"John, I get it. I'll square up soon."

"Good," John said. Will heard the clattering of John's telephone in its cradle and the dead air that followed. He cursed and sensed that someone was behind him. Robert stood at the door, his left eyebrow raised.

"That asshole still bugging you?" Robert asked.

"Not bugging me," Will said and shook his head. "It's fine, thanks. Just a bit behind on the bills this month."

"Aren't we all?" Robert laughed. "Tough for everyone these days. You know my brother's out of a job now too. Last round of layoffs at the mill got him this time. Not like it used to be, I'll tell ya," he continued, rubbing his hands on a rag. "I remember when my pappy worked there, shift change happened and we'd be down there sometimes to get him, and shit would that place spit out so many goddamn men. Not anymore," he said, shaking his head in time with the wiping of his hands.

"It's happening everywhere, manufacturing is dying they keep saying," Will shook his head as well. "Sorry to hear about your brother like that. What's he gonna do?"

"I dunno. Probably look for something in construction. He used to do some carpentry on and off before he started at the mill. Hard to start over at 55 or whatever he is now." Robert shrugged.

"That sucks."

"Yep." Robert shrugged again. He said it affirmatively, as if confirming a fact that Will already should know to be true and required no further conversation. His brother's plight didn't seem to bother him all that much, or at least Robert didn't appear to express it. To Robert, life did occasionally suck, but that was to be expected. As Will had heard him opine on a few occasions, one had to ride out the hard times to enjoy the good.

Knowing that Robert would neither want nor engage in any further elaboration about the difficulties his brother might be facing, Will asked: "That Sable getting close?"

"Yep," Robert said. "Give me another hour."

Robert had worked with Will since he had taken over the shop, and had even been with Will's father for ten years before that. Other technicians had come and gone, but Robert appeared content with the job. Will appreciated his hard work and had hardly heard the man complain, even when Will had to approach him and ask to hold his check for a week a few months back when the cash flow was even worse than it was now. Robert had simply shrugged and said that was fine, that he knew Will was good for it.

While Robert worked on the Sable Will decided to take stock of what remained for fluids and filters. Once completed, he returned to the office and rummaged through the manila folder in which he kept financial documents and located the deposit slip from last week. The checking account for the shop only held a few thousand dollars, far short of what was needed for payroll and the outstanding bills to parts suppliers and utilities. The next few weeks would hopefully be busy and bring in enough cash to help keep the shop afloat. Since school had just ended, parents and teachers alike would look to have their car serviced before their big summer trips to Niagara Falls, Acadia National Park, or Montreal. Will knew from years past that he could count on at least a small bump in business around the end of June and beginning of July.

The problem was — or at least, one of the problems was — every year everything cost more: the prices of parts went up, the prices of supplies went up, the cost of labor went up, and, without fail, taxes went up. The only thing that bucked this trend was profits, which, as Will had calculated, steadily dropped with the same frequency. Politicians of all stripes continued to preach their messages of economic growth, growth that Will figured must be going to other states or other regions or other cities or other towns. Derryfield certainly wasn't receiving it.

Robert finished with the repairs on the Sable and took it for a test drive. While he was out, the phone rang again and Will answered it with his usual enthusiasm: "Good morning, Derryfield Auto, how can I help you?"

"Mr. Boucher?" asked a woman on the line.

"Yes, this is Will, how can I help you?"

"I'm calling from Pleasant Lane Nursing Home, the billing department." The woman didn't identify herself but Will recalled seeing her before in the administrative offices of the nursing home. He immediately found her voice on the telephone unpleasant, equal parts saccharine and frustration. Will didn't envy the woman her position and he could tell she didn't like making this call, but her attempt to masquerade her displeasure was unsuccessful and it only further annoyed him.

"Yes?" Will asked, though he already knew what she was calling about.

"I understand your mother's bill is past due. Please understand that it's important that we are paid in a timely manner in order to provide the services our residents require."

"Yeah, I know, I know. I'll have it to you shortly."

"And how soon will that be, Mr. Boucher?"

"A few days. Maybe a week. I've got to clear some things here, and then will have a payment to you."

"Good," she said. "The outstanding balance is $453. I expect we will have it by this time next week. Goodbye." She did not wait for Will to respond. By the time he was finding the words he wished to say in response the line was dead and humming in his ear. He dropped the phone back into its cradle and frowned. He thought of having a drink. It was close to noon, and surely quitting time someplace. Thoughts of drinking brought forth memories of his father, many of them unpleasant. Will instead turned back to the books and wondered what he could do to save the business from bankruptcy.

CHAPTER FIVE

Erica thought her parent's house looked different. She had been there a week prior, at the gathering right after the funeral, but even in the late morning light its white siding was duller and the pavement of the driveway had faded since then. She felt as if her brother's passing had left some mark on the dwelling, that his death had sullied not only her memories of the place but her perception of it in the present.

As she slowed to pull into the driveway, Erica glanced up and down the street, but saw no one nearby. The O'Connors to the right and the Trudeas to the left were either away or keeping a distance, as neither neighbor presented on their front porch or yard. Erica remembered most of the neighborhood to be near her parents' age with adult children of their own. She had hoped they would be there, to ask how she was doing, to delay her entry into the house. She lingered for a moment by the car and then headed for the door. To Erica's surprise the yard was freshly mowed. As she expected, the front door was unlocked.

"Mom? Dad?" Erica called out as she entered.

"In here," Judy said from the kitchen.

The shades were drawn in the entryway in an effort to block the sunlight and the heat from entering. If not for Erica's familiarity with the interior of the house she would have been forced to wait for a minute as her eyes adjusted to the interior gloom. While the house did feel a few degrees cooler than outside, the temperature difference was not enough to bring about comfort and Erica unbuttoned the top button of her shirt.

The front hallway was missing some of its framed photographs. Her parents had long ago designated this space for all of the family photographs, and by Erica's estimation approximately eighty cluttered one wall, a sea of faces and places in colorful display against the white wall of the hallway. But at least fifteen were missing now, the blank spaces between pictures evidence of their absence. Erica remembered that they had raided these photographs for a collage for the funeral and realized her parents must not have put the photographs back up yet.

As Erica rounded the corner to the kitchen she saw a collection of dishes — white, light green, and tan — piled high in the sink. She could hear a television on low. The small boxy television sat on the kitchen table, its two antennae raised to the sky, a proposition she could only perceive as a cardinal sin given her mother's insistence throughout Erica's childhood of turning the television off during mealtimes and forcing family conversation. The kitchen reeked of cigarette smoke, a scent Erica hadn't known since she was eight, before her mother quit smoking. A cigarette hung between the index and middle finger of her mother's right hand, the lit end smoldering in the hazy light of the kitchen. The purple polish on her mother's nails was chipped and her blonde hair darker and slicked back down her head and the nape of her neck from a recent shower. While she was never a large woman, Erica thought her mother looked smaller than ever, a measly 120 pounds or so on her frame.

"Mom," Erica said, unable to stop the concern washing into her voice, "why are you smoking?"

"Erica, I don't need it now, not from you." Judy kept her attention on the television and waved her left hand over her shoulder, as if she were shooing an insect away from her face.

"Mom, I just..."

"Not now."

"Are you going to get those photographs back up on the wall?" Erica asked and pointed with her thumb over her shoulder, back towards the hallway.

"Yes," Judy said.

"When?"

"When I get to it. It's been plenty busy around here. I just want to sit for a bit." Judy remained fixated on her television, where CNN anchors discussed OJ Simpson's arrest and arraignment for murder. The tales of some celebrities killing and dying a continent away was more alluring to her that what she had here: only memories of a son now laid to rest.

"Think he did it?" Judy asked.

"Would he have run if he hadn't?" Erica responded.

Judy said nothing more and instead just nodded her head. She remained transfixed on the television and raised a cup of tea to her mouth without taking her eyes from the screen.

"Is Dad around?" Erica asked.

"He's out back. Didn't feel like going into work. Finally putting some of that sick leave to use I guess — he mowed the damn lawn too," Judy laughed without any mirth and took another drag on her cigarette. "See if he'll come in for lunch."

She did not turn to Erica and instead stared at the television where the anchors continued to discuss the murders of Nicole Brown and Ron Goldman. Erica stared at the back of her mother's head for a few moments, as if doing so would prompt a response and break her mother's fascination with the television and the cigarettes. But Judy did not turn.

Erica left the kitchen and exited through the rear screen door. The lawn out back had also been recently cut. Erica was shocked to see that even the grass abutting the house was short; her father had taken the time to break out the weed whacker and shorn down the vegetation too close to the house to mow. Erica's father, Sam, sat on one of the lawn chairs in the yard, his back to the house. Only his mop of gray hair was visible above the top of the chair, his usual crop cut now beginning to appear shaggy and in disarray. He did not turn as Erica approached. As she drew near she cleared her throat loudly.

"Hi Dad," she said.

He turned to look behind him and said: "Hi honey." His face was red from exertion and still slick with sweat. He had unbuttoned all of the buttons of his polo and a large tuft of graying chest hair poked out from the shirt.

"Lawn looks really good." Erica pulled up a lawn chair next to him and sat.

Sam sat back in the chair. "Thanks, honey. Felt like I had to do something. Thought it might as well be that."

"Well it looks good. Good job."

Sam said nothing more so Erica asked: "How's uh, how's Mom?"

"She's fine, I think."

"You know she's in there smoking, right?"

"Is she?" he responded. "I said something to her the other day." Sam looked at her with a blank face. The lines of her father's face were more pronounced to Erica, as if what she was viewing was not his actual face but an artist's interpretation, a caricature or sculpture of his face exaggerating his age lines.

"You OK?" she asked.

"Yeah. I'm fine. As well as can be," Sam spoke slowly and Erica caught herself leaning over in her chair towards him as she waited for each syllable.

Sam was tired, not just from the mowing but from life in general. Though the events had added additional gray to his hair, he had survived the recession of the late '70s and early '80s. Sam had expected a break in his later years, after attaining a supervisory position at Seabrook and seeing two children out of the house and in successful careers. He had not expected the death of a child. It cut him more deeply than anything else had, even more than the death of his mother and father. The loss he felt was all encompassing, a dizziness in his head and a hollow in his heart made because a part of his future had been extinguished in a moment. The world, however difficult, had made sense to him two weeks ago. It no longer did.

Erica sat with her father. For a few minutes, neither spoke. Erica sat back and enjoyed for a moment the warmth of the sun. The sky overhead was clear and a pair of robins were flitting about the large oak tree in the far corner of the yard. A rope swing hung motionless from one of its limbs. A few white birches stood nearby, guards of the forest's encroachment back into suburbia. Closer by, to the left of where they sat, stood the back shed, a ten by ten structure Sam had haltingly built across one spring and summer. It's red siding — painted to match the house — was long flaking and the entire structure appeared to list a few degrees to the left.

Sam broke the silence by asking: "How's the Gazette? Still standing after your absence?"

"Yes," Erica said and laughed. "Still standing."

"What are you working on now?" he asked without turning to her. He spoke with hardly any intonation, the words stripped of color and variance. She could tell he was engaging with her, but not totally. His mind was still on Nate.

"Just fluff. 'Local interest' they call it. " She shrugged. "The kind of stuff on page 8, behind the news that sells."

"I see, I see. It's good that you're back."

"Sure. I mean, it's fine. Just, seems like a waste in some ways. There are more important things going on than who won the local beauty pageant or when the newest phase of road construction will be done, you know?"

"Maybe," Sam said turning to her. "Maybe it's something more. These stories, the local interest, they're important to someone, right?"

"I guess. I just wish they had me on something else. I finally got on district and then I'm bounced. It feels like a step back. I thought I had earned my place, but I guess not. It's just not what I want to be doing right now. One step forward, two steps back."

Sam nodded but said nothing in return.

"When are you going back into work?" Erica asked.

"In a few days. A few days. I just need to, regroup, you know? Yeah, regroup," he repeated in an effort to convince himself.

"What are you going to do in the meantime?"

"Take care of some things around here. Maybe repaint the shed, try to straighten it out a bit. Something's off with the way it's leaning."

"Great idea. Will you need a hand with that?" Erica asked.

"No, no. I'll just get what I can done. Seems like a good time as any now."

They sat again in silence. Erica glanced over at Sam. He laid back with his eyes closed. She could see the rhythmic flaring of his nostrils as he breathed. His face was at rest, expressionless.

"If you need anything Dad," Erica said, "let me know. Ok?"

Sam opened one eye and glanced over at her. "Sure thing sweetie."

"I've got to head out; I still have to run a few errands before I get into the office."

"Be safe," Sam said. He smiled to Erica in a manner that expressed little happiness: while the corners of his mouth raised he did not reveal his teeth, and his eyes remained placid.

Erica nodded and leaned over to kiss him on the cheek.

When Erica re-entered the house the smell of cigarette smoke was even worse than before. She forgot to catch the screen door behind her and it slammed back into its frame. Judy glanced over and then immediately back to her television. She still sat at the kitchen table, the cigarette in one hand now joined by a slice of toast in the other. The burnt edges of the toast matched the pile of ashes growing in the ashtray before her.

"Mom," Erica said gently, feeling as if she didn't wish to disturb her mother again. "Mom, I've got to go, OK?"

"Sure," Judy said without even turning away from her television. "You talk your father into coming in for lunch?" she asked and motioned towards the toast in her hand.

"No, sorry Mom, I didn't."

Judy huffed. "He'll come in when he's hungry then."

Erica closed the front door shut behind her and glanced up and down the street as if she expected to find someone watching her, witnessing her attempt to do what she should, visit her parents and offer them her assistance. But no one was there. No neighbors were outside to witness her good deed and provide the positive reinforcement she craved, support she would have received from Nate had he been here. A part of her knew that what she was doing was right, the right thing to do, but she didn't want to be doing it. Her parents were clearly in need, but Erica did not know what they needed (other than a son). She didn't like seeing them this way. They appeared as alternate versions of her parents. Her mother's good cheer and focus was replaced with cigarettes and apathy. Her father's drive and humor replaced with solemnity and lawn chores. She knew that the memories of her brother was all she held now, and did not want the burden of the memories of her parents to be so similarly important in this moment, as if she was required to protect them all at once in her recall, as though their identities could slip away through her forgetfulness. The loss of Nate was enough, but as she so often did, she felt the need to support her family. Erica was certain that if not for her efforts, her family would have long since have dispersed into separate tribes, now more so than ever.

Erica pushed the feelings aside and climbed into her car. As she expected, firing up the Ford was enough to distract her to a degree. Driving had always helped her relax. As she pulled out of the driveway, she tried not to think about how Nate had died in his car, out on Route 101.

CHAPTER SIX

The weather overhead was not identifiable as individual clouds but was instead a gray backdrop for a day that hid the sun. Time stood still for Corey and Alex, for as the day progressed the afternoon was the same as the morning: a cool colorlessness in which all shadows were absent. Though rain was threatening it did not fall and the two determined to carry as much timber back to Fort Barren as they could manage.

The underbrush, fed by the rains of spring, was thick this late in June. The branches and bushes kept scratching their arms and legs, and both boys wished they had had the foresight to wear pants rather than shorts. Occasionally the underbrush would thin out under a few taller trees, but it always returned after the small clearings, like each patch of grass or moss was simply an island among an ocean of thicker growth.

"How do all deer and bear and things walk through this stuff?" Corey asked. He shifted the boards in his hands and slowed to allow Alex to do the same.

"I think they find paths or trails. Or walk through like plains, big clearings. I remember Mr. Parsons talking about it in science class."

"We should look for one of those trails then out to the Fort. It would at least make it easier to carry these boards. Maybe we could find a deer too, or baby deer. How cool would that be?" Corey asked.

Alex grunted in agreement.

"Well let's look for one after we drop these boards."

When Alex did not respond Corey added, "It will be fun. If we find an easier way we can use that more. We might find some animals too!"

"Sure, OK," Alex said without any enthusiasm. Alex hated when Corey got like this, one minute doggedly on the task at hand, the next

47

bored with it and fixating on something else. They had started the day with hauling boards, after which Alex had assumed they would continue construction. But the thought of finding game trails had enticed Corey and Alex could tell Corey was no longer interested in working on Fort Barren. Rather than argue, Alex knew it was better to go along with Corey for now and try again tomorrow at working on Fort Barren.

The Fort's back wall was now complete, and, at Alex's insistence, they had brought out a tarp and installed two supports to raise a temporary roof. They hadn't sat under the tarp during a heavy rain, but they had remained relatively protected underneath it from a drizzle the other day. They stacked the new boards under it and Alex shouldered his backpack again, filled with their two hammers and a box of nails, too valuable and important to leave behind in the forest. At Corey's insistence they set off around the Fort to try and find a game trail.

The grayness of the day muffled sound as well as color. The noises of the forest were distorted and gauzy. The two noticed that even their voices sounded strange. Whenever one talked the sounds reflected back from the gray air. Alex insisted they stop after a few minutes so he could rearrange the contents of his backpack and find a suitable walking stick to help with the trek.

Neither was entirely certain what to look for, but once they saw it, they knew they had found it. At the far end of a relatively large clearing where the older trees towered overhead and left little sunlight for the brush underneath, the two saw a tight grouping of smaller trees, shrubs, and grasses. Cut into that collection of plants was a narrow path, the earth below it a dark brown in contrast to the vibrant green elsewhere, just like the path they had worn from Alex's yard a ways into the forest. As the two boys approached the trail they noticed it snaked its way deeper into the brush, beyond their sight.

Once they found a game trail, at Corey's insistence they had to follow it. The trail was not straight: it continued to wind back and forth through the forest. The underbrush grew in close beside it and formed a tight natural corridor with barriers of vegetation on both sides. It was difficult to see far beyond the brush to either side given the thickness of the growth and the low light of the day. After ten minutes of walking down this newly discovered trail the two began to hear a low rumbling sound they thought might be a river. As it grew louder they recognized it as nearby cars on North Road. They continued to follow the trail and, when it crested a small hill where the underbrush thinned, the roadway became visible through the final thirty meters of forest. To their right sat the Overpass to Nowhere, a bridge of North Road rising over nothing but bare dirt.

"So no deer, sorry man," Alex said.

"It's cool," Corey responded. He pointed to the overpass and asked, "When do you think they will finish it? The highway I mean."

"My dad says in twenty years. He says they don't know what they're doing and that's why it's not finished. Says the highway won't come through here until he's dead. Then he always laughs, thinks he is so funny."

"We should go explore under the bridge. Maybe there's some animals living underneath it."

"Eh, I don't think so," Alex responded. He looped each thumb under the strap against his shoulders and tugged on his backpack. "It's all pavement, or concrete or something. What could live there?"

"I don't know. Maybe there's hobos living under there. To get out of the rain and the sun. We should go check it out, just to be sure."

"I don't think that's such a good idea. I mean, what if we run into some hobos. What if they try to rob us or something?"

"Well, maybe there is some materials we could use for the fort," Corey replied.

This was more appealing to Alex. He considered it and said, "OK, at least for a quick look. Not long though, OK?"

"Sure," Corey said, "we'll be fine." He reached in front of him to move a branch about head height out of the way and began down the hill towards the Overpass. Alex watched him get halfway down the hill and then followed. When Corey reached the edge of the bushes he stopped and looked up and down the road.

"Alex," he said, looking over his shoulder, "I think we should stay away from the road. What if someone sees us or something. I don't think our parents, well, my dad, and your parents, would like that, if we were out here I mean."

Alex took a moment to push his glasses back up the bridge of his nose with one hand and said, "Yeah, good idea. I don't wanna get into trouble." The two crept along the bushes near the edge of the road. In about five minutes they came to the foot of the overpass.

It stood approximately twenty feet above them, and, as they had heard, rose over nothing but a patch of dirt, rocks, and some discarded chunks of concrete. Graffiti colored both sides, blue and yellow and red signs from multiple artists bleeding together into some type of modern art installation in a post apocalyptic world, the streets covered in dirt and the concrete crumbling. Corey and Alex laughed at some of the more vulgar language and the spray-painted penis on the wall.

"I don't see any hobos," Alex said and shrugged, "we should probably head back now."

"Maybe they're hiding," Corey offered. "Maybe they ran when they saw us."

"I don't think so, Corey. I didn't see any when we were walking up. Plus, wouldn't a hobo have a tent or like a shopping cart or something? They always have a shopping cart right, for their stuff." Alex wrinkled his nose and asked: "Why does it smell so bad down here?"

"The bog." Corey pointed at the underbrush beyond the overpass. "I'm pretty sure the bog is right past this stuff, and it always smells."

Alex continued to walk under the overpass and towards the brush on the other side.

"Ew, gross!" Alex yelled. Corey jogged the few steps to Alex and looked to where he pointed. The corpse of a deer was pushed up against the concrete of the overpass. The two boys could tell it had been dead for some time. Flies continued to buzz around the carcass and a host of maggots writhed about the abdominal cavity, the matted fur and darker viscera moving in time with the squirm of the pale larva.

"That's disgusting!" Corey said, without much disgust in his voice.

"What do you think killed it?" Alex asked. He poked at it with his walking stick and yelled "Eww!" again when dozens of maggots spilled out of the torn chest of the carcass, a cascade of wriggling white against the dull brown of the fur.

"I don't know, maybe it got hit by a car?"

"Maybe. Maybe a bear got it — or maybe the Bog Monster!" Alex said. His voice rose in pitch and Alex raised his arms over his head and lumbered towards Corey.

Corey laughed. "Stop being stupid."

"Well it could be!" Alex said.

"There ain't no bog monster."

"How do you know?"

"I heard it eats people whole! Like, if it had attacked that deer, there wouldn't be anything for us to see. Or at least like, only a leg. The Bog Monster would have eaten the rest."

"Nah, that is just made up shit," Corey said.

"Maybe. Maybe it was the Bog Monster that the squirrels were running from? Like it scared them all off?" Alex asked. Though offered in jest, the idea scared Corey. He had imagined it but had not voiced it that last time at the fort when the squirrels had come past in such numbers. He hadn't mentioned in then, and didn't mention it now, as if refusing to speak of it would not give the idea power, could in some way keep the monster he believed could be at fault further at bay.

"No, no way, Jose. In New Hampshire?" Corey scoffed as if this idea was inconceivable, "It's not like the Himalayas out here, those mountains can hide the Yeti."

"Maybe. But maybe it is out here. 'Member the guy that went missing last year? I think it was Mark's uncle, I heard it got him."

Corey remembered that Mark's uncle had gone missing last summer. Mark was a year younger than them though they occasionally hung out. Mark wasn't close with his uncle, but it seemed as if the whole town had searched once the man was reported missing. He was still missing to this day. Corey had asked his father what he thought of it all, and Ted had shared that Mark's uncle had likely left for "greener pastures" or "warmer weather", likely down south. Either way, he hadn't turned up.

"No, I heard it from Billy at school, about the bog monster. His cousin told him about how the mills and stuff have been dumping stuff into the waters, it like mutates the fish and things in the river. That's how the bog monster was born."

"Born?" Corey asked.

"Well mutated like."

"Sure." Corey rolled his eyes.

The two explored the rest of the overpass but found little else of interest: a small ring of fist sized stones surrounding a campfire long cold; a collection of crumpled blue and silver beer cans and other refuse; and a single weathered red and white sneaker. The two wondered aloud where the its mate could be and almost brought it home with them in hopes of finding an owner, but were convinced otherwise when they realized the unlikelihood of success and potential that the shoe was likely covered in some type of hobo germ.

"We should get back soon Corey," Alex said. The gray day still refused to provide any indication of time. He glanced down at his watch and added, "it's already five. I gotta be home by six."

The trek back was less exciting than the trek in, but also seemed to both to be much quicker. The anticipation of the unknown, not knowing where they were going or what they would find as they followed the game trail had elongated time, stretched that malleable property to its limit before it snapped back and both realized they had to get home.

Neither boy spoke much on the walk back. Each focused on the brush nearby and where they would take the next step. It was not until they were within sight of some of the houses on Alex's street that they were able to walk side by side. Neither spoke, and Corey enjoyed these moments. It seemed to him as though everyone wanted to talk all the time. Silence was something to be avoided through any action or conversation. But he didn't always want to talk and sometimes just wanted to think, even with his best friend around.

As the two walked up Alex's porch steps Mrs. Marino was there to greet them. Corey had only ever seen her in one kind of outfit, and today was no exception: a pair of blue jeans and a single colored blouse, this one a dark green.

"Well I hope you two had a fun day," she said as she ushered them into the house. "I'm glad you are home in time for dinner Alexander. Last year I would have been shouting up and down the street looking for you. Getting that watch really was smart."

"Yeah, yeah," Alex said as he grinned sheepishly. Corey smiled and stifled a laugh.

"Thanks for getting Alex back home, Corey," Mrs. Marino said.

"What time do you have to be home?" Alex asked.

"I dunno," Corey lied. "My dad didn't say."

"Think you can stay for dinner? I think we're making pizza

tonight!" Alex gave Corey two thumbs up and flashed a smile.

"Yeah, maybe, I think -" Corey started.

"Did you ask your father if you could stay for dinner?" Mrs. Marino asked. She raised one eyebrow as if to punctuate her question.

Corey looked at the floor between his feet. "No, Mrs. Marino."

"Well I am going to have to call him then, Corey. He'll be worried sick about you if he doesn't know where you are."

"No, no, it's OK," Corey said, "Really, Mrs. Marino, he's probably working late anyways."

"I'll call all the same," she said as she grabbed the phone off the wall. She turned to the desk near the phone, opened the small bound book filled with numbers of friends and family and began to run her finger down the page looking for the number to Corey's house. As she did so Mrs. Marino remembered that Corey was standing there, so she held the phone against her shoulder and asked him for the number. He provided it reluctantly and pouted as she spoke with his father.

"Hi, Ted? Yes, it's Marlene. Yes, Corey is here. OK. OK. I'll send him right over." Alex's shoulders dropped.

"You heard, Corey, you've got to head home," Mrs. Marino said.

"Sorry Alex," Corey said.

"Bummer man," Alex replied. "Can you come over tomorrow?"

"Yeah, I think so." Mrs. Marino helped Corey collect his belongings and return them to his backpack.

"OK, you run home now," Mrs. Marino said and patted Corey on the head. "Maybe we'll see you tomorrow."

Corey waved at the door and then slipped his thumbs under the straps of his backpack and skipped down the porch steps. There were few street lights this far from downtown. At the far cross street approximately seventy yards away one light struggled to cast a cone of yellowed light on the pavement. Though more difficult to see, the same layer of clouds from the day blocked out much of the light from the setting sun or a rising moon. From each house Corey passed the windows projected rectangles of light into the burgeoning night. Corey imagined they cast a warmth and slowed his step whenever he walked through one. He took that time to glance into the windows from a distance and to examine what he could of his neighbors interior life. He saw the Johnsons — Mr., Mrs., and their kids, Jill and

Wanda — sitting at their kitchen table laughing about something. They all laughed the same, their heads tilted back and their golden hair rocking in the motion. Corey watched Mrs. Polanski stand at her kitchen sink while Mr. Polanski walked through their kitchen and into another room. Another house held Mr. and Mrs. Harrington, both old and gray and bespectacled, both hunched over a book as they sat beside each other in what Corey guessed what their living room.

After a few minutes Corey approached his house. The kitchen window and living room window to the right of the building were lit, casting out rectangles of light similar to those of the other houses. Without realizing what he was doing, he avoided those areas of light and stood in the darkness to peer inside the windows as he approached. He could see his father inside sitting on the living room couch and illuminated by the glow of the television. Corey watched his father's face but did not see him smile or frown. He sat still, entranced by whatever the TV displayed. His white undershirt contrasted sharply against the dark green couch he sat on. Corey watched for another minute before he glanced up and down the street and reluctantly entered the house.

CHAPTER SEVEN

Will hated the nursing home.

His distaste began with the parking lot. The Ford's tires bumped over the ragged cracks and bulges of the broken pavement as he pulled in, the old springs creaking in protest but easing the ride all the same. Will parked the Ford between two lines long since faded by the sun. The lot was empty save for a late '70s Chevy. Will exited the Ford, careful to navigate around the browned grass and weeds poking up along many of the cracks in the pavement. The lot reminded him of the people inside, similarly warped and broken and forgotten with time.

The air inside Riverview Nursing Care carried the scent of alcohol and disinfectants layered atop the odors of shit and another scent, a touch of sweetness that Will believed was the smell of people dying. He came in here often and always spied the same people in the same beds. Most lingered for years on the doorstep of death, too strong or too stubborn or too stupid to walk through.

Will recognized the middle-aged woman behind the desk but could not recall her name. He was not sure if he ever knew it. They all seemed similar, the employees here: the young ones were eager to talk, ready to help the patients and happy to engage with the few family members who visited. The veterans, those who had worked in the facility for more than a few months were more taciturn. Will imagined they had seen enough piss, shit, and death to make a soldier pause.

The woman behind the counter said, "Hi," nodded to Will, then bowed her head back down into the soft-cover book splayed out across the desk. Will spied Stephen King's name on the cover but couldn't make out the title. He mumbled a response and hurried around the corner and down the hallway to his mother's room. The hallway was spartan, the walls painted a lime green, the pine floor marked with twin grooves formed by the shuffling of feet across the years. Will fought the urge to glance into the rooms he passed, and failed, as usual, by the second door. The faces and bodies in the rooms he passed all told a similar story.

Many sat in beds, a bundle of blankets up around their waists, even with the heat. Others sat in wheelchairs, blankly staring at a television, the window, a wall. More disheartening were those with enough wherewithal to stare back at Will, those with minds sharp enough to recognize that the confinement they faced was not just this building, but by now, their bodies.

Will slowed and then stopped before the door to his mother's room. It lay open and the sounds from a television set on low were barely audible. He hated this place, but felt drawn to it nonetheless, in order to visit his mother. Not long after his father had passed, his mother had fallen and broken her hip. Though only a little over sixty, the injury had proved severe and required hospitalization and then a course of in-patient rehabilitation in a nursing center. Whether this had accelerated her — at that point, undiagnosed — underlying Alzheimer's or simply revealed it, the short rehabilitation stint had transitioned into long term care as his mother's deficiencies and diagnosis became clear. Will paused at the door for a moment, cracked the knuckles on his left hand, and entered the room.

Norma, his mother's roommate and the woman in the first bed, was dying, and appeared to be doing so more quickly than the others here. Her breathing was labored, quick, a moist ticking that echoed in her chest, as if her inner workings were audibly failing. Her gray hair hung close to her shoulders. The visible sections of her scalp beneath her thinning hair were pink with darker moist blotches of mottled brown, like a decaying leaf in the dead of winter. Her eyes followed Will as he walked across the room, but she said nothing, nor moved in any way other than the regular rise and fall of her chest.

His mother sat alone in the far corner, her head cocked towards her right shoulder, her attention transfixed on some scene outside the window. The long black hair Will always pictured her with was now cut short at the shoulders, the dark strands now overcome by the lighter grays. Her hair was mussed as it usually was. His mother was always rubbing her head and ruffling her hair now, and it usually ended up into a mess before lunch, looking like some haphazardly manufactured helmet resting upon her head.

Will approached her and looked out the window in the direction of her gaze. He saw only the broken parking lot, the scrubby grass and trees beyond it, and the blue sky above.

"Mom," Will said as he drew up next to her, "what are you looking at?"

Mildred turned slowly, and looked at him for a moment with a blank face. It was the moment Will hated most about visiting her, hated more than the sights or even smells of the dying: the moment before she recognized him, the moment when the illness seemed at its worst. It was taking her slowly, one piece at a time, one memory washed away at a time as he watched, week by week.

"Oh, Billy, come here baby," she said, waving her hands to bring him down to her. He leaned in and hugged her gently, awkwardly, one arm around her right shoulder, and kissed her wrinkled cheek. "How I've missed you!" she said. "I haven't seen you in so long. How are you?" she asked.

"Good, Mom, good. Things are good."

"How's the shop? How's business?"

"Well, you know, Mom. Good days and bad. Business is great one week and slow the next. But we're surviving."

"Good, good Billy. I miss your father," she said, any pretense of transitions in conversation long gone from her repertoire.

"I know, Mom. We all do."

"How's Daisy?" she asked. She always asked about Daisy, his sister.

"I don't know, Mom. I haven't spoken to her in a while."

"Why?" Mildred rocked back and forth in her chair as she waited for an answer.

"She's in California, Mom. She's busy, I haven't heard from her lately."

"What's she doing out in California?" Mildred asked. "Why would anyone want to be out there?"

"She got a good job offer Mom, remember?" Will said, knowing that Daisy's desire to get away from their father, away from Derryfield, away from New Hampshire, had propelled her as much as the job offer. "She's working a job out there in television, sound mixing or something on some of the television shows."

"Oh," Mildred said, surprised by information she had been told numerous times. "Well you should call her." She shook her head slowly from side to side to express disbelief that Will hadn't thought of that solution yet.

"Good idea, Mom. I will."

"Good," she said and patted her lap. "I'm glad we got that sorted out. How's the shop?" she asked.

"It's good. Pretty busy. Just tough time of year. Hot as -" Will started to say, remembering his mother would prefer he not curse "it's very hot, and lots of people off on vacation, so not as busy as I'd like."

"Things will get better." Mildred patted Will's hand gently and smiled.

"Thanks, Mom. How are things with you here? What have you done today?"

"Oh, the usual. They keep me busy." No matter the activities planned, her answer was always the same. Will couldn't tell if the answers were the same because she couldn't remember what she had done that day or simply didn't care. He assumed it was the latter.

Will sat with her making small talk and circling around to the same points in conversation multiple times. After ten minutes or so, Maureen Mitchell, the nursing director, a short woman who always appeared to be anxious about something, walked into the room and spoke to Will.

"Mr. Boucher," she said, "I'm glad you're here, we have a few things we need to discuss."

Mildred's brow furrowed and she clasped her hands together. "Who is that?" she asked.

"Just someone who works here, Mom," Will said. He stood up and nodded to Maureen. "I'm going to go talk with her. I'll come by to say goodbye before I leave, OK?"

"Where are you going?" Mildred asked as the furrow in her brow deepened.

"Just down the hall, Mom. I'll be right back."

"OK." Mildred sighed deeply, the tension leaving her raised shoulders and her face returning to an indifferent stare as she returned her attention to whatever it was outside the window that had transfixed her earlier.

"Right this way," Ms. Mitchell said as they entered the hallway. Her legs moved quickly but Will had no problem keeping pace with her as short as she was. She continually looked left and right into each room as they walked, looking to Will like some over sized child anxious about crossing the street and religiously checking her surroundings. She led him down the hall, past the small lobby at the entrance, and around a corner to the suite of administrative offices.

She ushered him into her small office and pointed to a seat opposite her desk where he could sit. Will took a moment to glance over the office, Mitchell's diploma from UNH hanging behind her desk, a reproduction of a Norman Rockwell picture on the far wall, and a photograph of a gaggle of penguins on the beach with the phrase "Walk the Talk" emblazoned below it. Her desk was nearly empty save for a collection of pens and pencils, a pad of paper, and a stack of manila folders lying on the corner of the desk nearest his seat.

"What can I help you with Ms. Mitchell?" He had called her Mrs. Mitchell once, but had been chided well enough that he hadn't made the mistake again.

"You know as well as I, Mr. Boucher. The bill for your mother. This is perhaps the part of my job I enjoy the least, but it's necessary. The bill is overdue again. You made a partial payment last month but the balance of $453 still remains. We receive some monies from the State, as you know, but that does not cover the full cost of the care she receives at a facility such as ours. We can't provide this service to anyone," she said, stressing the word, "if we are losing money on residents in our care. The bill for April is still due. When can we expect payment?"

Will knew that there were other facilities that might be able to care for his mother. But none were as well maintained as Riverview, nor located in Derryfield. His mother had spent most of her life in Derryfield, had moved here when she was just a child, had married, had children, and lived here since; it made sense to him that she would spend what remained of her life here as well.

"I spoke to your assistant or whoever on the phone the other day. By this time next week," Will said. He ran his hand through his hair and sat back in his seat. "I have some outstanding accounts of my own that should be coming in, and that should be plenty to cover what remains of that bill."

Ms. Mitchell studied the collection of writing instruments before her and, after a few seconds, grabbed one quickly, her hand darting out as if the pens and pencils were food about to be whisked away by a waiter. She scribbled something on the pad of paper on her desk.

"Please be mindful of May's bill as well, Mr. Boucher. It's due by the end of this month."

"I understand," Will said.

"I appreciate that you understand that. I will be expecting the remainder of April's bill by this time next week. May's is due by the end of this month."

"Of course."

Will waited for Ms. Mitchell to say something more. She sat tall — well as tall as someone as short as her could — her spine straight and untouched by the back of the seat, her hands clasped together on her desk.

"Thanks," Will said, unsure of what else to say. Ms. Mitchell nodded as he rose from his seat and left her office.

Will slowly walked down the hall back towards his mother's room. He kicked each leg out and focused on the feeling in his feet as his weight shifted from one to the other with each stride. He needed to calm himself, release the anxiety he felt; there was no need to alarm or upset Mom any more than she usually was in this place. The staff — well, most of the staff — really tried, but by the time Mom had made it here, she was too far along to identify Riverview as anything but not home.

When he returned to the room Mildred was transfixed by the television and whatever daytime soap was on. The volume was low enough that Will could barely make out the voices. Mildred had pulled her wheelchair directly in front of the television and sat only about two feet from it. Norma's eyes were closed, and she looked like she could be dead but for the rhythmic rise and fall of her chest. This time Norma was ignorant of Will's entrance into the room and did not stir when he spoke.

"Hi, Mom," Will said. Mildred remained focused on the television, so Will repeated himself.

"Hi, Mom," he said a bit louder.

"Oh, Billy!" Mildred said. "How I've missed you! I haven't seen you in so long!"

Will smiled. The initial moments of the smile were true, an expression of happiness for his mother's honest joy in seeing him. The smile remained on his face for a few more seconds in an effort to mask the concern he felt, the kind of smile that as a mother she would know was forced.

"It's good to see you too, Mom," he replied, forcing the smile but meaning every word.

CHAPTER EIGHT

The local office of the New Hampshire Department of Transportation was located in Durham in a small brick building a few miles from the university. The drive there from Derryfield had taken Erica down Route 101 and past the site where her brother had died. The road in that section was two lanes — one running east, one west — with oncoming traffic hurtling in the opposite direction at over 50 miles per hour. Erica slowed as she neared the spot, adorned with a gleaming white cross, like so many of the other sites where drivers and passengers had perished.

If not for the highway, the area could be confused as picturesque. The land was relatively flat, many of the nearby hardwoods reaching their limbs high into the sky, the forests having recovered two generations ago when the people of New Hampshire — as did the rest of the US — began to shift away from agriculture as the primary profession. What eliminated any further appreciation was the smell, the stench that nearly always wafted up from the swampland scattered about the Pilwilla River.

Erica grasped the wheel tighter as she neared the spot — her knuckles turning a bone white like the cross beside the road — and pushed down on the accelerator. She had stopped there once two weeks ago, a few days after Nate's passing. Her mother had insisted on having the cross placed there, though the family was only nominally religious, regularly attending Mass only on Christmas and Easter. When asked about it, Judy had mentioned the dozens of other crosses scattered about the highway as if the presence of those was reason enough to place one for Nate.

Erica arrived at the DOT in Durham a little before 12 PM. The parking lot seemed too large for the small building, its dozens of spaces containing only a few late '80s Ford Escorts and a Jeep Wrangler.

It looked to Erica like an oasis of blacktop in a sea of green, the grass ringing the lot at least six inches tall. As she exited her car she realized the size of the lot was likely due to the potential for the actual vehicles servicing the roads to access the lot; tri-axles, dualies, and more, whatever large vehicles moved the men and asphalt and tools and equipment needed to maintain the state roads in this corner of New Hampshire.

The air was again hot and heavy. A few wispy clouds did little to block the sun and did not suggest the storm that the meteorologists were predicting would be rolling through in the late afternoon. Inside the office was considerably cooler; Erica could hear the hum of an air conditioning unit. It was what one might expect of a small state's satellite office: light tan tiles on the floor, off white walls, a drop-ceiling with white panels surrounding the fluorescent lights affixed to the ceiling. A row of cubicles ran along one wall, with two offices in the rear. The other wall led to restrooms and a larger room Erica assumed was a break room.

"Can I help you?" the receptionist said in an exasperated tone. She raised her eyebrows and sighed, as if this intrusion was too much of a burden.

"Erica Couture," she said, holding out her hand, "I'm with the *Gazette*, have a meeting with Gerald at 12."

The receptionist did not take her hand. "I'll let him know you are here."

Erica sat in one of the metal frame chairs while she waited. She was steadily producing articles for the *Gazette*, like stories about a new community center, a new housing development, or the fund raising efforts of the Derryfield Lions Club, but had yet to draft anything on Route 101. Karen had inquired a few times about "the road construction story" as the two of them worked their way down the list of approved topics, and each time Erica had assured her she was still on it, and that she believed it may even become a multi-part article spanning a few days in the week.

After a few minutes of waiting a man emerged from one of the rear offices. He wore a pair of khakis and a wrinkled blue polo shirt with short sleeves. She guessed he was in his early forties, old enough to be in charge of the local office of the DOT but not enough years in state service to be up in Concord yet.

"Erica, nice to meet you," Gerald said. "I don't believe we've met before."

Erica shook his hand. "We haven't. I've been here before, a few years back, but spoke to Susan Moss."

"Yeah, Sue. She's up in Concord now. Got a promotion a year or so back, working right with the Commissioner. Again, I would have been happy to speak with you further over the phone."

"I know," Erica said and smiled. "It's just that the phone is so impersonal. There's something to be said for in person interviews that allows us at the paper to better flesh out a story. Plus, it's not that far to get here — only took me about half an hour."

"I see. Well why don't you come on back to my office, it's a little more comfortable back there."

His office was small, ten feet by ten feet, a metal desk placed prominently in the center. A single window let in some natural light, which was somewhat blocked by the air conditioning unit sticking out its bottom half. Gerald settled in behind the desk and motioned for Erica to take either of the two seats in front of it.

"You mind if I record this?" Erica asked as she sat, placing a tape recorder on the edge of the desk.

"I do, sorry," Gerald said, breathing in quickly between clenched teeth. "Don't have the OK from the Commissioner for recording. I mean, it's on the record sure, but no recording." He shrugged.

"I understand," Erica replied. She reached into her satchel and rooted around for a pen and pad. She did so slowly, slightly exaggerating the movements in hopes that he might grow uncomfortable with the extended silence and instead just agree to recording. After a few protracted seconds, Erica wielded a pen and pad and then returned the recorder to her satchel.

Often a bit nervous when meeting an interviewee for the first time, any anxiety Erica might have felt was washed out by the anger simmering inside her. She knew, intellectually, that her anger was likely misplaced — the DOT had not killed Nate, no matter how its work (or lack thereof) on Route 101 had contributed to his death. Though knowing this, she felt the anger all the same, and it helped propel her forward.

"So," Erica began, "we're working on a story at the *Gazette* on the current construction projects across the area. Looking to give our readers an idea of what to expect, both in terms of delays while the construction is ongoing during the summer tourism season, as well as anticipated improvements to the roadway. What in particular should we be telling the readers?"

"You've seen the press release from earlier this year, right? I think it was April," Gerald did not wait for a response and instead thumbed through a stack of folders on his desk. He pulled out two sheets stapled together and handed it to Erica.

"Thanks," Erica said before glancing over it, briefly reviewing the bulleted list of work projects and expected start and end times throughout the summer. "I think I've seen this."

"So you know we have some important expansion projects throughout the state, and in particular along the seacoast. Route 1A needs some work, though that will be put off until the summer season has passed."

"And how are the projects coming along this summer?" Erica asked.

"Very well. For the most part, summer is a time for some significant projects for road improvements. We usually lose at least four months of the year to the winter season, when our primary role becomes snow removal, salt treatments, sand applications and the like. It's not that we can't continue large projects, it just becomes much harder. Mud season follows that, and our primary goal moves to repairing the damage from winter and the freeze/thaw process throughout the spring. Summer gives us the time and manpower to really tackle larger projects. We always have to be mindful of the increased traffic with tourism, but it's something we try to plan around."

"How about Route 101? What's the status of 101?"

"It's a work in progress. We had hoped to have the expansion done years ago but expect it to be done in the very near future."

Erica felt her frustration rising in her chest, a warmth and tightness that caused her to grind her teeth. She had feigned patience for only a few minutes with this man and it was already to long. What she wanted was answers.

"Many people have died on that road," she spat. "By my count, at least 100 people have died on 101 since 1980, and many more injured. That's all primarily on a stretch of 101 about 15 miles long. That's an extraordinary fatality rate, 6 per mile. The Highway of Death. What gives?"

Gerald looked flustered for a moment, his mouth slightly agape, his eyes somewhat unfocused, but he regained composure quickly. "It's a complicated project," he answered, his voice low. "Funding is piecemeal, holdups in the legislature. It's a busy road, the main artery to the coast for much of south central New Hampshire, and as a two lane road, the potential for significant collisions is high."

Erica nodded to Gerald to continue.

"We've been trying for years to improve it — tried to get approval for a new Interstate running that stretch, Interstate 92 they were gonna call it. Tried to make it a toll road too, to expand it. Also was shot down. Always an issue with funding from Concord — or from D.C. We've finally secured that funding and expansion is currently underway, but for the recent environmental hold up." He took a breath, gathering more composure, and continued. "The expansion of the roadway into a four-lane divided highway should significantly decrease the rate of accidents and fatalities on the roadway."

"Why hasn't anything been done in the meantime?" Erica asked. She fought to control her voice, keep it level, professional.

"But we have; we put up the flashers where the road pares down to two lanes, the speed limit drops, we diligently ensure that the road is well marked, and the signs have been placed there for a few years informing drivers of the increased fatality rate. Until the funding issues are resolved, as well as the current environmental hold up, we've done all we can."

"What do you expect for a decrease in accidents following the expansion?"

"Significant. A significant decrease. I don't have the projections right in front of me, you understand," Gerald said, waving his hands about as if to show to Erica again they were empty, "but I recall it being significant. If you look at comparable highways, well, not comparable, but divided highways, the fatalities per mile are nearly always lower than undivided highways. It decreases the probability of head-on collisions, or near head-ons, especially when traffic is looking to pass. It's just a much safer design for a highway. It's unfortunate that 101, especially in that section, has been an undivided highway for so many years."

Erica heard footsteps and voices in the main space of the building behind her, some of the work crews arriving back to the office at midday. The noise distracted her, eroding what little control she had maintained over her anger.

"Unfortunate is quite the fucking understatement, wouldn't you say?"

"Excuse me?" Gerald said, raising his eyebrows in time with his voice. "I don't know what you are expecting out of this interview Ms. Couture, but you shared on the telephone that you wanted an overview of construction in this part of the state. If you have no other questions about that, I presume we are done here."

"Yeah," Erica said, "I appreciate your time Gerald,"she added as a force of habit more than a genuine expression.

As she ventured forth back into the sunlight, Erica saw the parking lot now held three large GMC trucks. Two men stood leaning in the shade of one, laughing and holding cigarettes. She swallowed her anger and raised her hand to them and walked over. Her experience prodded her forward, urging her to speak to the men to at least hear their thoughts on 101.

Ignoring their height, the men could have been twins. Both wore blue jeans and a gray t-shirt emblazoned with NH DOT under an orange reflector vest. Both grinned out of the corner of their mouths when Erica appeared, the motion slightly shifting the bushy beard on each chin. Both were slim, but wiry. The first stood well over six feet, the second no taller than Erica, five six or so.

"Hi," Erica said as she drew closer, "I'm Erica Couture from the *Gazette*. Can I have a moment of your time?"

The tall one spoke first: "Sure Ma'am, long as you don't mind us smoking that is." He laughed, as did his companion, both revealing a broad and honest grin slightly stained brown from years of cigarette smoke.

"I'm Drew," the tall one said. "This one here's Jack. What can we do ya for?"

"I just have a few questions if you don't mind."

"This OK with Gerry?" Drew asked. "I think we're supposed to check with him for shit like this."

Erica lied. "I just finished up speaking with him, he said I should talk with you guys as well."

"Sure," Drew said, taking a moment for a quick drag on his cigarette, the end glowing bright in the shadow, "shoot."

"I'm just wondering what you think of 101. The road, the dangers and all."

"Heh," Jack said before coughing once to the side and spitting a wad of something into the shaded pavement beside him. "Highway of Death huh?"

"Yeah. You guys deal with this sort of stuff all the time — what's your take? Why hasn't the road been expanded all these years?"

"Well shit, I don't know much about that," Drew answered. "I mean, it's all up to Concord and all what gets funded. And all we do is-"

"Well I'll tell you this," Jack interjected, "it's pretty fucked." He nodded and opened his eyes wide. "Excuse my French," he added. "All those folks dying, pretty uh... crazy things happening out there."

"Yeah," Erica said, unsure of what else to say in response. "Why though — why so many fatalities?"

"Road's narrow and all. High speed." Drew shrugged.

"Strange shit happens out there too, ya know," Jack added. When Drew started to protest, Jack turned to him and nodded his head to quiet him. "You heard it well as me Jack, don't bullshit her."

"You don't need to be sharing made up shit with a reporter," Drew said and sighed.

"I didn't make any of that shit up — you heard it same as me!" Jack replied. "There's shit out there you can't explain man."

"What do you mean?" Erica asked. She looked from one face to another, trying to read the expressions hidden behind smoldering cigarettes, squinted eyes, and bearded faces.

"This like, on the record?" Jack asked.

"No, doesn't have to be. I'm just curious. Always interested to hear a story. What sort of strange shit is happening out there?"

"Well, I ain't seen anything myself," Jack said, taking a drag on his cigarette and leaning in slightly towards Erica, "but I've heard plenty of people who have."

"Who?"

"Some of those folks who got in wrecks but survived. I don't know 'em personally really, just spoken to some."

"OK. What did they say?"

"Seen strange shit out there. Something spooked em off the road. Plenty of them off that road not cause of oncoming traffic's what I'm saying."

"What did they see?"

"I don't know for sure. Not sure they knew either. Maybe a ghost or something." Drew laughed at that remark and shook his head; Jack ignored him.

"I see," Erica said, pursing her lips and nodding.

"I knew she wouldn't believe your bullshit," Drew said. He laughed again and clapped Jack on his back.

"I ain't bullshitting you. Honest lady," Jack said and held up his cigarette-free hand. "You don't believe me, go talk to some of those folks who've been through the wrecks. Drew," he said turning, "what was that guy's name again? David something."

"Jesus Jack."

"Ha, not Jesus. Come on, what was his name?" Jack urged him on. "You always remember names better than me."

"Bellows I think," Drew said, shaking his head, before returning to his cigarette.

"Yeah, David Bellows. We was behind him a ways on the highway a few years back. We came up on the wreck. Helped him, his leg was all crushed, tried to stop the bleeding and all. He came by afterwords — after he was out of the hospital — bought us a few rounds as thank you, you know? Showed off his new leg, had it amputated you see from the accident."

"And?" Erica asked.

"And he told us something spooked him off the road. Wasn't sure what it was. Heard rumors about others seeing stuff too. Never have myself though." Jack shrugged and finished his cigarette in one long drag. Drew made eye contact with Erica and shrugged.

"Where's David Bellows from?" Erica asked.

"Over in Portsmouth I think," Jack added.

"Listen, that all you need? You heard his story," Drew said. "It's time for lunch, and I'd like to get out of this damn heat."

"Yeah, that's all. Thanks," Erica replied.

"No problem," Drew said. They both stomped out their cigarette butts then started towards the office. Erica turned and looked down at the pavement as she walked back to her car, unsure of what to make of Jack's story.

CHAPTER NINE

The heat continued throughout the month of June with only an occasional day of respite, so on many days, Corey and Alex found themselves retreating at midday to the air conditioned living room of Alex's house. Even in the forest the heat and humidity was too much; if Mrs. Marino would let them they would all go down to the lake to swim, but on the days that she refused to take them, the boys stayed inside during the middle of the day to escape the heat.

They sat together now on the floor of the Marino's living room, Corey with his legs crossed on the beige carpet and Alex with his legs folded underneath him. The television sat on a small table at the far end of the room, a coffee table with scratched legs lay behind the boys, with a yellow couch and a leather recliner chair behind that.

As usual, the best thing on television this time of day was Nickelodeon. The phone rang but neither boy moved. *Aaahh!!! Real Monsters* was more interesting than a phone call.

"Corey," Mrs. Marino yelled from the kitchen, "your father called."

Corey twisted and turned towards the kitchen. Mrs. Marino yelled: "He's got to work a second shift, so why don't you stay the night here."

"OK," Corey yelled back. He heard Mrs. Marino say something more to his father before she hung up the phone.

"Should I go home to get a sleeping bag, or maybe like some new clothes?" Corey yelled towards the kitchen.

"Not unless you want to honey," Mrs. Marino said as she stepped into the threshold of the living room. "We've got plenty of sleeping bags here and I'm sure you can borrow some clothes from Alex tomorrow if you need them."

"Yeah, definitely," Alex said. "We've got tons of sleeping bags. I used a couple of them last year when I went camping, remember?"

Mrs. Marino returned to the kitchen and Alex turned to Corey. "Corey! We can watch *MonsterVision!* It's a marathon of hidden island movies tonight!" Alex clenched his hands together and rocked back and forth on his knees, unable to contain the excitement he felt.

"Have you seen any of the movies before?" Corey asked.

"Nope! But they're going to have that guy from Gilligan's Island host... the silly one, I can't remember his name. All night movies and popcorn!"

"That'll be wicked awesome," Corey said and smiled.

"But don't tell my mom!" Alex warned, leaning over towards Corey and lowering his voice. "She'd tell us to be in bed before the second one started. We'll watch the first one and tell her we are going to bed. Then we can wait until she and my dad go to bed, and we can head down to the basement and watch the rest!"

"Do you want to get popcorn or something?" Corey asked.

"Definitely. Let's go down to the store and get some snacks. How much money do you got? Should I ask my mom for some allowance?"

Corey emptied his pockets and disbursed a few crumpled single dollar bills, a handful of silver and copper colored coins, and a single red bottle cap.

"That one gets me a free Coke," Corey said, holding it out so that Alex could see it. The inside of the cap had fine black printing inside that said "1 Free Coke."

"Nice!" Alex said. "Where'd you get that?"

"My dad gave it to me. He won it a week or so ago."

"You going to get another one?" Alex asked.

"Yeah. You going to get popcorn for tonight?"

"Hell yeah!" Alex answered and then looked over his shoulder for fear of finding his mother behind him. He'd been caught a few times already cursing, thankfully just the familiar four letter words his father sometimes spat, and each time his mother had chided him and told him that consequences would follow, up to and including being grounded. But she had not heard this one, so Alex scrounged up another few dollars from his room and the two walked down to the nearest convenience store.

Mark's Convenience was a small building sitting on a lot that had enough room for approximately 12 parking spots squeezed between trees to the right and bushes to the left, with only a small clearing on the right for deliveries to pull in and access the side door. The building itself was oddly shaped, much wider than it was tall, but disjointedly so; the far left of the building had a black topped sloped roof rising approximately 20 feet in the air, which met another roof a few feet shorter which trailed away and more than doubled the size of the store. It was clear the building had not been built in one sitting, but in at least three stages, each stage adding additional space as the sole commercial property in this part of town grew alongside the neighborhood. Heavy vegetation rose up behind the store but was not visible from the street, though Corey and Alex were familiar with it due to their explorations around the neighborhood.

The automatic doors at the entrance of Mark's slid open soundlessly. Alex turned to Corey and said: "Let's enter the holodeck." Corey smirked. As they entered, the heavy heat of the June afternoon gave way to the air conditioned climate inside. Both boys became more aware of the sweat their bodies had produced in the short walk. The cool and dry air washed over them, and both, without realizing the other did it, began rubbing their suddenly cold arms.

The interior held more than seemed possible from the outside. Rows of merchandise — candy, canned goods, batteries, milk, an assortment of basic tools, water, and bread, among other necessities — ran from the rear of the store to the front, with just enough room between rows for one person to maneuver and find what they needed. The register sat immediately to the left of the door and the restroom to the right. Jerry, a high school senior both boys vaguely knew from his time working at Mark's, looked bored behind the register, his right elbow on the counter and his chin resting in his right hand. Jerry glanced at the two but did nothing more to acknowledge their entrance. The drink displays were pushed far against the right wall, just beyond the bathroom.

"I'll get popcorn," Alex said, "grab me a Moxie, OK?"

"Sure thing," Corey replied.

Corey surveyed the row of refrigerators displaying dozens of different cold beverages. He grabbed a Moxie for Alex and considered grabbing one for himself, but remembered the cap his father had given him good for one free Coke. Corey glanced through the four rows of plastic coke bottles and stared at where the overhead lights reflected off the deep brown of the soda, a glare that shifted as he moved his head or jostled the bottles. He chose the upper row on the right; it felt lucky to him, like another winner.

Jerry took an extra minute to cash them out as he was unsure of how to process the free soda. Once the transaction was completed, Alex stuffed the candy and popcorn into his backpack. Going from inside Mark's back to the summer afternoon was even worse than the reverse; the heat was stifling and Alex found his glasses beginning to fog in the humidity.

As soon as they exited the store Corey cranked the soda opened and, before he even took a sip, checked the underside of the cap. It read: "1 Free Coke."

"Alex! I won again!" Corey yelled. He held his right hand holding the cap aloft like it was a trophy.

"No way in hell you did," Alex said. Alex craned his neck and stood on his tiptoes and said, "Let me see it! I can't even see it!"

Corey smiled a held his palm out before Alex, the cap upturned to reveal the message inside.

"Damn!" Alex yelled, shook his head, and smiled at Corey. "You're one lucky son of a gun."

"It's not luck," Corey teased, "it's skill. You have to know the right ones to pick. You've got the feel it, sense it, to figure out which ones are the winner."

"Sure, sure," Alex said before he punched Corey's arm.

"What the hell man!" Corey yelled, "that shit hurt!"

An old woman walking into the store stopped mid-stride and frowned at Corey. Corey didn't notice her immediately, so Alex elbowed his arm and nodded his head over towards the woman. Corey glanced over at her, eying her long mauve skirt, heavy sweater, and wrinkled face contorted into a disapproving glare. Corey tried to stifle a smile, but feeling that it would escape, he opted to turn his back on the old woman and move away from her. When Alex caught up with him after a few steps Corey said: "Geez, didn't see her there."

Alex laughed and looked back over his shoulder to see the woman shaking her head as she entered the store.

The two walked towards downtown and talked about whatever was most interesting in the moment: the best Magic: The Gathering decks they could assemble with the few cards they had; the optimal way one would fight a T-Rex; and which version of Harrison Ford would win in a fight between Indiana Jones and Han Solo. Thoughts of tomorrow or yesterday were entirely absent from their minds. Without even meaning to, without realizing it, what only mattered to them both was now, how the sun felt on their back, how the soda tasted in their mouth, and how their friendship mattered in their heart. They walked down to the circle and started their way back towards Alex's house when they heard a man shouting.

"Hey," Will Boucher yelled to the two boys as they passed, "can one of you give me a hand for a second?" Will held a large cardboard box in his hands that was filled to the brim with boxes of oil filters, each emblazoned with the yellows and reds of marketing and a string of numbers identifying the filter. Will's tendons bulged out from his forearms and looked like serpents coiled up to his elbows.

Alex and Corey looked at each other, each expecting the other to volunteer. Corey shrugged and jogged the thirty feet to open the door.

"Thanks," Will said before stepping inside and placing the cardboard box on the floor of the office. He turned back and nodded to the two.

"Name's Will. Thanks for the hand."

"I'm Corey," Corey said. "That's my friend Alex."

"Nice to meet you both." Will squinted his eyes and looked intently at Corey. "You Ted's son?"

"Yes, sir," Corey replied. As they talked, Alex walked a few steps towards them.

"Look like your father," Will said, and then quickly added, "Jesus, I sound like all the old farts in this town — I've heard that enough myself."

Both Alex and Corey laughed at Will's refrain.

"You mean people say you look like your dad?" Alex asked.

"Yeah, yeah they do. Or at least used to. Guess that's bound to happen when you follow in his footsteps like I have."

"You work here, right?" Alex asked.

"Yeah. My old man used to run the place and now I do."

They each stood there a moment with nothing more to say. "Well don't let me keep you, you two look plenty busy," Will said and gestured at the soda and bags in the boys' hands. "Thanks, by the way," Will added, "be seeing you around." He nodded again at the two and entered the office.

By the time they got home, Alex's parents had already started dinner: cheeseburgers and hot dogs on the grill, the boys' favorite. Each had a hot dog and they cut a cheeseburger in half and shared it. After a shower — mandatory in Alex's house after a day of play — the two popped some microwave popcorn and settled in for *MonsterVision*.

MonsterVision was a favorite of both. Each week the show presented a number of horror movies from years past, movies they were usually unknown to them. The most difficult thing about watching MonsterVision was finding the time to watch it; it was on too late to reliably watch during the school year, even if it was on a weekend night. However, Alex's parents were much more lenient during the summer months, and Corey made it a point to stay over as often as he could on Friday nights to catch the marathons of monster movies — mostly B-movies from years past, with stop-motion animation and brave heroes that saved the women they loved.

The first movie, *Creatures the World Forgot*, chronicled the lives of prehistoric tribes. Neither liked it; it didn't have enough monsters. The next movie, *Mysterious Island*, was much better received by the boys: it included monster crabs, giant birds, bees the size of cars, and even an enormous octopus. Midway through the next movie, *Jason and the Argonauts*, Alex was asleep. Corey didn't notice until one of the commercial breaks, when he stretched, yawned, looked over at Alex, and saw his eyes closed and his head rolled to his left, onto his pillow.

By the time *The Valley of Gwangi* was airing, Corey was nodding off. His exhaustion gelled with the images from the films, and he was surprised to see that his mother, Sandra, was in the movie. She wore a white hat and was riding a horse. He sat up and leaned forward and thought of waking Alex. He wouldn't believe that his mother was in the movie — she had never told Corey that she was an actress.

He watched as she rode off with two cowboys, one tall, wearing jeans, a duster, and wide black hat, the other short and slim and with a similar outfit except for the red and white handkerchief pulled across the lower half of his face. The three rode together in a canyon, the tan walls reaching up towards a thin streak of blue sky. A roar emanated and reverberated from deeper within the canyon. The trio rode on, but his mother fell further and further behind the other two, until only the man in the hat and the man in the handkerchief remained on screen.

A scream woke Corey. He startled and raised himself up on one arm and struggled to pull the sleeping bag off of his legs. It resisted briefly and stuck to him, the sweat from his legs adhering to the sleeping bag in a few slick patches. The television cast a dim blue glow across the room, not enough to dispel shadows but enough to give those shadows definition. Alex still lay beside him, asleep.

Corey turned to the television; on it, a dinosaur attacked an elephant in a rough hewn stone stadium. The nearby crowd ran from the scene. The women screamed and the men clutched their hats. Corey searched the scenes for his mother. When he didn't find her after a few minutes, he turned the television off. The sudden darkness surprised him. He crawled back to his spot on the carpet and waited for sleep while he tried to keep the image of his mother out of his mind.

CHAPTER TEN

A car horn sounded outside and Will put down the crossword puzzle he was working on. The fan blowing warm air across the office sputtered at the end of its cycle and began turning to circulate across the rest of its 150 degree arc. Will rubbed his hands on the thighs of his jeans to ensure he removed the majority of the oils before opening the door and heading outside. As he approached the vehicle, a sky blue 1988 Ford Taurus missing one hubcap — like a pirate missing an eye — Will caught a glimpse of a familiar face.

"Erica?" he asked.

Erica turned to him, smiled, and stepped out of her vehicle. He hadn't seen her often since high school, but the years hadn't made much of a difference. The features of her face were more defined, her jaw sharper and brows increasingly angular and figure fuller, a woman now, not a girl, but her hair was the same: shoulder length brown with bangs across her forehead. They had dated in high school during their junior year, a relatively long — by high school standards — relationship. They had amicably drifted apart the summer following their senior year, when each had found someone more interesting at the time. Will's memories of Erica were all pleasant and he looked back on their time together as the type of formative dating relationship that had helped him grow.

"Hi, Billy, how are you?" she asked.

"Good, good," he said. "Will now, I mean, that's what I prefer now, if you don't mind."

"Not at all, Will. Knew you were here now, but didn't think I'd see you back here all these years later," she smirked as she said this, lightening the words and making it clear she meant so with at least some humor.

"Well, neither did I. Seems life's always taking you places you don't expect."

"Ain't that the truth," Erica responded. "You in touch with any of folks from our class?"

"No, not really. Just sort of drifted apart after graduation. I'm in touch with a few guys from college." Will shrugged, but feeling the need to share that he did still have friends, though he rarely saw them nowadays said, "most of them are down in New York. But how about you, what are you up to ?"

"Still working over at the *Derryfield Gazette*, staff reporter."

"I thought I saw your name in the paper, I mean, I thought I recognized it, just wasn't sure it was you."

"Yeah," she said and laughed, "just me. Sorry to disappoint." Will laughed alongside her.

"Worked in a few different departments. Reporting on whatever I'm assigned."

"That's good," Will responded. "Hey, how's your mom and dad? How's Nate?" As soon as the question had left his lips, Will was certain he should not have asked it. The change in her demeanor was instantaneous; Erica took half a step back and began to clench both of her hands. The smile on her face vanished and the laugh lines at the corners of her eyes disappeared. Her face was blank and expressionless. The change only lasted a moment. A smile re-appeared in the right hand corner of her mouth and she lifted one eyebrow; her hands relaxed and she shifted her foot forward again. If he had turned away in that moment he would have missed the signs of her sorrow, trying as she did to mask it.

"I'm so-" he began, but stopped as she returned to the friendly disposition she had expressed the moment before. "Is, uh, is everything alright?" Will asked.

"Nate passed a few weeks back."

"Shit, Erica. I'm sorry, I didn't know." Will took a step towards her one arm held out in an awkward handshake or awkward hug. She ignored the gesture and said, "Thanks," while nodding.

"Really, I'm sorry, he was a good kid."

"He was." Feeling the need to offer some explanation, she said, "It was an accident, up off 101."

"Damn," Will said, but wasn't sure how else to respond. He

wondered how he had missed it. Must not have been on that tow, and with so many fatalities so far this summer, he must have overlooked it. The silence that filled the space between them grew more uncomfortable with each passing second.

"Well, what can I help you with? Your ride acting up?"

"Yeah," Erica said, mouth pursed. She crossed her arms over her chest, and any levity expressed earlier was now gone. Will sensed the change, and identified it not as hostility, but indifference. Where moments before she had been happy — even excited — to see an old high school once-boyfriend, Will's comment had ripped off whatever scab had been forming in her mind about the loss of her brother. She was emotionally bleeding. Will couldn't see it or smell it, but he could feel the blood.

"What seems to be the trouble?" Will asked, now painfully aware of what her real troubles were.

"I'm getting a noise from the front down the road. Sort of a hum up front."

Will took a few steps forward towards the front of her vehicle and asked: "At all speeds? Does it get worse the faster you drive?"

"I don't know." Erica took two steps backwards towards the rear of the vehicle, communicating with her position that she was comfortable with Will examining the car. Will glanced at the passenger side front tire and rested his hand atop it in order to feel the wear of the tread and the remaining depth. There was considerable tread left on the tire but it was worn unevenly. The bumps across its surface were about the size of his hand and sporadic, as if the tire was a boxer who had taken a few good hits and the bruising and protrusions were the damage that remained. Before saying anything he walked to the other side of the vehicle and felt the driver's side tire as well. It had the same gradated bumps across its surface.

"Tires all are chopped. Could be the alignment. Maybe the suspension. When'd you last have it aligned?" Will asked.

"I have no idea. It would be a while ago."

"Should probably get it in to check at least. Could be the suspension too." Will placed his hands with elbows bent on the hood and above the wheel well and then extended his arms quickly to compress the front suspension and observe its rebound. It bounced up and down a few times, more so that it probably should.

"Yea, could definitely be the suspension. It seems a tad weak, but I can't tell all that much just out here. Might need a new set of tires too, unless you can live with the noise. We should really get it in and take a look. A two minute review next to the pumps is only going to provide so much information, you know?"

"Yeah, I do," Erica answered. "Well, when can you get it in?"

"Come on in the office and I'll check the calendar," Will said, knowing that nearly any day would do. He turned without waiting for Erica and began to walk back towards the office. He heard her footsteps fall in behind his. The bell hanging overhead rang as he pushed open the door and rang again when it closed behind Erica. Will stepped behind the desk, its surface covered with catalogs, papers, folders, and repair orders. He began casting them aside in search for the calendar.

"Is that?" Erica asked, grabbing a news magazine he set aside, "is that the *Weekly World News*? You read this?"

Will smirked. "Just for fun. It's hilarious the things these people come up with. Bigfoot sleeping with the President, the Loch Ness monster in telepathic communication with the Pope, those sorts of things. It's fun."

"It's not exactly the height of journalistic integrity."

"Hey, hey." Will laughed. "Ease off me. I read the *Gazette* too you know."

"Well I'm glad to hear our readers have such diverse and sophisticated tastes."

"Yeah, yeah," Will responded, drawing out each word. He continued to rummage with both hands through the papers and folders on his desk until he found the shop calendar.

"Well," Will said as he scanned through the calendar, "tomorrow is pretty well booked, but I can get you in Friday, if that works for you."

Erica already had the calendar in her purse out and open, and thumbed through the week. "I need to confirm with a coworker that I can get a ride in on Friday and back here, but that should work."

"Great," Will said, "so I'll pencil you in." He began to write her name into the calendar and then added, "I can probably give you a ride in and back if that helps."

"No," Erica said smiling, "I wouldn't want to inconvenience you."

"It wouldn't be an inconvenience at all. It's only a few minutes down the road. Robert can watch the shop for that long at least."

"I heard that!" Robert yelled from the shop. Will smiled and stifled a laugh.

"Sure then, that'd be great," Erica said. "If you could give me a lift into the *Gazette* I'd really appreciate it."

"I'll see you then," Will replied.

She left and Will followed out the door a few minutes later after yelling to Robert about the need to pick up parts at NH Autoparts. The parts store was only a two miles down the road, but getting out of the shop every once in awhile felt too good to pass up to regular deliveries. NHAutoparts sat at the end of a small strip mall built in the early '80s. The sign had long since passed middle age and at night only enough letters to spell "N A toparts" were illuminated. The drivers curried parts in battered and rusting S-10s that many likened to "Frankenmobiles", as when something went wrong with one, Burt, the owner, was likely to make do with whatever part would get the vehicle running for another week, even if it wasn't the right part.

Will was not surprised to see Stanley Lewis and Jason McCarthy standing at the parts counter. Jason's job was to stand there and answers phones, but Stanley just enjoyed the company. Stanley was something north of 75 and appeared every year his age: his hands were perpetually clenched, the knobby knuckles bulging from his thin limbs. What hair remained on his head was shock white, and his ever present grin revealed teeth yellowed with age. At his age, Stanley was old enough to have even retired from his "retirement job" as a driver for NH Autoparts. But even retirement from that gig didn't keep him off the premises; he spent most days shooting the shit with staff and customers at the store, and his nights in one of two bars downtown, sipping on one — or at most two — beers throughout an evening.

Jason stood a foot taller than Stanley and his thick forearms sported an assortment of tattoos. Will wasn't sure what they all were, though a few of the larger were obvious: a cross, a skull, a four leaf clover. Will thought that Jason might have served some time in prison; Will picked up that kind of vibe off him, though it didn't matter. Jason knew cars well, and knew what parts were needed.

"Hey," Will said as he approached the two.

Stanley kicked one leg out to rotate on his stool and said: "Well if it isn't Boucher the younger. How the hell are you?"

"Fine, Stanley," Will answered. "How are you?"

"Out of bed, so that's good in my book. Ready to fight and fornicate," he laughed at his own joke and smiled at Will and Jason.

"Hey Will," Jason said. "What do you need?"

"A big bag of twenties would do — hell, even a bag of tens. I'm not a picky man."

Jason laughed. "I'll see what I can do — anything else other than that?"

"Need a tie rod for a '91 Cavalier."

"Let me see what we've got," Jason said and walked back into the small warehouse behind the retail store. NH Autoparts had enough warehouse space to store the more common parts used on the more popular cars, but anything for an odd repair or a unique vehicle would not be available. Will figured they'd have the tie rod for the '91 Cavalier in stock.

"Will, let me ask you about this," Stanley said as Jason walked away. "I keep telling Jason here," he said, pointing at Jason's back as if he needed to identify him because there was another Jason present that might make the story confusing, "that this State is going to hell. I mean, I love it, but it's happening. It's going to hell."

"Let me guess," Will began, having heard Stanley's complaints more than a few times before. "Too many flatlanders moving in, voting in the Democrats, tax and spend and damn America. I get it right?" Will asked.

Stanley laughed. "See, you get this. It's getting worse every year. All these Massholes keep moving up here, voting liberal, trying to turn this place into Taxachusetts as well."

"Hey, hey, hey," Jason yelled from the next room, "I'm sure some of them are, but not all of them. You know I'm from Mass, right?"

"The enemy in our midst!" Stanley shouted with glee before again laughing at his own wit. Will couldn't help but appreciate his exuberance and laughed as well. They could hear Jason laugh from the warehouse before he moved deeper into its rows of auto parts.

"Is that really a fair criticism?" Will asked Stanley. "You were born and raised here, right?"

"You got that right."

"And it's changed plenty in your seventy something odd years, right?"

"Well, yeah," Stanley began, "but the change was good, you hear? We got automobiles everywhere, planes in and out of every city, hell, we went to the moon. But it's not like that now — it's like we reached a peak you hear? We reached a peak and now we're just backsliding."

"Nah," Will said. "Hate to break this to you Stan, but every generation says that. Wasn't your father bitching about how you and your generation was ending the world too?"

Stanley paused for a moment to consider his answer, rocking back and forth slightly as he did so. He took in a deep breath. "Well yes, he complained. But it's different nowadays. I mean, the world's changed. People went soft."

"Sure, they're always saying that."

"Yeah, yeah," Stanley muttered as he rubbed his chin. "Whatever. Anyways, how's business?"

"It's OK. Just a lot of things to juggle right now. Tough to keep everything under control at the shop. Plenty of tows this time of year though, lots up on 101."

"Jesus yeah, another fatal up there the other night, huh?"

"That's what I heard. Roger Simmons's boy. I wasn't up on that one, someone else got the call. Seems like a new one every week."

"Highway of Death and all," Stanley added and sighed.

"They really have to finish that expansion project," Will said. "What was it, let me guess: speeding, drunk?"

"The Simmons kid?" Stanley asked. "Nah, no way was that kid drunk, or likely speeding. Police haven't said as much, at least not yet. He was a good kid, came around here a few times getting parts for his Ford. You know his parents, right?" Stanley asked, not waiting for a response: "You ever see Roger at the Hilltop or the Granite Goose? That family's straight as the day is long. Just a terrible accident I guess."

"They're all terrible up there on 101," Will said, shaking his head.

Stanley grunted in response, a sound that communicated agreement and understanding in a single syllable. Neither man spoke, the only sound that of Jason rummaging about in the back room and the gentle hum of the air conditioning units filtering the air.

"Well, at least you can thank God Governor Morrill has kept things tight," Stanley said, referring to the governor. "The economy's finally looking better."

"Yeah," Will replied. "Let's hope. I could certainly use the boost."

Jason stumbled out of the stockroom and cursed under his breath. "Sorry Will," he said, "Can't find it. I could have sworn we had one back there, but maybe it got misplaced. I'll ask some of the driver's to keep looking, but put in an order for one as well."

"Thanks Jason," Will said.

"You ain't gonna ask me to go look for that shit, are you?" Stanley asked.

"I wouldn't dream of it," Jason answered.

"Listen guys," Will started, "I'd love to stay and listen to you two flirt," Jason scowled and Stanley laughed, "but you know how these things go. The minute I step out that door at the circle is the minute work stops." Will smiled and both Jason and Stanley laughed now. "Catch you later," Will added.

The ride back to the shop felt longer than the ride out. He thought not of the missing tie rod, but of Erica and life before college, before his dad had passed, when leaving Derryfield seemed like the best choice he could make, when the future held promise for something new and different. Now he wasn't sure what the future held, but he was sure it would include bills he couldn't pay and a mother he couldn't help.

CHAPTER ELEVEN

David Bellows was tall — a little over six feet — with short reddish brown hair that continued from atop his head to wrap around his chin in a closely-trimmed beard. He stood slightly off kilter and each step he took was just out of time, like a marionette performance that was close to emulating a human stride but was falling just short.

David had needed almost no convincing to meet with Erica when she called and asked if he would agree to share his memory of his accident on Route 101. Erica had expected some resistance or at least hesitancy, but David seemed eager to divulge what he knew. Erica knew that some people needed coaxing or needed to be convinced that what they knew was worth sharing. Others spoke to her easily; they were ready to spill their secrets, and with only a little prodding burst forth with their tale like an overinflated balloon. Oftentimes, she found one of the most important part of the job was not just listening, but making others want to share their stories. No matter their outlook, in the end, most spoke to her. The request for a story and the interest in a someone's personal narrative, Erica believed that there was something universal about it.

David hobbled over to the small table Erica occupied and pointed to the cream colored prosthetic leg jutting out from underneath his jean shorts.

"Sorry for making you wait," he said, smiling "as you can see, I'm one foot in the grave."

"Yes, I noticed," Erica responded before laughing along with him. "Thanks for agreeing to meet with me."

They shook hands and Erica added, "I didn't pull you away from your work, did I?"

"Nah," David said as he settled down into a chair across from Erica, waving his hand as if he could brush away the pointless question.

"Now that I'm running my own insurance agency, I can get out whenever I want. A bit more pressure, owning the business and all, but the freedom's nice."

"I can believe that," Erica replied. "You want anything? Coffee? Well, iced would be better today. Either way, on me."

The had met halfway, David driving over from Portsmouth and Erica from Derryfield to speak to each other at a small diner in Stratham, *The Early Bird*. This late in the morning the crowd was beginning to ease and most of the tables and booths were empty, those employed having long since eaten breakfast and arrived at work and those retired or on break now on to some summertime adventure.

"No, nothing for me thanks," David replied.

"Of course. Well thanks again for coming out here. As I said on the telephone with you, I'm a reporter for the *Derryfield Gazette*, working a story on Route 101. If you don't mind, I'd like to ask you some questions about the accident you were involved in a few years ago."

"If I minded, I wouldn't be here," he said and grinned again as he rubbed his hands together. "It wasn't pleasant, but I've got nothing against speaking about it. Helps... what's that phrase they use? Exorcise the demons I guess, deal with the trauma or whatever. But before I go on, can you tell me more about what the story's gonna be about?"

"Yeah, of course." Erica leaned back into her chair. "I'm working on a story for the *Gazette* on the history of 101. I know there have been many serious accidents on it over the years, and I'm looking for your recollection of it — of your accident. I know a little bit about what happened, because I reached out to DOT, spoke to them, and some of the guys over at DOT said they were there to help you back when it happened. I'm just looking to learn more about that. The accident, the cause, the aftermath. Your story, if you will, of Route 101."

"Yeah, sure," David said, this time rubbing his beard, "that's what they said, the guys at DOT. I mean, I don't remember it much, the accident. Don't remember much immediately after the accident is what I'm trying to say. Doctors told me the guys from DOT saved my life though. Just my luck they were coming down the highway a mile or so behind me, saw the crash, got out and helped me. Stopped the bleeding on my leg, but it wasn't enough."

"No?"

"Dash came down and pinned my left leg and mangled it all to hell. I don't remember much after the, well, collision, but the docs tell me they tried to save it. But it was too far gone. So now I got this," he added, pointing again at the flesh-colored plastic calf that disappeared into his sock and shoe.

"Can we start at the beginning? When was the accident?"

"Sure, I mean, it was... Christ, about seven years ago now, it's hard to remember everything. But, well, I was coming back from the beach, had just dropped one of my friends, Steve, off at his house. It was late, after dark — 9 maybe? So I got back on Route 101, I was heading west back towards Manchester."

"You drive that route often?"

"Oh yeah sure. I mean, whenever I went out to the coast. I was living in Manchester at the time, so at least a dozen times a year, probably more."

"Sorry to interrupt. Go on," Erica said.

"So I was heading back to Manchester, just cruising along 101. And then, well then something got up on the road, right in my way. I tried to avoid it, ended up off the road, in the crash and yeah, minus one foot."

Erica leaned in — this was just what Drew at DOT had mentioned. "Something got up on the road? What was it on the road?"

"A deer maybe?" David paused. "I don't know." His brow furrowed and he looked down between his feet, one tapping slightly against the linoleum floor, the other lifeless. "I didn't get a good look at it. But bigger I think actually, maybe a moose, maybe even a bear. Moved up quick off the shoulder onto the road. I tried to get out of the way. I got out of its way, but I got myself in the way of a tree down the opposite side. Then, the crash. Next thing I remember is waking up in the hospital later that night." He shrugged and looked at Erica briefly. "Is that what you wanted to know?"

"Yes, like I said, just looking for your story." Erica paused, her attention focused inward as she considered David's words. "Did you get a good look at what it was? Or hear anything?"

David looked at her quizzically; she was uncertain if he was going to answer or was searching his memory, so she added: "I'm just trying to understand it, to place myself there."

"No, I mean. Just a flash here I think. Maybe if the crash hadn't been so bad I'd remember more." He shrugged and frowned. "Just something up on the road. Not a car, that's for sure. It was big, but it moved fast, came up off the embankment right across the road. I got out of the way and — BAM! — next thing I know I wake up in the hospital. Thank God I had already dropped Steve off, so no one was in the car with me. Sorry I can't help you more, especially after you made the trip out here. That's just about all I can remember."

"It's alright," Erica said. "I understand. I get a small snippet here, another part of a story there, its all apart of this process. Together it'll make a story."

"You know that other reporter from the *Gazette* came around and asked me the same questions back then."

"What? Who was it?" Erica felt her eyes widen and tried to hide the expression on her face.

"Real old guy. Right ready for retirement I think. Stewart. That was his last name. Can't remember the first. Always called me 'Mr. Thompson' so I called him Mr. Stewart back."

"Can you recall his first name?" Erica asked.

"No, sorry. Just the Stewart. Old guy, nice, but seemed a bit... intense I guess," David added. "He asked me the same sort of things. Told me he was doing sort of the same thing you are: interviewing folks who had accidents out on 101. Trying to put together a story on the accidents out there, all the deaths. I don't think anything ever came of it, at least I don't remember seeing anything in the paper."

"I'll check into that, thanks. Do you mind if I follow up with you via telephone if I have some more questions?"

"No, not at all. Can't promise I'll pick up depending upon how work is, but I'll certainly give you a buzz back."

"Thanks," Erica said as she gathered up her belongings.

Erica focused on the short stretch of 101 she drove on westbound back to Derryfield. The traffic was heavy going eastbound with hordes of residents and out-of-staters heading to the 11 miles of New Hampshire beaches for tax-free summer vacations. At times, the traffic heading east came to a near stop, and Erica glanced at many of the faces as she passed: most drivers appeared annoyed or exasperated, their faces red from the heat or the humidity or the traffic. The line of cars before her unfurled across the green landscape like a rainbow scar in the land, purple and blue and red and yellows bumper to bumper as far as she could see in the opposite lane.

When she arrived back at the office, Erica checked with a few of the other reporters to see if any knew of an old reporter named Stewart. Karen immediately suggested it likely was Andrew Stewart, a reporter for the *Gazette* long since retired. Most of them knew Stewart — or at least of him — but only distantly; he had retired about seven years ago, just as Erica was hired at the *Gazette*. Erica did not recall ever working a day with him, though it was possible: those early days, introductions, learning the process at the *Gazette*, unlearning all the useless things she had picked up at school, had left little time to learn names and make friends. If she had met Stewart then, she didn't know him now. No one Erica asked on the floor could recall a story he had written about 101.

Searching the archives also proved fruitless. Loading the microfilm into the readers was tricky and time consuming, and as she had no way of knowing if and when Stewart might have written a story on 101, Erica could only blindly reel through, hoping to spot his name or the phrase "Route 101." She began seven years ago when everyone said Stewart had retired, and worked backwards. She managed to leaf through two years and though she found many articles written by Stewart, none focused on 101. His taste — or assignments — was eclectic. She glanced over articles on local crime, the presidential primaries, Concord politics, and New Hampshire tourism, all penned by Stewart.

The stories she found and skimmed on 101 — none written by Stewart — repeated a common refrain, written by the local reporter assigned the coverage that month. Every year saw a number of single car accidents resulting in significant injuries or death. Most occurred on a narrow stretch of 101 along Raymond, Derryfield, Epping, and Brentwood. The authorities suggested alcohol or inattention was a factor in most, as was speeding. No story mentioned any other causes.

Frustrated at her lack of success, Erica poked her head into Frank's office later that afternoon. The office was small, and made even smaller with the cluttered shelves and bankers boxes pushed against every wall. The desk top itself was clear but for a pad of paper and mug nearly overflowing with pens of all colors. Frank sat hunched over his desk and his arms were tucked under his torso. The posture accentuated his shoulder blades, which strained against his thin checkered shirt.

He looked up at her in the doorway and said: "Good work last week on the piece on the opening of the new Wal-Mart. Tied in well with the adverts they were running."

"Thanks Frank," Erica said, unable to hide all of the sarcasm she felt.

"No, really Erica. I received some good feedback, both from readers and from upstairs. We're here to inform the readers of what's happening in the community; Wal-Mart opening over on Beech is a significant accomplishment. The tax revenue, the employment it will provide in the community, all significant to Derryfield."

"Sure," Erica said, hoping to change the topic, "I'm working on a piece right now about construction across the state, particularly Rockingham County."

"Yes, I recall that was one of the topics suggested for you and Karen. And?"

"Well I heard that Andrew Stewart, a reporter from a while back, may have written something a few years ago about 101."

"God damn, haven't thought about Andrew in a while." Frank crossed his thin arms over his chest and smiled. "Smart son of a bitch, talented writer; also stubborn as hell. What's this about a story you heard he worked on?"

"Something about 101 — the fatalities out there."

Frank's demeanor changed. His arms tightened across his chest and the smile left his face.

"Do you really think you should be working on a story on 101?"

"Why?" Erica asked.

She stared at him, daring him to look away. He did, and said, "I'm just concerned about your objectivity on this Erica. Given all that has occurred as of late." He cocked his head to one side and pursed his lips.

"You put me on this assignment Frank. Said I could have a little freedom, some prose about New Hampshire. I know this. I'm fine. There's a good story here."

Frank frowned but did not immediately respond.

"So do you remember anything he wrote on this? On 101? On the fatalities out there?"

Frank tilted his head up and stared at the ceiling. While it looked like he may have been consulting a list of articles written on the tile above him, Erica recognized this tic as Frank's attempt at recollection. After a few moments he dropped his head and looked back to Erica and said: "I don't recall any story he wrote." He took a breath to consider his words then continued. "Though I'm uncertain of the wisdom of you pursuing this, I'll honor my word to you. I said you would have the freedom to pursue what you want, within some limitations. But don't let this take up too much time, you understand? This should be no different than anything else you are working on."

"Sure."

"Did you look back at our coverage of 101 the last few years?"

"Of course," Erica said and sighed. "I pulled what I could find, the usual dailies on accidents and deaths as they occurred. I'm envisioning something different, a longer piece about the history of 101, the causes of all those deaths."

When he said nothing, Erica asked, "What about Stewart?"

Frank grunted. "Call him. If I remember right, he covered this same sort of thing years ago. Became a pet project of his but I don't think anything substantive came of it. Nothing published by the *Gazette* I can recall. He should be able to bring you up to speed on what he looked into."

"You got his number?"

"Yes, give me a moment, I will get it for you." Frank opened the desk drawer nearest his right leg and began shuffling through the files.

Erica returned to her desk and turned on her desktop personal computer. A few minutes later Frank stalked over to her, handed her a slip of paper with a phone number and address on it, and said: "Please say hello for me."

Erica took the number and said, "Sure Frank, will do."

Frank sauntered back to his office and Erica punched in Stewart's number. She listened to the ringing of the telephone over the din of hushed conversations and typing emanating from the newsroom.

On the seventh ring, just as Erica was considering hanging up the phone, a man answered.

"Hello?" he asked, cautiously, as if whoever was on the end of the line was a threat.

"Hello, Mr. Stewart?" she asked.

After a pause: "Yes. Who is this?"

"I'm Erica Couture. I'm a reporter over at the *Derryfield Gazette*. Do you have a few minutes to speak with me?"

Erica listened to another pause, this one a bit longer. Though only a few seconds it felt longer, uncomfortably so as pauses so often do in conversation, as if a momentary lack of words is some breach of manners.

"Regarding what, Ms. Couture?" Mr. Stewart asked.

Erica continued: "Well, this might sound odd, but I'm working on a story on some of the motor vehicle accidents out on Route 101, and some of the people I've spoken to have mentioned your name. Said that you spoke with them after the accidents. I was hoping to speak with you about the same, about what you learned. I checked with some of the others in the office, but they don't remember any story — I certainly couldn't find any in the archives when I checked."

Erica heard only breathing. It was labored and sounded to Erica out of tune, like a clarinet with a cracked reed.

"What is your interest in the story now, Ms. Couture?" Stewart said. She inhaled quickly in preparation to speak an answer but instead listened to Stewart as he coughed repeatedly into the receiver. After he caught his breath he said: "I am sorry, Ms. Couture. I have been feeling a bit under the weather, as nice as it is this time of year."

"I'm sorry to hear that Mr. Stewart." She used his last name as he did hers, and didn't think of asking to use his first. "I'm just following the story; trying to understand why 101 has claimed so many lives. I won't take much of your time, I can promise you that."

Mr. Stewart laughed. His laughter was short, shallow, and rapid fire, much like his breathing, and it brought with it a coughing fit in its wake. After a few hacking coughs Mr. Stewart said: "I am an old man and do not have much time, if you understand Ms. Couture, but time is all I have these days. It is a perverse state of being, getting old. Though it is better than death, I would avoid aging if I were you."

Because she was not certain what to say in response, Erica laughed.

Mr. Stewart grunted. "I am at 34 Rosen Street. Come by tomorrow at noon and we will talk."

"I'll see you then," Erica said. She began to set down the phone but stopped as Mr. Stewart continued to talk.

"And Ms. Couture," he said before hanging up, "try to keep an open mind about this."

CHAPTER TWELVE

Corey liked Mimi but never felt quite comfortable at her house. Every piece of furniture was enclosed by a thick plastic covering which made Corey self-conscious about any dirt he might track in or any mess he might make. He never knew Mimi to scold him about it, but it felt more like school than home. He could never quite relax for fear of doing something wrong.

Mimi herself was short and squat and powerful even in her old age. Besides her silver hair, Corey recognized that she was unlike other old people he encountered; she wasn't unsteady on her feet or slow in her actions. She moved with deliberate purpose and was always busy with one project or another, be it her garden out back, mending clothes, or repairing something in her house or garage.

Mornings at Mimi's were spent with some chore or another; afternoons were set aside for inside work and Mimi's shows. This day, Corey was at Mimi's just in the afternoon, and they spent it watching television and sewing. Corey helped sporadically, but the sewing never held his attention for more than a few minutes at a time. He kept thinking back to the dead deer in the swamp. Like most boys his age, he had seen his fair share of dead things: a roadkill raccoon two years ago, a finch dropped by a neighborhood cat last spring, and a squirrel in the field behind his backyard last summer. The process of death and decomposition was intriguing enough to Corey that he had checked in on the squirrel each day. He wasn't sure what had killed it, but he was sure what had taken the remains: insects. Ants had started it, a veritable army of ants, their black specks countless as they swarmed over the body, crawling within the pink flesh and over the brown fluff.

The flies came next, followed the day after by maggots. Corey had watched with an interest that bled into revulsion as the maggots swarmed beneath the flesh, a pulsating marrow white that spilled over the small squirrel corpse onto the ground around it. Within a week, nothing remained of the squirrel except a skeleton, a pile of desiccated skin, and tufts of fur. Corey thought again about the deer, and wondered what killed it and what shape the corpse was in now. Perhaps worth checking out, if he could convince Alex to do so and if he could gather the courage to venture out there again. Something about the Overpass to Nowhere made him anxious.

"What do you think of this program, dear?" Mimi asked. She gestured at the flickering screen with the needle and thread in her left hand.

"It's fine Mimi." In truth, he didn't care for any of the afternoon soap operas, but knew that Mimi watched them rather religiously and, if prompted, could and would go on at length about the trials and tribulations — her words — each character was facing. Even at only 12 years of age he found it somewhat ironic, that a woman so prim and proper as Mimi would watch without hesitation a show depicting the lives of people so thoroughly amoral. At least the drama was interesting, with all the shouting and fighting and backstabbing going on between the people on the screen.

Corey shifted in his chair and thought about telling Mimi about the deer. There was a chance she would tell his dad about him being so far in the swamp; he'd only get an earful about being careful and staying close to the house and wouldn't get any conversation on the deer itself. But it must have been something big out there, some carnivorous creature able to hunt down and eat half a deer.

Weighing the options, it seemed worthwhile to mention it to Mimi, to seek an explanation from some adult, and Mimi certainly had knowledge about the area. He had heard her say plenty of times how she was born and raised in Southern New Hampshire. Perhaps she knew what it could have been that killed the deer. Corey leaned forward and said: "Mimi?"

"Yes, Corey?" she answered. She dropped her hands to her lap and glanced over at him.

"Well, I just..." Corey began and trailed off.

"What's bothering you?" Mimi asked. She set down the needle and thread in her hand on the small table beside her and sat patiently, a small smile visible at the corners of her wrinkled face.

"It's nothing really. Have you ever, Ms. Mimi, have you ever heard of like, strange things out in the swamps?"

"Well, what do you mean?" Mimi asked. She cocked her head and squinted her right eye nearly completely shut. "What do you mean by strange?"

"Like, well, a creature or something out there. I don't know," Corey shrugged. "Are there any alligators or anything out there? Something big that could eat a deer?"

"No alligators," Mimi said and laughed. "Far too cold for them here in New England. There are bears out there, and supposedly some wildcats too, though I've never seen one myself."

"Could one of those get a deer?"

"Of course. Both bears and wildcats eat meat you know, so I wouldn't put it past either to go after a deer."

"What else? Are there other things out there that could get something big like a deer? I mean like, big things that could get a deer. Snakes maybe?" he suggested and squinted at Mimi, recognizing that the suggestion was far-fetched.

"Well, I don't know of any big snakes out there, but there are always stories, you know, of strange things. I've heard it said that the Indians thought the swamps were places close to the afterlife, and strange things would walk among the swamps. Maybe just stories." Mimi smiled at him. "Why do you ask?"

"It's just that-"

The phone rang and Mimi moved to grab it. He could only hear her side of the conversation but recognized that his father was calling to summon him home. When Mimi returned to Corey his backpack was already on his shoulders and he was slipping on his sneakers.

"My dad, right?" Corey asked.

"Yes." Mimi smiled at him again. "It was nice to see you today. I'm sure I will see you again soon."

"Yep," Corey said on his way out the door.

"Careful crossing the street!" Mimi yelled after him.

Corey rolled his eyes: he could see his house from Mimi's front porch and only had about 100 feet of space to cross diagonally across their empty residential road. Corey heard a car moving on another cross street, but the early evening was otherwise filled only with the sounds insects and birds and or nocturnal creatures marking their territory or looking for mates in the coming darkness.

Once inside his house Ted hollered to him from the kitchen. He stood with his back to the entryway. A pot of something light brown or dark red bubbled on the stove top — either soup or sauce, Corey could not tell, but likely poorly done either way. His father's best meals tended to be the ones delivered to the house.

"Help me get some supper going in here, Corey," Ted said. He had peeled off his top shirt to reveal only a white t-shirt stained yellow at the armpits over a dirty pair of blue jeans. He must have just gotten home and immediately began on getting supper together before taking a bath.

"I already ate at Mimi's," Corey responded as he placed his backpack down.

"Good for you. I don't care if you already ate, I've got to get something and I want a hand dammit. So give me a hand."

"Yes, sir," Corey said.

"You go ahead and chop this pepper." Ted handed Corey a green pepper. "I'll work on the onion."

"Spaghetti sauce?" Corey asked.

"Indeed," Ted answered. Corey grabbed the nearest cutting board and knife and worked slowly to cut the pepper into strips and small sections to be thrown into the sauce. They chopped in silence for a minute until Ted cleared his throat and asked: "So what'd you do today?"

"Played with Alex. Had lunch with him, some grilled cheese, it was good, his mom always puts two kinds of cheese on it, I can't remember what it's called, a white one and a yellow one. Then we worked some more on the fort, then Alex left with his family to go see their grandma in Massachusetts so I went to Mimi's house for the afternoon."

"How's that fort coming along? You going to let me see it one of these days?" Ted smiled and raised his eyebrows to emphasize the question and communicate his interest.

"Yeah, once we are done. As long as you promise not to tell anyone. It's a secret, we don't want everyone in school to know about it. Then everybody would want to be part of our club, or they'd ruin the fort or something. It's better if it's just us, me and Alex."

Ted nodded. "Now the Marinos are down in Florida most of next week Corey, so you'll either have to come into the mill with me or stay with Mimi if she's up to it."

"Sure," Corey said. He finished up chopping the pepper and moved the cutting board with the pieces towards the bubbling sauce. As he did so, he stumbled slightly and the pieces of pepper rained off the cutting board and onto the floor. The green cubes spilled across the tan tile and skittered underneath the stove and refrigerator.

"God dammit Corey, why'd you do that?" Ted yelled.

"I'm sorry!" Corey reached for the paper towels while Ted continued to curse under his breath.

"I keep telling you to be careful, but you never listen. Why don't you listen to me Corey?"

Corey's eyes began to water and he squeezed shut his eyes and wiped at them with the back of his hands. He knew crying would just bring more criticism from his father. It seemed as if they were never operating on the same wavelength, as if Ted's anger came when Corey was most vulnerable and Corey's sullenness arising when Ted tried to be accommodating. The differences between them had expanded since his mother had left, not detracted.

Corey's anger and frustration were too much, and even knowing it was likely to result in some kind of punishment, he yelled. "I wish Mom was here! She wouldn't be so mean!"

Ted's face hardened. His lips became a thin line, his jaw set. "You can say whatever you want about your mother, about how nice she was. But where's she now Corey?" Ted did not wait for an answer. "I don't know. She left. But she's not here, dammit. I am. And you damn well better listen to me."

Corey said nothing in response, preferring instead to study the tiles between his feet.

"Jesus, I know this isn't what you want," Ted continued, "and believe me, it's not what I want either. I didn't expect this anymore than you. But I expect you to listen to me god dammit and to be more careful in the kitchen. Do you understand me? You could hurt yourself. You're using the knives in here for Christ's sake. You've got to be more careful."

"Yes," Corey said. He furrowed his brow and worked quickly with the paper towels to pick up the scattered pepper pieces on the floor. Ted stood above him, hands on hips, head at a disapproving angle as he watched Corey clean.

"I wish Mom was here," Corey muttered again as he cleaned.

"And I wish we had a million dollars. Wishes don't do us much good, you understand? We just have to get by with what we got for now, OK? Another word of this and you're grounded."

"Mom wouldn't ground me!" Corey yelled.

Ted raised his voice in response: "Enough! Enough of this, do you understand me?"

"Yes, sir."

"And that's it. Grounded for a week."

Corey felt the urge to respond but knew that doing so would only invite further punishment. Instead, he cleaned the kitchen while Ted finished the sauce and boiled some pasta. Though Corey wasn't hungry, Ted made him sit at the table with him. "Family time" he called it. Said it was important for the two of them to sit down together and catch up, find out what was going on in each other's lives.

Unprompted, Ted would always begin these discussions by sharing with Corey stories about his day at the mill. Every story revolved around one of three things: the ongoing layoffs or retirements of men older than his father; an injury someone sustained, usually described comically though the injuries themselves often sounded horrific, missing fingers or mangled hands; or, most likely, the incompetence of management. The stories he told were occasionally more interesting, when Ted was in the mood to share about the hauntings at the mill or the things — like giant catfish — that supposedly lived near the dam.

Ted had risen quickly in the ranks of the mills to become a foreman. He was responsible for the first shift of the Washington Mill No. 1 in Derryfield. Generations prior the mill had been the economic center of town, the largest employer and the factor that led to Derryfield being one of the larger towns in New Hampshire, even now. Washington Mill No. 1 was one of only two buildings in the complex still in operation at the mill, and much of the work was now powered by electric drives rather than the hydro power from the Pilwilla River. New equipment, particularly computer controls, improved paper consistency (and some reduction in odor) and further reduced the need for human labor. Each passing year fewer and fewer men remained employed there.

"It's a damn shame," Ted said, pointing at Corey with a sauce encrusted fork. "With the way things are going, this place isn't going to be around for you." He speared a mouthful of pasta and sauce and between chews continued. "You've got to figure you'll be doing something else. The mill won't have a job for you. You understand?"

Corey nodded but said nothing. He wished he could leave the table, or even ask to leave, but he knew his father would not permit it and would in fact be offended by the request. He had tried in the past, but his request had only resulted in a louder and more strident speaker.

Ted enjoyed these lectures, and since Laura had left, the frequency of lectures had increased. Ted wasn't the kind of man to engage in introspection, but had he been, he might have realized he now feared his son leaving as his wife had, and by speaking to Corey every night and imparting his wisdom, he sought to make himself invaluable to the boy, or at the very least prepare him should he leave some day. Most of these lessons were about how hard Corey would have it: the world had changed, it wasn't like it was when Ted was a boy, and no matter what Corey did, he wouldn't be prepared for it. Ted continued on in this fashion for another ten minutes, providing his insights into the world as it worked now, the changes in the economy, and how the damn politicians were ruining it all, only interjecting at times to point his fork at Corey and ask, "You understand me, right?" To which Corey would respond, "Yes, sir."

By the time he had finished his lecture Ted had also finished his plate of spaghetti. He pushed back from the table, stretched his arms above his head, and said, "You run along now. Start getting ready for bed. I'll clean up."

Corey followed his instructions and began preparing for bed. As he brushed his teeth he stepped out into the hallway and watched his father. Ted began to load the dirty dishes into the dishwasher and sealed up the leftover sauce and pasta. Corey remembered when his mother would be in there with his father, each one doing their part, perhaps talking to one another as they did so, occasionally laughing at something Corey couldn't quite hear.

By the time he was ready for bed, his father was in the living room in his usual spot on the couch. Ted's legs stretched out, an empty Budweiser on the coffee table and the TV on low. The individual noises from the set were indistinguishable, a low hum that fluctuated with the intensity of the bluish glow from the screen. When Corey walked in, Ted's half-closed eyes peered over towards him.

"Goodnight, Dad," Corey said from the doorway.

"Goodnight," Ted responded and then blinked his eyes slowly and sank deeper into the cushions of the couch. Corey returned to his room, tried not to think of his mother, and hoped for sleep.

PART II
JULY

CHAPTER THIRTEEN

The drive to see Stewart took Erica down Deer Run Road and past the new thirty house development that was under construction. As she looked to her right, she saw that the trees that once dominated the area, standing tall above the occasional house, were all but gone. A huge sloping hill of brown dirt took their place. The hill was criss-crossed with packed pathways clearly the work of heavy machinery, and a few hundred feet back Erica could make out small mounds of dirt she assumed were the beginnings of holes for foundations. She remembered the times she and Nate would run through those woods, climbing trees and crossing creeks, and felt a pang of nostalgia mixed with grief, knowing that such things could never happen again now that both the forest and Nate were gone.

Past the diminished forest and the Town's transfer station lay West Derryfield. At one time the two communities had been separate, and the vestiges still showed: West Derryfield had its own town square, a satellite fire department with one engine, a general store, and post office. In the center of the town square stood a weathered stone statue of some Revolutionary era hero. The general store shared a roof with the post office, which was but one room manned by a clerk who accepted mail and dispensed stamps, envelopes, and managed a few P.O. boxes. All the mail that was delivered was brought across town to the main post office in Derryfield.

After passing through the center of West Derryfield the zoning returned to residential. Most of the houses along Stark Street, the main drag in West Derryfield, were colonials and stood close to the road. Those on the avenues running off Stark Street tended to be newer and set back from the road, with longer driveways, larger garages, and fewer trees in the lawns.

Mr. Stewart lived in an older neighborhood off Stark Street which

Erica guessed was built in the 1950s. It was definitely post-war, a small square house no bigger than 1500 square feet with a small lot to match. She parked on the street. Erica grabbed her notepad with one hand and closed the car door with the other. She made sure to lock the door to her Taurus and walked towards the house along the narrow brick path cutting through the grass. She checked her pager and patted her pocket to make certain she had a few pencils within, feeling for the familiar impression of the instruments.

As she walked up the drive Erica figured there couldn't be more than six feet of grass on each side of the little structure, the thin lines of turf merging into a backyard shaded by a single tree just peering over the roof of the house. Judging by the age of the house, the tree must have been planted soon after its construction. The grass of the yard was a deep green, cut short, running right up to the blue siding. A collection of odd shaped rocks in a heap of no discernible pattern sat in bed of mulch in the front yard no bigger than a desk. An aging Buick sat in the drive, the green paint at the wheel wells falling away to reveal a reddish rust that was spreading like an invading force across a map.

She rang the doorbell and waited. At first Erica heard nothing. No one called out. After a few seconds she could hear someone moving about inside the house, a rhythmic shuffling that grew louder the nearer it came to the door. The door opened a crack but Erica could not see into the gloom. It opened another half a foot, and then was thrown open more widely to reveal Mr. Stewart leaning over a slate gray walker.

"Good afternoon. Ms. Couture, I presume," Mr. Stewart said. His hair was nearly gone, what little remained only a few wisps near his temples. He was thin and wide. His arms were spindly, and Erica wondered how long he could remained hunched over the walker. The swell of his midsection was apparent even under the buttoned shirt he wore. His slacks hung tight around the waist and loose at the ankles, and matched his shoes and his buttoned shirt. His face was wrinkled and spotted, but his eyes were clear and did not waver while turned towards Erica.

"Good afternoon," she answered. "Thank you for agreeing to meet with me, especially on such short notice."

"Of course. I remember the game. Always deadlines, rush, rush, rush. I do not rush about anymore these days, but I remember." Mr. Stewart started to turn back into the house but then paused. "Would you prefer to come inside, or sit on the back porch? It seems too nice a day to avoid enjoying it."

"Why don't we sit outside."

"I will ah, go through the house. Less walking, easier on the hip. You can go around back outside. Either side of the house will get you there," he said and laughed once. He smirked at her and Erica couldn't help but smile back. She started down the steps of the small porch and heard the door close behind her. Erica walked past the battered Buick in the drive and took a moment to peer inside: the leather of the driver's side seat was cracking in places but the rest of the interior of the vehicle appeared untouched, even pristine, beyond a few coins glinting in the center console cup holder.

The grass in the backyard was not as well tended as that in the front or sides, and the concrete of the patio coming off the back door was cracking. The tree she had spied from the front was central to the backyard; its branches reached up to the blindingly blue sky like the hands of a congregation of some church praising the spirit of nature. Three brown wicker chairs were positioned around a small circular table. The tree cast enough shade to cover the patio, and Erica found it relatively comfortable in the shade. She sat in the chair closest to the side of the house she had walked around and waited for Stewart. She heard a clattering at the back door and Stewart hobbled out with the walker still in front of him.

"That's a beautiful tree you have back there," Erica said. "Must be nice to have the shade on days like today."

Stewart grunted an affirmative response while he positioned himself above a chair opposite Erica and lowered himself into it.

"Now where are my manners. Can I get you anything? Water, tea?" He leaned forward and grasped the handles of his walker and readied himself to stand back up.

"No!" Erica said, perhaps a bit too harshly. "No, no, not necessary. I'm OK. Thank you though."

"Of course. If you need anything, please let me know. I do not have much for beverages aside from water and tea, though I may have some instant coffee hiding in one of the cupboards."

"Thank you but I'm all set." Erica set down her notebook and retrieved a pencil from her back pocket. "As I said on the phone the other day, I'm working on a story on 101, all the fatalities out there. I understand you were working on something the same a few years back, or at least were interviewing some of the people who survived accidents on the road. Can you give me any insight? What did you learn?"

"Mmmhmm," Stewart responded. He rubbed the left side of his jaw with his right hand. Erica heard something crack, uncertain if it was one of Stewart's knuckles or some other joint. He seemed unaffected by it and continued to rub his jaw.

"Well," he began, "you were informed correctly. I did look into this very phenomenon. I would say for the last ten or so years of my time at the *Gazette* it was on my mind and I was interviewing persons involved. Nothing more than something to do every other month or so, but a story to chase nonetheless. One I could not shake."

"What got you started on it?" Erica asked. She scribbled notes as he spoke and enjoyed the occasional burst of summer breeze that coiled through the backyard.

"Someone I knew met their end on that road. I was disheartened, but, though I hesitate to use the word given the circumstances, intrigued by it as well. Even going back many years, that highway has been the site of many deaths. So I began to make inquiries, speak to those involved, to pull records from DOT, the local police forces, even the *Gazette*'s archives, whatever material I could access."

"And what did you find?"

"It has been that way for a long time; the deaths, that is. Only getting worse, and I realized that back in the late '70s."

"The rate of fatal accidents," Erica said.

"Yes that, and non-fatals too. Significant accidents. They call it the Highway of Death of course. A dreadful name, but apt."

"If it's so bad, why hasn't the State fixed the road already and expanded it? I've been around and around on this. I get some of the political difficulties with funding, but it's inexcusable. I assume you spoke to DOT or Concord about it? I'm looking for the full story here, both the political aspects of it and the personal."

Stewart cleared his throat, the cough somehow both wet and

scratchy at the same time, and said: "I am sure the condition of the road contributes to the rate of injuries and fatalities in that area, but that is not the reason why there are so many accidents out there Ms. Couture, nor is that the reason I found it so compelling."

"What do you mean? Like the wildlife crossing the roadway? I know about that, I realize that there is quite a bit of wilderness that 101 cuts through. I've spoken to a couple of people who have been in accidents on 101 and I get that some of the accidents were caused by animals crossing the road at inopportune times. That can happen on any road though, and I don't see how it is significantly worse on 101 than say up on the Kancamagus. Not enough to explain the number of deaths on that road."

Stewart shook his head. He pursed his lips and inhaled deeply as if to start speaking but stopped himself and exhaled. "Something more than that as well. The frequency of significant accidents goes far beyond what one would expect even with significant wildlife crossing. But more important is the timing: the accidents on 101 started in earnest nearly 30 years ago. Per capita, there have been significant deaths on the road for nearly 30 years, and it just keeps getting worse year over year."

"Sure, because of the increase in traffic over all those years." Erica shrugged. "The road should have been expanded years ago."

"No. There have been strange things going on in that part of the state for decades." He coughed again and took the time to glance around before turning his eyes back to Erica.

"How familiar are you with the so-called Exeter Incident."

"Excuse me?" Erica asked, her features scrunched together in confusion.

"The Exeter Incident. The sighting of, well, something out there in the skies back in '65. An unidentified flying object if you will."

"What does that have to do with 101?"

"I am certain that they are in some way connected."

Erica had to fight the urge to roll her eyes. No wonder the man had retired. Though he still appeared sharp in some respects, something was not only wrong with his body, but his mind.

"Mr. Stewart," Erica began, "I appreciate you taking the time to speak with me today, but this doesn't really seem relevant. I was told you might know more about the accidents on 101. I know you've spoken to a number of people that were involved in accidents on 101. I'm interested in hearing what you heard from them or what other information you may have gathered about the condition of the highway or the efforts to expand it. The tale of some UFO sighting of thirty years ago doesn't really interest me."

"But it should," Stewart said, his voice growing louder, losing the hesitancy she had come to expect of him. "I understand that you don't believe me. That is fine." Stewart waved his hand before him as if shooing away a fly. "I know that you have investigated this to some degree, given your comment yesterday on exploring the archives, but I urge you to look further. Consider the numbers and timing of fatalities, pull them yourself. You will see accidents on that stretch of road significantly increased in '65 and have been increasing since. Others know about this, Ms. Couture. It is not, as I am sure you might be thinking, just the ramblings of an old man."

When Erica did not respond he continued, "At the very least, I challenge you to do this: speak to Rebecca Corville. She will tell you what she saw."

"Who the hell's Rebecca Corville?" Erica asked. She didn't like the way this conversation had gone, as it now seemed as though the drive out had been a waste of time.

"A woman who lived out near Exeter and was a young girl back in '65. I have spoken to her a number of times. Last I knew, she was living here in Derryfield. For all of her faults, she is consistent with what she remembers."

"And what is that?" Erica asked. She didn't appreciate the game Stewart was playing, stringing her along like a fish on a line, giving her an occasional bit of additional information while denying her the truth.

"You have already indicated to me you are disinclined to believe what I shared with you on this point. I think it is likely better if you speak to her directly, without allowing my recollection of her story to color your opinion."

"Sure, I will," Erica said, not certain if the words were a lie. She closed her notebook and dropped it into her satchel before thanking Stewart again for his time.

"Let me remind you Ms. Couture," he replied as she stood up from her chair, "you don't have to believe what I am telling you to recognize the story there."

CHAPTER FOURTEEN

Will used his left hand to rub his eyes while he rested the right atop the steering wheel. The exhaust work that day had left him tired; he didn't mind welding, but doing it overhead left his arms feeling heavy even hours later. He had only slept a few fitful hours before Lonnie called and had requested a tow out on Route 101 in the pre-dawn morning. Another fatal. Already so many fatals, and the summer was just beginning. He thought of his conversation with Sergeant Herbert: "No wonder they call it the Highway of Death," he had said.

Will yawned once and turned the radio up a few more notches. Should have had half a cup of coffee, he thought. The hours at the shop and those driving the wrecker were too much to reliably maintain. It felt as if he might finally get enough sleep one night to feel rested but a call would come in for a tow and his hopes of a restful night were dashed. The compiled fatigue felt like a weight on his shoulders, as if he couldn't lift his arms above his head. Will drove slowly, making sure to open his eyes wide every few minutes in an effort to better hold back his weariness.

When he arrived at the scene Officer Wilson, a newer recruit whom Will had only met once before, was directing traffic and pointed down the embankment towards the accident. The slowly revolving blue lights of the cruisers gave everything a cold glow that reminded Will of the inside of a bar. The onlookers in their motor vehicles added to the perception, each craning their necks to the side as they rolled past the accident scene, looking like bar patrons perturbed by the entrance of someone they didn't recognize into their dive.

Will pulled the Ford over to the shoulder, leaned his head out the open window and said: "What do we got?"

"Uhh, a fatal, a single car accident," Wilson yelled as he waved traffic by. "The uh, the scene is clean. Check with Dougherty. I'm pretty sure it's ready. The vehicle, just needs a tow back to the lot." Wilson smiled as he spoke and directed traffic. He gesticulated excessively when he held one hand out — the arm ramrod straight — to stop vehicles. This was all still new to him, or at least new enough that a shit detail at one in the morning wasn't enough to eradicate his enthusiasm for the work. Will figured it would in time.

"Got it," Will said. He raised a hand and Officer Wilson nodded back.

Will pulled the wrecker along the shoulder at the top of the embankment and across from the accident scene. A wood paneled Ford Country Squire lay on its side with a stream of oil and coolant hemorrhaging into the soil through the half-heartened attempts to stop the ecological degradation with some pads and kitty litter. The driver's side brake light still glowed dimly in the night; the passenger side was broken, the shards of its red casing visible in the sand behind the station wagon.

Officer Dougherty stood nearby. He took a drag on a cigarette. The end burned brightly in the darkness, and Dougherty nodded to Will. Will nodded back and walked over, but glanced back at the accident, recognition appearing in his mind like a sudden squall, forceful and unexpected.

"Jesus, wait, I think I know that car. Is this Stanley Cooper's car?" Will yelled to Dougherty.

"What's that?" Dougherty asked and took a step towards Will, his cigarette dangling at his side.

"Is that Stanley Cooper's car?" Will asked again.

"Well, I'm not supposed to say anything, we still have to notify the next of kin you know..." he shrugged. He pursed his lips and nodded to Will.

"Fuck me. I just talked to the guy the other day. What happened?"

"Not sure. Looks like he just went off the road. Maybe drunk, maybe fell asleep at the wheel, maybe had a stroke or heart attack or something while driving. The MD will get on it most likely, should have a report in a few weeks."

"Wow." Will sat, crossed his legs, and dropped his hands into the sand at his side.

"You alright?" Dougherty leaned over towards Will.

"Sorry, sorry," Will said. "Just bringing back memories. Not particularly good ones."

"It's alright, Will, I get it. Seems like all the old guard are uh... moving on, finding their peace."

"I guess it's that, if you could call it that. Peace I mean."

Dougherty shrugged.

"You'll be OK getting this one in?"

"Yeah, yeah, not a problem. Somebody's gotta do it. Just hard to believe, like I said. Was just talking to him the other day."

"It's fucked man. Can come at you just like that," he said and snapped his fingers, "out of nowhere."

"Yeah," Will said. He grabbed the tow hitch, began un-spooling it, and walked down the embankment sideways while he kept his flashlight trained on the ground below him. The vehicle was even more damaged than it appeared from the road. The passenger side was buckled in at least 12 inches towards the center of the vehicle and the body of the car around the point of impact was crumpled and jagged. The roof was caved in and the driver's rear wheel was entirely missing.

As Will leaned over with the hitch in one hand, the crickets quieted. Their chorus of summer faded out like a diminuendo at the end of a song, as if those writing the song or those singing it weren't sure how to end it. The roar of passing cars was distant beyond the rise of the embankment to the road. Will heard the sound of something splashing in water far to his left, beyond the Country Squire.

He stood up quickly and the hitch in his hand almost struck his knee. Will didn't see the thing — at least at first. He sensed it, a presence, a movement beyond the glow cast by the headlights of the Ford.

"Hello?" he said. No one — or nothing — answered. The leaves of the nearby trees rustled in the breeze.

"Hello?" he said again, this time louder, his voice nearing a shout. He waved the flashlight back and forth, its weak beam disappearing beyond twenty feet. "Is someone there?" His mind went to deer or bears. It was likely some large mammal moving about off the road, more frightened of the sights and sounds of the nearby cars than Will was of it. He glanced around once more but saw nothing. He crouched back down and returned to the Hyundai in order to attach the tow hitch and pull it out of the ditch.

Then he heard it. The noise it made was low and guttural and reminded Will of a pig, if the pig was the size of a truck and was working to stifle its sounds. The sound was deep too, something he not only heard with his ears but felt with his gut. The reverberation within him brought with it fear. Will immediately felt his heart beating faster, felt the hair on his arms rise up, and noticed his hands begin to shake. He thought of the .38 in the glove box. Will dropped the hitch in the sand and ran the twelve steps back to the truck and into the cab. He fumbled with the glove box and pushed aside a stack of paper and receipts to uncover the silver bodied pistol with a worn brown handle. He looked back through the windshield when the firearm's grip rested tightly in his right hand.

In the foggy distance where the cone of headlight met the darkness of the summer night, Will saw it move. All the colors were washed away at that distance, and Will could only tell that the thing — whatever it was — was dark, a dark gray or dark blue or dark brown. It was large even at this distance, at least the size of the Country Squire, and the outline of its form in the dim light made it appear hunched over, face to the ground. It moved slowly, but Will did not sense in its lack of speed any hesitancy, but instead a measured confidence that reminded him of a cat effortlessly moving about, prepared to spring upon its prey at any moment.

Will held the .38 in front of him but did not point it at the creature. Instead he watched the thing in the distance. His chest rose and fell every second. His breaths were short and shallow. In spite of the heat Will felt a chill.

The thing continued to move across his vision from left to right. Just as it reached the edge of the light cast by the Ford's right headlight the creature became still and the guttural snorting stopped. The appendage it held close to the ground — what Will assumed was its head — suddenly swung up and pointed towards the Ford. As it did so, it came closer to the headlights, and Will was able to make out more detail.

The creature's head was not symmetrical. Multiple markings that appeared to be eyes lay scattered across its lumpy head. He could discern no pattern to their arrangement. At the center of the bulk was one dark orifice. That hole puckered and Will heard the same low snort as before. Movement behind and under the head drew Will's attention and he saw multiple smaller appendages hanging from the underside of the creature, each contorting and flexing like the arms of someone experiencing a seizure. Bits of its skin appeared translucent and fluttered like feathers as it moved, reminding Will of a snake in the midst of shedding its skin.

Will raised his right arm and tried to sight down the .38. His hand continued to shake so he raised his left hand to help steady the weapon. It still wavered in the air so he lowered it and watched as the thing took one lumbering sinuous step forward. Will turned the key over and the Ford's diesel engine coughed, sputtered, roared, and then spit a cloud of smoke out its tailpipe. He jerked the shifter into drive and, in the process, banged his hand against the steering wheel. The horn bleated.

The thing moved back out of the headlights and retreated into the darkness. It took only a second before its dark body blended away into the night. Will pressed the accelerator to the floor and the Ford complied. It climbed the embankment and Will jerked the steering wheel to the right to keep it from careening into the road. The Ford stayed off road and Will didn't slow until the shoulder had narrowed and the Ford began to crowd into the travel lane. He cranked the shifter back into park and the Ford groaned, shuddered, but came to a stop.

A motorist in a small Chevrolet — a older man with graying hair and glasses — laid on his horn and flipped Will off as he drove by. "Watch where you're going fucker!" he yelled.

Will pushed open the door and spilled out onto the shoulder of the road. He stepped away from the Ford and reached down to steady the .38 and was surprised to see it was not in his clenched hand. Will bent at the waist, hands on his knees, and vomited. He heard footsteps and looked up, saliva dripping from his lower lip, as Dougherty came jogging over towards him. Dougherty's gear — his service weapon, radio, flashlight, baton, and more — clattered with each step.

"Jesus, Will, you alright?"

Will held up his hand to indicate to Dougherty to stay back before vomiting again. His stomach felt tight but empty. Will rubbed his mouth with his forearm and spit away from the road in an attempt to get rid of the taste of vomit.

"You OK?" Dougherty asked.

Will looked to his left into the darkness down the embankment and began stepping backwards. He continued to scan the darkness before he felt Dougherty's palm on his shoulder.

"Easy there," Dougherty said, "you're getting awfully close to the road." He nodded over his shoulder to the cars slowing and passing by. "What's the matter? Is it because it's Cooper's ride down there?"

"No." Will shook his head. "I... There is something... something is something down there. Something big."

"What, you see a deer or something? That's what's got you spooked?" Dougherty smiled and patted Will's shoulder. He reached down to his belt and scooped up his flashlight and directed its beam down the embankment. The dim circle of the flashlight illuminated the crashed Ford and some of the snapped immature trees leading to the area in which the it lay.

"I don't see anything down there," Dougherty said. "It was probably just a deer, got spooked and ran once you started up your truck."

"No, no." Will shook his head and continued to scan the darkness down the embankment. "Not a deer... I don't even fucking know what it was. It's big, way bigger than a deer."

"You feeling alright Will?"

"No, definitely not."

"You been drinking?" Dougherty asked. He leaned in towards Will. The smile on his face vanished, an artifact of his police training activating. Without immediately realizing the change Dougherty was no longer talking with an acquaintance, but fully on duty.

"No! I haven't been fucking drinking." He finally turned away from the embankment and looked over at Dougherty. "You didn't see that thing? You didn't hear it?"

Dougherty didn't smell alcohol, and Will was steady on his feet. Confident alcohol wasn't at play, Dougherty's face softened and he smiled at Will. "Will," he said softly before again patting Will's shoulder. "I didn't see anything, just you tearing ass back up to the road. You sure you're OK? You been sleeping well lately? Too many late night tows?"

"Dammit Dougherty you aren't listening to me. There was something down there!"

"I believe you Will," Dougherty reassured him. "So you saw something down there." Dougherty looked behind him at the road, and, finding the traffic wasn't too bad, said to Will: "How bout this. Let's go check it out, make sure nothing's down there. Sound fair?"

"I don't know," Will said, "that thing was fucking huge. I don't think it's a good idea."

"Relax. So it's a deer, or even a bear or something. It's like to run off, and even if it doesn't" he added and patted the service weapon on his hip, "I've got this. Let's go take a look, OK? It'll be fine."

"No," Will responded.

Dougherty flicked his flashlight back on, pointed it towards his feet, and began to step down the embankment. He walked at an angle and led with his left foot, his left hand directing the flashlight and his right atop the holster for his service weapon. After a few steps he turned his head back towards Will and said: "You coming?"

"No. I don't think this is a good idea."

"It's fine." Dougherty continued down the embankment. Will watched with increasing anxiety as Dougherty descended and began sweeping his flashlight back and forth across the roadside. Will relaxed his hands when he realized they were clenched tight enough that the pressure of his fingernails on the palm of each hand was painful. Dougherty's flashlight illuminated the wrecked vehicle as well as the trees and other vegetation surrounding it. The beam of light otherwise dissipated into the dark of the night.

"I don't see anything down here Will!" Dougherty shouted. "Must have run off!"

"That's fine!" Will yelled back. He thought his voice sounded too high so he cleared his throat and struggled to get enough saliva in his mouth to spit the unpleasant taste out.

"That's fine man," Will said. "It's OK. Forget about it."

"See," Dougherty said as he climbed the embankment back towards Will. "Nothing to it. Just a bear or deer or something. I've been there too. Been on edge, seen something move in the corner of my eye, freaked myself out." He laughed and clapped Will on the shoulder again. "Happens to us all."

"Sorry," Will said. "I've just got to go. Call Tony or somebody for this tow, OK?"

Dougherty's face dropped and the playful, reassuring tone in his voice disappeared. "Shit, that's gonna keep us out here at *least* another 30 minutes," he said, emphasizing the word least.

"I know, I'm sorry. I've just, got to go. Don't feel good. Sorry, I'm sorry," Will repeated. He backed up towards the cab, keeping Dougherty and the darkness behind Dougherty and down the embankment in his vision. He walked backwards slowly and collided with the Ford. Without turning around Will found the door handle with his right hand and hopped back up into the cab. He slammed the door shut, pivoted in his seat, cranked the truck over, push the pedal towards the floor and didn't look back.

CHAPTER FIFTEEN

Besides a few "yes, sirs" and "no, sirs", Corey hadn't spoken to his father much in the past week. He thought he should apologize — to at least placate his father and earn some measure of freedom back — but each time he thought he would be ready to do so he remembered his anger and thoughts of apologizing were incinerated, only remembered hours later after his father had left for the day. He was at least thankful that Mimi had agreed to watch him for the week; it beat sitting in the break room at the mill all day.

Unfortunately, though Mimi was adept in the kitchen, her repertoire was small. Corey didn't know if this was because her tastes had narrowed over the years or she had simply forgotten other recipes she once may have tried to make. For Corey, this meant that lunch every day was some kind of meat pie. It wasn't bad, and for the most part Corey didn't mind it, but the fact that she — and now he — was eating it every day was beginning to test even his 12 year old patience.

The other big downside to staying with Mimi (besides not seeing Alex, had Alex been around and not in Florida visiting relatives) was the lack of any interesting television. While Mimi was happy to leave the television on for most of the day, she only had basic cable and was wedded to the idea of keeping the station tuned to channel 4. Besides the news, she only watched the soap operas on during the afternoon hours and scheduled her summer days accordingly. The morning was for any chores, be it cleaning, repairing, painting, or yard work (of which Corey would be pressed into service and help). Then, when the sun reached its apex, Mimi would shepherd Corey inside and prepare the meal of meat pie. The afternoon was then spent watching As The World Turns and General Hospital, usually while stitching or mending or knitting. Corey wasn't sure the difference between those, but knew that Mimi always had something she was fixing or creating with thread and a needle.

Mimi hadn't asked why Corey was spending the week with her. Corey figured she may have spoken to his father about it and knew that he was grounded, but he was relieved she didn't ask him about it. They were sitting and eating the day's meat pie with *General Hospital* on in the background when the doorbell rang.

"Be a dear and get that for me please, Corey" Mimi said.

Corey pushed his TV tray aside, slipped off the plastic covering on the over-sized chair in the living room, and scampered over to the front door. The door had a small window with frosted glass about five feet high. As he approached, Corey could not see any figure through the window. He opened the door expecting to find a package and the retreating back of a UPS driver. Instead, Alex was standing there smiling.

"Alex!" Corey said and stepped out and hugged him.

"Hi Corey," Alex said into his shoulder.

"What's up?"

"Not much," Alex said. "Just got back and I was kind of bored, so I figured I would see what you were doing."

"Just eating lunch now, want to come in for a little bit?" Corey raised his shoulders and eyebrows in unison.

"Sure," Alex answered.

They each stepped back and Corey yelled over his shoulder: "Mimi! Can Alex come in?"

She kept her eyes on the television. "As long as he takes his shoes off dear, that's fine."

"How was Florida?" Corey asked.

"Really hot," Alex said. "Really really hot. I thought it was hot up here in the summer but it was even worse down there. The plane ride was neat though."

Alex came in and told Corey about his adventures down south with his aunt and uncle. Alex had snorkeled in the ocean, watched the storms come in every afternoon, and had even taken an air boat ride into the swamps and seen swarms of alligators.

"Were you scared?" Corey asked.

"Nah," Alex said and laughed. "I mean, they were big, but they're kind of dumb. Stayed away from the boat. I guess they keep growing all their life so they get bigger as they get older, just keep getting bigger. But they taste good! I had some gator jerky!"

"Wow."Corey paused, then said in a lower voice: "You think it was an alligator that is out there in the swamp — an alligator that got that deer we saw?"

"Nah, I don't think so," Alex said. "They don't live this high up right? Like they don't get up to New England, right?"

"I don't think so, but maybe?" Corey said and shrugged.

"Something is out there. It could be a bear you know. Something big enough to eat a deer. Or maybe a wolf, or a pack of wolves."

"Yeah, maybe."

"I heard from Peter Lincoln that his neighbor two houses-over's dog went missing," Alex said.

"Yeah?"

"Yeah. Something got it he thinks. Something in the swamp." Alex spoke in a hushed voice and glanced quickly over his shoulder. If Mimi could hear them — and if she was even interested in the conversation — she made no sign of it. Her hands moved in her lap as she sewed, and every few seconds they slowed as she glanced at the television screen and focused on it for an update on the program she was watching.

"It's fine," Corey said and nodded towards Mimi. "She's pretty cool."

In the last week, Corey had realized that Mimi didn't have much in the way of toys, but she did have some old board games. Corey and Alex took out checkers and played while they discussed the rest of Alex's trip.

As he was getting ready to head back home, Alex asked: "Let's work on the fort more?"

"Yeah," Corey answered, "as soon as I'm not grounded anymore. This Friday should be the last day, or maybe tomorrow. I think I'll be ungrounded by next week. My dad's just being a jerk lately."

"Sorry," Alex said. "At least Fort Barren will be awesome when we're finished!" Alex pumped a hand in the air as if he had just won something, and to his mind, perhaps he had: he had a fun project and a best friend to complete it with.

Corey smiled. "Yeah, it will be the best. We'll have to camp out in it when we are finished. Get a bunch of snacks and stuff."

"Definitely," Alex said. "See you later, man."

Corey shut the door, turned, and said to Mimi: "Thanks for letting Alex come over."

"Of course dear," Mimi said as she set down the needle and black thread in her hands. "A boy needs to spend time with his friends. When I spoke to your father earlier this week he told me you are grounded. So let's just keep Alex's visit to ourselves, all right?"

Corey grinned. "OK. Thanks Mimi."

They spent the rest of the afternoon sewing and watching television, each new show chronicling the misadventures of some group of attractive people. As the afternoon wore on, Corey grew hungry, realizing he had never finished his meat pie. It took no convincing for Mimi to heat it back up in the microwave and sit him down at the table; as she was often saying to him, a growing boy needs to eat. They sat together in the living room with television trays before each chair, the television set providing its usual background noise, Mimi now with a book in her hand.

"Mimi, can I ask you something?" Corey asked.

"Of course child, what is it?" Mimi said.

"You've lived her a long time, right?"

Mimi laughed and set down her book. "Well, young man," she said, emphasizing the phrase, "it depends upon what you think a long time is. I've lived in Derryfield all my life."

Corey set down his spoon. "How long is that?"

Mimi tut-tutted and said: "You know you ain't supposed to ask a woman her age, right?"

"Uh, no, why?" Corey asked.

"It's not polite. But I'm an old lady, so that's fine."

Corey nodded but did not understand.

"I'm sixty-seven years old. Been living here in Derryfield since 1927. Lot's changed since then. Lot's stayed the same too, thank God, but lot's changed."

"Well, you ever hear any stories about the well, uh," suddenly Corey didn't feel like asking. He felt foolish and young, as if he were entertaining an idea that was fit for an elementary school kid, not someone about to enter 8th grade in September. He had to ask someone though, so he said it quickly, the words tumbling out of his mouth one after the other: "Have you ever heard about a monster in the bog?"

Mimi laughed and for a moment Corey was afraid she was laughing at him and poking fun at his ignorance or his fear. But it was a warm laugh and she crinkled her eyes shut and smiled; she wasn't laughing at him but at the idea and a collection of memories that bubbled forth in the cauldron of her mind, their aroma long forgotten but familiar.

"Oh sure," she said as she put down the jeans she was folding and sat down next to him. "I've heard of tales of the Brown Stump Bog Monster, something that crawled out of the run-off from the mills. Heard stories about the witch over at the end of Dartmouth Street, the killer at the old Pine Isle Park, or 'bout the hauntings at the butchery on Main Street — supposed to be built on an old Indian burial ground." She laughed once again and smiled broadly, her large cheeks wrinkling even further in the expression. "Every place has got its tales, you hear? Some true, most probably not. Somebody been telling you stories lately?"

Corey took a bite from his meat pie and dropped his head as he chewed. He chewed slowly and thought of what he should say.

"Sort of. I, uh, well you know I told you a while back, I saw a deer out there that was all eaten up, and I thought it might be the bog monster that got to it."

"Hmmm," Mimi said. She leaned back in her chair and the clear plastic underneath her crinkled and squealed, and reminded Corey of the noise a new set of sneakers made on the gym floor at school.

"Well honey, I'm sure there's something out there that could get a deer — a bear perhaps, or maybe some coyotes, but I don't think it's a monster. What makes you think it's a monster out there?"

"Just stories I guess," Corey said and shrugged again. "I heard some of the guys at school talking about it too. Some of the 8th graders. The 8th graders from last year," Corey quickly added so as not to confuse Mimi about which set of 8th graders he meant.

"Well, I doubt it was a bog monster out there. I'm not certain such a thing even exists. But if you see it, you stay away, you hear?"

"Yes ma'am," Corey said.

"Can't be up to much good if it's tromping about in the bog out there. Plus," she began but was interrupted by the sound of footsteps on the porch.

Corey heard his father's footsteps only a moment before the bell rang. He couldn't articulate how he knew it was his father. The time — a few minutes beyond five PM — certainly lent credence to such a belief, but there was something about the cadence of the steps, the rhythm in how the heel rolled to the toe that Corey was instantly able to attribute to his father.

Ted knocked on the door and called out to Mimi. The spell of silence between Corey and Mimi was broken.

"Hello Theodore," Mimi called out. She placed a hand on each arm rest and pushed up to stand out of her chair. She opened the door. "How was your day?" then stepped back and allowed Ted to enter the house.

"Fine, Mimi, thanks," he said. Corey began to gather his things and considered that he never heard his father call Mimi anything but Mimi. Other adults he always had another name for: Uncle Jerry was just Jerry for him; Grandpa in Connecticut was Mark. He wondered why Mimi was still just Mimi for his father.

"How was Corey today? He behave?" Ted asked.

"Of course, of course."

Ted grunted a response but didn't bother to look over at his son. "Thanks again. I'll take a look at the Buick on Saturday, OK?"

"Thank you Theodore, you don't have to. I really enjoy having Corey over."

"Sure," Ted said. He glanced at Corey, said nothing, and then looked back to Mimi. "Come on Corey, let's get home."

Corey slung his backpack over his shoulder. "Yes, sir."

As he walked out the door Mimi leaned over and whispered to him: "We'll talk more next time you're over."

Corey nodded to her and she smiled again, the same crinkled face and old eyes.

CHAPTER SIXTEEN

Rebecca Corville — "Becki" she had immediately insisted, with an "i" — leaned over a plate of French fries and glanced at Erica. Erica didn't know Becki personally, but after asking around the newsroom about her, Erica realized she knew Becki's situation well enough. Becki lived in a trailer at Murmuring Birch, a trailer park on the west end of town. Once her memory was jogged, Erica realized that Becki's name was a frequent addition to the local crime section of the *Gazette*, usually for alcohol or drug-related offenses. Becki was out now, and clearly enjoying the food available to a free woman.

The figures Stewart had mentioned to Erica were accurate: accidents on 101 had increased significantly from 1964 to 1965, and had increased nearly every year since. That alone still didn't make any clear connection between the "Incident" and the accidents, but Erica had asked around the office about Stewart. Those that had worked with him remembered him as a solid reporter. His explanation (or half-hearted start of one) seemed far-fetched, but it was the thread that was now loose, and though she was certain it wouldn't lead anywhere, Erica was determined to pull it.

So she sat with Becki at Willi's Burgers, a seasonal roadside joint that sold perhaps the greasiest — but cheapest — burgers in town. There was no indoor seating; only a collection of picnic tables and assorted lawn chairs of different colors and sizes scavenged from estate sales and yard sales. The building in which Willi made his burgers was small, no larger than a garage, with a single window for ordering and receiving food. The white paint on its side had long since been stained an off-white and was peeling in more places that it was not. The grass surrounding the lot thinned to packed earth where cars parked and people ate. Willi, years prior an old man, his white hair thinner every year, was faintly visible inside the shack, leaning on the front counter with a cigarette hanging from the corner of his mouth, the end of the cigarette glowing with each inhale.

"You talk to that other guy who's come around a few times, what the fuck was his name... St. Pierre?" Becki twirled a French fry in a cup of ketchup and nibbled on the fry in a succession of quick bites.

"Stewart? Andrew Stewart?" Erica asked.

"Yeah, him. You talk with him? He was always coming around and pestering us. Never liked that guy. My parents didn't either, God rest their souls." As she said this Becki made the sign of the cross; Erica was amused to see a small splotch of ketchup appear on the right shoulder of Becki's t-shirt.

"Yeah, I've spoken with him. Don't know him, never met him before speaking to him a while back. He suggested I speak with you."

Becki grunted and chewed on a French fry. "What for? Why you care about it now? This shit happened like, 30 years ago, right?"

"Yeah," Erica said, and sighed. "I'm uh, doing a follow up to see where those involved are now, what they remember of the Incident. So I'd like to hear about what you saw, or what you think happened."

"Well, it was a long while back, don't remember much really."

"You lived over near Exeter then, right?"

"Yeah. Over on Hill Road. Remember it being a big commotion. My folks saw it, you know. I didn't, don't recall why. I think I was asleep. But don't remember seeing it. Was a pretty big deal though, plenty of reporters came along, asking questions of my folks and others in the neighborhood."

"Marjorie and Paul, right?" Erica asked after consulting her notes.

Becki nodded her head and downed another French fry.

"Did Marjorie and Paul — did your parents talk to you about it?"

"Not really," Becki answered.

"Any idea what it was?"

"I sure as hell don't know what that thing in the sky was."

"Well why don't you tell me what you remember?"

Becki confirmed many of the details Erica already knew from her review of the initial stories from three decades ago: including who in that neighborhood saw the Incident and what they shared with each other and the reporters. It was a big deal back then, with the Cold War nearly as hot as it ever got, so people weren't sure if the UFO was something from the Soviets or perhaps even something from another planet. Even with prompting, Becki had difficulty remembering the names of those she had talked to, aside from her parents.

When Erica asked Becki if she knew of any other important details, anything else that stood out to her, Becki said: "Well, I think it had something to do with that... well, that thing in the swamp, you know?"

Erica was taking notes absentmindedly when Becki said this, listening but not listening to what she said. The sun was too warm to focus more energy on a conversation Erica was certain was useless. But this surprised her and she sat up, leaned forward and interrupted Becki's stream of French fry flavored narrative.

"Excuse me," Erica said as she raised her hand, "what did you say? Something in the swamp?"

"Yeah, whatever that thing was out there. Saw it when I was a kid you know, was 11 or 12, I can't remember. Must have been 12, I think it was right when I was starting seventh grade. Just a few weeks after the whole *Incident*," she exaggerated the word in an effort to mock it and disarm it of its connotations.

"What, what did you see?" Erica asked, her pen still.

The movement of Becki ceased. A host of smaller details, things Erica hadn't even noticed, at least consciously, slowed and stopped. Becki's right leg no longer jumped; the slight rock of her head as she talked or ate stilled; her hands did not reach for a fry. The pause between Becki and Erica grew long enough to be uncomfortable and Erica leaned forward to add to her question when Becki spoke.

"I don't know what it was. It was tough to see." Becki was staring at Erica but she saw something else, something made live in her mind through memory and emotion. "It was big, bigger than a bear. Smelled too. It was fleshy, like a pig, you know?" Becki shifted her head and looked at Erica again; Erica nodded. "Not sure what it was, but it scared the shit out of me. I ran home. Never saw it before then or again. I figure it must of been a passenger or something on whatever was in the sky that night back then, you know? Or maybe like a soldier that jumps out of planes, uses a parachute, you know, what are they called-"

"A paratrooper?" Erica asked.

"Yeah, like one of those."

"You think whatever you saw came from the UFO in the Incident?" When Becki nodded, Erica asked, "Why?"

"Well, like I said, it happened just a few weeks after the whole sighting. I figured what else could it be?"

"Did you tell anyone?"

"I mean sure, my parents at first. Once they figured I wasn't fibbing, they said it was a demon or something being religious like they were. I told some girlfriends." Becki paused and looked down to her plate and seemed surprised to see the fries. She took a moment to trace another line in the ketchup with the French fry and then curled it into her mouth in one piece.

Between chews she said, "Plenty of other people've seen it too, you know."

"Like who?" Erica asked.

"Well, a bunch of the folks that are regulars over at Hilltop. Winnie said he'd seen it. Him and Oscar talked about it plenty. So did what's her face... Nora, Nora Wilson said she'd seen it back in the '70s or '80s I think, I can't remember."

"Did you tell Stewart?"

"Probably," Becki answered between chews. "I don't know. He was kind of an asshole you know? Why, what's it matter?" Becki's activity returned: her leg rocked, her head bounced with each syllable she spat forth and fries began to disappear into her mouth.

"It's just something new to me. I'm surprised."

"Well I saw what I saw," Becki said between bites. "I don't care if you believe me. I saw that damn thing."

"I didn't say I didn't believe you." Erica jotted down some of the details Becki had shared and kept her face expressionless.

"Sure, whatever," Becki said. "It's all a bunch of bullshit anyways. People saw some weird shit, shit in the sky and some shit in the swamp, and nothing ever came from it. Who knows what the hell it was. Maybe we were all high." She laughed too loudly at her own joke, and some of the other patrons nearby looked over at their table. When Erica saw the stares she lowered her head and focused on her notepad.

Erica sat with Becki for a few more minutes, but obtained nothing but the same information she had received earlier. Erica could tell that

Becki had achieved whatever she had hoped to get out of this interview. She began answering questions with a yes or no and did not elaborate any further. The plate of fries garnered more of her attention so, after a few more clarifying questions which received simple responses, Erica left Becki to enjoy the remainder of the plate.

On the way back to her car, Erica checked her pager: nothing. She also checked her watch: only 12:30 and she didn't have to be back to the office for at least another hour, which gave her enough time to try Stewart. She drove down the street to the nearest pay phone, dropped in a quarter, and dialed Stewart's number. He answered on the third ring, told her he would welcome her to visit, and that she should see herself out to the backyard porch.

Twenty minutes later Erica found him sitting on the porch, admiring the single tree.

As she sat down she said: "I'll be honest with you Mr. Stewart. I'm not sure why you wanted me to speak with Rebecca — Becki — Corville. I pulled the figures and you're right, accidents did increase on 101 in '65, though there were occurring before then as well. Becki told me a story about seeing some creature in the swamps in Exeter. I don't see the connection here. Even assuming there was something like Becki describes, what the hell does it have to do with the accidents on 101 today?"

"Well," he said, clearing his throat, "if you have a moment, let me start at the beginning. First, the Incident, you know it wasn't really in Exeter, right? It was in Kensington, just south of Exeter." He did not wait for an answer and continued, "But that's not really important. It was one hell of a thing. One hell of a thing. How long have you been doing this?"

"Reporting you mean?" Erica asked.

"Yes, ma'am, reporting."

"Seven years," she answered. Stewart nodded his head in approval.

"So you've seen your fair share of them. Well this one, the whole Exeter Incident and everything surrounding it. This was one that comes along infrequently. Back then, I thought I understood the world and what it held. I am less certain of that now, with the benefit of all those years between it. And this was something that makes you wonder — made me at least. It was the sort of thing that gives you sleepless nights."

Erica raised her eyebrows. "Why's that?"

"Because I'm not sure any of us had the story right. Something happened that night. Something, I — nor anyone else I spoke to — was able to explain." He sat quietly for few moments and continued to rub his jaw. Erica had the foresight to wait; she would let him tell this story at his own pace.

"What do you know of the Incident?" Stewart stressed the last word.

"I'm familiar with the basics — a few people on the ground, including a police officer saw something in the sky, a UFO."

"Yes, that's what they said, or at least what we reported then. Certainly was a UFO — it was flying and it was unidentified — that moniker sticks. So the question that follows is: what was that object?"

Stewart again paused. Erica could tell from his posture that he was thinking, either searching his memory or considering his words. He leaned over slightly and continued to rub his jaw. His eyes were unfocused.

"I figure it was one of three things. One, it was a celestial body or phenomenon. Just the moon misidentified or a comet. I think that's the most unlikely option given the numerous eye witnesses who thought something strange was going on. Two, it was an aircraft, either a civilian flight again misidentified, or a military flight, perhaps something classified which then leads to the unidentified nature of the sighting. Quite likely. Or three — and this is the potential most interesting and most unlikely — it was a craft from another world. Unlikely, but still a possibility."

Erica was scribbling in her notepad when Stewart stopped. She looked up and brushed her hair out of her eyes. He leaned forward slightly and nodded when she made eye contact with him.

"I spoke to everyone on the ground back then," Stewart continued, "the officers, the witnesses, people walking their dogs the next town over, you name it. But there was something more going on. A flight, a sortie, whatever it was called," Stewart said, waving away his confusion with a swipe of his hand, "went up from Pease. It was meant to get close to whatever it was in the sky, get a visual ID from the air."

"And did it?

"Well, that's classified." Erica inhaled more deeply as if to begin speaking, but he cut her off with a wave of his hand. "I tried FOIA requests. I have for years. Always rejected. They keep telling me it has to be kept confidential in the 'interest of national security'."

"That seems to eliminate your first option. If it was just some natural phenomenon it wouldn't be classified," Erica said.

"Correct," Steward responded. "But I kept on it, as best as I could. Talked to everyone I could find. Not only the witnesses to the Event on the ground like I said before, but anyone who had worked at the airbase around that time who was willing to talk with me. Most would not. A few who retired out of Pease — last duty they had prior to 20, 25 years — a few of them settled here. A Sergeant Brown. One of them was named Hutchinson. I had a few drinks with them when I could, and learned only a bit more." Stewart paused and watched with some interest as Erica summarized what she was told and set it down in her notebook. When she finished she looked back up at Stewart expectedly. Her eyebrows were raised and she nodded to Stewart as if to continue, but he remained silent, his eyes focused on the sole tree in the yard.

"And?" Erica asked, "Who did you speak to? What did they tell you? And how is this connected to the accidents?"

Stewart dropped his chin to his chest. He continued speaking, but did so in a lower, quieter voice, and did not make eye contact with Erica.

"I, well," he began. "I am not sure I am comfortable telling you. The little I was told was shared in confidence. The persons I talked to do not believe it was a traditional aircraft. It certainly wasn't a commercial flight. The staff at Pease would have been all over that, been right up on radar — and it was not something the Air Force was flying. Something was in the air that night, and from what I heard it was not something anyone could identify. Maybe it was Soviet and came over the Arctic; maybe it was alien. But it was not American, and it was flying over god damn Exeter, New Hampshire. I sure as hell cannot figure out why."

"Did any of this make the print?" Erica asked.

"I tried to, well, I tried with some of it," Stewart replied. "The story was very hot at first, all over the papers, even on the local television news. We ran it in the paper through the fall of '65 into '66.

But it quieted down, and people were not so interested in it anymore. 'Wouldn't sell' my editor said. Vietnam really began, boots on the ground, real escalation. It became a war then. The Incident just did not have much story left in it at that point."

"So what did you do?"

"I did what we all do, Ms. Couture. I set that aside, and began in earnest on the next story. I had deadlines, a desire to write and a family to feed."

"But you said you followed up, right?"

"Yes, but not, shall I say, officially. This story, the Incident, was one that remained in my mind, no matter what I did to banish it. In the minutes when I could not sleep I would remember it and wonder — do you ever have those moments?" He didn't stop for her answer, and said: "I would catch myself thinking about it while driving, the last few miles gone from my memory. It was not enough to be my white whale — I am happy where I am, I had a successful career, a family — but it was at least my, I do not know, my white marlin. I never did feel that I had really figured it, and given my current condition," he said, pausing and taking a moment to look down at himself, "I doubt I will."

"I appreciate you sharing all of this," Erica began, "but how does this connect to the accidents on 101? You think something from the 'Incident' is causing those accidents?" Erica could not hide her skepticism which was fast turning to annoyance. None of what Stewart was telling her made sense.

"Precisely," Stewart said. "The figures alone suggest that. The eyewitness accounts, however varied and unreliable, support the same inference: something came out of or was caused by that thing in the sky, and it has been affecting that part of the state for years, primarily the area along Route 101."

Stewart quieted again and stared at the tree. Erica nodded her head and glanced at her watch.

"Thanks for your time," Erica said as she gathered up her pencil, pad of paper, and purse, "but I have to get back to the office."

Stewart raised his hand and smiled as she turned the corner to the side lawn. Erica was walking back to her car, shaking her head at the old man's continued foolishness and her curiosity which had led her down this path to a waste of time, when she heard Stewart call out to her. She glanced back and was surprised to see him turning the corner near the front of the house, hunched over the walker once again.

"Ms. Couture," he said. "I would be remiss if I did not mention one more thing to you. If you keep looking into this, avoid the staff at Pease, particularly those there now. I find they do not take too kindly to inquiries of this nature."

CHAPTER SEVENTEEN

"Oh Billy!" Mildred said. "It's so good to see you! How have you been?" She looked good, better than most days. Her hair had remained well styled into the afternoon, and a stack of pages lay before her with some scribblings that Will glanced at as he sat down next to her. He thought it looked like attempts at a journal, musings that her mind had managed to expel through the confusion and forgetfulness, a stream of lucidity from a lake of Alzheimer's. Will was pleased to see he could only identify a minimal tremor in her hands.

Will tried to smile, but his efforts, so often successful previously, failed him now.

Mildred leaned forward in her wheelchair and frowned. "What's the matter Billy? Is something wrong?"

"I'm just," Will said before running his hand through his hair and in that moment thinking of his mother, who must do the same countless times each day to result in the mess her hair usually became. "I don't know, Mom. Just tired. It's been busy."

"You don't look so well, Billy," Mildred said in a tone Will remembered well from his childhood, one of mixed concern, chastisement, and a touch of guilt. It seemed mothers always had that tone available, a verbal weapon which never rusted and was never out of ammunition.

"It's OK, Mom. Just haven't been sleeping well."

"Sleep is very important. Your father always knew that. If you can't get all the sleep you need at night, you should look to take a nap. Either before dinner or after work, one of the other. Not both though. Either after work or after dinner."

"Yes, Mom," Will said. This lecture was one well known to him, having heard it throughout his youth.

"I've been trying, Mom. I've just been having some bad dreams. Well, nightmares honestly. But really, it's nothing Mom. I'll be fine."

He smiled, enveloped his right hand into the left, and cracked the knuckles of his right hand.

Mildred leaned forward even more, and for a moment Will was concerned she would fall out of her wheelchair and he would be forced to catch her before she struck the ground. Instead, she rested her hands palms down on her knees and stared at Will and said, "I know my son better than this. What's bothering you?"

It felt unusual, confiding in a mother who was so often the one in need of support.

"Just had a rough tow, Mom. Got the better of me, couldn't sleep that night and haven't sleep well since."

"What happened?"

"Nothing, was just out on 101. Late night tow," he rubbed his eyes, then said, "thought I saw something. Some animal or something out there. I don't know what. Just, I don't know, spooked me."

"What did you see?" Her tone caught Will off guard. He sensed an urgency but well controlled; not the sporadic concern he heard from her often these days, motivated by memory loss and confusion, but instead an interest in what he was saying that reminded him of how they used to talk.

"Nothing, Mom," Will lied. The conversation was already unnerving him, and he found himself repeatedly squeezing the armrest of his chair with each hand. "Nothing, just a bear I think. Scared me. Didn't expect to see something so big so close to the road."

Her eyes, so often blank, sharpened. "You've seen it, haven't you."

"What? Shit!" Will yelled as he banged his knee against his mother's wheelchair in his haste to reposition and lean in closer towards her. "Seen what Mom?"

She leaned towards him, her hands wrapped tight around the armrests of her wheelchair.

"That thing out there. That damn... thing."

"What thing? Out where, Mom? What do you mean?"

"That thing in the swamps. That thing your father saw."

Will had heard of people being knocked out of their seats by words, but had always thought it to be an over exaggeration, something old men told each other as they sought to one-up the other when the future held little promise and grandiose stories of the past is all that seemingly mattered. When he learned of his father's death four years ago, he had fallen out of his chair to the floor and had realized that some part of that saying was true. News could knock you on your ass, literally. His mother's words now nearly did the same. He startled back and had to kick out a leg to keep himself seated.

"What, what do you mean?" His voice sounded loud and too highly pitched, the anxiety he felt unexpected and doubling back to raise his concern even higher.

"The time your father saw that thing off Route 101, down by the swamp."

"What did Dad see? What are you talking about Mom?" Will asked.

"That... I don't know what you'd call it. He never did describe it all that well to me." She looked off above his shoulder, but not in the unfocused way she so often did; she squinted her eyes and clenched her jaw before continuing: "He said it was big. Moved quietly, too quietly for its size. Hunched over like. He only ever talked to me about it that one time, a few nights after he saw it. But he looked just like you do now."

Will leaned forward and tried to lower his voice: "What, I mean, how, how did he look?"

"Like you do now. Run down. He didn't sleep the few nights after. Something about your eyes — look the same as his afterwords. The whole thing shook him up. He tried telling Oscar, but he didn't believe him."

"He told Oscar what Mom?" Will asked. He thought back to what he remembered of "uncle" Oscar. The man had been a frequent visitor at the Boucher's for many years; as much as Winston and Oscar liked to drink, they seemed to like to do so even more together. Christmas, 4th of July, Labor Day, Easter — you name it, the two would be seen at one of their houses (or the Hilltop bar) with a beer in hand. Will remembered Oscar as always friendly, in a distant and uninvolved sort of way. While his father would take the time for a game of catch or to give a hand with a school project, no matter his level of intoxication, Oscar was always on the sidelines, watching with a beer in his hand, never offering Will more than a greeting or an occasional story about what had happened over at the Mill or how the Patriots were shaping up for next season.

"About whatever Winston said he saw out there. Oscar called him a damn drunk fool," she said matter-of-factly.

"Well I mean, Mom..."

"He was, no one is perfect. He was a drunk. But he didn't touch a drop after that. Scared him sober, whatever that thing was, whatever he thought he saw. At first, I thought I should have thanked it for that, but the scare, the fear, stuck too. He wasn't so well after."

Will stood up and took a few steps towards the door. He turned quickly on his heel to start back towards his mother.

"Jesus Christ, Mom. Why the hell didn't you tell me about this?"

"You weren't here. I'm sure he would have told you too if you were home. But you know your father, he didn't like to share much. Didn't talk much about Vietnam. Didn't want to talk much about this either. You can't blame me for that Billy. That's just the way your father was. You know that."

Will wanted to continue to ask his mother questions, but the interruption of the entrance of one of the staff members gave him pause.

"Hello," the woman said. Will saw her name tag read "Dolores." She was thin enough that it concerned Will, and when she smiled, Will recognized the yellowed teeth of a smoker. Any doubts about that identification disappeared when Dolores stepped closer and Will smelled the smoke on her. He recognized her as one of the employees but was otherwise ignorant of her role at the nursing home or her familiarity with his mother. She carried in her hand a small translucent plastic cup.

"Hi," Will said with a nod. "Can we have a minute please? We're just right int he middle of-" Will wasn't how to describe it to the woman: a lucid conversation with his sick mother that brought with it things he had never heard before.

"I am sorry to interrupt," Dolores said, "it's just that it is time for Mildred's pills. It will only take a minute."

Will hesitated. "Oh sure, fine." He stood up from his seat and backed up to allow Dolores access to his mother. Dolores moved around him in small steps, her feet pattering on the tile. She leaned in and spoke directly to Mildred.

"Time for your pills, dear."

Mildred held out her hand and took the cup of pills. Dolores held out another small cup filled with water and aided Mildred as she swallowed the pills with a cup of water. Will was surprised to see Mildred do so with relative ease, her hands somewhat steady as she raised the water to her lips.

As Dolores stepped back from Mildred, she turned and nodded to Will.

"Are you feeling alright?" Dolores asked. "You're quite pale." She squinted and leaned in, revealing a slight frown a mixture of disapproval and concern. As she leaned in, Will saw in greater detail the wrinkles that lined her face and the wispy facial hair that hid inside them. He backed up, her sudden closeness too much to accept alongside the confusion and fear he felt over his conversation with his mother.

"Just not feeling well," Will said. "Something I ate."

"You're not feeling well, Billy?"

"I'm fine Mom."

"Oh Mildred, this is your son?" Dolores asked. Her frown disappeared, replaced by a smile of approval for a son visiting a mother in a nursing home.

"Yes," Mildred responded. "My son. The spitting image of his father." Mildred paused and took a deep breath as she glanced at the ceiling. "He was just telling me that he saw the same thing his father did, a-"

"A uh, coyote." Will spoke over his mother and then said again: "Actually a moose. Was east of here a bit."

Dolores raised an eyebrow and nodded.

"Surprised me," Will continued, the words tumbling out of his mouth as he sought to explain away his mother's comment and his sudden nervousness, certain as he was that Dolores could sense it. He suddenly felt his shirt sticking to his armpits as a single drop of sweat rolled down his side.

"I was just out on a call, I'm a tow driver. Didn't expect to see one. Surprised me is all."

"Really!" Dolores said. "How big was it? What was it doing"

Will looked over at his mother and back to Dolores and said: "Oh, real big. Much bigger than a deer, it actually frightened me. It was just trotting along."

"Wow, I've never seen one in person," Dolores said. "I hear they keep heading farther up north, north of the notch. Getting away from the development going on down here. Not enough forest and such."

"Yeah, yeah," Will said and nodded.

The silence that followed lasted a beat too long before Dolores said: "Is there anything I can help you two with?"

Will looked over to Mildred. Her attention was focused out the window while she picked at her pants, rubbing the fabric between thumb and forefinger.

"No. But thank you. If there is anything, I will be sure to grab one of the staff." Will smiled at the woman to reassure her. She smiled back slowly, hesitantly, recognizing that something was odd, but not certain what it was or how to approach it.

"I'll be right around the corner," Dolores said as she walked towards the door, "right at the nurses station. Call me if you need anything."

"Will do, thanks." Will smiled again, thinking to himself as he did so to moderate the smile, not too large or eager, but broad enough he hoped to convey acknowledgment of her words and his receptiveness to them.

When Dolores had left Will turned to his mother and asked: "Mom, what were you just saying, before she came in the room? Dad saw something out on Route 101? What do you mean?"

She turned back to him slowly. "What? What Billy?" She looked around for a moment, her eyes briefly resting on every significant thing in the room: the television set, the door to the shared bathroom, the bed, and the feet of her roommate, visible past the edge of the curtain barrier. Mildred seemed to have lost not only her place in the conversation, but her bearings in the room.

"Mom," Will said urgently, leaning back in towards her. "You were telling me that Dad saw something, something that spooked him out on Route 101."

"Huh?" She scrunched her face up in confusion. "What are you talking about Billy?"

"Mom, you were just..." Will slumped back into the chair. Mildred furrowed her brow and stared at Will. After a few moments Mildred's expressions softened and she smiled at Will.

She reached out and patted his arm and said: "It's so good to see you Billy, how are you doing?"

CHAPTER EIGHTEEN

The notes and papers scattered around Erica centered from her lap and spilled across her couch, coffee table, and even onto the floor. She didn't believe Becki or Stewart or the bullshit theory that something from the Exeter Incident was connected to the accidents on Route 101. But enough people had mentioned seeing large animals on the road that Erica thought perhaps there was something to it, and that she should follow up with some of the others Becki had mentioned to get their story.

Working was not the best way to spend a Saturday night, but it kept her mind off of things she'd rather not think about, bobbing in the waters of her mind like crocodiles ready to strike and drag her down into the depths of depression. The job was no longer — had maybe never been — exactly what she wanted, her parents seemed lost, but most of all she missed Nate.

They had been especially close as children and had been born not even two years apart. They grew and played together, spending as much time in the woods behind their house as they did renting videos or playing board games together. There had been a few years when she had grown frustrated with him, particularly when she first started high school, but once he had started as a freshman they found themselves spending more time together again at after school events and football games. Both played soccer, and they enjoyed the time with one another before and after practices and games, each sharing some tip about the game or gossip about the team. Erica stopped staring at one of his pictures on the wall and tried to focus on the work before her.

The apartment was small but suited her. The front door opened up into the largest room in the apartment, a twenty by thirty foot space including her kitchen, dining area, and living room. A hallway in the center of the far wall led to the sole bedroom, flanked on one side by the full bath and on the other by a room that was too small to be a comfortable office and too large to be a reasonable closet. She preferred to work in the living room anyways; the two windows looked out over Vermont Street and let in enough noise to remind her that she was near others but not enough to break her concentration; it was a comforting feeling that gratified both the introverted and extroverted aspects of her personality.

The brick apartment building sat a block back from Main Street. The first floor set up for commercial spaces, with the three floors above that residential. Erica had watched as a number of business had entered the spaces on the first floor, but none of them lasted. Killian's Electronics had survived a year, even with the scores of kids Erica had seen walking in and out. A toy store had followed soon after, the owner's likely hoping to draw upon the same traffic as Killian's, but that place had only survived for a few months. Romano's, an Italian restaurant staffed by an older woman and who Erica assumed was her three sons had held on for nearly two years after the toy store closed but even it succumbed to the development down on Beech Street that was leeching the life from Main.

She set down her notes, stretched her arms, and thought of calling up her parents and offering to pick up dinner but was afraid she would just find them no different than when she last saw them: disinterested in much else and largely indifferent to her presence. She had no desire to experience that now. She picked her notebook up to return to her work for now but was startled when the phone rang. She nearly dropped the notebook in her lap as she lurched off the couch towards the telephone. She picked it up on the third ring and said: "Hello?"

"Hi, Erica?"

"Yes?"

"It's Sarah, you up for a drink? I'm heading out in a few and thought you might want to join in."

"Uh, I don't know." Erica sank back into the couch and moved the phone from her left ear to her right. "I was just thinking of staying in tonight. It's not still raining, is it?"

"No, Erica, it's not still raining!" Sarah said as if she were scolding a child. "Get out here, it's been awhile since you've been out with me."

"It has been, but, I wasn't planning on going out tonight," Erica said, her voice sounding soft even to her ears.

"We're heading to The Granite Goose, OK? It will be fun!"

"I don't know, Sarah, it's just that-"

"Come on! First drinks on me, OK? We'll get some apps too. Some fries or something equally greasy and tasty. OK?" Sarah stressed the last word and her voice rose in pitch, as if to convince Erica that it would not only be OK, but would be an exciting time.

"Fine, fine," Erica said. "Meet you there in... 40 minutes?"

"See you then hun," Sarah said.

Erica quickly showered, dressed in one of her favorite jeans and paired it with a dark blouse, then ran her fingers through her hair a few times. She thought of putting on makeup but couldn't muster the energy enough to care. She needed a drink right now and a painted face wasn't going to change that.

Her car was parked behind the apartment building, off Vermont Street. She considered driving down to The Granite Goose, but knew that she wanted to drink more than she should if she were to drive home. She thought better of it and called the local taxi service to arrange a ride. Derryfield was large enough to have a taxi service, but not large enough to have one that could be mistaken as reliable. While the service ran 24 hours a day, the fleet of taxis servicing Derryfield were few enough in number that one could never be certain to catch one on the street and ready to accept a fare.

The air outside was warmer than she had expected and Erica realized that she had forgotten she had started the air conditioner in her apartment earlier that night. She should probably turn if off — her landlord would bitch about it if he knew — but she didn't care and leaving it on would keep the apartment that much cooler for her return. The colder her apartment was, the better, for she enjoyed the feeling of slipping under the covers and wrapping herself in blankets; she could never sleep as easy without the weight of a few blankets atop her.

The street stretched away in a straight line in both directions for over a mile. Erica knew the land had been cleared and settled centuries ago, but wasn't certain if the center of Derryfield had originally been so flat or had been shaped that way by human hands. A few cars rolled past and Erica spied a group of people about 20 yards across the street walking away from her. One couple walked hand in hand while the others moved around them like circling planets. Even at this distance Erica could easily make out their laughter.

The white and green striped cab arrived a few minutes later and Erica recognized the driver as one she had ridden with a year or two ago. An older man, somewhere in his fifties, with a shock of unruly gray hair that suggested he didn't spend time in front of the mirror and a set of wrinkled and stained clothes that suggested he didn't spend time on laundry. At least he didn't smell, Erica thought. He grunted a greeting as she slid into the car.

"Where to?" he wheezed. He glanced in his rear-view mirror back at her, both eyes squinted in an expression that either signaled poor vision or discomfort.

"Heading to The Granite Goose, please. Thanks." A dumb name, she thought, but the beer was cheap and the food decent enough. She looked out the window as he pulled away, the vehicle creaking with each bump and dip in the road. Something rolled around and thumped in the trunk with every turn.

Downtown was hurting. Erica preferred not to think of it as dying, as that suggested that Derryfield could die, that the town itself could somehow be erased from the map. But she knew that each year a few more business shuttered up as the jobs that once formed the core of Derryfield's industry — the jobs in the mills — disappeared overseas or to modernization. The world was moving forward in a flurry of advancement, development, of globalization, while towns like Derryfield were left behind. It seemed as if New England had once been the center of the New World, but it didn't seem that way any longer, and the empty mills the next block over were a constant reminder. Erica imagined this is how the weavers must have felt a hundred years ago when the mills first sprang up along the river. The forcible extinction of one lifestyle for another.

Thankfully the cabbie didn't care to converse. When they reached The Granite Goose, he turned halfway around and muttered the total to Erica. She was surprised to find his disinterest carry over to the final transaction, as she had expected he would at least perk up when he asked for money.

Once she was out of the cab, Erica spotted Sarah waiting outside, a lit cigarette in her hand. She wore a denim skirt and white tank top and a pair of earrings that reminded Erica of wind chimes, something Sarah would never wear at work. When Sarah saw Erica approaching she lifted the cigarette to her lips, took one long draw, then dropped it to the pavement and rubbed out the butt with her toe.

"Erica," Sarah said as she drew near, "this is Clarissa," and pointed to the woman standing to her left. Clarissa stood even with Sarah, a few inches taller than Erica. A swath of blond hair ran over her shoulder and curled across the front of one arm. She smiled at Sarah and held out a hand.

"Pleasure to meet you," Clarissa said.

"Same," Erica said and took her hand. "How do you know Sarah?"

"We're cousins," Sarah replied, "can't you tell?" She leaned towards Sarah, reached her arm across her and pulled her into a sideways hug.

Erica laughed and between laughs managed a breathless "No." Clarissa pouted and exaggerated the motion. "Well let's drink," Erica said, "I certainly need one." Clarissa and Sarah laughed and fell into step behind Erica. The small lot beside The Granite Goose was entirely filled, as were the few parking spots on the street nearby. Even across the parking lot Erica could hear noise from inside the bar, a multitude of music, voices, laughter, and glasses melding into a sound of social activity. It was one of the few businesses that was doing as well both prior to and after the problems at the mill. People needed a place to drink whether the times were good or bad.

The smoke in the lounge hung in the air in a haze reflected a portion of the illumination cast by the dingy lights above. Beneath the smoke, she could smell sweat and stale beer. Erica was not surprised to see it was crowded: only a few stools were empty around the bar and she saw no tables near the entrance open. Most of the crowd appeared young and many sat in groups of three or four. Erica believed them to be students from the nearby John Stark College.

Inside it was louder; louder than she remembered or thought it would be. A jukebox in the far corner was blasting some song by The Police. A few people stood around it, beers in hand, swaying slowly to the music. A young woman Erica did not recognize walked up to her and smiled. The right breast of her shirt was emblazoned with the outline of a goose. A name tag pinned to the left stated "Lisa".

"You looking for a seat at the bar, or a table?" Lisa asked. Sarah and Clarissa looked to Erica.

"Table," Erica said.

Lisa led them to a table along the far left wall, one of the few that was unoccupied. The party had to weave through the crowds both standing and sitting. Most held some kind of drink in hand, and all talked loudly to be heard over the music, loud enough to be overheard by Erica and the others as they passed. She heard snippets of conversation, each more intriguing than the last:

"...so then, I turned to her, and I said, go fuck yourself..."

"...nah, it didn't come down right on the house, hit just the garage..."

"...you see that accident down on 101, another fatality..."

Sarah managed a smile as the three of them settled into their seats, each woman finding a place for their purses before they reached for a menu.

"Let's get a pitcher of beer," Sarah said. "I love it when it's on draft."

Sarah liked beer and was quick to tell everyone she drank with that she liked it. Erica wasn't sure if Sarah felt the need to tell everyone this in an effort to convince herself or because she honestly thought this was a detail worthy of repeated mention to anyone who saw her imbibe.

Their waitress arrived a moment later. Erica recognized her and realized that time had not been kind to her. Her blond highlights were evident only in the final eight inches of her hair, and that by her scalp was instead a dark burgundy. A small name tag read: "Susan." Susan's polo shirt was stained and slightly wrinkled, though because of the glossy appearance of the stains Erica was not certain if the stains pre-dated Susan's shift or were acquired during it.

"Hi, name's Susan. What do ya want?" she asked. She raised her eyebrows as she spoke and sighed the words as much as she spoke them. Normally, Erica would have been annoyed at the waitresses annoyance; instead, she understood Susan's lack of enthusiasm and felt a kindred spirit amongst the merriment of patrons in the Granite Goose.

"A pitcher of Bud," Sarah said. She glanced at Clarissa and Erica and nodded to both as if to inquire about their interest and express her desire.

"You got it," Susan said, "anything else?"

"And let's get some French fries at least, OK?" Sarah said.

"No, no, I want poutine!" Clarissa yelled. Erica glanced sideways at her and back to Sarah. Sarah either ignored or didn't care about Clarissa's lack of volume control and voiced her assent to this idea. When pressed, Erica nodded.

"You see the game yesterday?" Sarah asked.

"Yeah!" Clarissa said. "I can't believe it, the Indians just turned it on towards the end."

Sarah turned to Erica. "What'd you think?" she asked.

"I uh, I missed it, sorry," Erica said. The pitcher of beer arrived and Erica was relieved, not only at the thought of drinking it but because of its use as a way to avoid some of the conversation. Anytime she didn't feel like talking, she simply sipped her beer.

"Lucky you. It was bad. Even Clemens looked bad. Not sure what you can do when he's pitching like shit."

"Sure," Erica said before she swallowed a mouthful of beer.

Susan brought the poutine over and dropped it off at the table without a word. The plate was stacked high with long golden fries, though those fries near the top of the pile were indistinguishable under the dark brown of gravy dripping down the plate. It reminded Erica of the pictures she had seen of active lava flows: the gravy was clearly a liquid but moved with such torpidity that it resisted the force of gravity and cling to whatever it touched.

Sarah and Clarissa immediately began pulling fries out of the pile and consuming them, gravy end first. The fries were the same as Erica last remembered them but the gravy was different. It was sweet, too sweet, and was extraordinarily thick even though it was so warm. The color was off; instead of the light brown she expected it was a dark brown trending into a gray.

"God dammit, what happened to this bar?" Erica asked.

"What do you mean?" Sarah said.

"Don't you fucking remember," Erica started and held her hands up, both clenched into fists, "used to be so much better. I don't know who the hell half these people are, and they're fucking slobs." Erica pointed to a couple three tables over: one of the woman's high heels lay six feet away from their table and she was half embracing the man next to her, with each resting their other hand upon the table to keep themselves upright. In the process one or the other hand knocked their basket of popcorn on the floor and the white kernels lay scattered across the floor in a constellation of snack food. Someone had evidently missed this new stellar phenomenon and half of the popcorn was flattened and ground into the floor.

"Can you imagine this shit a few years ago?"

"Well, no, I guess not," Sarah said, as if this was the first time she had ever considered the possibility and arrived at a conclusion. "But, I don't know, it's fun. They aren't hurting anyone."

"Yeah," Clarissa added, "seems like fun! I didn't realize you kicked it this hard up here in New Hampshire."

"It's not -" Erica said and then dropped her head and stared at the table. She closed her eyes and shook her head slowly. This wasn't right — this wasn't what she remembered of The Granite Goose and it wasn't how it should be.

The alcohol sat heavy in Erica's stomach. She took another bite of fries but it tasted of grease. Suddenly she wanted to be home, wrapped in a blanket, sitting on her couch with the television on or a book in her hand.

"Sorry Sarah," Erica said. "Nice meeting you Clarissa." She slung her purse over her shoulder, reached into her wallet, and put a ten dollar bill on the table.

"What's going on?" Sarah asked. She raised her eyebrows in concern and leaned over the small table and waited for an answer. Clarissa ignored the conversation and in one swift motion snagged another fry off the plate and tossed it into her mouth.

"Sorry, I've got to go. This is just, I just thought I was up to this, but I'm not. Just too much going on right now. But thanks. I'll see you on Monday."

Erica did not wait for a response. She turned on her heel and walked towards the exit. When she pushed open the wooden door a cloud of haze unfurled around her. The music followed and Erica imagined the notes might be visible if she looked hard enough. As the door swung shut behind her the music faded and at the same time the hazy air dissipated into the night sky.

She thought about getting a cab but the air had already begun to cool and her apartment was less than half a mile away — an easy walk in this weather. Besides the occasional passing car, the streets were empty and relatively quiet. Most of the storefronts on the ground level were closed or empty; all were dark. The few buildings with two or more stories — almost all of those an aged-red brick — were occupied, the second floor apartments casting light from the windows out onto the street. The light from the apartments did not diffuse easily into the night air. The lingering humidity confined the casted light into distinct cones illuminating patches of gray concrete and crumbling asphalt.

Her thoughts drifted on the summer breeze to her brother. His death seemed at once both so real and not; the pain and heaviness she felt, a ball of anger and grief clenched and folded upon itself inside her, was there and given life anew whenever she thought of him again. She would have liked to see him on a night like tonight; catch up, see how his classes or internship was going, just grab a beer and make fun of townies. Now she would never have those conversations again with him and that realization came in waves, a repeated pounding at her heart and mind that was eroding parts of her away.

As she neared her apartment, Erica spied a man sitting on the sidewalk. He sat with his legs splayed out in front of him and his back against the wall. Erica thought of crossing the street to avoid him, but with her apartment only a dozen or so yards beyond and on the same side of the street, she thought it best to continue on and enter the building.

As she neared, the man looked towards her and twisted to put his right arm against the wall behind him and his right foot under his body. In the low light Erica could not identify the color of the man's eyes or short-cropped hair. As she drew closer, he stood and Erica saw he had a few inches on her and at least fifty pounds.

"Hey, you got any spare change?" he asked. His tone lacked the hesitancy of a question, but was instead replaced by an immediacy tinged with frustration, as if the words soured and he was forced to spit them out in a staccato to reduce the time they remained in his mouth.

"No, sorry," Erica said. She stepped into the street to give the man a wide berth. The sound of her shoes on the pavement seemed louder now, or she was at least more cognizant of it. She hoped the pace had not changed.

As she drew alongside him, the man leaned in towards her and sneered, an expression signaling not distaste but contempt. Erica could tell he was young, though he didn't look it. His face was pockmarked and his teeth yellowed. Drugs most likely. Erica did not step back. She held her keys in her hand and without looking away from the man threaded a few of the keys through her fingers in a makeshift weapon.

"Excuse me," Erica said and held his eye contact. After a moment he relented, or at least relaxed: he took a step back and his shoulders dropped while his hands dangled at his sides.

Erica kept the man in the edge of her vision as she glanced down and located the key to the exterior door of the apartment. The building only held three units, but her landlord had the foresight to lock the exterior door and provide each tenant a separate key. Once she was inside she closed the door behind her and breathed a sigh of relief as the lock clicked shut.

When she glanced back out the door she saw the man walking away. She was used to dealing with drunks — hell, her Uncle Jimmy was always plastered at any family get-together of any size — but the drugs was something new, or at least the amount of users in New Hampshire was. Perhaps a story to write someday. For now, she couldn't shake the story on Route 101; something was there, something more to learn and write about, and perhaps something related to Nate.

CHAPTER NINETEEN

Corey scored big. After purchasing another (free) soda at Mark's Convenience the other day, he had spied one of the beer distributors unloading a stack of pallets next to the rusty green dumpster. Although a few of the pallets were broken, most were in good condition and could be a source of free wood for Fort Barren. Corey had called Alex and convinced him to meet him that morning behind Mark's to see the loot and get it to the Fort.

"This is great, Corey," Alex said as they stood surveying the pile, "but how are we going to get all this stuff out to the fort?"

"I don't know man. I just saw it and thought we should get it before the trash man takes it away. Do you think your mom or dad would drive out here to pick it up and drive us back.?

Alex tried to hold back laughter but it spurted out between his lips in a short burst of high-pitched squealing. "No way," Alex said as his laughter quieted. "No way at all. My mom wouldn't want any of the stuff in the car. She'd throw a fit if I even tried. You remember when we had mud on our shoes that time after the reservoir?"

"Yeah, yeah," Corey said. "So what do we do?"

"I don't know." Alex shrugged. "Just start lugging it back a piece at a time I guess."

"Man..." Corey said, his voice trailing off, "that's going to take forever."

"Maybe we can get some help? We should ask Jordan Potter maybe, or we could maybe ask Steve."

"We can't. If we tell anyone, they will want to be part of the club. We've got to do it ourselves. It has to be ours. Then we are the only bosses."

"I guess," Alex said, and that ended the debate. They both glanced around to be certain that no one was watching them. The street was empty and the parking lot held only two cars. Though the pallets were sitting by the dumpster and almost certainly meant to be hauled away as trash, both felt it was nearly stealing, but neither wanted to ask permission to take the pallets on the off chance that they would be told no.

With a shrug, Alex grabbed the end of one pallet and Corey grabbed the other. The two carried the lumber back a piece at a time. Each trip took nearly 30 minutes winding through the forest behind the store and along the paths they had discovered. They stacked each pallet beside the wolf pine supporting Fort Barren and discussed how best to use the salvaged wood. After five trips Jason — one of the clerks at the store the boys knew — saw them grabbing another and yelled them off.

After they carried the last one, they had lunch. Neither felt like working on the Fort. Carrying the pallets out had been work enough for one summer day. As they finished up their hot dogs and chips, Corey suggested they go down to the bog and see what they could find.

"We shouldn't go out to the bog," Alex said.

"Why not?"

"I told you: my mom says we should stay away, it's too dangerous. Says there's quicksand or something and we could drown."

"So? You listen to everything your mom says?"

"No," Alex said and emphasized the word, "but you know what Jason said, right? And Terry too. About the Bog Monster. They've both seen it. And you saw the deer we found. There's something out there. "

"You believe them?" Corey asked.

"Well, maybe. I mean, I think they're both kind of jerks, but who knows what's out there."

With that, Corey knew how he could convince Alex to come with him to the bog. "Well, let's go look," he said. "If we discover something out there we'll be famous and we can name it after ourselves."

"I don't know," Alex said. "You really think so?"

"Well sure," Corey responded. "Isn't that what scientists do all the time when they discover a new animal? They pick a cool sounding name and then translate it into... Greek I think, some old words like from school, and then that's the name everyone has to use."

The thought of discovering a new species, of locating a cryptid, of making his mark in history, was enough to override Alex's concern over his mother's expectations for their travels. A liberal coating of bug spray later, the two boys were ready to travel to the Bog. They passed Fort Barren and traveled down some of the same paths, near the highway and alongside the Overpass to Nowhere and continued on to the shore of the Great Bog. They spoke as they walked.

"You know what I heard from Robbie," Corey said, referring to another neighbor he occasionally played with when Alex wasn't around, "you gotta be careful at the carnival. The, uh," Corey stammered, snapping his fingers to help with the recall in perfect unrealized pantomime of his father, "those people who work there, the carnies, my cousin heard from a friend that all the carnies are like, murderers and stuff, and he told me all about it. So the carnies live and work on the carnival, and move from town to town I heard, just murdering people and stealing babies."

"What? They steal babies?"

"Yeah," Corey continued, "to grow them up in the carnival, to teach them and make more carnies. Otherwise there wouldn't be no carnies, and the carnival wouldn't exist."

"No way," Alex said. "No way that's happening."

"I've been there, I've seen it."

"You've seen them steal babies?" Alex asked. He raised his eyebrows and looked over the top of his glasses at Corey, unknowingly mimicking the same expression of incredulity his father had given him so often.

"Well, no," Corey began, "I haven't seen them steal the babies, but I've seen the carnies. They're like, rough people. Kind of dirty. Like hobos. They have long beards, even some of the girls."

"Ew, the girls have beards?"

"Yeah, that's why I think they need to steal babies. Like they can't have babies of their own, but they need to get new carnies, so that's how they do it. They just steal normal people's' babies and raise the babies to be carnies."

"Maybe," Alex said, then raised his hand in front of his face and tried to waft the sudden stench away. It was intense, and didn't so much infiltrate the nostrils as it assaulted the brain. Corey felt as though the brackish scent was swirling around in his skull and the beginnings of a headache formed behind his forehead.

A cloud of insects now followed them. The bug spray they had applied worked to dissuade some of the mosquitoes and black flies, but a few were able to overcome its effects and every couple of seconds the boys were forced to swat away an insect dive bombing an ear, nose, or mouth.

"This place smells like shit," Alex said.

"Yep," Corey responded.

"What are we even looking for?"

"I don't know for sure. Just look for signs of the Bog Monster, or maybe treasure, or who knows, maybe we could find even more materials for the fort. Just think — people don't really go out here, it's unexplored land, so we could find anything." He stressed the word anything in an attempt to add importance to the idea.

"There's quicksand out here, right? Shouldn't we have like, rope or something?"

"Shit," Corey said. "I don't have rope. What if we get long sticks or something. That should help, right?"

"I guess," Alex said. They searched for a few minutes to find sticks long enough to help in case one of them got stuck in quicksand, light enough that they could carry them, but thick enough that they felt it would hold up to the task. Each ended up with a limb about six feet tall and the thickness of their wrist. They walked further into the Bog and used the limbs as walking sticks, poking and prodding at the ground in front of them with each step.

They weaved their way through the marsh. The Great Bog lay to their right and the sun overhead shimmered in spots on its surface. On the far side the boys could see evergreens forming a natural barrier encircling the bog.

"What do you think lives out here?" Alex asked. The question startled Corey, not because of what was asked but simply because of the unexpected sound of Alex's voice; after just a few minutes without conversation the sounds of the bog had permeated his mind and pushed from his consciousness the idea of conversation.

"What?" Corey responded.

"What lives out there? Like, birds of course, but what else? Snakes and stuff, right?"

Corey stopped and turned back to Alex. "Yeah, sure, I guess. I mean, I guess we'll find out, right?"

"You think the thing out here killed that deer we saw a while back? Maybe it was just a bear. Do bears live in the bog?" Alex looked over both shoulders quickly, afraid he might find a bear sneaking up on him from a blind spot.

"Maybe. I don't know. Maybe it got hit by a car or something, then it just got chewed on by like rats and stuff."

Alex shrugged his shoulders, nodded his head, and followed after Corey again. "I don't like this," Alex added.

"Well let's keep looking." Corey moved forward. The scent from the Bog had become something in the background, a taste that lingered but no longer offended, when the two began to smell something new. This new scent complemented that of the Bog but was stronger and thicker in the air.

"You smell that?" Alex asked.

Corey coughed and said, "Yeah. What do you think it is?"

Alex shrugged and they continued forward. The marshy waters extended to their left and melted into the broken trees and grassy bends of the far bank.

"This is stupid," Alex said. "Why are we friggen out here? It smells bad and there's nothing but frogs and snakes and bugs. Probably a dead one somewhere stinking up this place. I wanna go home."

The sound of traffic had long since dissipated. Now a chorus of mosquitoes and black flies and crickets filled the void, the encompassing buzzing sounding like the vehicles on the highway over the ridge. They continued forward, Corey leading and Alex reluctantly following.

Corey stopped and held up a hand. "Alex, you hear that?" he asked. "Where'd all the bugs go?"

"What do you-" Alex started to say before he realized the silence that now surrounded them. The cloud of insects was gone and nowhere in sight. Alex leaned towards Corey and whispered: "Where did they all go?"

"I don't know..." Corey said. He glanced to his left and surveyed the still waters, then glanced to his right and peered through the underbrush. The silence scared him. It reminded him of the silence of the early morning after being awakened by a distressing dream, before the sun had risen or any people or animals or birds were out and the only things liable to be on the prowl were up to no good. It was the silence that betrayed no activity — an absence of sound and absence of life. And here, by some trick of acoustics, even the noise from the highway was imperceptible.

A splash sounded nearby, close enough to startle both of them, ripples from the brackish water cascading over their shoes. It was much louder, and likely larger, than a fish. Both boys would have fallen to the ground had they not had a hand tight around their walking sticks. The waters of the marsh undulated in ever expanding rings from a point thirty or so feet from the boys. The swamp was still and silent besides the water lapping against the shore. Corey glanced over his shoulder. Alex stared back with wide eyes, his eyebrows disappearing under the locks of his hair.

Alex mouthed *what was that?* Corey shrugged. They stared at the rippling waves. The water was silty and dirty, and even right at the shoreline the bottom was not visible. Seeing anything in the water that did not surface was unlikely. Corey turned to Alex.

"Maybe it was-" Corey began to whisper, but was interrupted by another splash, this one closer. Close enough to wet the boys' legs.

They ran.

CHAPTER TWENTY

After stewing over it for a few days, Will tried to call Oscar Kelly. Unfortunately, it didn't appear as though Oscar had a phone. The white pages had no listing for an Oscar Kelly, and when he asked the operator to provide him a number, she likewise was unable to find one. Will considered asking Lonnie or one of the other guys at the Department if they had a number for Oscar but decided it would be best to save any favors he might have earned for some other future request.

Will recalled that Oscar had — at least ten years ago — lived in one of the apartment buildings in West Derryfield. While considering which one he should try first, he remembered one place where Oscar almost certainly would be at: Hilltop Bar, the place Will's father and Oscar had forged and sustained a friendship since at least Will's birth.

Hilltop Bar in Derryfield sat about 50 feet off Hill Road. Though it sounded aptly named, Hilltop Bar only sat about two thirds up the small rise in the north-western part of town, dwarfed by the nearby Mount Majassic. This was not the only way it which if fell short of expectations. But, the beer was cheap and usually cold. Its parking lot was dirt and in the drier months of summer often kicked up dust with every tire and foot. Will deliberately picked his feet up a bit higher than normal in an effort to minimize any dragging and resulting dust. The building which housed the bar and kitchen was low and squat, a single door at the center of its slate gray siding.

Will was familiar with the place, having driven his father home a few times when Winston was unable to do so himself and the bartenders wise enough to call a ride for him. When the bartenders at Hilltop called the house while Will was in high school, he was always quick to respond. For them to call the house meant Winston was beyond simply drunk, and likely either asleep or nearly so from the alcohol. Will hadn't been back to the bar since the summer before he started college.

The bar was just as he remembered it. The heavy curtains covering the two windows in the front let in little light. The glow from the fixtures overhead gave the interior the feel of twilight; one could see and move easily about, but coming inside the bar on a sunny day required patience to allow the eyes to adjust. Being one of the few full smoking bars left in Derryfield, the constant haze inside didn't help with the sight lines either. A single long bar made up most of the main room, with only two tables and three booths crammed into the far right wall, clustered around the doors to the single use bathrooms. Two of the booths were occupied with two persons each, but Will couldn't identify them between the dim light and smoky air.

Five sat at the bar and a dirty mirror reflected their faces to Will. Three were mill workers, easily identified by the dark blue shirts they wore with their name tags sewn on the chest. The other two sported heavy tans and thick forearms, making Will think they were likely outdoor laborers. He recognized everyone's faces but couldn't place names.

The bar itself was a darkly stained wood pockmarked with decades worth of scratches and chips. The stools at the bar were similarly worn, the cushions flat and matted from the accumulated weight of patrons. A kaleidoscope of glass mugs hung from hooks bolted into the ceiling above the bar. Most had name plates attached nearby. Will saw his father's still in its usual place, third seat from the left, two hooks back. Even from ten feet away and in the poor light Will could see the layer of dust on the mug.

Will recognized the bartender, Jerry Marchand. Jerry had been old nearly twenty years ago, when Will first met him. His wrinkled face was tan and his frizzy hair was still the same salt-and-pepper combination Will remembered from years past. He wore a black apron slung over his chest and leaned on the bar, talking to a man Will recognized but couldn't name or place.

"Billy Boucher!" Jerry said in a loud voice, and more quietly to the man in front of him, "Excuse me, I've got to say hi to this guy." Jerry leaned over the bar in towards Will and smiled a nicotine stained crescent.

"Jerry," Will said. "How are you?"

"I'm well, quite well. Been a long time. What would you say, five, seven years?"

"Something like that."

"Listen, never got to say anything to you about your old man, and sorry if this isn't the time or place, but didn't see you at the funeral or service. Just wanted to say, he was a good guy."

"Thanks," Will said.

"What the hell you been up to? Well I mean, besides the shop and all. Hear you are taking care of things down there. How's your mother holding up these days?"

"Not all that well," Will said through gritted teeth.

"Sorry to hear. You look a little beat, need a drink?" Jerry asked.

"No thanks. Not tonight. I'm looking for Oscar."

"Oh, really?" Jerry said. He stepped back from the bar and said: "He's only in a few nights a week now, but you're in luck kid. He's sitting over at one of the booths." Jerry motioned with his thumb towards the far wall.

Will waved a cloud of smoke away from his face and made his way back towards the booths. As he approached he saw a young couple leaning over their drinks in one booth. In the other, the one tucked in the corner, Oscar sat with his back against the wall, facing Will. Oscar had occasionally dropped by the shop, especially in the weeks immediately after Winston's death, but his visits had become less frequent as the years went by. Will hadn't seen him in at least a year, and going by memory and perception, the last year had not been kind to Oscar. From what Will could, Oscar had gained at least thirty pounds, most of it in his abdomen and face. The beard always marking his face no longer looked imposing but was instead unkempt and splotched with gray.

Oscar's eyes remained on his booth mate. As Will drew closer he was able to see around the wall of the booth and he spied a familiar curl of brown hair.

"Erica?" Will asked. She turned in the booth and nodded at him. The line of her mouth wavered but instead of a smile formed into a one-sided smirk.

"What the hell are you doing here? With Oscar?"

"Jesus, Billy?" Oscar interrupted as he slid out of the bar and held his hand out to shake Will's. "Damn good to see you. What the hell are you doing here?"

"Hi, Will," Erica said. She looked tired to Will, less colorful than he remembered from just the other day. The dim bar lights, the smoky air, and a long day at work all conspired to add years to her face.

"I'm here looking for you," Will said to Oscar. "What are you two doing?" he asked.

"Well Erica here — she's a reporter for the *Gazette*, you know, had a couple questions for me."

"Yeah, I know Erica, Oscar. We went to school together."

"You both went to Bartlett High School, right?" Oscar asked.

Both Erica and Will nodded. "Well how's about that," Oscar said and laughed. "A little reunion we got ourselves here. I went there too, back when it was just Riverside Elementary."

"Join us, join us!" Oscar said. He sat back down, scooted further into the booth and patted the bench for Will to sit down. Oscar peppered Will with questions, asking him about the shop and his mother. Erica sat quietly and finished off her beer. After another few minutes, she interrupted and said, "Well, let me get everyone some rounds. I said I'd get you Oscar, and I may as well get Will here."

The two thanked Erica as she walked over to the bar and signaled to Jerry. When she was out of earshot, Will said, "I've got some questions for you about Winston."

"Sure thing. Ask away."

"Well," Will said. He took a deep breath in before continuing, "I'm honestly not quite sure how to ask it. So I was talking to my mother, and I don't know if it's just her Alzheimer's acting up, but she mentioned something about Winston that just... left me wondering."

"What about?" Oscar leaned back and waited for Will to continue.

"I expect this will sound kind of crazy, well, first, let me backup. She said it in relation to him being sober the last few years before he," Will paused, not certain what word to use, "before he died."

"Yeah, he was. Still got down here, but it was nothing but pop for him."

"Really?"

"Swear on it. Surprised everyone."

"Jesus," Will said, shaking his head. "Well, I don't know if its related to that, but my mother said Winston... saw something out on Route 101. Like, scared him sober."

Oscar leaned further back in his seat and his eyes narrowed. Pursed lips replaced his easy grin.

"Yeah..." Oscar said, adding nothing more.

"Well... did he say anything to you about that? Do you know anything about it?"

"Only what he told me. Why do you want to know?"

"I'm just trying to understand what motivated the change, you know, to drop alcohol after all those years."

"You got the time line about right, from what I can remember," Oscar said, rocking back and forth on the booth seat a few times. "I 'member it pretty well. I came in after shift one afternoon, probably back in '91, to find your old man sitting at the bar, a warm beer — flat too — sitting in front of him. Never saw that before, he never had any trouble finishing them before that. But anyways, I asked him what the hell was going on, and he looked at me with these eyes all wide, could practically see more white than anything else, you know what I mean?"

Will nodded.

"So, he starts in about this thing he saw off Route 101. I figured he was drunk, either when he thinks he saw the thing, or when he's telling me the story now, or knowing him — no offense — but probably both, and I try to laugh it off. Offer to buy him another round. He says no. Just like that. No, he said. Never did touch a drop again, far as I know."

"Thanks," Will said. "What did he-" he began before Erica came sauntering back from the bar, three glasses of amber beer in hand.

"Hope you all like PBR — wasn't sure what to get," she said.

"Honey," Oscar said, "I ain't turning down a free beer from no one." He smiled and reached out a hand to take one of the glasses from her. Erica sat another one in front of Will and slid into the booth next to him before taking a sip from the last remaining glass.

"Better on tap, huh?" Oscar said.

"So where were we?" Erica asked.

"Honestly," Will said, "I was just getting ready to go. I can't stay long." He felt overwhelmed by the confirmation of his mother's story and his father's sobriety. Will didn't want to stay in the bar with the scent of smoke and beer and desperation.

"Nonsense!" Oscar yelled a bit too loudly. The couple in the booth across the room craned their heads around the booth walls to stare at Oscar for a moment.

"Billy here was just asking me about his old man, about him getting sober. Same kinds of stuff you were."

"What do you mean?" Erica asked. She sipped her beer but kept her eyes above the rim of the glass and on the two men as Oscar answered.

"The stuff you were asking about. That story his old man told, the one about the thing off Route 101. A drunk dream or something, but scared him sober all right."

Erica brought her glass down with such force that it knocked loudly against the wooden table and a few drops of PBR sloshed over the side. Erica was worried for a moment it would break, but the glass held firm.

"He what?" Erica asked. "Are you two pulling my leg?"

"What?" Will said. "Why are you asking about my father?"

Both leaned away from the other in the confined space of the booth. Will sat with his back against the wall and Erica nearly spilled out of the booth entirely and had both legs under her, ready to stand and leave.

"You two ain't working together on this story?" Oscar asked.

Both Erica and Will went to answer and spoke over one another in a jumble of negative answers and half-formed sentences. Oscar shook his head and took a large gulp of the PBR.

"What the hell kind of story are you writing?" Will asked. "Why's my father in it?"

"Listen," Erica said, "it's not specifically about your father. It's about 101, all the accidents out there, and what could be causing it. I'm just asking around, trying to gather stories. That's it."

"He wasn't involved in an accident out there."

"No, not as far as I know," Erica replied. "But I heard from someone else that your father had one of those stories, that he had seen something."

Who?" Will asked. He leaned forward and continued, "Who told you that?"

"A source. Just someone else who had heard the story."

"A source? That's it?"

Erica shrugged and said: "Why are you asking Oscar here about it?"

Will nearly did not respond, the urge to rise and leave growing even stronger, but instead said, "Just asking about my father, I told you. Catching up with an old family friend."

"Quite the damn thing," Oscar interrupted the two.

Erica leaned over the table and asked, "What do you think it was Oscar? What Will's father saw?"

"Well, I always heard stories. Just drunks you know," Oscar said and waved his hand as if dismissing the tales. "People around the bar sharing stories about something out of the mills, the pollution in the water, all that dumping. Mutated something out there, can you believe that? Like one of those old science fiction movies, with the mutated ants or whatever it was," Oscar said. "Who the hell really knows," Oscar said, then laughed and drained his beer.

Will looked at the beer before him but didn't touch it. He didn't like Erica asking questions about his father, and he didn't like the stories Oscar was telling him. The little he had heard settled into his mind and brought forward the fresh memories of the thing he had seen on the tow. Will suddenly became aware of the sensation of an empty stomach, of nicotine laced air in his nose, of the sweat on his brow, of the pressure in his head. He wanted to get home, before the sun set, get to sleep and forget what he had seen and what he had felt and what Oscar told him just now.

Will slid out of the booth and said, "Thanks Oscar. If I want, how can I get in touch with you?"

Oscar grunted and said, "Don't have a phone right now. Here at the Hilltop ain't bad. Or try me at home, 24B Richards, the apartment complex you know, over behind the fire station."

"Thanks," Will said. He nodded to Erica.

"Good seeing you Billy," Oscar said and raised his hand. "Good to see a Boucher in here, it's been a while. Hope to see you again soon."

CHAPTER TWENTY-ONE

Erica was driving to relax. An iced coffee in the cup holder, the radio turned up loud enough to drown out the sounds of the engine, the windows open; nothing beat a car ride in a summer evening to put her at ease. When she reflected on this, she assumed that the focus driving took (enough to occupy her mind, but not enough to fill it) allowed her subconscious to ruminate on other things.

She knew the white cross lay ahead, the marker set down by her parents to memorialize Nate's life and death. Before his passing, she had always found the occasional cross along the highway distasteful somehow, the pure white cross — often ringed in flowers or a wreath — out of place beside the pavement and the exhaust, an affront of spirituality alongside the callous industrial scar cutting across the land.

She could have gone to his grave, to where his body lay, but it seemed to her more appropriate to go to where he was last alive, as though if any part of him remained, some spark of his being was still present, it would be here, where he last drew breath. She wanted to go and speak to him, to catch him up as to how her life was going. She also felt a need to share the bullshit she had heard, the nonsense about UFOs and aliens in the swamps.

Beyond speaking to Nate, Erica also hoped to get a sense of the area that held the mythical beast she had heard so much about. She didn't believe Stewart's or Becki's or Oscar's stories, but that didn't matter. What did was getting a feel for the highway, the river alongside it, the bog — all the elements that brought to mind whatever it was that caused these people to believe they had seen something incredible. If she was going to write it, she needed to understand it. Frank at the *Gazette* had been pestering her for a few days now to turn something in on the construction story. Her repeated excuses wouldn't buy her too much more time; she needed to put together whatever it was the story would be and get it to the editors.

When she passed mile marker 26 heading east she pulled onto the shoulder of the road. Her headlights illuminated Nate's cross a few hundred feet away. The white wood gleamed in the light. Erica turned off the ignition and grabbed a flashlight in one hand after tying a long sleeve shirt around her waist by its sleeves. She scooted out the passenger side door and heard frogs chirping nearby, a summer chorus sung to the stars and moon. As she expected, the air smelted brackish, here where the swamps between Derryfield and Epping drew so close the road.

She walked along the highway for twenty feet before spying something of a path down the embankment. The embankment might obscure some of the sky to her left, but she certainly felt safer off the highway. As had been repeated to her numerous times over the last few weeks, it wasn't known as the Highway of Death for nothing. Her flashlight cast a small circle of light at her feet and illuminated some calf high grass and occasional sapling struggling to take root in the poor soil. She wondered if she might see any plants she recognized. Maybe that minor in plant biology would finally come in handy; she didn't expect to be working as a gardener or florist anytime soon.

Though she was familiar with the road and the general area after the ceremony when they planted the cross, she had never been out here at night on foot. Once she was down the embankment she unfurled the shirt around her waist and alternated slipping each arm into a sleeve while the other held her flashlight. She chided herself for wearing sandals in this terrain and closely watched the small circle of light cast by the flashlight in hopes of avoiding a fall. As she trundled through the brush, the vegetation scratching her legs and crunching underfoot, she thought she heard a similar noise further from the road. Erica stopped and listened for a few seconds but heard nothing besides the sounds of the frogs and a car passing by. She ignored the uneasiness in her abdomen and assumed it was just her stomach protesting the burger she had eaten for a late dinner.

The moon hung high, a pock-marked half crescent amid a scattering of stars. Though she recalled it from her youth, she couldn't see the Milky Way proper. The lights of the cities near the seacoast proved too bright for that sort of sight-seeing this far east. Still, she stopped walking for a moment to admire the stars and the moon when she heard the crack of something breaking and the shuffling of something moving in the distance to her right, further away from the road. She thought that perhaps she should climb back up the embankment and just walk along the highway to Nate's cross, traffic be damned.

"Hello?" Erica asked. "Is someone there?" She pointed her flashlight to her right and was dismayed when its flickering beam only projected about sixty feet from her. The light illuminated a few scraggly trees bare of any leaves, standing upright like disfigured men at attention, knee deep in the dark water of the bog. She noticed a ripple in the surface of the swamp and swung her flashlight back and forth in hopes of identifying its source. She was concerned for a moment, Becki Corville's story resonating in her mind, the words she so easily scoffed at over a plate of fries at noon a few days ago suddenly substantial and made solid in the darkness and relative silence. After a few more seconds Erica shrugged — the gesture more in an effort to calm herself then communicate to anyone — and turned back to navigating her way through the weeds.

She enjoyed the outdoors, in moderation. She had been camping with her family a few times in her youth, but it always was more trouble than it was worth. A hike for a day, during the day, was more her style. Though she knew the road was just up the embankment to her left she felt isolated. The embankment was too straight to be anything other than man made — it stretched before her as far as her eyes could see in the low light — but other than that, her surroundings were wild.

As she walked parallel to the highway Erica heard a series of splashes to her right, each following the other in quick succession. She stopped and turned back to the swamp. The yellowed beam of the flashlight reflected off the rippling water, small undulations bobbing outward in concentric circles. Again, besides the water, all the flashlight revealed before succumbing to the darkness were some bent trees. Erica stopped moving and listened for a moment. She could hear nothing but the slowly diminishing sound of the water and the occasional vehicle on the highway above.

Erica stepped closer to the embankment and began looking for an easy path back up to the shoulder and Nate's cross. The grass and weeds continued to reach at least eight inches above the ground, the

DOT road crews apparently deciding not to attempt to mow on this steep of an incline. She nearly stumbled once but caught herself with an outstretched arm. The ground was moist and Erica wiped her hand on her shorts. Another car passed above, its tires humming and engine coughing, and in the silence that followed, Erica heard another splash in the waters behind her, this time closer and louder.

Now she was certain she was hearing the movements of some creature. Her mind immediately returned to her conversations with Becki and Oscar. Suddenly being out here beside 101 at 10 PM seemed foolish, an invitation to a danger she didn't believe in yet couldn't help but fear in some way. The darkness and relative solitude again gave weight to the stories. Erica sighed and then rubbed her head and slowly inhaled and exhaled. She needed to focus.

Knowing even a cursory look for whatever otter or stork was likely making the noise would help calm her, Erica scanned her flashlight back across the swamp, then froze. The beam illuminated an enormous creature no more than 40 feet away. It stood low to the ground and its pale bulk was not captured by the weak beam of her flashlight. Its skin hung in flaps and appeared to be sloughing off its frame. Erica could not tell if the moisture dripping off its skin was bodily fluids or water from the swamp.

For a moment, Erica's mind went blank but for the creature before her, as if its visage was enough to derail conscious thought. As the thing before her registered in her mind, her hands trembled and she nearly dropped the flashlight; her mouth became dry; her breathing quickened. The creature listed to one side and a cavernous maw in the center of its mass widened. The edges of the maw quivered as it bellowed.

Erica ran. As she ran a car passed by and she heard for a moment the sounds of its radio cranked above the roar of its engine and the noise of its tires on the road. Those sounds muffled that of the thing behind her. Erica glanced over her shoulder as she climbed the embankment to see it scrambling up the incline further down the road, as if it was chasing not her, but the car that had just passed.

Erica lurched up the embankment and glanced to her right to track the creature, instead only catching Nate's cross in her flashlight. She turned and ran along the shoulder towards the Taurus and had the presence of mind to pull her keys out of her pocket and ready the key to the car. She jammed the key into the Taurus and in one fluid motion tore open the door, hopped into the car, and slammed the door shut behind her. She fumbled with the key as she tried to slide it into the ignition, glanced up through her windshield, and in the soft light of the moon saw the thing bounding along the road.

Erica cranked the key and the engine roared to life. The Taurus bucked forward when she depressed the gas pedal. It fishtailed in the sand, the creature only a few feet beyond the passenger side of her car, before the front tires gripped the pavement of Route 101. Erica glanced at the rear view mirror and saw the creature hurtling after her. The rear lights of the Taurus bathed it in a red glow. Though the thing moved quickly, it was not graceful; its gait was uneven, a long stride followed by a staccato of smaller steps. Its flaking skin waved in the air as it propelled itself forward.

Erica slammed the gas pedal to the floor and rocked in her seat as the passenger side tires dropped off the pavement of the shoulder of the road and into dirt. She jerked the wheel to the left and bounced again when the tires pulled back up onto asphalt. The thing following her was closer, the wet maw at the center of its mass a darker red glow from her taillights, its body just a few feet from the rear bumper of her car. Erica kept her foot on the pedal and the vehicle's speed climbed past 30 mph, then 40, after which the creature behind her faltered, slowed, and disappeared in the darkness behind her.

She continued driving east on Route 101 for a few more miles and glanced in the rear view mirror every few seconds. Her knuckles were bone white from her grip on the steering wheel. She became aware of the sound of her radio tuned to NHPR and stabbed with one hand at the knob to turn it off. In the relative silence that followed she listened to the roll of the tires on the pavement and the sound of her heart in her ears. She wasn't sure where the beating in her chest ended and the sound of circulation in her ears began; it was as if one bled into the other and combined to cause the shaking of her hands.

This is what Becki saw, she thought; this is what Winston had seen. *Holy fuck, whatever it is, that thing is still around.* She had no idea what it could be; she'd never seen, nor heard of, anything like it. She'd thought Becki just a washed up waitress, a townie whose brain and stories were fucked by the passage of time and an overindulgence in cocaine. She figured Winston was much the same, a drunk whose stories had grown with his waist line and alcohol dependency. But Erica was wrong — whatever Becki and Winston and others had seen was really out there, was still out there today.

Erica pushed the Taurus over 70 mph and hunched over the steering wheel. Home was towards Derryfield — west — but she had no intention of driving west on Route 101 and back towards the creature out there. She drove for miles until she reached Hampton Beach. Route 1A was nearly empty. The beach, often filled with so many people in the summer that the sand wasn't visible under the brightly colored umbrellas, towels, and chairs, was empty. The dark purple of the surf at night crashed into the sand. The arcades and pizza joints and ice cream stands along the coast were silent and shuttered, another reminder of the missing crowds.

Why the hell haven't I heard about this thing until now, Erica wondered. A giant creature out in the swamps. Surely even more must have seen it, more than just the drunks, dopers, and deadbeats at the Hilltop. They must have told others about it. She had lived in this area her whole life, and the first she had heard of it was only a few weeks ago. Now she had seen the damn thing. She wondered if it could have contributed to Nate's accident.

She drove south over the inlet. The white bulbous dome of the nuclear power plant glowed in the night across the estuary. The water reflected some of the light, making the wide river mouth brighter than the sky above.

Erica drove for another few miles and then turned back towards Hampton. She stayed on Route 1A, the sea to one side and that thing to the other. She drove and waited for dawn.

CHAPTER TWENTY-TWO

"It was probably just a turtle," Corey said. He and Alex were sitting in Fort Barren, the closest they had been to the Bog in the last week. Fort Barren was now weather tight, or at least constructed well enough that a 12 year old boy considered it weather tight. Corey and Alex had spent one rainy afternoon in it and, after installing a blue tarp over the carefully laid roof boards, found only one leak in the rear of the Fort where the tarp was torn.

That was fortuitous, as their fever to build the fort had finally broken. The windows were only rough squares cut in the wall and the door in the floor didn't line up very well, but additional construction seemed like a lot of work; it was complete enough for playing, so that's what they did. Neither boy was sure why or when they had decided the Fort was done enough. If they had taken the time to reflect on it, they may have realized it was the anticipation and the allure of building, the dream of what the fort could be, that had initially pressed them forward. Once what was imagined began to take shape and the limitations of their work made clear, their motivation went with it.

"Maybe," Alex replied. "Did you see a turtle?"

"No," Corey said, louder than a whisper but not by much. "But it could have been. I mean, we didn't see it, but it could have been."

"Must of been a snapping turtle then. I heard those things are really big."

The sun was on its back end journey to the horizon and the light was beginning to change to a warmer orange hue. Alex peered at the sky between the tree branches over head and said, "We should probably head back for supper. It's getting pretty late."

Corey agreed so they climbed down and walked back to Alex's house. Alex's backyard emptied right into the edge of the woods. The carefully manicured grass Mr. Marino painstakingly mowed every

Saturday and watered every afternoon after he got home from work ended at a berm made of wood chips; the forest began past the berm with a few trees as thick around as an oil barrel and many others much smaller. The boys spilled into the yard laughing, both dirty and sweaty, both ignorant of their condition in the way that only children can be.

They were startled when Mrs. Marino yelled to them from the back porch: "Where have you two been? I've been calling for you two for twenty minutes! Dinner was ready twenty minutes ago!"

"Jeez, sorry Mom," Alex said, "we didn't realize it was so late."

Mrs. Marino ignored her son and turned to Corey. "Your father's been calling too, worried sick about you. Says you were supposed to be over at Mrs. Gagnon's. She's been calling here too, looking for you." For some reason, one Corey had never identified, Mrs. Marino was one of the few persons that called Mimi by her last name.

"Ah shoot," Corey said, mindful of the audience. "I forgot."

"That's not the kind of thing to forget young man." She put an arm around Alex and shepherded him towards the back door.

"You know the rules, Alex," Mrs. Marino said, turning back to Alex. "Back home in time for dinner at 7."

"Sorry Mom, we lost track of time."

"How did you lose track of time?" Mrs. Marino grabbed her son's arm and waved it back and forth. "Where is your watch? Why did we buy you a watch if you are never going to wear it?"

"Sorry Mom, I forgot."

Corey started up the porch steps to follow Alex into the house but Mrs. Marino stopped them both and said to Corey, "No, off to home with you. I told you your father is looking for you. Called here twice. Get yourself home now."

"OK," Corey said morosely. "See you later, man," he said to Alex.

Too tired to run but too anxious to walk, Corey jogged home. It took only a few minutes. He slowed into a brisk walk as he approached the house. He could see the light on inside the kitchen and living room so he circled to the side entrance to enter the kitchen.

Ted was inside, sitting at the table.

"Where have you been?" Ted immediately asked.

"I'm sorry, I'm sorry, I forgot. I finished lunch at Mimi's and I was out playing with Alex and we lost track of time and — "

"Corey, fer Chrissakes, I don't have time for this," Ted yelled. "I tell you to be at Mimi's for meals at the very least, I expect you to be there. I get home and you're nowhere to be found. Even the Marinos have no idea. You've got to listen!" he stressed the last word and drew it out as he said it, as if he was speaking to someone unfamiliar with the language.

"I'm sorry Dad, I just forgot!" Corey cried.

"Sorry is not good enough! I can't have you out and not know where you are! No playing with Alex for the rest of this week. I've had enough of this with you."

Yelling Corey could take; losing TV privileges was expected occasionally, like when he forgot his chores; but losing time with Alex was too much, a punishment that far exceeded what, to Corey's mind at least, was a minor infraction, a mistake and nothing more. He felt his anger rising inside him and yelled: "Why can't I see Alex! This is unfair!"

"Jesus Christ! I work a 12 hour day and come home and you are nowhere to be found! You're supposed to be with Mimi, she tells me you've been MIA since lunch, and I call the Marinos and find out you're with their kid but they can't find the two of your either! I can't have this!"

"I hate this Dad! I wish Mom was back! She would let me play with Alex! Why do you have to be so mean to me? I hate you!"

Ted leaned in closer and grimaced. Corey could tell he was very angry: the muscles to his jaw bulged and his face reddened. "You can hate me all you want, but you will respect me. I'm the one keeping a roof over your head and putting food on your plate. Remember that. No one else is here. Your mother isn't here. Now get to your room. You're grounded. No TV while you're here. No seeing Alex. You'll stay at Mimi's while I'm gone, or hell, I'll bring you to work and you'll sit in the break room all day while I work. That'd be plenty fun. I've had enough of your attitude, you understand?"

Corey ran. He was out the door before Ted even processed that Corey was heading not towards his room but in the opposite direction. Corey skipped down the gray cement steps, hit the patchy grass at a run, and circled between their house and the Jackson's next door. Ted followed after him but by the time he made it to the door Corey had already disappeared into the gloom of twilight.

"Corey!" he yelled. "Get your ass back in here, right now!"

Corey heard his father's voice but ignored it and ran faster. He knew he couldn't run to Mimi's or Alex's house. His father would undoubtedly visit those places first and, if he resisted, likely drag Corey back to the house. He wanted to be anywhere but there right now. The only place he could go was Fort Barren. His father knew he and Alex were building a fort in the back woods, but didn't know exactly where. As soon as Corey had entered the woods he slowed his pace and began walking. The gloom of twilight was quickly becoming the dark of night and the level of light was even lower under the foliage. Corey walked slowly and waited for his eyes to begin to adjust. The shapes of the trees and bushes gradually became more distinct, but regardless he walked confidently to his destination; the hundreds of trips to the Fort with Alex provided all the experience he needed to travel there even in these conditions.

After a ten minute walk he arrived at the Fort. The sun had set and only a dim orange glow to the west remained as a memory of its presence. The rolling sounds of crickets and other insects surrounded him. He climbed up the boards of the ladder Alex and he had installed up the tree and pushed with one hand to open the trapdoor in the floor. The old door hinges creaked and squealed in the quiet of the night. He hauled himself into the fort proper and let the door fall shut behind him. It was darker inside the fort, but after a minute his eyes began to adjust to the low level of illumination from the stars and moon that bathed the area.

Corey sat on the floor of Fort Barren and cried. The tears surprised him. He had cried often when his mother first left, and after the first few holidays — and the first birthday — she had not called. But eventually he came to expect her absence, and crying over it no longer seemed worth it. His father often chided him if he caught him crying, so Corey had worked to avoid it. But the tears came fast and heavy now, along with great heaves of his body as he sucked air in.

He sat and cried, not even certain at first what he was crying about. Certainly the fight with his father was a part of it, even the majority of it; but even at 12 years old, Corey recognized that the tension he felt around his father was so often because of his mother's absence.

Something had changed about their relationship after his mother left. He didn't know if his father blamed him, but the anger and frustration Ted always carried was often directed towards Corey, something he had rarely experienced before his mother left.

After a few minutes, Corey wiped his forearm across his face to remove most of the snot and tears and then lay down on the floor and rested his head atop his hands. His stomach rumbled and Corey wished he had eaten something before making his dash out to the fort. He did not intend on sleeping but the darkness coupled with the relief he felt after crying was enough for him to slip into a light sleep.

A sound in the bushes woke him. For a few moments he was lost, the unfamiliarity of Fort Barren at night a new sight for his groggy mind. A second later he recognized the Fort, remembered he had hiked out to the fort to escape his father, and the fright began to bleed off and his heart began to slow. But then the realization of his sudden alertness and the sound that prompted it circled back into his conscious mind and with it, the fear returned. Something was in the bushes at the edge of the clearing. Something large and heavy, moving slowly through the brush.

Corey crept forward on hands and knees and raised his head high enough to peer over the damp wooden edge of the open window, the window nothing more than a rough square cut in the boards of the wall. The moon overhead cast enough light to illuminate the forest's outlines: trees and bushes were visible but their constituent limbs or leaves were not. A patch of stars shone brightly through the canopy overhead. The air was heavy with the scent of rotting vegetation from the swamp. Corey wrinkled his nose at the pungent odor.

Another sound came from the edge of the clearing, and this time Corey was able to really listen, not just with the always awake, reptilian portion of his nervous system that had stirred him from sleep, but with an alert mind. What he heard was a wet sloshing sound, like a boot pulled from a puddle of mud, but louder. Much louder. So loud that he swore he could see the bushes tremble in time with the sound.

After a few seconds of silence, the sound occurred again, and then again. Rhythmically. An organic rhythm, a cadence Corey immediately identified as biological, as something sniffing or coughing or breathing. His hands tightened on the window sill. Small splinters from the cut boards pierced two of his fingers, but he hardly noticed. Without realizing it he held his breath.

The sound occurred again, louder, and to his left. Whatever was out there was moving beyond the small clearing. Another bush trembled, and this time Corey saw what moved it: a long bending appendage of some larger creature.

All at once he became aware of the fullness of his bladder and the dryness of his mouth. The need to urinate was immediate, an overriding urgency that he fought to relegate to the backdrop of his consciousness as he sought to understand whatever it was in the bushes. He remained focused, licked his lips, and thought, *this is the fucking Bog Monster.*

Corey's immediate thought was to run, a primal instinct vaulting up from deep inside his mind. He turned towards the trap door but before he reached for it his conscious mind, the part of him that could reason even in this dire situation, recognized the danger in doing so. The sound of the hinges would surely alert the thing out there to his presence. Better instead to wait for it to pass. He turned his body slowly back towards the window and stared at the vegetation at the far end of the clearing. Again, the plants rustled and a large indistinct form became visible in the low light. Something fell from it and slowly flitted down to the ground like a sheet of paper caught in a breeze.

As Corey watched, the thing turned towards him and paused. The odor in the air grew stronger. Corey was not certain how he knew it had turned towards him — there was no eyes he could see, no visible face. He could still only see a large form among the bushes at the far end of the clearing. But some part of him could sense it reaching out, probing the tree, searching for something. He remained still and again held his breath.

When he thought he would no longer be able to remain still and hold his breath, the thing in the bushes turned away from the fort and tromped off through the underbrush with surprising speed. He could hear the crunch of leaves and the pops of breaking branches. It moved quickly now. Corey immediately lost sight of the creature and after a few seconds could no longer even hear it. He was not certain how long he waited there, having to pee, listening for the return of the monster from the bog. Certain he would piss himself if he waited any longer, he carefully opened the hatch, mindful of the noise it made, and climbed down the tree. He moved halfway around the tree (away from the direction he had seen the thing in the bushes) and pissed against the tree. The relief was instant, and after finishing, another layer of fatigue enveloped his mind and mixed with fear that had taken root.

He ran home in the dark, frightened of every noise he heard along the way.

CHAPTER TWENTY-THREE

When Ted woke he found Corey asleep at the kitchen table. The dried crusts of a peanut butter sandwich lay before the boy, the jar of peanut butter still open on the table and a few slices of bread half-spilling out of the bag.

"Corey!" Ted yelled. His voice sounded with a mixture of anger and relief. Corey jolted awake, nearly knocking the remains of his sandwich off the table.

"Just where the hell did you run off to? You cannot be running off at night out of this house!" Ted yelled.

"I'm sorry. I was mad and just ran to the fort out back."

"You're lucky you're home now," Ted said as he walked a few steps closer to Corey. "I was gonna call the goddamn cops on you if I didn't see you home before I was out the door this morning. You're also lucky I've got to get to my shift, cause I'm tempted to give you the belt but I don't have time for that now."

Ted thought about yelling more at Corey, but had a hard time getting any angrier at his son and was instead just happy he was home. He remembered running away a few times himself from his house growing up, in similar circumstances, when his old man got drunk or in a foul mood, sometimes both at once. *Got to let the kid have some way to blow the steam off,* Ted thought.

Ted reached into the bag, removed a piece of bread, slathered the bread with peanut butter, and took a bite. He did this while standing close to Corey, too close for Corey to be comfortable. Corey leaned away slightly but resisted the urge to move from the seat. In a few quick bites the bread was gone and Ted moved to the refrigerator to take out materials to assemble his lunch.

"Dad," Corey said, barely above a whisper. He looked down at his lap as if the words he was looking for might be there. "I saw it."

"What's 'it'?" Ted said, not bothering to look up as he slapped a thick layer of mayonnaise on a piece of white bread. He dropped a few slices of turkey atop the mayonnaise.

Corey sat quietly for a minute. "There was something out there, by the fort last night. I think it was the Bog Monster."

Ted wrapped his sandwich in foil, dropped it into his lunch pail and turned to face Corey. He shook his head and said: "I don't have time for this shit. I get it, you want to run off, you need some space or whatever. I get it. I was a kid your age too. I'm pissed at you, but I get it. You don't gotta lie to me about some shit in the swamp. OK?"

"Dad I'm not-"

"No, Corey. I said enough. Don't lie to me. I've had lies a plenty for the last few years from those in, well, those who used to be in this house. I don't want any from you, you understand?"

"Yes," Corey said, dejected. He slumped his shoulders and looked to the floor. "I understand."

"Good. Now get over to Mimi's. And you stay there, all day. I swear to God, I hear you take a step out of that house today, and I will drag you to the mill everyday and have you sit in that damned break room. I warned you about that before; this is the last warning. You understand that too?"

"Yes," Corey said again, "I understand."

"Good. Then get your ass in gear. Don't have time for a shower or fresh set of clothes," Ted said as he glanced disapprovingly at Corey's grass and dirt stained shorts and the ring of sweat at the neckline and pits of Corey's shirt. "You'll just have to deal with it today," he added.

Ted grabbed his things for work and walked down the street with Corey. He escorted Corey directly to Mimi's. When she opened the door and started saying hi, Ted interrupted her.

"Sorry Mimi," he began, "don't have much time. I gotta get to work. You got him today?" She nodded, so Ted continued, "No playing outside today. No time with Alex. He's grounded. Put him to work. Keep him busy. I'll explain later. Hell, he can explain it. I'll be back after my shift."

Corey walked into the house past Mimi.

"Thanks again," Ted said. "You're a real lifesaver, you know that?"

"He's a good boy," Mimi responded. "I like having him around."

"Well I appreciate it. I'll see you at 3:30 or so."

Mimi took one look at Corey, then ordered him into the shower. After the shower she even appeared with a set of new clothes for him to wear. The shirt was a little too big, and the pants didn't quite reach his ankles, but at least they fit around his waist comfortably. Corey wasn't sure where Mimi had gotten the clothes from, and when he asked her, she only replied that she had kept it tucked away in an unused drawer for circumstances just like this.

They had breakfast together, a bowl of Cheerios for each. Mimi didn't ask Corey for an explanation, which bothered Corey. He expected her to ask about it, and when she didn't, her disinterest, feigned or real, made him more conscious of his own anxiety and preoccupation with the events of last night.

He had finished nearly half of his bowl before Mimi said, "So what's bothering you Corey? Your father made it clear something happened. Do you want to talk about it?"

"I, well, not really, I guess." Corey did want to talk about it, but just thinking about it made him uneasy.

"Why not dear?" Mimi asked. She scooted closer to Corey and leaned towards him. Corey was mindful of the fight with his father and the fear he had felt at seeing whatever it was out near Fort Barren. The emotions of those two events bled together in his memory now, a soup of anger and fear and anxiety.

"Well, I got into a fight with my dad. Just about the same stuff as always, stupid stuff. Forgetting to be home when I'm supposed to. He was yelling at me so I ran out of the kitchen. Out into the yard I mean, outside. I just didn't want to hear him yelling anymore so I ran and the only place I could run to was out to the fort cause I knew he would find me if I ran someplace else so I ran out to the fort." Corey paused to take a breath and expected Mimi to make a comment or chide him on his impulsive actions. Instead she listened and waited. "That's why I'm grounded."

"I see," Mimi said. "But that's not what is bothering you, is it?" She smiled and waited for him to speak.

"No," Corey said, shaking his head. He stared at the half-empty bowl of cereal but did not find any relief there. "So I was out there right, in the fort. It's out behind Morrill Street, out towards the highway and that bridge thing they haven't finished. Well anyways, I ran out there, got inside the fort and I was sleepy I guess, cause I fell asleep. Then I woke up and, well, I saw something, Mimi. I saw something out by the fort."

Mimi leaned back in her chair and whistled. "What did you see?"

"The monster," Corey whispered. "I saw it. I told my Dad, but he didn't believe me. I saw it out there, wasn't a bear, wasn't a deer, I saw the monster. The Bog Monster."

Mimi clasped her hands across her stomach and leaned back in her chair. "Sure you weren't sleeping and didn't dream it? Could have been a dream."

"No. I'm sure it wasn't a dream. I was all the way awake. I saw it, swear on my life."

"Well. You seem pretty sure about that. What exactly did you see?"

Corey took another bite of his cereal and contemplated his response. Describing what he had seen was a challenge, not only because the words he thought of did not seem sufficient, but because he recognized that he had to be careful with what he said. The memory playing in his mind was hard to believe; he could only imagine that whatever he shared would be even more difficult for Mimi to believe.

Corey finished chewing his mouthful of cereal, swallowed, and said: "I saw it at night so it was tough to see. But it was close. And it was big. Really, really big." He paused, swirled his spoon in the milk, took a deep breath, and continued. "Like the size of an elephant. Well I'm not sure, I've never seen an elephant in real life, but I think as big as an elephant. And it smelled, sort of like the swamp, you know?" Corey glanced over at Mimi. She looked back at him over the tops of her glasses. She nodded. "That bad smell we get sometimes on the really hot days when it comes in on the breeze down by the swamp, like that, but closer. It was quiet though. It didn't make much noise. And it was gray, but kind of blurry almost, like it was covered in leaves or something."

"So what did you do?" Mimi asked. Corey told her about how he had stayed hidden in the fort while it had passed by, and after he was certain it had moved on, had run home in the dark.

"Do you believe me?" Corey asked after he finished the story.

"Of course I do," Mimi said sweetly.

"No Mimi," Corey said. "I mean, really believe me. Not kid stuff, not make believe. Not like Santa Claus or the Easter Bunny or something, like, for real I mean."

That was enough to prompt Mimi to set down her spoon. "Well, to be honest, I'm not sure, Corey. That's quite a tale. I've heard plenty in my day. Like I've told you, I've heard other people tell me about the monster in the bog, along with the witches up at the end of Dartmouth Street and the ghosts at the old Franklin Mill." She counted off each on one of her wrinkled fingers. "Every place has stories like that. I believed most of it as a kid," she continued, "when I was your age. Then, like most adults probably do, I didn't believe it for a long time. But now, now I'm not so sure, you hear? I've seen enough to realize that I haven't seen it all. And I don't have all the answers. So to answer your question in a roundabout way," she said, nodding her head, "I do."

Corey took a deep breath and smiled. Knowing that someone believed — even if it was only Mimi — was an incredible relief, as though the knowledge, the memory of whatever it was in the swamps was a mental burden and one that was lessened by being shared. The relief, though significant, was only slight; knowing that something was out in the bog sparked a need to act on that knowledge.

"Well, what should I do?" Corey asked and shrugged.

"What makes you think you should do anything?"

"Well, I don't know. Shouldn't scientists know about it. What if it's dangerous? Couldn't it hurt somebody?"

"All good questions," Mimi said. "But what would you do about it? Do you have proof to bring to a scientist? Do you know how it is dangerous? Or how to keep people safe from it?"

"Well, no, I mean, no, I don't know. I don't have like a picture or anything."

"Then you need to be careful Corey," Mimi said. She leaned towards him and looked him in the eye. "Things like that have been out there longer than you ever have. Older than you; probably older than me. Who knows what it is or what it does. So stay away from it, you hear?"

"Yes, Ma'am," Corey said while he started to think of everything he could do to track it, get proof, and share it with his dad and the world.

"Well, let's think on it. The two of us. The grass out there isn't going to mow itself, nor will the weeds pull themselves up. Your father said to get you to work."

So that's what they did. Mimi wasn't comfortable with Corey using the lawn mower because she was afraid he would injure himself somehow (though he had told her, again and again, that he routinely mowed the lawn at home on the weekends as one of his chores). Pulling weeds was mindless work, requiring only identification of the weed and a little pull to remove it from the garden. Mimi lined her flowerbeds with red, earthy wood chips. These made maintaining the plants easier, but stubborn weeds still poked through, and she liked the beds to look clean. Corey enjoyed the work for what it was, especially now as he did not have to focus much on it and could instead replay what he had seen and heard in the swamps and consider what he would do next. He fell into an easy routine of pulling a weed every few seconds with one hand as he mindlessly searched for another weed with the other.

Corey didn't come to any startling realization, or concoct a plan to find the creature. But just thinking about it, mulling it over in his mind, helped to ease at least a portion of his anxiety. They didn't talk about it anymore that day, and when Ted returned to get Corey that afternoon, he didn't mention it to his father again. Their dinner together was without conversation. Corey cleaned the dishes, brushed his teeth, and went to bed without a word to his father.

That night, as Corey waited for sleep, he thought back over what he had seen and what Mimi had told him. He already knew her warning would not stop him from seeking it out again, to find proof or get a picture of it to share with the world.

CHAPTER TWENTY-FOUR

Stewart did not seem surprised to see Erica on his doorstep unannounced.

"Why Ms. Couture, it is a pleasure to see you."

She had thought over what she would say, how she would introduce the topic, ease him into the idea that she had seen *something* out along route 101, something that defied her understanding of the natural order. Instead what came out was: "I saw it. I fucking saw it. Whatever the hell is out there."

Stewart didn't say anything in response. He nodded and grimaced, his teeth — stained a light brown from years of use and clearly not dentures, a detail Erica had somehow missed in her prior meetings with him — showing for a moment between his thin lips.

"What the fuck is it?"

"I wish I could tell you that Ms. Couture, I really do. It is something I have been puzzling over for years. Please, come inside."

Erica followed him into the gloom of the house. The front door opened into a carpeted living room. The brown carpet was stained a deeper shade in a few areas. The room was otherwise spotless, the single couch holding only a blanket on one end, while a recliner was pushed against the far wall across from the television set on the near wall. A few pictures hung behind the recliner; Erica could tell they were family portraits. All of the shades were draw down in an effort to block the summer light and heat. Stewart motioned for Erica to sit on the couch as he hobbled towards the recliner. He sighed as he lowered himself into the chair.

"Can I get you anything?" Stewart asked. He began to lean forward to get back out of the chair.

"No!" Erica said. She realized her tone was sharp, her voice curt, and she considered apologizing but instead said: "Have you seen it?"

Stewart leaned back into the chair and shook his head slowly. "No, I have not. Years ago, I spent a fair amount of time out on the highway and the surrounding area. There were moments that were... charged, shall I say, but I never saw what is out there."

"What do you think it is?"

"I can only speculate," Stewart answered. "But I believe it is directly connected to the Incident and thus something that was on whatever craft appeared in the sky that night. Perhaps some type of Soviet experiment, some sort of biological test or biological weapon, or, though it is unlikely, something from another world."

"That's ridiculous..." Erica said. "I... fuck."

"Yes." Stewart nodded.

"Who else have you told? Who knows about it?"

"I have not told many. I spoke of it with a friend of mine. I brought it up with a state senator and the Chief of Police in Derryfield. I do not think they believed me. I tried with Pease as well and they were... less than pleased about my inquiries. Besides those," Stewart continued, "Rebecca Corville, as you know. Nora Wilson. A few of the regulars — at least back in my day — up at the Hilltop."

Erica held her head in her hands.

"If you would indulge me for a moment," Stewart said, leaning forward in his chair, his hands on his knees, "What did it look like? What did you see?"

Erica closed her eyes for a moment before looking back to Stewart. He returned her gaze but soon realized she wasn't seeing him, as Erica considered her memory of the creature and the words she would use to describe it. It was a reaction he had not seen in some time but one he recognized nonetheless.

"It was big. Very big. And fucking fast," Erica added, exhaling quickly, her pulse rising as she thought back on what she had seen. "Something was wrong with its skin I think, like it is sick. It's hard to explain. It didn't run like anything else I've ever seen, its gait was... broken, or uneven maybe, I don't know why. I think it came right out of the water, it was shiny like it was wet. It chased me — I ran to my car and it chased me and then it chased my car."

"Thank you," Stewart said. "Whatever is out there — assuming it is one creature and not many — is strange. The eye witness accounts I have heard are similar, but never quite identical, though perhaps that can be explained by the stress and the-"

The beep of Erica's pager interrupted Stewart. Erica glanced down and saw her parent's number. She had given them her pager number years ago with a warning they should only use it in emergencies. She had received a page from them only once before: when Nate had passed. The fear she felt recounting her memory of the thing redoubled and changed to become fear over the pager and the reasons why her parents might page her.

"Shit, I'm sorry," Erica said. She jumped out of her chair and made towards the door. "I have to go, it's an emergency."

"I understand," Stewart said. "Please, see yourself out. My door remains open for you."

The drive from Stewart's house to home took her less than ten minutes. Her father was on the front porch and rose when Erica came bounding up the driveway. He said without any enthusiasm, "Hi honey, how are you?"

"Is everything alright? Why did you page me?" She tried to calm her voice and control her breathing.

"I'm sorry to do that, I didn't mean to alarm you. You didn't need to come over right away, I just wanted to talk to you about mom. I'm just worried about her."

"What is it?"

"Well," Sam said. He grimaced for a moment and bared his bottom teeth, as if he had tried to smile but the concern he felt had shifted the display to more appropriately express his emotion. "She's not good, honestly," Sam said. "She's still out of work, hasn't been very... responsive lately, just sort of coasting. She just doesn't seem to be in a very good place. I've tried to talk to her about it, to cheer her up in some way, but she's been ignoring me."

"Where is she?' Erica asked.

"In the living room," Sam said, gesturing over his shoulder. "I was hoping you could speak to her, help her out." Erica entered the house with her father two steps behind.

The living room was a few degrees cooler than the entry way; the blinds were drawn tight and allowed in little light. Most of the illumination came from the television and and the doorway behind her. The

TV near the far wall was tuned in to a news station; two well-mani-cured and well-dressed torsos above a desk discussing some issue.

Judy sat in a recliner in the center of the room. An ashtray sat upon the right armrest. The plush of the armrest grasped at the sides of the ashtray where Judy had forcefully pushed down on it to create an indentation. A half-dozen dirty glasses and a stack of plates atop a TV tray sat to the left of the recliner.

"Mom?" Erica said hesitantly. She took another step forward and reached out her arm like one would when meeting a new animal, to give it an opportunity to sniff.

Judy shifted in the recliner to look over at Erica.

"Hi," Judy said.

"Hey mom, how are you doing?" Erica stepped forward and sat on the couch near Judy's left side.

"Fine, you?" Judy's eyes returned to the television set and sat back into the recliner. The plush of the headrest ballooned on either side of her head and partially obscured her face.

"I'm," Erica hesitated, not certain what to say in response, thoughts of Nate and 101 and the creature and Stewart all on her mind, until she blurted out, "good. I'm good Mom." Erica glanced over at Sam. He shrugged and raised both eyebrows.

"What have you been up to? Back to work yet?"

"Does it look like I've been back to work?" Judy asked.

"No, but Mom, it's probably a good idea don't you think? Get back on the horse so to speak?"

"I will when I'm ready. I'm not ready, OK?" Judy spoke quietly but spat the words out and glanced over at Erica. She held her gaze for only a moment before looking back at the television.

"Is there anything I can do to help? Do you want to talk?"

"No, I don't want to talk," Judy said, sneering the last word. "I've had enough of talking and sharing and crying and all that other bull-shit. I just want to be left alone. Your father is kind enough to give me that these days." She turned back to the television and reached out to grab the nearest glass. Given the dim light Erica couldn't be certain what it contained. When Judy swallowed a small sip and squinted her eyes and grimaced slightly Erica figured it was likely vodka.

Erica remained silent, uncertain what to say. Nothing had

prepared her for this moment, one in which she needed to act as something more than a child for her mother, where she needed to provide comfort and assistance and a kick in the ass. Erica thought back on the things her mother had told her when she was nervous about going to school, or her first job, or moving off to college.

"Mom," Erica began as she leaned forward into her mother's line of view, "I get it. You're hurting. We all are. We all miss Nate. It won't go away — it doesn't go away, it's terrible. But we have to get up and keep moving. Nate would want it that way. Us remembering him but keep on doing what we are doing."

Judy shifted in her chair but said nothing.

"Mom, please. You have to get back to work, back on with everything else. I need you. Dad needs you."

"Sure," Judy said.

"How long are you going to do this Mom? Just sit in the house?"

"Just, just give me space," Judy spat, not even bothering this time to turn away from the hum of the television.

Erica sighed and walked into the kitchen. Judy clicked the remote and the sounds of the television grew a little louder. Sam followed her into the kitchen.

"What are you going to do, Dad? Do you think we need to call Dr. Richards or something?"

Sam sighed. His shoulders dropped with the exhalation. "I don't know. Maybe. She's just... just needs some time I guess. I'm keeping an eye on her. Making sure she's getting a couple meals a day. She's mostly just sitting in the house."

"How much can you do? You're at work — what — 8, 9 hours a day at least, right? And then the commute over to the plant, too."

"I know, I know," Sam said. "I'm here as much as I can be. I mean, she really wants to be left alone, but I figure being around her is good right now. It's probably what she needs."

Erica nodded and moved closer to hug him. As they embraced she said: "Thanks Dad. Thanks for taking care of her." They each stepped back and Erica continued, "I'm sure she'll be back-" Erica was going to say back to her old self but realized that her mother would likely never be that way again, or at least not for a long time. Nate's death had hurt them all terribly, but had wounded Judy worst of all. Judy had wept so hard and for so long she had barely made the service, and even then had to be nearly carried out by Uncle Frank and Aunt Cindy twice just to get some air.

"How are you holding up?" Sam asked her.

"OK, Dad, OK?" Erica tried to smile but it was forced and a moment too slow.

"It's getting to you as well, isn't it?" he said and moved towards her with his arms wide. Erica accepted the hug and held him close, but didn't find the words to explain that her malaise was caused not only caused by her brother's death or her mother's depression but also due to the thing she had seen off Route 101. The sudden genesis of anxiety over some shit she saw in the swamp made her angry, seemed to cheapen her grief in some way. If her anger over Nate's death could be displaced so easily, how genuine, how deep was it?

Sam hugged Erica for a few seconds and then stepped back and held her shoulders. "What is it that's bothering you?" Before Erica could respond he quickly added, "How's work going?" realizing the second question was less direct and more likely to encourage a response from Erica.

"Work's fine. Just trying to, you know, get back in the swing of things. They've got me working on some filler stuff, local interest. It's fine, I just want back on crime like before."

Sam nodded and said, "Mmm hmm."

"But I'm fine, thanks, just a little overwhelmed with everything right now," Erica added.

"It's good to get back to work," Sam said. "It's a good routine. Being productive and all," he added. "It helps me stay focused."

"Yeah," Erica said. The thing off route 101 continued to bother her, as if it had left the swamp and its bulk now inhabited the dark corners of her mind, ready to chase away other conscious thought. It frustrated her; she wanted to focus on this moment now and on what her family needed, but all she could think of was the thing out there.

"Hey Dad," she began while the anxiety grew inside her, both a function of recalling in more detail what she had seen, the taste of her fear building in the back of her throat, and the realization she was about to speak of it to her father, "you ever see anything, well, like strange, or, or out of place out on the highway? Out on Route, Route

101." She stumbled over some of the words and her mouth suddenly felt very dry.

Sam's face scrunched up in an expression of both concern and confusion; concern over the emotion of his daughter and confusion over her question. "What do you mean? Like an odd car? An accident?"

"No," Erica responded. The words were becoming harder to verbalize. "Not like that. More like, I don't know, any wildlife sightings, anything that stuck out to you?"

"Well, I once saw a moose out there. Quite the sight, those babies are big. Is that what you mean?"

"No, Dad, it's just... I don't know how to explain this." Erica shook her head.

"Take your time." Sam took a step away, slid one of the kitchen chairs over, sat down, and motioned for Erica to take a seat at another. She did, slowly inhaled and exhaled and focused on the feeling of expansion in her chest, then continued.

"I don't know what it was, what I saw." She looked at the wall behind him and studied the criss-crossed blue and green lines of the wallpaper, wallpaper likely older than she was. "It was big, Dad, really big. Bigger than a moose. I didn't get a real good look at it, but it wasn't like anything I've ever seen before. It was gray and.. I don't know, kind of, well indistinct. I can't think of a better word."

"When did you see it?"

"Just the other day. I was out on 101 and decided to visit Nate. Well the cross I mean. It seemed like the right thing to do. So I pulled over, was walking along the road, and this thing came out of the bog."

"Are you feeling OK honey?" Sam asked. He squinted his eyes and said, "Have you been sleeping well?"

"Yes, well, I mean, as well as can be expected," Erica tumbled over the words. "I'm fine. I just, just saw something that really scared me. I don't, I can't explain it."

"Well grief takes all kinds of forms you know." Sam pursed his lips and nodded his head as if this statement was particularly profound. "The mind responds to stress in different ways. You knew about Mrs. Martin, after her husband died, right? She was complaining of dogs in her yard, yelling about them all day and night, peeing all over her grass she said, and then when she finally got a good night's rest, she was able to process her grief or what have you, that was the end of that. No more imaginary dogs in her yard." Sam clasped his hands together and smiled toothlessly, an upturn of his mouth intended to convey reassurance.

"I didn't imagine it Dad, Jesus," Erica muttered. She stood and said, "Why the hell did I even mention it to you. I don't know what the fuck it was," she said, surprised at herself for cursing so strongly in front of him, "but I didn't imagine it. There's something out there."

"OK, honey," Sam said. The words were innocuous, but his tone was patronizing, that of a man sure his daughter was mistaken, not feeling well, had imagined the whole thing.

"Don't-" Erica began, but then thought better of it. "Forget it. I'll see you later," she said as she stood up and headed towards the door. The anger she felt towards her father in that instant mixed with the grief and fear she was still experiencing, a cocktail of emotions that drove other thoughts from her mind including, for at least a while, thoughts of the creature off 101.

CHAPTER TWENTY-FIVE

The morning was busy with a few drop-offs for routine oil changes and one waiter — someone waiting with their vehicle, rather than dropping it off — for a set of new tires. Will ignored a message from John Schmidt, and was otherwise happy to be back at work from the weekend, and not just for the opportunity to make some money (with the hope of gaining ground on his outstanding bills). The weekend had not been relaxing.

Will found the Derryfield of his youth lonely. His sister was across the country, his mother in a nursing home, his father dead. What friends he had had during his time in Derryfield had moved on or simply moved apart. They were in Boston, New York, even as far as Colorado. As a result, Will had little to occupy himself with socially, and whenever he paused and allowed himself a moment his mind would immediately turn to the thing he had seen. He had mowed the lawn and fixed a hanging shutter on the house and watched the Sox play a double header, but otherwise his mind tended to drift back to the swamp, like some stellar body drawn towards a black hole, unable to escape its pull.

By the time Will received the phone call he was happy to be busy, handling three cars in various states of disassembly along with a thought towards the noon hour and where he might get lunch. It didn't leave much room for thoughts of anything else. Will picked the phone up on the third ring, making sure to wipe at least some of the grease and grime from his hands onto his pants. "Hi, may I speak with Mr. Boucher please?" the man on the line asked. He voiced the words in bursts of sound, every three or four syllables interrupted with a beat of silence regardless of the word.

"Speaking," Will said, "how can I help you?"

"Great, thank you Winston — you don't mind if I call you Winston, do you?" the caller asked. The pacing of the words was the same, just slightly off-tempo, like the man was speaking a foreign language or overly conscious of his speaking and trying too hard to choose his words. Will could sense the man grinning on the other end of the line; the lift in pitch and tempo were enough to communicate the feeling.

"I do in fact," Will said, "as he passed away over a year ago."

"Oh," the man replied. The pause this time came after a single syllable and lasted more than a beat.

"Who is this? What do you want?" Will asked.

"I'm sorry to bother you Mr. Boucher — I assume you are a relative of Winston Boucher's?" Will offered no response and the man continued: "My name is Jordan and I was looking for Winston because I understand he had some outstanding debt. That debt has been sold to our company, and-"

Will hung up the phone. Telephone calls like this had been very frequent a few months after his father's passing, but had become less frequent as of late. Though he had managed the business finances fairly well, Will's father had always been an impulsive buyer (and for many years a drunk). For reasons never made clear to Will, in the years before Winston's death, when Will was in Connecticut, Winston had began to purchase all sorts of survival and safety gear. The garage at the house was still filled with some of them — MREs, flares, water purification tablets, first aid kits, and solar blankets. It seemed as if once the man decided to stop drinking himself to death, he tried to prevent his death through any other means possible.

Unfortunately, many of those purchases had gone on a number of credit cards, and, even after hiring a lawyer and going through probate court a number of the debts persisted. Will thought it a poor legacy for the man. The shop — or what remained after Will had taken it over — was better. Many of the old man's old customers still came to the shop, drawn as much by Will's efforts as the Boucher name.

After glancing to the parking lot to ensure there were no customers walking in, Will retired to the restroom. He fumbled with the door behind him. The single uncovered bulb hanging overhead was too bright for the small space, and cast deep shadows in the far corner of the room. He ran the tap, splashed his face, and cleared his throat then spat into the sink. Will watched for a moment as the tan phlegm from this throat swirled in the dirty basin before it slipped into the drain. Its color reminded him of the thing from the swamp.

Whenever he closed his eyes he saw it. Even in his memory it was indistinct, parts of it hidden in darkness and shadow, as if an imagined representation of it was too much to conjure. The concerns of the previous week — his mother, the shop, finances — were still present, but had receded further back in his mind. Will's bowels gurgled and he eyed the toilet but the sound of someone entering the office banished that thought from his mind. He dried his face and tried to banish the thing from his mind as well.

Betty Brown was waiting in the office wearing her trademark capri pants, a style Will didn't believe had been in fashion since the '60s. She was in her early sixties, about Will's mother's age, and wore her auburn hair in a large bun atop her head. She frowned at him, a frown that often marked her face but usually expressed a sort of bemusement rather than actual dismay. Betty and her husband Peter were longtime customers and had been having their vehicles serviced by the Bouchers since they moved to Derryfield in the late '70s. Will had gone to school with their eldest son Scott. They had traveled in the same social circles in a few classes and on the soccer field, but had drifted apart following graduation.

"Hey Betty," Will said.

"Hiya Will. Hot as hell in here," she said, motioning to the small office. "No AC?"

"I wish." Will shook his head. "What brought you here today?"

"Well, I got some strange noise coming from the damn Chevy." She pointed over her shoulder with her thumb to her '86 Chevrolet Celebrity pulled up next to the pump. "Can you take a listen?"

"Sure thing."

The Celebrity's light green paint was slowly fading under the New Hampshire elements and had begun to take on an almost gray tone. Betty slipped into the driver's seat and turned the vehicle over. After the roar of ignition, the V6 began puttering, the sound marred by a rhythmic squeal. Will nodded to Betty, waved his hand across his neck to signal her to cut the engine, and waited for her to step back out.

"Sounds like the serpentine belt. Could be something it works on, like the pump or pulley starting to act up, or might just be the belt that needs to be replaced. You remember when the belt was last replaced?"

"God no," Betty said. She ran the back of her hand across her forehead to wipe away the sweat. "It would have been here, but we're not the best record keepers. Would you have anything that would show if we got it done?"

"I can check, but no promises. My old man kept quite a few receipts going back over the years, but his filing system left something to be desired."

Will returned to the office and Betty followed.

"Make yourself comfortable," Will said as he motioned towards the chairs, "I'll pull the boxes that may have the record." Will went back into the garage. Robert was elbow deep in the engine compartment of a Ford Escort. Will climbed up a short ladder next to the door to reach the crawlspace above the office. The area was no bigger than eight feet by eight feet, and was crammed full of banker's boxes. When Will had first returned to Derryfield after his father had passed, he had glanced through a few to confirm the boxes were full of old records, mostly receipts and carbon copies of repair orders. The boxes were generally segregated alphabetically, though on a few occasions while looking for a particular repair order Will had realized that his late father's filing system was far from perfect. Will pushed around the boxes, coughing away some of the dust that rose in the air, and once he found the box labeled with a "B", carefully carried it down the ladder and back to the office.

"Found the box it might be in," Will said and held up the dusty cardboard box to show Betty. "I'll see if I can find anything on the Celebrity." He set it down on the desk and started looking through it.

"How is Scott?" Will asked as he leafed through the box. "I haven't seen him around town in quite a while."

"Oh, he didn't tell you? He moved to Connecticut."

"No, I didn't realize that." Will flipped a few more manila folders over; none were labeled Brown.

"Why the move to Connecticut?"

"Well, after the accident, he really wanted a change I think. Both in his living situation, and his career. It was a big change."

"Wait — what do you mean after the accident?" Will stood up from the box and narrowed an eye at Betty.

"Oh," Betty said. "I thought you knew. Last year about this time, Scott was in a pretty bad accident out on 101. He was hurt, had a concussion the doctors said. I'm sure I told your father about it; it must have been just before you came back to town."

Will's stomach tightened at the mention of 101.

"Shit, I'm sorry. I didn't know. No one mentioned it to me."

"That's fine," Betty said as she waved a hand, "I know you had plenty on your plate after he passed — your father I mean."

"Yeah." Will sighed.

"The whole thing shook Scott up quite a bit. He took a few weeks off, then quit his job at the grocer's, and found a new job working for a bank down there."

Will nodded his head and tried to focus on the files before him, but his thoughts kept returning to 101. Immediately after reading a name on one of the manila envelopes the visage of the thing off the highway would appear in his mind's eye. Will realized that Betty was still talking to him though he had not heard a word.

"I'm sorry," Will said as he placed the top back on the banker's box. "I can't seem to find it here. I can't get to the Celebrity today, but do you want to drop it off tomorrow?"

"Sure, that'd be fine, hun," Betty said.

Will stood in the open doorway and raised a hand as Betty drove off. Once her car was out of sight, the circle was quiet. Will imagined the heat likely contributed to the lack of activity; it was too damn hot and humid to be outside doing much of anything unless one had to be. Too hot to be working, but not working or otherwise staying busy only invited further thought on the thing he had seen.

The phone rang in the office and was a welcome interruption. Jason was on the line, explaining to Will that the muffler he had ordered earlier in the week was in, but all the drivers were out; if he wanted it soon (and he did, he wanted to get the car done and out the door), he better drive down and pick it up himself. A drive would be good. Clear his head. Will told Robert to watch the shop, grabbed the catalog to be sure the part number matched, and hit the road.

The late July day was another scorcher and the seats of his truck were hot to the touch. Will was thankful he was wearing pants if for no other reason than to lessen the heat radiating from the vinyl seats against his legs. He briefly considered AC, but instead rolled down the windows knowing that the AC would have only just begun to cool the air in the cab by the time he arrived at NH Autoparts. The lot there was empty save for a battered F-150 that Will knew belonged to Jason. The small fleet of S-10s were out, delivering parts across Derryfield and potentially traveling into the surrounding communities. Will knew for a big enough order they'd go out to Exeter or Newmarket or even Lee.

The stool where Stanley sat for so many years was empty. It hadn't been moved. Will wondered how long it would stay there as some sort of memorial for the man. Perhaps not the kind of memorial one would dream of, but fitting nonetheless for Stanley. Will didn't want to say anything of it, as thinking of Stanley immediately made Will think back to the thing he had seen in the swamp.

"Hey, Jason, Burt in?" Will asked.

"Nope, you missed him. Was in earlier this morning, but once the first deliveries were out he was out the door too. Said he might be back, but had to run up to the store in Exeter."

"Ah, got it. How things going here?" Will asked.

"Fine, fine. Just a little lonely without Stanley here, you know? He'd laugh if he heard me say it, but I miss the old bastard."

"We all do."

"Sad how he went, though I guess no way is all that good, right? Who knows I guess. Too tired and fell asleep, one too many beers out, and that's all it takes. People forget how dangerous driving is."

Will nodded and Jason continued, "But is kind of, ominous I guess. You hear about the whole Highway of Death thing, don't expect there's much truth to it, but then, bam, Stanley's gone."

"Yeah," Will said, uncertain what else he should say. The pause in their conversation was just a little too long, making both men uncomfortable.

"Well, I'll grab that muffler," Jason said.

"Thanks," Will replied.

Jason slipped off his chair, started for the stock room in the rear, then turned on his heel and said: "Hey, I heard you were at the scene? They really gave you the tow for him, well, for his vehicle I mean?"

The anxiety in Will's stomach returned; more threatened to

surface so Will took a deep breath and tried to focus on the feeling of the cool air in his lungs.

"Yeah."

"You didn't hook it though?" Jason asked.

"No," Will answered and thought of an excuse for his behavior. "I just realized it was his, you know, and shook me up a bit. Christ, I remember him from when I was just a kid, dicking around the shop."

"Something like twenty years here, from what I've heard. Long before me. I get it man, that would've shaken me up too, if I was there, where it happened and all."

"Yeah," Will said, pushing away thoughts of whatever the fuck he had seen out there, and instead focusing on his memories of Stanley. "Hard to see him go. He was a fixture here. Place won't be the same without him."

"And his shitty jokes." They both laughed at this, an honest laugh sharing both humor and a sense of grief.

"I'll be right back with the muffler."

"Thanks Jason."

Jason returned in a minute with the muffler. Will checked to be certain the part numbers matched, confirmed they did, and said his farewell to Jason. He placed the muffler in the bed of the truck to return to the shop. The route was serpentine like many roads in the Northeast, laid down following the contours of the earth rather than some design or plan. As he drove he passed the on ramp to Route 101 and tried to not dwell on the conversation about Stanley.

CHAPTER TWENTY-SIX

Most everyone Erica had talked to about the Incident said little of import and knew even less. Most had only confirmed the broad strokes of the story she had read before: back in September of 1965, a few people saw something in the sky, and most of them came across at the time as trustworthy witnesses. Time often had a way of softening memories; the details lost form and dribbled away, leaving only an impression no greater than the story as it was originally told — in this case — nearly thirty years ago. But others' memories were not so much softened as crystallized. What these people shared had been drawn into focus over the years, but the focus appeared imagined rather than grounded. The details were too sharp and bright, like a garish sign blazing in the city, advertising to all its inauthenticity. The only sure conclusion was that no one knew what it was, and thirty years later, while the world had moved on, it seemed as though everyone's understanding of the Incident hadn't. Or at the very least, people didn't want to understand differently: the stories told were known and comfortable. It was fitting she thought. The world had moved on, and New Hampshire hadn't.

Getting the story to page — whatever that story was — was proving difficult. Erica hunched over her desk and stared at the off-white space of the document on her computer screen. The empty space was offensive to her. It promised opportunity as a blank canvas ready to accept her story, but at the same time it highlighted her failure to put together a reasonable sentence on it. Maybe there had been something unusual in the sky above Exeter in 1965; even with all she learned, Erica still had her doubts. But there was something in the swamps near Exeter in 1994. Of that she had no doubt. What that meant she hadn't yet determined.

Whatever she had seen, had heard, had smelled, had crowded out other thoughts in her mind. Her brother's death only a few weeks back felt like a distant memory. She thought that the Incident and the story she was drafting were now inconsequential. Something was in the swamp out on 101. Something that had frightened her and was still frightening her, but also, on another level beyond or above or within that fear, intrigued her. She was not sure whatever the hell it was she saw out there. So she sat, looking at the off-white screen of her computer monitor, and replayed it in her mind as best she could.

"Hey, hey, Erica, you OK?" Frank asked. Erica's attention rebounded back to the present and she glanced at Frank bending at the waist and leaning towards her.

"Sorry Frank," Erica said as she ran her fingers through her hair. "I've just... it's been a stressful week."

"You and me both. You know how much I got reamed over that correction we had to run on the House of Corrections story? I forget sometimes why I love this job."

"Yeah." Erica smirked at Frank. "Sorry."

"Not your story, not your error, not your fault," Frank said. "No need to be sorry. But I've been meaning to say, I've been keeping a close eye on what you and Karen have been putting out. Good stuff so far. Local interest, the New Hampshire advantage and all that. Readers are liking it too." He smiled wide, the off-white crescent of teeth appearing over sized on his narrow face.

"Great to hear," Erica said with too much sarcasm.

Frank raised his eyebrows. "How's that story coming along?"

"On 101?"

"Yeah, you were working up something lengthy on it you said, right? You working on something else I don't know about?"

"No." Erica tried to muster a laugh but could only manage a huff and another smirk.

"Then yes, how's that coming along? You talk to Stewart?"

"Yes, I talked with Stewart. He directed me to a few others, locals mostly, townies, who had stories about the highway as well."

"When will you have it to me? I've given you some latitude to pursue this," he added, "but I think I've been plenty patient here. I wanted this a few weeks ago and I've got nothing from you on it yet. I've got pages to fill and I sure as hell need you on other stories as well. This local stuff with Karen is just a filler for now, you know that, right?"

"I know, I know," Erica said. "It's just taking longer than I expected — it seems every thread I pull leads to something new. You said long form, I'm trying to get what it needs."

"What's the hook?"

"Well, you know its called the Highway of Death, has had all those fatalities over the years." Frank nodded his head and motioned with his hand for Erica to continue.

"Well, I think there's something more to it — the rate of fatalities that is, the underlying cause of it all. See," Erica turned and began flipping through the stack of folders on her desk in which she had arranged her research to date, "the fatalities go back decades, and it appears that it really started to get bad in the mid-sixties."

"OK..." Frank said.

"Every year it seems worse. I've spoken to a number of people who have been involved in accidents out there, to get their recollection of what happened. And there's quite a few who have mentioned seeing something out there. Something in the swamps along the highway."

"I don't follow. What the hell do you mean something in the swamp?"

"I just," Erica started, "I just think there could be something more to this. A few people have talked about seeing something out in the swamp. It's hard to explain."

"It shouldn't be hard to explain — your job is to explain things."

"It's just that..." Erica wasn't sure what to say. "Frank, I think I saw it too. Something out in the swamp along 101."

"What?" Frank raised an eyebrow.

"I think I saw something. I was out there off Route 101 about a week ago, and I saw," she paused momentarily, uncertain what word or words would best describe what it was she saw and felt that night, and finally settled on the entirely frustrating "something." She continued: "I don't know what else to call it. It was big, really big. Bigger than a moose. And gray, it came right out of the water. Came for me."

"What do you mean, came for you?"

"It ran towards me. Not away. It wasn't frightened of me, like a deer or something might be. Didn't run from my light. It ran towards me." She only became conscious of her expression after she finished the sentence and was done imaging the scene in her mind. She realized she was staring at Frank — no, through Frank — eyes wide, jaw slack.

"Are you feeling well?"

Erica saw Cathy at her desk watching a dozen feet away. Cathy was frowning, and quickly looked away when Erica caught her eye.

"Yes I'm fine." Erica turned back to her computer and placed her hands on her keyboard.

"You sure? I told you earlier I didn't think it was a good idea for you to focus on this kind of story."

"Jesus Frank, I'm fine."

"Good. I've been patient with you," Frank said. "Slow start back and all that. But I need you to get your ass in gear on this one, OK?"

He waited for a response, and when he didn't get one, he added, "I need more from you than what you've been giving with Karen on this local stuff."

Erica pecked at her keyboard and did not respond. She hadn't received any significant criticism from him since her first year at the paper. It didn't sit right with her now; she had pumped out local stories everyday for the past few weeks. Her coverage before her leave of absence had been well received. She yearned to get back to crime. Speaking in anger wouldn't help that, so she held her tongue.

"Come with me," Frank said and turned on his heel. He started to walk away, not bothering to check if Erica followed. She did.

He led her through the newsroom floor over to the flight of stairs up to the next level, where some more of the editors had offices, as well as the executive staff.

"I've tried to give you plenty of latitude lately Erica, but I'm always feeling the pressure too." He said this without turning around, and she was not certain if he was saying this for her benefit for for his. "It's not an easy time at the paper right now. Though more people keep moving to Derryfield, our number of subscribers is flat if not down. We need to do all we can to reverse that."

Eugene Weber sat at his desk, back to the door, facing towards the large single window in his office. The walls were adorned with numerous pages of papers framed, alongside awards from one organization or another extolling the virtues of the *Gazette*. Erica had met Weber a few times, mostly at significant functions at work: retirement send-offs, the parties when a reporter or editor won an award, or those times they celebrated securing a grant for one project or another. She had only exchanged a few words with him, but liked him well enough.

Weber ran the paper, or at least claimed he did. He had bounced around the upper echelons of editors and was now its managing editor. Rumors abounded about his connections with the publishers, the Gilmores. Weber had worked at the *Gazette* since at least the 1950s. He was an old man, and looked every year of it. In contrast to Frank, Mr. Weber (he preferred titles) was short, squat, and gained an inch on his waist every year. Only wisps of white hair remained atop his head, but as if that lost hair had migrated south, his eyebrows were enormous fuzzy white caterpillars. They traversed his face each time he emoted. A rumpled suit covered his frame in a way that couldn't be described as wearing it. He wasn't comfortable in it and pulled at the cuffs a few times before addressing Frank and Erica.

"Yes, Mr. Harris?" he asked.

"We need to have some words with Eri — Ms. Couture," Frank said, correcting himself for Weber's benefit. Weber sighed as if this was all too tiring, as if looking out his window was what he really preferred doing at this time.

"Still an issue?" Weber asked.

"Yes," Frank said.

"I've been here a long time, Ms. Couture. I've seen quite a bit in my time. Seen this paper rise and fall, along with the city itself. You know what that tenure gives me?" He fidgeted as he talked, constantly shifting his weight or stretching his fingers or adjusting his suit. Erica had heard Mr. Weber would occasionally pontificate in this way and pepper an employee with rhetorical questions. She disliked it — and it soured her earlier impression of him immediately. The prior pleasantries from occasional brief meetings fled from her memory.

"No," she said. She didn't feel like guessing.

"Patience." Silence filled the room. Weber leaned back a little more in his chair, appreciating his own words, perhaps even impressed by them. Erica glanced over at Frank but his eyes were on Weber.

"But I listen to those I place in positions of authority," Weber said and pulled on his tie. "So when Mr. Harris tells me he is losing his patience with someone, I likewise lose my patience. I understand you've been through some personal troubles. That's behind you, and you now have to focus on the work."

"Sure," Erica said searching for the appropriate words to respond. "I just have been rattled a bit."

"No, go on," Frank said, motioning with his hands, "tell him. Tell him what you told me."

"Tell me what? Is this more about your leave of absence?" Mr. Weber said between a fit of coughing.

"No, it's nothing," Erica said. She felt the anger rise in her. She hadn't thought about sharing what she had seen, what she felt, with Frank. It just came out, and she already regretted telling him. She did not want to share it with Weber.

"What?" Mr. Weber asked. Weber leaned forward and pushed some papers away to make room to place his elbows on the desk. If he wasn't adjusting his person he was adjusting his desk.

"I just, well, I was out off Route 101. I wanted to be out there at night." Her mind was filled with too much: thoughts of the thing in the swamp, the damn story that still wasn't finished, the import of this meeting and its potential effect on her employment, all of it filling her mind like a pot with too much water and now, with more pressure, boiling over. She felt like she was rambling. But she continued: "So I was out, researching." She didn't want to tell them about Nate's cross. "And I saw something, not sure what. An animal or something, it freaked me out. It's not — " she almost said not a big deal, but it was, "not anything for the story really, I don't think. I'm not certain what it was," she added, trying to minimize it now that it was out of her mouth.

Weber's fidgeting stopped. He leaned back in his chair.

"What?" Weber said again.

"I just saw something. Freaked me out. Threw me for a loop." Erica felt as if she needed to downplay what she saw or provide reasoning for her feelings then, and now. This angered her more, doubling her fury over the conversation she didn't want to have with two men who were passing judgment on what she was now saying.

"When?" Weber said, now reduced to single syllables.

"Last week. Tuesday."

"Where?"

"Out on Route 101, mile marker out towards Exeter, still in

Derryfield. Just off the highway."

Her curiosity got the better of her and Erica said, "Why? Why do you care?"

"I'm... intrigued, Ms. Couture. Do you anticipate it being a part of this story you are working on? About the highway?"

Frank raised an eyebrow and looked quizzically at Weber.

"It might. I really don't know. I'm not sure what it was, or how it fits, so to speak," Erica said.

"You put her on this story, right Mr. Harris?" Weber asked.

"Well," Frank began, uncertain how to answer the question, ultimately deciding upon, "Yes, sir."

"Then let her work it, for now at least."

"So you believe me?" Erica said.

Weber laughed in response.

"Belief has little to do with it, Ms. Couture. It sounds though, that you have an interesting story to tell. It might be true, it might now. But it will sell papers." He turned to Frank and said: "How long has she been on this Mr. Harris?"

"Nearly a month." Frank sighed.

"Ms. Couture, remain productive on the other topics I have seen you working on with Ms. Truell. In addition, remain working on this story about 101. Write something that intrigues the people."

Weber waved his hand towards them to signal for Erica and Frank to leave his office. He began to turn his chair but stopped mid rotation and added, "Please keep me updated on this, Ms. Couture." He nodded then turned his chair the rest of the way so that all Frank could see was the green vinyl of its back.

Erica suppressed a smile. "Yes, sir."

CHAPTER TWENTY-SEVEN

A patch of grass lay between Corey and freedom. Ted's anger had sub-sided enough that Corey would no longer be grounded come Saturday. The only thing that remained was all of the day's chores, foremost among them in the summer: mowing the lawn. Ted was working to repair one of the gutters that was hanging loose from the eaves of the roof while Corey mowed. The backyard was done. All that remained was the front yard between the fence and the driveway.

The week with Mimi hadn't been that difficult. Corey had helped her around the garden and her yard, pulling weeds and moving a bunch of small limbs that had fallen in a heavy thunderstorm on Thursday. Corey wasn't sure why, but Alex did not stop by Mimi's while he was grounded. Corey had tried on two occasions to call Alex, but each time Mrs. Marino picked up the telephone and, not wanting to get ratted out for calling Alex's while he was grounded at Mimi's, Corey hung up.

Corey hadn't spoken again to his father about whatever he had seen. He was certain now that he couldn't convince his father unless he had something more substantial to show him, some proof of what-ever it was that lived in the forest and swamps by Fort Barren. As soon as the lawn was done, he planned on gathering Alex and heading down to the Fort to find evidence he would need to prove his father wrong.

As soon as he had finished the front lawn, Corey hustled inside and called Alex. Alex picked the phone up on the second ring.

"Alex, sorry, I've been grounded, it's a long story, I'll tell you to-day," the words spilled out of Corey's mouth and over one another as he frantically spoke. "Can you hang out today?" Corey asked.

"Yeah, yeah I can. Yeah I know you were grounded," Alex answered. "I sort of was too. I think your dad talked to my dad or something."

"Bummer."

"Yeah it sucked. See you at the corner in five?"

"Yep," Corey said and hung up. He yelled to his father and told him he was heading out to play. Ted grunted in response from the top of the step ladder but didn't bother to turn away from affixing the gutter back to the house.

As Corey expected, Alex was waiting for him at the corner of Morrill and Pine, underneath the massive oak tree between the Robertson's and the Smith's houses. The oak cast a significant pool of shade below that made the temperature under it feel a few degrees cooler.

"So you were grounded too, huh?" Corey said as he approached Alex.

"Yeah." Alex let out a large sigh. "My mom said I need to pay more attention to the time, be back home on time, you know the deal."

"That sucks." There was no easy transition, no comfortable way to begin the conversation, so Corey just said it, "Alex, I like, I saw it."

Concern showed on Alex's face, a furrowing of his eyebrows above the rims of his glasses, a pursuing of his lips. But he said nothing. Corey continued, "I saw it last week. I couldn't see you 'cause I ran away when my dad was yelling at me so he grounded me last week. But when I ran away I ran to the fort, and I was out there at night, and the monster came by. I saw it man."

"Bullshit." Alex didn't laugh at the curse. Neither did Corey.

"I swear, I saw it. I was out there, in the fort. I woke up at night and it was just out in the bushes. Out a little ways from the fort, Alex."

"You woke up?" Alex asked. "Probably just a dream then. It's just stories, right? The whole bog monster thing."

"It's not a story! I saw it Alex!"

Alex shook his head. "It's just a story, the older kids at school told it just to scare us."

"Why don't you believe me?" Corey yelled. His surprise pooled with the sudden anger he felt. "You heard it with me when we were down by the bog!"

"Eh, I don't know." Alex looked away from Corey, down to his feet. "We just heard a fish or something." He continued to look away from Corey, preferring instead to peer down the street, as though he was expecting something more interesting to come down the road.

Corey realized that Alex was scared. Scared that he could be right, that he had seen it, that something was out there in the bog. Scared that if he accepted that, it would make him vulnerable to it in some way, as if ignorance of it was a shield against it. The realization came swiftly and surprised him.

"Let's go to Fort Barren. I'll show you where. There's got to be prints, like tracks in the mud or something, or broken bush branches. I've got to find some proof to show my dad. I will show you, you'll see. It was just out there, just beyond the clearing where the fort is. I'll show you!"

"I don't wanna go back out there. It's full of bugs and smells like shit. I don't even like the stupid fort. All that work and it's just a stupid platform in the tree."

The words hurt Corey. He and Alex had spent hours working on the fort together, planning the adventures they could have at and stage from their hideaway in the woods.

"It's not just a stupid platform," Corey said forcefully. "It's our fort. Don't be a baby, let's go out there and check for signs of it. We could be famous or something when we find proof. It's during the day now, we'll be fine. Don't be so scared about it."

"No, don't be an asshole. I don't want to go out there anymore. It's all bullshit." Alex shook his head to emphasize the point and stared at Corey.

"No!" Corey yelled. "You stop being an asshole!" He reached out and grabbed Alex's arm. Alex pushed Corey back with both hands. Corey took a step back to regain his balance. Then he hit him.

The punch connected cleanly with the side of Alex's face, throwing him in turn off balance and to the ground. Alex landed on the earth next to the sidewalk, a patch that was more dirt than grass beyond the edge of the shadow cast by the oak above. Alex looked up at Corey, his eyes little more than slits behind his glasses. The frames sat at an odd angle on his face, still there with the help of the strap across the back of his head but askew. Alex slid them back into place while still on the ground.

"I'm sorry," Corey said. He looked down at his balled fists at his waist and back to Alex. The pain in his right hand surprised him. He hadn't thrown a punch since last summer, when one of the older boys from a few streets over kept throwing rocks at them. He had never thrown a punch at Alex, and it scared him, to realize that he could be moved so quickly to violence against his friend.

"I'm sorry," Corey repeated. The anger he had felt as a pressure in his chest was already fading but the heat in his face remained.

"Screw you," Alex said as he scrambled up. Corey held out a hand to help him but Alex ignored it. After standing up, Alex brushed some of the dirt off his shorts and took a step back from Corey.

"Screw you man, go to hell." Alex wiped at the side of his face and inspected his hand to see if it carried any blood. Alex turned and started to walk towards his house.

"Wait," Corey yelled after him. He took two steps forward but didn't follow any closer. Chasing Alex didn't feel right, not after the punch. He was ashamed of his own conduct and could feel his face grow hot.

Alex didn't wait. Corey watched him walk away. As the distance between them grew, Corey sat down in the shade of the tree. His chest and face still felt very warm and his breathing was quick and shallow.

He was certain now that he had to return to Fort Barren to find evidence of the creature he had seen. He had to show his father and Alex that they were wrong to doubt him. He knew he would have to apologize more to Alex — and likely his father as well — but he figured that bringing them some proof of the creature or convincing them to come to the Fort to see evidence of its existence was the only way to convince them and return things to the way they were before.

Corey's determination to venture out to the Fort was weakened by fear. Fear not only that he would find signs of the creature, but that the thing itself was still there. But any fear he felt was now outweighed by his anger and frustration. He reasoned that whatever it was, it was unlikely to be out during the day; with all the countless times he had been out in that stretch of forest, he had never seen it until that night the week prior. So he hiked out to Fort Barren, determined to find proof to show Alex and his father.

By the time he reached the clearing near the pine tree of Fort Barren, Corey's courage — if anger driven action could be courage — was beginning to wane. It did not wane enough that he left, but enough that he moved slowly along the outside of the clearing, keeping near the bushes and eyeing the area nearby for anything unusual. A complete revolution around the clearing assured him that there was nothing there beside the usual squirrels and birds. Corey moved to the fort.

Fort Barren was as he had left it: trapdoor down, tarp tied down on the roof. Though he couldn't be certain, it did not appear as if anyone else had used the place since last week. Certainly not Alex given that he had also grounded and afraid to come out to the Fort. Corey climbed carefully up into Fort Barren and slowly dropped the trapdoor behind him so as not to make any excessive noise.

From his vantage point in the fort, Corey scanned the edge of the clearing again and tried to look past the undergrowth deeper into the forest. To the north, west, and south the trees grew thicker and thicker and after a few hundred feet Corey could see no further into the vegetation. To the east, the trees were thinner, but the rolling hills which lead to the bog cut off any extended surveillance. Assured again that there was nothing nearby, Corey climbed down and approached the line of scrubby growth at the edge of the clearing where he had seen the creature moving.

He searched for any sign of the thing: a footprint, a path through the brush, a large scale, or perhaps a feather. He scanned the area and found nothing. He was certain whatever he had seen had moved behind or through the bushes he tramped through now, but he could find nothing that indicated that any creature of any significant size had been there. While he knew that the storms from the end of last week could have washed away some evidence, he expected to find something — anything — that would vindicate him.

Corey began to search in an expanding ring, eyes focused on the ground. He stopped every minute or so to orient himself towards Fort Barren to ensure he was near where he saw the creature moving. But there appeared to be no sign of it. A deer run he and Alex had found earlier in the summer opened up nearby. Corey imagined it may have moved down the run, but it still didn't explain why he couldn't find anything where he knew the creature had been.

A new noise rose above the chatter of birds and whisper of wind in the air: sirens. Coming from the direction of the highway to the east, down the hill and over the next rise. His plan to find evidence of the creature frustrated, Corey set off for the sirens to see what all the commotion was about. He walked slowly and took the time to consider how else he could find proof of the thing of the bog.

The sounds of the passing cars grew steadily louder. Far to his left, just peeking over the nearby crest of small hill, Corey could make out the gray concrete of the Overpass to Nowhere. The sun was beginning its final descent over the horizon to his back. Corey's shadow grew larger before him. The trees came to an abrupt end where the median off the highway began. He skirted around a small swampy patch of earth fed by a culvert that ran under the highway. The blacktop of the road stretched to both his left and his right, disappeared over the crest of the hill to his left and a curl to the east on his right.

A hundred or so feet away a green station wagon lay upside down in the stubbly grass beside the road. Corey could tell from the scrapes and divots in the earth and the extensive damage to all sides of the vehicle that it had rolled across the grass before it came to rest where it was now. The front two windows were either smashed out or remained retracted; the windshield was a spiderweb of broken glass, and the front fender and some other long piece of metal Corey could not identify had been amputated by the crash and now lay beside the vehicle.

The green of the station wagon — now scratched and scuffed on every panel of the vehicle — was contrasted by a streak of red running down the driver's side door. Corey wasn't sure if he was imagining it or actually seeing it, but the streak appeared to still be wet, the color trailing down the door and dripping off into the earth. A tarp lay over a mound a dozen or so feet away from the vehicle. Corey could see a pool of red underneath the tarp.

A Derryfield police officer stood nearby, turned mostly away from Corey, one hand on his hip as he directed traffic with the other. Corey recognized him: a tallish man, broad around the shoulders and hips with his blond hair in a buzz cut. Officer Mitchell or Marty or Manning. Corey remembered he had come into the school last year and talked about saying no to drugs.

Another officer stood next to the first. He was quite a bit shorter, but just as solid. He wore a blue cap atop his head and kept removing it to wipe at his brow. They were close enough that Corey could hear their conversation, but they had not yet realized he had come out of the forest behind them.

The second officer said: "Jesus, another fatality?"

"Yep," said the first as he waved traffic on. "This guy was gone immediately, nearly took his head right off. EMTs were ready to call it. Staties came, took pictures and all that. Already got Richards coming to put what's left on ice."

The second shook his head. "Highway of fucking Death, that's right."

"Yep," the first responded.

"They gotta finish the expansion work, finally make this place safe. Or at least safer."

As the first officer directed traffic he shifted his stance, and glanced up and down the roadway. As he looked towards the overpass, he spied Corey. "Hey, kid, what you doing?"

"Nothing," Corey said. He turned back to the accident and remained fixated on the long streak of blood splashed against the exterior of the driver's side door.

"Hey kid!" the second police officer and began to walk down the slight slope towards Corey. "This is a bad accident, you've got to get out of here, OK?"

"I got this," the second officer said to the first, "you stay on the traffic."

When Corey didn't respond, the second officer yelled out again. "You shouldn't even be this close to the highway anyways? Get out of here."

"I'm just looking," Corey said, "I won't get any closer."

The second officer stepped up alongside Corey. "What's your name kid?" The officer's name tag read "Ford." Officer Ford removed his cap again and wiped at his brow. Corey could see beads of sweat on the man's brow. He stunk, a funk that Corey identified as the same kind of smell that wafted off his father after a long day of working in the sun.

"Corey Barrington." He glanced at Ford then looked back to the accident. Ford put an arm around Corey's shoulder and tried to direct him to turn and not face the accident.

"Your parents know you're out here Corey?" Ford asked.

Corey shrugged.

"This highway is dangerous. You shouldn't be out here at all, especially without a parent. Cars are going off the road all the time."

"I was just out playing and I heard the sirens."

Ford nodded and stepped in front of Corey to block his line of sight towards the accident. Corey could see a pair of men in slacks and white t-shirts hustling down the incline with a stretcher lined with vinyl between them. They set down the stretcher and walked up to the tarp near the station wagon. One lifted it up part way and grimaced.

"What are they doing?" Corey asked.

Ford kneeled down next to him. "Moving the body. The driver died on impact." He glanced over his shoulder at the scene, then back to Corey. "You should get out of here, OK?"

Corey watched over Ford's shoulder as the two men donned long gloves that reached up to their elbows. They pulled off the tarp and Corey saw what was left of the man: his limbs were at strange angles and his clothing was damp with blood. Corey could not believe how much there was scattered about the car and all over the body. Even at this distance Corey could tell that the man's head was only partially connected to his neck as it lay at an almost ninety degree angle to his shoulders; something had nearly severed his head.

Ford encouraged Corey one more time to leave, and this time Corey listened. The visage of the dead man fought in his mind for primacy over the creature he had seen. Neither won, and Corey's sleep was restless.

CHAPTER TWENTY-EIGHT

Erica's anxiety increased the closer she got to Derryfield Auto. The thing she had seen did not occupy every waking thought, but it came close. It was like when Nate first died. She would wake up, and in those first few second of the day her mind would be free: no memory of the terrible news, no recognition of the loss, no feeling of grief. But a moment later all memory, recognition, and feeling would ricochet through her mind and body and leave her breathless. It was much the same now, except that moment after waking, when she became conscious again of what she had seen, her mind was not filled with grief but with fear.

Her father had not believed her. Frank had not believed her. Stewart seemed to believe her, for what it was worth, but he had no clue what it could be either. This far removed from it, from the sounds and smells of the swamp along route 101 in the darkness, Erica was even beginning to doubt her own experience. *Maybe I was just too stressed, or too tired, or too consumed with grief,* she thought. *Maybe Dad was right, and I just imagined it.* But the fear she felt in her chest was strong and still, days later, remained too strong. It wasn't like the dread of a nightmare washed away by the light of consciousness. The more awake she was, the more afraid she became.

She had a need to understand whatever it was, to put the thing to paper and in that way minimize, rationalize, and compartmentalize it and the despair she felt. Others needed to know of it; the readers of *Gazette*, the people of New Hampshire, hell the people of the world. She needed more than she had, and unsure of where to go, she circled back around to those who had set her on this path.

Erica had tried to reach Oscar, but hadn't found him at the Hilltop and couldn't reach him by telephone. She had considered stopping by the Mill, but hadn't found a time that worked. She wasn't even sure what shift he worked. She had even called Becki Corville a number of times to try and set up a meeting, but even the offer of a free meal wasn't enough to entice Becki to another session with Erica. Becki had refused, saying she "didn't have time for more grab ass." Erica assumed Becki was looking again for the bottom of every bottle she found. Even Stewart had been uncharacteristically gruff, telling her he couldn't meet and was "under the weather."

So Erica turned to the last person she thought may know something about that thing. Will had asked Oscar about what his father Winston had seen. Maybe Winston had shared the story with Will. Maybe Will had seen it too.

They had been close once, dating during their junior year of high school. She remembered the time fondly. AP classes, three seasons of sports, the school newspaper, and afternoons spent driving around town with Will. They had been each other's first, and that shared experience was enough to color her memory of Will favorably. The relationship had ended, as not many do, rather naturally. Erica had spent the summer after their junior year up north of the notch working as a camp counselor while Will had remained in Derryfield working at the shop. They had drifted apart and, when the school started in the fall, began seeing other people. There had been no fight, only a few tears, and then understanding and mutual respect. Erica expected that history would only help her with this conversation.

Erica parked her car in the lot out front and stared at the door into the shop. The blue letters in all caps, exclaiming DERRYFIELD AUTO had long ago begun to chip and flake away. Each letter was visible but only as a desiccated shell of its former self; the first R in Derryfield, for instance, was lacking its bottom extension and only the off color white underneath it made it clear it was not a P.

Erica sat in the car and told herself, for the dozenth time, that she had to ask Will about what she'd seen. It was stupid, she knew, to bring it up with him. He might think her crazy, or worse yet, foolish. But his judgment she could live with. Not understanding what she had seen, not knowing what to do next, those things she could not, and any hope of better understanding it was a hope worth pursuing.

Erica entered the shop to find Will behind the counter, scribbling away at a pad of paper. "Hi Will."

"Hi," Will replied. He smiled and she smiled back. Both expressions were brief and perfunctory. Will set aside the crossword puzzle in his left hand.

"Taurus OK? Still problems with the suspension?"

"No, no, nothing like that. Taurus is fine." Erica stood a few feet back from the counter and looked at Will. He glanced at her and nodded his head, unsure what to say. "Uh, good. Glad to hear it. What can I help you with?" he asked.

"Will," Erica began. "I've got a strange question to ask. I know it's odd, I just... need to find out more." Will shrugged. Erica took a deep breath, looked over Will's shoulder at the wall behind him, then back to him. "Do you believe your father saw something out there on Route 101? Like what Oscar said?"

Will picked up the crossword puzzle and set it to the side and shuffled some purchase orders across his desk in an attempt to buy time to formulate an answer that wouldn't make him sound stupid or foolish or crazy.

"Erica... I, I don't know. I mean, I guess I think he thought he did, whatever that means. What does it matter now anyways?"

"What if there was something out there. Some... creature, I don't know. Something that's just out there. Hidden or unrecognized or undiscovered."

"Is this for another story? You chasing around the myths of New Hampshire or something?"

Erica considered for a moment lying to Will. It would be easy enough; he had already provided the cover. A simple yes and he might talk, give her the information he had, avoid the whole complication of actually seeing a monster out alongside Route 101. Instead, she said, "Would you believe me if I said I had seen it?"

Will turned and fully faced Erica and looked at her — really looked at her — for the first time that day. Her hair, normally brushed straight down past her shoulders, was frizzy and bunched up by her neck. She was pale, as if the summer sun had not yet kissed her skin. She did not smile, or frown, but instead clenched her jaw, awaiting his answer. Her eyes were glassy and reflected the glare of the overhead fluorescent lights reflected, two rectangles of white positioned above her pupils.

"Yes," Will said, without emotion.

Erica stared at Will and noted his stillness. His shoulders rose and fell with each rapid breath. He leaned forward and held out his hand for support against the desk. Erica was surprised to see his hand shaking. His knuckles turned white as he grasped the desk.

"You've seen it, haven't you?" Erica wiped at her eyes and clenched her hands at her side. "The same thing your father did. The same thing I did. The thing Oscar talked about. You've seen that fucking thing too. When?"

"Erica..." Will trailed off and turned away from her, a tactic that was familiar enough from their time together over ten years ago.

"No," she said, her anxiety turning to anger. "Don't do that. Tell me the truth."

"I don't know what I saw," Will muttered. "It was late. Who knows what it was?"

"When?"

Will looked over his shoulder, glanced around the office, and finished the survey by studying his shoes. "A few weeks ago," he mumbled.

Erica cursed and let out a sigh. "Fuck, I thought maybe I was losing it. I thought I was losing my mind. But something is really fucking out there." She ran her hands through her hair. "Aren't you going to say something?"

"What? What do you want me to say?"

"What the hell are you thinking? What the fuck was that thing?"

"Erica... I... I don't know." He glanced over his shoulder again. "Please, keep your voice down. I, well, I don't have time for this. I've got enough shit going on right now."

"What? You've got enough going on right now?" Her anger swirled out of her through her words and her tone and her extremities. She raised her arms and then pointed a finger at him. "What the fuck is out there? What the fuck is that thing? We've got to deal with that! Do something about that! What do you mean you've got shit going on?"

"I don't have time for this. I've got a mother in a nursing home with a bill I can't pay. I'm struggling to keep my father's business — my business — afloat. I don't have time to deal with some fantasy out there in the goddamn swamps."

"Fantasy? God dammit Will." Erica stomped up to the desk and said, "We both saw this fucking thing. You can't just ignore this."

"I'm not, I'm just... not dealing with it right now. I've got other things to deal with."

"What do you think is going to happen?"

"I don't know and I don't care."

"This is a miracle, or a scientific discovery or something. I don't know. But this is fucking big, Will. This is huge. And it scares the hell out of me. I don't know what the hell it is. We've got to do something or tell someone."

"Tell them what?" Will glanced again over his shoulder into the shop; in the second bay about twenty feet away Robert leaned over the open hood of a Buick, his back and head visible, his arms within the engine compartment. AC/DC roared over the boom box sitting atop Robert's toolbox. "That we saw a monster out there? Some kind of... thing living out there? An undiscovered creature?"

"Exactly! We tell them what we saw!"

"Who?" Will growled. "We call up the Weekly World News? Think we get on Ricki Lake? Who the fuck is going to believe us?"

"I... I don't know. We just have to get this out there."

"You want to write a story on this? Get a Pulitzer for your work on the bog monster of Rockingham County?" Will sneered. His anger surprised him, coiling out of the depths of his fear and confusion.

"Jesus, yes I was working on a story about Route 101." Erica shook her head. "But I didn't know about this thing. And that's not the point. This goes beyond that. You know the Chief. We should talk to the police. There must be other sightings, or people who have seen this. We have to do something."

"If anyone — I mean anyone, was taking this seriously, don't you think we would have heard of this?"

"There's been rumors for years," Erica added. "You heard Oscar. Some other regulars at the Hilltop have talked to me about it too. People who have seen it or claimed to see it. Going back years Will, I mean years. Like thirty years or more. Something has been out in that swamp for years."

"And?" Will asked.

"And what? We need to tell someone. The police at least, maybe the governor? I don't know. We have to do something!"

"OK," Will said, raising his hands palms up momentarily in a gesture of defeat and then placing them back down on the desk.

"OK yes? You're ready to do something? We've got to at least tell someone, right?"

"Listen," Will added. "I appreciate your concern here. And it's admirable really, I get it, you want to get the scoop here, get the story out. It's what you do, what you like." Erica began shaking her head and Will continued: "Really, I get it, I do. This just, isn't me, OK. I've got other shit to deal with."

Will crossed his arms and leaned back.

"I expected better from you," Erica snapped before she walked out the door. Will watched her go and tried not to think of the thing he had seen.

PART III
AUGUST

Will knew the man was not a regular customer just because of the way he parked his car. He pulled it in nose first, right up to the shop and next to the door. Those that were customers knew to pull in parallel so that Will or Robert could easily drive the vehicle around back to get into the garage. The vehicle was unfamiliar to Will as well, which is not to say he didn't recognize the model (most anyone would recognize the boxy shape of the Mercedes 400 class), but it was one he hadn't worked on nor one he recalled seeing around town. The Massachusetts plate by itself was enough to signal a stranger was here.

Will continued to talk on the phone with Ms. Phillips when the man walked in. Will glanced up and nodded to him to acknowledge his presence and pointed at the phone. Will was certain he wasn't a customer when he walked in. He wore a pressed pair of slacks and a button up shirt — which itself didn't eliminate him as a customer — but combined with lopsided grin and the folder under his arm, Will knew the man would likely be looking to sell him something as soon as he was off the phone.

When Will was finished with the conversation with Ms. Phillips he asked, "Can I help you?"

The man took a few more steps forward and stuck out his hand.

"Name's Peter Rath," he said. "You can call me Peter. It's nice to meet you." Peter's hair was cut short and appeared thinner on the tops than the sides. Peter's blotchy scalp showed underneath the thinning hair. Will guessed he was in his forties.

Will took his hand and said "I'm Will, how can I help you?"

"Well, I'm hoping to speak to you about your business and this property."

"I'm in the business of fixing automobiles. Do you have one that needs fixing?" Will asked.

"No, nothing like that." Peter smiled, but it was a movement of only his lips in an effort to bare his teeth, and the action did not engage his eyes.

"I'm a *developer*," he said, emphasizing the word. "I'm looking to purchase some land nearby, perhaps even on this circle, and wanted to discuss that with you."

"What for?" Will asked.

"I'm always keeping my eyes on property that could be developed into something more." Peter stressed the word developed with the same tone he used with developer. "Are you interested in selling? I took the liberty of pulling the deeds, and don't see there is any mortgage. That true?"

Will cocked his head to the side and squinted at Peter. "Could be. Not sure I appreciate you looking into that."

"Please, let me assure you Mr. Boucher, it was all just part of a review for possible business opportunities. I only inquire into public documents to obtain as much relevant information as possible regarding the properties in which I am interested."

"Why my property?"

"I can envision something more here than just a garage. A convenience mart perhaps, with a bank alongside and a McDonald's."

"We've already got Mark's Convenience in the neighborhood. It's been here years, does fine by us, don't think we need another." Will crossed his arms over his chest.

"Southern New Hampshire is changing Will," Peter remarked. "Derryfield and the County are growing. I expect in a few years time this whole circle will be built up." He turned to look out the windows to the circle and the cars that rolled through it. "Lots of opportunity. Now would be a good time to sell."

As the two men talked, Anita Johnstone, a longtime customer, entered and sat in one of the waiting room chairs. She glanced for a moment at the two then picked up one of the magazines — likely months old at this point — on the small table.

"As you can see," Will said, "I have customers to attend to. Is there anything I can help you with related to an automobile?"

"I don't think so," Peter said. He reached into his breast pocket and pulled out a business card. He did not hold it between his index finger and thumb, instead opting to hold it pressed between his index finger and middle finger. He unfurled his fingers and held it upright, his palm towards the ceiling, offering it to Will. Will did not take the card so Peter placed it on the desk.

"There's my card," he said. "Give me a call once you've thought things over. Thanks for your time."

When the man had turned, Will picked up the card and threw it into the trash.

"Good afternoon Will," Anita said. She peered intently at Peter Rath as he passed. She wore a pair of loose slacks and a billowy cotton shirt that hung loosely on her small frame. Will wasn't sure her age, but knew she was old; she had been old when he first met her while he worked in the shop during high school. Anita was a lifer of Derryfield; she was born in Derryfield, went to school in Derryfield, had worked in Derryfield's public library for her entire adult life, and after retiring, had returned in a volunteer position at the library.

"Who was that?" Anita asked.

"Some guy looking to buy this property tear down the shop and build something else," Will said. "Not interested in selling though."

"This place's been here a long while." Anita nodded. "I remember when your father started the shop, back in the late fifties. Wasn't a decent mechanic in town until he moved in."

"Lot of history here I guess." Will patted the desk. "You bringing the Buick in today?" Will asked, though he already knew the answer as Anita had no other vehicle.

"Yes, for the brakes. The rear I believe." She handed him the keys to the Buick. "The weather is nice enough, I am just going to walk home. It's important to stay moving, especially at my age." Will was tempted to ask; he knew she was north of seventy, but not sure by how much.

"Please do call once the repairs on the Buick are complete," Anita added.

"Will do," Will responded.

He pulled the Buick around and set it up on the lift to access the rear brakes. First he removed the wheels, and then he removed the drums. The drums proved to be beyond saving: the rust and wear of years of friction had reduced the shoes past their safe operating limit.

The work helped to occupy his mind. Will was surprised to find himself focused more on this Peter Rath than that thing he had seen off the highway. Will was still stewing about the developer when Robert sauntered over to Will and the Buick. Robert could see the tension in Will's frame. His shoulders were high, he kept rubbing his hands together, and he bounced his right leg up and down on the ball of his foot whenever he stood and worked on the brakes.

"What next?" Robert asked. He wiped his grease stained hands with a rag that was well on its way from a rust red to an oily black. "I finished up with the Chevy. You want me back on the F-150?"

Will glanced at the clock on the far wall: 4:00 PM. Only an hour left in the workday to finish any repairs they had started. Otherwise, the vehicles they were working on would sit in the bays and complicate work tomorrow. Will didn't turn to Robert but said, "Yeah, let's try to get the F-150 out the door today."

"Sure thing. I think I might order a pizza from Derryfield Pizza to bring home tonight. You want something from there?" Robert asked, hoping that the question of food would perk up Will. "I'll see if that new girl, Jessica can deliver it. She asked about you the other day you know."

Will grunted as he yanked on a drum.

"My cousin knows her, went to school with her. I think you should meet her. I hear she's an artist or something, I think you'd like her," Robert added.

"What are you, match-maker now? No, I'm fine," Will said, again not turning to face Robert.

The phone rang and Will answered it on the third ring.

"Heya Will," Lonnie said over the speaker. "Don't know if you heard, we got a two vehicle accident up there on 101. You got time for a tow today? I've got Patrick's on the way up here to pull one of 'em, figured I'd leave the other for you."

4:00 PM. Plenty of time until sundown. Still, he didn't like the thought of being back out on Route 101. Not unless he had to be. Not unless he was there on his own terms and ready to face that thing out there.

"No, sorry Lonnie. No can do right now. Too much at the shop we still gotta get out."

"You turning wrenches today?" Lonnie asked.

"What days am I not?"

Lonnie laughed. "No problem. I'll call over to Lee Auto and get them to tow the other. Catch you next time."

Will returned to the garage and continued working on the brake job on the Buick. One pair of the rear hardware was nearly rusted in place so he had to pull hard on the return springs to get them off and the shoes after that. As he pulled and yanked, Robert yelled over to him. Will could tell by his tone alone that something wasn't good; it was too high, too reedy for Robert's usual guffawing.

"What is it?" Will asked as he approached, rubbing his hand on a rag.

"This radiator's shot." Robert pointed at the innards of the Ford. "I was trying to get the goddamn belt off and managed to ding the radiator pretty good. Sorry. Not what you wanted to hear, I know."

"Fuck," Will muttered.

"Yep."

"Well get it out." Will didn't need to say anything more. Robert knew he had fucked up; he knew Will wasn't pleased. The best he could do was work to fix the problem as quickly as possible.

Robert popped the drain, emptied the coolant in a catch basin underneath the car, and unhooked the brackets for the radiator while Will called the owner. Will dreaded making these calls, the ones in which he had to disappoint a customer not because something was broken, but because someone at the shop had screwed up. He'd comp the cost of the radiator and the extra labor to replace it, but he always felt as if he was letting them down and that the shop should do better.

Robert had the radiator out within the hour, just as 5 PM approached and his pizza was delivered to the shop. Will inspected the damage: a quarter sized gash in the fins of the radiator dribbled fluid. He carried it out the back muttering under his breath. The pavement behind the shop extended only twenty feet or so and thin knotty trees surrounded it. A small stream ran through the back of the property and emptied into a similarly small pond nearby. With one heave Will threw the leaking radiator at the dumpster beside the building. He found the loud crash of it slamming into the dumpster satisfying.

"What the fuck!" he yelled. Just what he needed. Another fucking job going south, another lift tied up for another 3 days while they waited for another radiator, another dissatisfied customer, another payment delayed while the bills continued to mount.

A cough caught Will's attention. A boy — the boy he had met a few weeks ago (Charlie or Caleb or something like that) sat on the grass between Derryfield Auto and the Snack Shack next door.

"Hi, Will," Corey said.

"Hi... uh, Corey, right?" Will asked, thankful the kid's name came to him. "Where is your friend? What are you doing out here?"

"Alex," Corey supplied. "He's visiting an aunt or something, I don't know. I'm just having some snacks from the store." He held up a small paper carton with fries. "I didn't want to go home or over to Mimi's — Ms. Gagnon's house."

"I see. Sorry about that," Will said, motioning over his shoulder with his thumb, "for the cursing and all. Just had a bad day." He laughed a mirthless laugh and added, "Bad couple weeks actually."

"Sorry." Corey shrugged. "Me too." He wasn't sure what prompted him to continue. "It sucks cause no one believes me. They act like I'm stupid or something. I know what I saw. It wasn't a moose or deer like they say. I saw something weird out in the swamps, but everyone I told thinks I made it up or something."

"What? What did you say?"

"I saw something, I don't know, a big animal or something out in the bog. But everyone thinks I'm lying, and I'm not. They think that just cause I'm a kid I'm making it up or something."

"When?" Will asked. "When did you see it?"

"A couple weeks ago."

"What did it look like?" Will stepped closer to Corey.

"Well, it was dark, and in the bushes, but it was big, really big. And it made this weird sound."

Will leaned in, hands at his sides, face blank. Realization appeared on Corey's face, first in his eyes: they widened as his eyebrows raised. His jaw then hung down slack and he inhaled quickly enough that Will could hear the breath.

"You've seen it too," Corey said.

"Yeah," Will said as he nodded. "Yeah. I have."

Though speaking of it scared him, sharing the knowledge of it with someone else still brought a smile to Corey's face.

"What is it?" Corey asked.

"I don't know. Does your friend, Alex, know about this?"

"Well, kind of. He heard it with me, when we were out in the bog. I told him that I saw it but he doesn't believe me. Well I mean he tells me he doesn't believe me, but I don't believe that he doesn't believe me. I just think he's afraid."

Will nodded. Corey added, in a voice a little lower, and little quieter, "But I am too."

Will turned slightly and watched traffic move through the circle. He wished that he was anywhere but here: facing a shitty day at work, standing outside the shop with a kid he hardly knew, talking about some monster he saw in the swamps.

"I, uh, I lied," Corey said. "Alex isn't seeing a relative. We got in a fight and I haven't been hanging out with him."

Will nodded, but sensed that the kid wanted to tell him more. "What happened?"

"Well. Like I told ya, he didn't believe me. Or said he didn't. But I knew he did. And it just got me really angry. I don't know why, but I punched him, right in the face. I wish I hadn't."

Will nodded, not sure what else to say.

"So what do we do next? About the... thing out there I mean," Corey said.

"I don't know." Will shrugged his shoulders and turned back to Corey. "I don't know."

CHAPTER THIRTY

In the daylight Erica could see that the marsh near her brother's cross continued out from Route 101 for over a hundred yards, broken only by a few scraggly leafless trees in the water, before winnowing down between the stands of healthy trees in the distance. It didn't smell quite as bad — at least at 8:30 in the morning — a change Erica attributed to the reduced temperature of the water after the cooler temperatures of the night.

She waited for a break in the traffic and then stepped out of her car. The Ford Taurus was pulled off the road beyond the breakdown lane and into the scrubby grass that was sporadically cut by the orange mowers of NH DOT. Erica took a deep breath and tried to ignore the mounting pressure in her chest. The daylight helped, but the memory of being here and seeing something unbelievable — and unbelievably frightening — was still fresh. But beneath the fear (or perhaps above it), her curiosity remained. So, she was out along the side of Route 101 in Derryfield at 8:30 in the morning retracing her steps from weeks ago in hopes of — well she wasn't quite sure. Perhaps hoping to find some sign of it or better come to terms with it.

Erica looked over to Nate's cross as though it could provide her some assistance before she walked down the embankment towards the marsh. She was careful to steady herself with her trailing right arm against the incline as the sound of the traffic above dropped a few decibels. She glanced once back up at the Ford and Nate's cross before she gritted her teeth and pushed on towards the marsh.

Though the temperature was already in the 80s this early in the morning, Erica had the foresight to wear a pair of hiking boots that rose a few inches above her ankles. She was immediately glad she had done so, as she sunk a bit into the mucky edge of the marshland which began to grasp at her footwear. The sun cut through the few wisps of clouds overhead and beat down on Erica; she raised her left hand to shield her eyes and stared out at the water before her.

She walked along the shore of the marsh, making sure to choose her steps carefully so as to avoid any spots where the mud looked wetter than usual. As she walked she looked for signs of the creature: a footprint, a patch of fur or skin, or some spoor. She recognized that she had no skills or training, no sure idea of how to conduct such a search or exactly what to look for; but she figured that a creature that large would leave unmistakable evidence, things that even her untrained eyes could detect. She walked this way for fifteen minutes when a voice sounded out above the din of the traffic beyond the embankment.

"Can I help you ma'am?"

The voice startled Erica. She had been so engrossed in watching her steps and looking for some sign of the creature that she had completely missed that someone else was nearby. Erica looked up and stared at the man. He stood about twenty yards away. He wore khakis tucked into a pair of green boots that nearly reached his knees and a long sleeve shirt despite the heat. Erica could see a sheen of sweat on his bare cheeks. A pair of binoculars hung from a strap around his neck and a walkie-talkie was clipped to his belt. He squinted at her now, eyes tight against the sun over Erica's shoulder.

"Excuse me?"

"I said, can I help you? Looks to me like you are looking for something."

"No, I mean, no thank you. I work at the *Gazette*, just out here on a story."

"I see," he said. He was tall, well over six feet with additional inches from his heavy boots. Erica guessed he was in his forties, but couldn't be sure and figured he could fall the decade prior or after; he had a sandy blond hair — cut short to his scalp — that would have hidden any grays. She didn't recognize him. The man continued to squint at her. He said nothing. His walkie-talkie squawked once but Erica couldn't make out what was said.

As Erica watched the man, another appeared behind him from around the bend of the embankment, twenty yards further back. This man also wore khakis tucked into knee high green boots, similar in many respects to the first man aside from his dark brown hair. He carried a long thin metal bar in his right hand and with his left hand steadied a canvas bag slung over his left shoulder.

The first man held a pair of binoculars up to his eyes and scanned the marsh.

"What are you doing here?" Erica asked.

"Hmmm?" the man said. He set the binoculars down and looked at Erica with a blank face.

"I said, what are you doing out here?"

"Bird watching." He didn't frown but pursed his lips. Erica could read the expression even from the distance between them; the man was clearly not pleased with her presence. Erica heard the sound of a vehicle pulling off the road on the embankment to their right. She glanced up and saw a white van stop and the passenger window roll down. The man standing near her waved the van away. The window rolled up and the van rolled forward another twenty yards past Erica.

"What's with the walkie-talkie? Gotta call in the birds you see?"

The man didn't respond. He walked a few steps closer to Erica and continued to scan the marsh. The white van idled atop the embankment. Erica's uneasiness — initially generated by her return to the area in which she had seen the thing — now centered on the strangers nearby and their unusual behavior. Though not a birdwatcher herself, she found their get-up, and the waiting white van, unusual. The marsh off the highway did not strike her as fertile ground to search for birds.

As she stood there, uncertain what to do next, a police cruiser pulled up behind the white van and a police officer she did not know — but at least recognized on sight — got out. He wore a short sleeve uniform and walked slowly. His utility belt hung at a slight angle with his firearm lower on his hip. He walked up to the passenger side of the vehicle and began speaking with whoever was driving it. Erica could not hear their words but watched the officer gesticulate with his hands, take something the driver handed him, then bow his head down to study it. A moment later he handed it back, nodded, and backed up a few steps.

The officer turned and yelled down to Erica.

"Ma'am! I'm going to have to ask you to leave now!"

"What?" Erica called back, not because she misunderstood him, but because she couldn't believe his words.

"I'm going to have to ask you to leave now!" He waved his arm as if he was scooping water and shoveling it up the incline. "Please come up here!"

Erica looked over at the man with the binoculars. He ignored her gaze and continued to study the marsh. Erica struggled up the loose silt of the incline to the scrubby grass of the embankment. The officer stood watching, hands on his hips. When she reached the top of the embankment he said again: "Sorry Ma'am, but I'm going to have to ask you to leave."

"Why?"

"These gentlemen are doing a study and they need the area clear. You really shouldn't be this near the highway anyways, its a safety issue." His jaw worked up and down slowly as he chewed on some gum or dip. "Your car nearby?" he asked.

"Yeah, it's up the road a ways," Erica said, pointing west. "What are they studying?" Erica leaned to her right and tried to get a better look into the van. The passenger window, tinted a dark impenetrable gray, was still mostly down. She could see a man leaning back in the driver's seat, slowly drumming his fingers along the steering wheel. He glanced over towards Erica and rolled up the window.

The officer ignored her question. "What's your name ma'am?"

"Erica Couture. And you?"

"Officer Stapleton."

"What are they doing?"

"Said they're studying the wildlife, the birds in the protected marshes. They've asked all civilians to clear out and frankly, you shouldn't be here, this close to the road, anyways. Not safe for you, but more importantly, causes a safety issue for those driving by. You could unknowingly distract a driver, and boom" he smacked his hands together, "another accident on the Highway of Death."

"They with UNH or something?"

"The EPA. Come with me please," Stapleton added. He walked back towards the cruiser. She followed and glanced down at the men at the edge of the marsh. The first continued to scan the horizon with his binoculars; the second was kneeling down and staring at the ground near his feet. His canvas bag was at his side and splayed open, revealing a plastic bin with multiple internal containers.

"This way Ms. Couture," Stapleton said. He opened the rear passenger door and added, "I'll drive you back to your car."

She sat in the back and he closed the door behind her. She had never sat in the rear of a cruiser before and she didn't like it. The grill between the front and rear seats made her feel as though she was incarcerated, as though she had done something that warranted her detention. Stapleton climbed into the cruiser. "Seat belt please," he said. He flicked on the directional as he waited for traffic to pass so he could pull the cruiser back onto the road.

"What were you doing out here?" he asked and glanced at Erica in the rear view mirror.

She thought about her answer.

"I work at the *Gazette*. I'm writing a story on the marshes and swamps of southern NH. Was looking to get some exposure to it."

Stapleton pulled onto the highway. As he picked up speed the metal of the grill began to rattle against the frame of the car. Erica could see the brake lights of the car in front of them activate for a few seconds as it slowed.

"Well, you should not be stopping on the highway for sightseeing Ms. Couture," Stapleton yelled over the noise. "I'm not going to ticket you today, but it's not the sort of thing you should be doing. Do you understand?"

"Yes," she yelled back. Stapleton nodded to her.

"That's my car, up there," Erica said and pointed at the Ford. Stapleton flicked a switch on the dashboard to activate his emergency lights, tapped the brakes, and started to pull off the road. He stopped behind the Ford and waited for traffic to cease so he could exit the vehicle. He helped her out and walked her up to her car.

"There's plenty of other places to see the water, Ms. Couture. Please stay off the highway, it's not safe."

I know, Erica thought, after the things I have seen, I know it's not safe.

CHAPTER THIRTY-ONE

Will wasn't expecting to find much of interest when he began tidying the house garage. It was a pointless venture, trying to clean and empty it of the junk his father had kept stored there, but he wanted to stay active in hopes that doing so would keep his mind off the problems of the nursing home, the shop, and the swamp. Idleness only left his mind free to wander, where it inevitably found its way back to ruminate on the things he feared most: his mother dying, the shop closing, that creature prowling about the swamp.

Will had made a half-hearted effort to clean the garage one Sunday a few months after his father's death, but after bringing two truckloads worth of space blankets, busted fishing gear, and rusted gardening equipment to the town dump, he had simply closed the door and ignored it. The garage was built for a single car, but over-sized. The right side kicked out another twelve feet with a slightly sloped roof and held a row of wooden workbenches that had years ago disappeared under an ever-growing collection of tools, gadgets, lumber, and camping and fishing supplies.

Will's mother had always kept the house clean. She — usually with the help of Will or Daisy, his sister — made sure the house was dusted every day, vacuumed every other day, and the floors washed every week. But the garage, the garage was Winston's domain, a place that Mildred did not enter save to get in the vehicle parked there. Will remembered her often making snide comments to his father to clean the place (usually when getting into or out of the car) but Winston had always shrugged it off and continued to add to the collection of materials in the garage. Though to Will it seemed disorganized as all hell, Winston always seemed to know where whatever he needed was.

Unfortunately, Will lacked the perfect recall of his father and could not easily place his hand on anything he wanted in the garage.

Though it wasn't a large space, the number of items stored there still made it difficult to easily determine what was present, while at the same time made it difficult to even get to it. The sheer volume of materials, one stacked atop another to nearly chest level, left little space for walking. Will wasn't certain where to begin, what to keep or toss. Another inventory of the space, some sense of what it contained, made the most sense.

He began to step through the materials and tried to keep mental track of the tents, space blankets, coolers, and tools he came across. In one corner of the garage, halfway behind a discarded bookshelf filled with an assembly of hand tools, Will spied the old desk that had once sat in the spare bedroom of the house which served as an office. After Will had accidentally kicked through one leg of it while roughhousing in high school, Winston had carried it out and made Will pay, in part, for the newer one that still sat inside.

Once in the garage, Winston had sawed off the splintered leg of the desk and placed a stack of bricks underneath to hold it steady. It was piled high with newspapers, a stack of documents with the heading U.S. NRC, and issues of the *Nuclear Plant Journal* for the years 1990 through 1993, the year of Winston's death. An issue or two came in the months after his father's death, and Will remembered calling up the service to cancel the subscription. He had not questioned the arrival of the magazine. He simply didn't have time to. When Will returned, he had to take on the responsibility not just for planning his father's service and assisting with his mother, but also for the business. He hadn't had the time or the energy to figure out why his father had ordered the magazine. He glanced at the covers of a few but pushed them aside and continued perusing the materials in the garage.

Behind the scattered *Nuclear Plant Journals* Will spied the dark leather of a bound notebook resting on the rear of the desk. He leaned over the mess on the desk and pulled free the tome. It was dusty and speckled in a few places where it had gotten wet. The leather cover was wrinkled in spots, and when Will flipped it open he saw that the first third or so of the pages splayed open and displayed text, while the final two-thirds remained closed and pressed tight, evidently because the writer had not reached those pages. The first page was dated 7/16/1990 in his father's hand. Will didn't know his father kept a journal; he certainly hadn't found any in the house. His father never struck him as much of a writer, though he was one to read a military thriller every once in a while. Will began to read the notebook with interest.

I saw something I can't describe, something in the marsh off 101. I don't know why I'm even spending the time to write this shit down, but I've got to record this somehow. I read something about how writing shit like this out is supposed to help.

So it happened on July 1, 1992. Right about at 9:30 at night. I was heading up for a call, and saw it, off the road. It was big. Long too. Ugly bitch. Had tentacles like an octopus. It stood there, off the side of the road, just eyeing me. It wasn't natural. Not like any animal I've seen.

The words struck Will with a physical force. He nearly tripped over the clutter on the garage floor as he stepped back in alarm. He clutched the journal tightly and glanced around the garage, as if someone might be there, and if that someone might disapprove of his reading the journal. Will extricated himself from the mess on the floor and marched over towards the near wall of the garage and leaned against it to continue reading.

He flipped ahead a few pages.

The thing is from Seabrook. It has to be. The timing can't be a coincidence. Seabrook came on line in March and this thing appears in June. Whatever radioactive mess that plant is pumping into the water created that thing.

They say the plant is a closed system, like the radioactivity can't get out. But of course that's what they'd say. That what they said about Chernobyl. That thing is evidence enough of it getting out. Once I've got proof, they'll have to admit that somethings wrong with that plant.

Will flipped forward pages again and read:

I've been out to the marsh three times now. I still haven't found it, or for that matter any signs of it. Mildred seems to be getting worse everyday. I hate to leave her alone but I've got to find this thing. I can't sleep at night, I just keep seeing it, even in my dreams.

I tried to explain it to her, but she didn't understand. Maybe she did and she's just too sick now. I can't be certain.

Oscar knows about it. I don't think he believes me, but he listened. He said I should call the kids, talk to them about it. Tell them about Mildred too, how she's doing. They'll call when they want to talk.

The entries went on like this for another fifty pages and filled the first third of the book. Across the pages his father's writing became more strident, the penmanship more haphazard. Will flipped through the covered pages and felt the indentations of the pen marks. The last page read:

Been out every third night for three weeks now. Still no sign of it. Dusk or dawn seems best. I can tell it's close sometimes, in the marsh or the bog, just below the surface of the water. I can feel it, tell it's near. But nothing I can bring back, to show them.

Mildred keeps pestering me about going out. Doesn't understand why I have to get this thing. She will once I've got it.

Fuck, Will thought. His mother was right. Whatever he had seen out there, so had his father had a few years before. Something that had motivated Winston to venture out into the swamp to find it. Something that had driven him to sobriety, when nothing else could.

Will was surprised to find himself sitting on the garage floor. He couldn't remember moving to sit. His legs were cramped and he felt an intense need to pee, both sensations large in his mind but only present now when he momentarily set the journal aside.

Will spent the rest of the afternoon leafing through his father's notes and the stack of journals and newspapers piled high on the desk. What Will had once thought to be nothing more than a bundle of combustible materials was clearly something much more. His father's research and journal spoke to Winston's focus on finding whatever it was out there and doing something about it.

A task his father hadn't completed before his death. But a task that Will could perhaps complete for him.

CHAPTER THIRTY-TWO

Ted was surprised when Corey asked if he could come into work with him. His son rarely showed interest in the Franklin Mill or his stories about work or the men and women he knew there. Corey always seemed more interested in his movies or games or running around with Alex and causing trouble. But he was not about to reject his son's interest, so he agreed, and packed them both a lunch.

"Finish up brushing your teeth and let's go!" Ted yelled. Corey came hustling out of the bathroom and they slid into Ted's truck. A few minutes later they were following the river down to the mills. Corey stared out his window and, between the passing trees, studied the waters of the Pilwilla. As they neared the mills the water became darker and deeper. Corey wondered what their depths might hold.

"So why now?" Ted asked.

"Huh?" Corey turned from the window and glanced over at his dad.

"I'm always telling you about the mill, hell, threatening to make you come if you can't behave." Ted paused, giving his words a moment to sink in. "So what made you want to come now?"

"Just want to see what it's like I guess. Like a career day."

Ted grunted. "OK, well we'll get you a good look. One rule though: you listen to the directions that we give you. It's an active mill. It can be dangerous. Don't go wandering off, and don't touch anything unless someone says you can. Understand?"

"Yes, sir," Corey replied. The trees thinned as they drew nearer to downtown Derryfield, replaced by houses and businesses that clustered there. The red brick of the mill buildings was visible above the tops of the trees.

The central building of the Franklin mills was three stories tall, with enormous windows running from knee height to well above one's head, built that way to allow a maximum amount of light into the structure over a century ago, before electric lights were an option to illuminate the interior.

After pulling into the parking lot, Corey was surprised to see how many people were filing into the mill. He recalled his father's comments about how many jobs had been lost in the last fifteen years; apparently there was still enough positions to employ the dozens of men and women that were walking in now. He realized then what it had meant to Derryfield when the mill had begun to suffer. He looked over the parking lot and saw that less than half of the spots contained a vehicle.

"Come on, let's go Corey," Ted said, both lunches in hand. Corey hustled after his father and followed him into the main lobby of the mill. The room held a collection of desks and a system of shelves against the far wall. The persons filing in chatted amongst themselves and walked over to the shelving, where they grabbed sheets of paper and slid them into a boxy machine bolted to the wall. After they did so, each person dropped the paper back into the shelves and walked through one of the far doors. Corey could see a large hallway beyond and stairs leading up.

"Dad, what's that?" Corey asked, pointing at the machine.

"Time card. Hey, Gloria," Ted yelled to a woman sitting at one of the desks. She was heavyset with long dark hair. A pencil peeked out atop her right ear. "Gloria! Can you keep an eye on my son here for a bit? Name's Corey. He wanted to come in, see the place in action."

Gloria stood up from her desk and sauntered over, smirking at Ted. "You clear this with Morris?" she asked, referring to the operations manager.

"No, I didn't Gloria. The kid told me this morning, and I'd thought I'd bring him in, let him get a taste of it. Learn what his old man does every day."

Gloria rolled her eyes and sighed. "He can sit here in the lobby. I'll keep an eye on him for a bit. He supposed to be here all day?"

Corey didn't like how they were talking, as if he was simply a task for them to delegate, as though he was not there witnessing the conversation.

"Yeah, he's here as long as I am. Brought him a lunch." A bell sounded in the office and Ted moved towards the time cards. "Talk to Morris for me, will ya?"

"Fine, fine," Gloria said. "I'll talk to him. Get him the tour, if you will."

"Thanks, you're the best!" Ted grabbed his time card, slotted it in the machine, and turned to Corey saying, "See you in a bit, OK? Gloria will keep an eye on you and I'll see you when Morris or one of the other guys brings you in for a tour, OK?"

"OK," Corey replied. Ted dropped his time card back into one of the shelves and slipped through one of the far doors and into the mill proper.

"Alright," Gloria said and sighed, "so you're with me for now Corey. Take a seat over there," she pointed to a row of chairs against the nearest wall, "I'll buzz Morris and see what we can do for a tour. You need any coffee or anything?"

"Uh, no thanks." Corey took a seat where she had pointed and watched as Gloria sat back down at her desk. A phone sat on one corner of the desk and a stack of papers spilled across the rest. She picked up a pen and hurriedly scribbled on one of the papers. Corey couldn't imagine how she kept it straight, but clearly some system was at play given how quickly she worked with the documents.

The next hour crawled by. Gloria occasionally answered the phone but otherwise remained focused on the things on her desk. Every few minutes she would glance up at Corey to ensure he remained seated in the row of chairs. Corey leafed through the magazines on the nearby coffee table while he waited.

Finally he had enough. Sitting in the lobby was getting him nowhere. He set down the magazine in his hands and approached Gloria. When she didn't immediately looked up, Corey cleared his throat.

Gloria looked up from the paper on her desk and said, "Can I help you, Corey?"

"Yeah. I'm bored."

Corey saw a flicker of anger register across Gloria's face before she quelled it. She looked down at her desk, then back to him and said, "Well, what are you expecting here? I'm working and you just got dropped in my lap by your father."

"Are there any people that have worked here a long time? Anyone

I can talk to?"

"Well sure. Most of us here are longtime employees, ten years at least."

"No, I mean like a really long time. Like fifty years maybe, or more."

"Yes," Gloria said. She ran her fingers along her desk causing her nails to click against the top in a repeated staccato. After a moment she said, "Ernest Jenkins has been here there abouts. Fifty years at least, maybe going on sixty. We keep saying he's got to retire one of these years, but he hasn't."

"Oh cool. Can I talk to him?"

"When he has a break, I don't see why not. Is there some reason in particular you want to speak with him?"

The lie came easily, mixed as it was with some truth. "One of my teachers at school last year was teaching us about the mills. I want to ask somebody about that, about what we learned about, like the history of it and all."

Gloria set down her pen and crossed her arms against her chest.

"That's a decent use of your time," she said, and added under her breath, "and will get you out of my hair at least. Let's go to the break room. I'll let Ernest know that you want to talk to him about the history of this place, OK?"

"Yeah. Will you let me dad know too, that I'm at the break room I mean?"

"Sure," Gloria said as she stood up from her desk. "He won't be on break at the same time, but I'll make sure he knows."

Gloria led him to the break room and left him there, telling him she would let Mr. Jenkins know that Corey wanted to talk with him. The room was smaller than Corey had expected, only twenty feet by twenty feet with a few tables and chairs and two vending machines up against the far wall. He took a seat at one of the tables. One of the vending machines dispensed soda; the other an assortment of salty and crunchy snacks. The door to the left of the vending machines was marked with a sign for the men's restroom, and the door to the right with a sign for the women's restroom.

After a few minutes of waiting, workers began to file into the room. They largely ignored Corey, preferring instead to sit at the other tables in the room, visit the restrooms, or purchase a drink or snack from one of the vending machines. Their conversations were filled with laughter and bitching and with colorful language Corey had not even heard in the worst moments on the playground. He liked it immediately. It was not only the language used but the creative combinations in which they were deployed.

One man walked in and came directly towards Corey and sat down at the table with him. The few hairs left on his head were a silver-white; his eyebrows — once a dark brown — were peppered with the same silver-white. He walked slowly and with an irregular gait, favoring more time on his right leg than his left. He groaned as he settled down into a chair and rubbed at his lower back with his right hand.

"You're Barrington's kid, right?" Jenkins asked. Corey nodded.

"Gloria said you wanted to talk to me?"

"Yeah."

"Well I'm here. Talk away."

"I wanted to ask you some questions, about like the history of this place. What you know about it and stuff." Corey shrugged as a way to reduce the impact of his request.

"Well I'm parched. Get me a soda kid, and I'll talk."

Corey slid off his chair and stood in the short line before the vending machines. After a minute he reached the machine, purchased a Coke, and returned with it to Jenkins. The old man grunted his approval. He cracked the can open, took a large gulp, and wiped his mouth with the back of his wrist.

"So what do you want to know?" he rasped.

"Uh..." Corey's mind went blank. The questions he had prepared were suddenly absent from his mind. He had considered being here, but now that he was, he was not certain how to begin.

"I wanted to hear like, any stories you know about the place."

"Stories?" Jenkins said before taking another swig from the soda. "I've got plenty of stories. This place is old kid. I've been here longer than any other fool here, but it's long older than me. My daddy worked here, and his daddy too."

"Do you know any stories about things in the mills, like strange things you've seen or heard?"

"Ha! You interested in the old ghost stories and such, huh?" He chuckled and slapped one hand against his knee. "I've heard plenty about that. You've got to understand, lot's of people been injured, even killed in this place. It's tough work, always dangerous with all the machinery and such."

"Well, not really. More like, stories of things outside the mills. Animals or weird things out there?"

"What? Something in the river?" Jenkins asked. He returned to rubbing his lower back as he waited for Corey to respond.

"Well yeah, and the marsh. Well the bog, downstream."

"Plenty of shit in the river that's for sure. It's gotten better, ever since the Feds passed those laws twenty or so years back, really cracked down on what we could just get rid of in the river. Made it a lot more costly to run this place, but better for the fish and beavers and all that I'm told."

"Did you ever see anything? Like a really big fish or turtle or something?"

"What are you getting at kid?"

The crowded room was growing hot. The other discussions in the room layered over one another into a general buzz that surrounded them. Corey didn't want to share with Jenkins what he had seen. He didn't expect the man to believe him, and didn't want him — or the others in the break room them — to ridicule him for it.

"My friend told me he saw something weird out by the marsh. Something big on the shore. I don't believe him but I told him I would ask about it at the mills."

"What'd he see?" Jenkins asked.

"Something big. Like bigger than a bear. But on the shore, moving near the woods. I asked him if it was a moose, but he said it wasn't."

"He see it near dark?"

"Yes," Corey said.

"Creeped along but he escaped by the skin of his teeth?"

"Yes, I guess."

"Ah yeah," Jenkins said, smiling. "I've heard that one. The Monster of the Marsh, the Beast of the Brown Stump Bog. Prowling around after dark. When'd he see it?"

"A few weeks back."

"Been a while since I heard that one. Last one was... Jesus, '85, '86.

Richard... can't remember his last name. Richard said he saw it. That guy was a clown."

"What do you think it is?"

Jenkins laughed. "It's a crock of shit kid. A stupid story that's been passed from rube to rube for years now. You ever hear of the serial killer with the hook for a hand? Or the ghost lady hitchhiking on Route 101?" Jenkins didn't wait for an answer. "Same shit kid."

Another bell sounded in the building and the workers began to file out.

"I've got to get back to shift. Thanks for the Coke kid." Jenkins stood up slowly. He grunted as he stood and rubbed his back again. He followed the group walking out, favoring his right leg again. In less than 60 seconds, Corey was alone again in the room. He sat there, waiting for his father or Gloria or someone else to find him while he thought about the thing he had seen and how he would prove to his father and Alex — and maybe even Ernest Jenkins — that it was real.

CHAPTER THIRTY-THREE

Will hoped, for the third night in a row, that the humidity was at its breaking point. The recent heat wave caused temperatures in the 90s with the air holding as much moisture as it could. It was heavy and sticky, even in the morning. Sleeping was difficult enough with thoughts of the thing in the swamp and his father's experiences with it. The muggy nights did not help. He woke every morning covered in a sheen of sweat, wondering how much his nightmares were contributing to it.

Thankfully a wind was coming in from the west that seemed certain to bring a change to the weather. Will knew it brought rain by the way the breeze turned up the leaves to show their undersides, like Marilyn's skirt in the iconic picture on the street. By 4 P.M. the sky overhead was a dark gray, the color of wet stone. A rumble sounded every few seconds, a rolling reverberation that traversed the sky as it shook the clouds. The rain would come soon.

After he signed in the visitor log, Will raised a hand to the woman behind the front desk, the same woman who sat there nearly every day he came to see his mother at Riverview. He still couldn't remember her name, she still wore some floral print scrubs, and she still had a Stephen King book on the desk before her. She nodded back but said nothing.

Will hurried down the hallway to his mother's room, keeping his eyes focused on the lime green floor. He walked quickly and with his head bowed, hoping that he would not run into Maureen Mitchell as he was still behind on the bills. He had caught up somewhat, and the outstanding amount was less than that from June, but he wanted to avoid the same tired conversation they had every time he ran into her.

When he turned into her room Will was surprised to see that the first bed was empty, the sheets gone, displaying the gray of the bare mattress. Norma's long battle had ended — or perhaps more optimistically had just landed her in the hospital. The sight of the empty bed caused Will to consider for a moment when he might find his mother's bed empty. Due to her failing health, Will was the designated power of attorney. Her doctor had made it clear to Will that his mother might live for another ten years in ever worsening health, or she could succumb quickly to the disease in a matter of months. The illness inside her brain that was wearing away at her mind could not be stopped. The best hope was for slowing it, by keeping Mildred active and otherwise healthy.

Mildred smiled when she saw Will but said nothing.

"Hey mom. What happened to Norma?"

"Who?" Mildred said and frowned.

"Your roommate." Will motioned over his shoulder with an outstretched thumb.

Mildred looked over at the bed and seemed to recognize for the first time that it was empty. She cocked her head and stared at the bed.

"I don't know. Maybe she's getting a shower."

Will shrugged his shoulders and pulled up a chair next to his mother. He had more important things to address with her right now. He sat down close to her and smiled, a smile he hoped was reassuring, one that he hoped would quell the anxiety he felt in his chest. Mildred smiled back and brushed at the hair on her forehead.

"Mom. Do you remember telling me about Dad seeing something out on Route 101?"

"No. What are you talking about?"

"Mom," Will said and leaned forward, as if moving closer to her would assist in some way to spark her memory, "try to remember. You told me about something Dad saw. Something that scared him out on Route 101."

"I'm sorry Billy," his mother answered. She frowned and repeatedly clasped and unclasped her hands. "I don't know what you're talking about."

"You said that Dad saw something strange out on Route 101 a few years back. You started telling me more about it a few weeks ago."

"About what? I don't, I don't remember." She waved her hands back and forth as if she was shooing away flies or the wisps of memory that confirmed her failing mental health.

"Please, think," Will said. "There was something you said Dad saw, out on Route 101. He went out in the marsh a lot, in the swamp out there, he was looking for something. Do you remember?"

"No, I do not!" she said, raising her voice. "Would you stop pestering me about conversations I don't remember?"

"What about him getting sober Mom? Why did he get sober? What did he tell you about that?"

"Oh Billy," Mildred said. She leaned towards him and smiled a sad smile. "Your father always drank, Billy, you know that. He loved us, but his weakness was always the bottle."

He tried to ask her about their last conversations a few other ways, but each avenue of questioning was blocked by the debris of her aging mind. He had hoped that by choosing the right words he could find an uninterrupted path to the lucid part of his mother that remained, the part that still appeared infrequently, but with enough force to dazzle him and remind him of the woman he had known as a child.

Nevertheless, he tried again.

"Mom, Mom," he said. "This is important, please try to remember." He stared into her blue eyes. She held his gaze and smiled at him in a grin that only appeared at the corners of her mouth and in wrinkles beside each eye.

"What do you need Billy?" she asked.

"You were telling me a story Mom, about how Dad saw something out on Route 101. I need to know more about it. It's important."

"Why?" she asked. She expressed her confusion not only in the tone of her voice — suddenly higher in pitch — but also in her face: she squinted her right eye nearly shut and grimaced with the right side of her face. "Why is that important?"

"I think, well, I'm not sure. But I think Dad might have been on to something, something big. It's hard to explain."

"I'm sorry, Billy, I don't remember."

Will hung his head and said: "It's OK Mom, it's fine."

They talked for a few more minutes, the conversation invariably looping back around to the few topics that seemed to always be at the forefront of her mind: the status of the shop, the weather, and Will's sister Daisy out in California. After working through the expected conversations a few times, Will waved goodbye to her and tried to slip out the way he had entered, eyes to the floor with hurried steps. As he approached the lobby he glanced up and saw the familiar brown hair and heavy-set build of Maureen Mitchell. She stood at the front desk speaking with the woman sitting there. Will walked towards the door and avoided eye contact.

"Mr. Boucher," Mitchell called out. Will grimaced, stopped, and turned to her.

"Ms. Mitchell."

"Do you have a minute right now?" she asked.

"Actually, I don't," Will responded. "I just popped in to say a quick hi to my mother and I've got to get back to the shop." He took another step towards the door but Mitchell moved towards him.

"We need to speak Mr. Boucher. The bill, again, is late."

"I understand," Will said. "Let's talk soon."

He stepped out into the parking lot and was frustrated to find her following him. The sky overhead was even darker then when he had entered the facility. Now it was a dark gray that hinted at purple, the clouds no longer a fluffy cotton from the morning but a swollen mass blocking out most light. Mitchell cleared her throat loudly and when Will turned she spoke.

"Mr. Boucher, you don't seem to be understanding what I am saying. We need payment. Your mother's care is expensive. If we don't get payment, we will have no choice but to discharge her to other care."

Will slowed his pace and turned back towards her. "I've been catching up every month," he objected. "The balance has been getting lower, right?"

"It has," Mitchell responded, "but that is not what is required of you. Every month you carry a balance is a month you are violating the policy of this facility. And every month you assure me that the past due amount and the current bill will be paid in full. And every month it is not. So we are yet again, having this conversation. This time, in the parking lot," she added with a note of disgust.

The rain came suddenly. One moment, the sky was threatening but it was dry. In the next, the rain was falling to the ground in waves so heavy that visibility was immediately cut to only a hundred feet. In a few seconds Will and Mitchell were both drenched. Their clothes clung to their bodies like a second set of heavy wet skin. Puddles formed on the ground. They grew quickly and began to connect and grow into one larger puddle until the pavement of the lot had disappeared below the pattering ripples of water.

Mitchell turned and ran towards the entrance of the nursing home while she raised a hand over her head in an ineffectual effort to shield herself from the rain. Will moved towards the truck, thankful that the rain had cut their conversation short. He climbed into the cab. His clothes and shoes squelched as some of the moisture oozed out of the fabric and plastics. The cab of the truck was a cocoon in the storm. Thunder continued overhead and with each gust of wind the rain shifted, at times striking the truck at an angle parallel to the ground.

Will sat in his truck and watched the rain. The water collecting in the parking lot swept towards the sewer grate near the sidewalk and out towards the Pilwilla River. Will thought about what he could do to pay all of the past due bills and what he should do about the thing he had seen in the swamp.

CHAPTER THIRTY-FOUR

For the fourth time in as many days Erica was at Paul Hutchinson's house. After considerable research, Erica knew Sergeant Hutchinson, U.S. Air Force retired, to be one of the Airmen not only still alive who had been stationed at Pease Air Force Base 30 years ago, but more importantly, one of the few still living in the area. Many of the officers and enlisted men had left once the base was closed and transferred to other active bases. She knew little else about the man, except that he didn't answer the phone, return messages, or spend much time at home.

The fourth time though was the charm. She knocked on his front door and waited while she heard footsteps inside. The house itself was small, older construction with bay windows, a tall chimney erupting from the roof, and a porch running the entire front of the structure. The whole thing was painted a dark gray. She could make out the top of a barn in the rear of the property, but the thick trees to either side obscured the neighbors and afforded the lot a measure of privacy.

She was surprised when an older black man opened the door. He was broad through the shoulders but slightly bent at the waist at an angle Erica could tell was likely permanent, brought on either by age or injury, making him only an inch or so taller than she. The man's hair and thick mustache were both graying. He glared at her and growled: "Don't want whatever your selling."

"Mr. Hutchinson?" she asked and put up a hand towards the door.

"I told you, I don't want whatever you're selling. Move along please."

"Mr. Hutchinson, please," Erica said quickly, "I'm not selling anything. I'm a reporter with the *Derryfield Gazette*, I just have a few questions for you please, if you don't mind."

Her outburst slowed his arm and he stopped closing the door to examine her more fully.

"About what?" he asked.

"I understand you used to work at the Pease Air Force Base. I just have a few questions for you about your time there."

"How'd you get my name? What is this about?" he snapped.

"Well, sir, I've been speaking to a number of people who worked at Pease. I'm particularly interested in the sighting back in September of 1965. I'm doing a follow up piece on it."

"The Exeter Incident?" Hutchinson asked. He sneered the words and looked disapprovingly over the tops of his glasses at Erica. "That was a long time ago."

"Yes. I heard that you were one of the Airmen who investigated the incident."

"Who told you that?" He didn't move to close the door, but he didn't open it any further either, preferring instead to leave it only cracked.

"I spoke with Andrew Stewart, and he said that you might have more to share on this."

"That asshole that works at the paper? Haven't seen his face in a decade or better, which is fine by me."

"He doesn't work there anymore Mr. Hutchinson, I followed up with him some weeks ago and he said you might be a person to talk to."

"He was wrong. I've got nothing to say about that. I don't know anything about it." He started to close the door again and Erica yelled out.

"But you were stationed at Pease, right? You worked there when the investigation was ongoing, right?"

"Yes," Hutchinson said, "I worked there."

"Can I ask you some more about your time working there? Who you knew? Did you know anyone who looked into the Exeter Incident?"

"Ma'am, I've got nothing further to say to you or anyone else on the topic of my military service. Please leave."

"I just have a few questions sir, I won't take much of your time." She smiled now, doing her best to project an interest in his response, an engagement with his words.

Hutchinson was unmoved. He glared at her. "I don't take kindly to people trespassing Ms. Hutchinson. I will only ask you this one more time: please leave."

Erica turned in frustration and cursed to herself under her breath as Hutchinson closed the door behind her. Other Pease servicemen she had tried to interview had reacted much the same: either unresponsive or uninterested in speaking to her. She settled into her car and glanced back at Hutchinson's house. She hadn't expected it to be easy, but she had — perhaps naively — not expected it to be this difficult. She had seen something out in the swamps; others had too. But few wanted to speak about it or the Incident.

The frustration she felt over this interaction bled into her current dissatisfaction with the job at the *Gazette*. She wanted back on crime. The piddly shit she was working on — besides the Exeter Incident Story — was boring her to death. They were the kind of stories any cub reporter could work. She knew Frank would be expecting a few more of that filler shit so she put the car in gear and drove towards the office.

The drive downtown always made her feel melancholy. At night at least the darkness hid the empty storefronts, the graffiti, and the cracked sidewalks. Derryfield's imperfections were ever present and undeniable in the daylight. She recalled the downtown from her youth in the '80s, when every storefront was bustling and there was always talk of expansion and business coming in and houses being built. Though the houses kept going up, the only stores erected were monstrosities of size and scope, a few miles away, and were slowing siphoning all the business from downtown. She ignored these changes as best she could and reminisced about the memories she had of Nate. A minute later she parked her car in the lot behind the Franklin Building and deciding that the stairs were a better option than the elevator, took the two flights up to the office. The office was, as one would expect on a Wednesday afternoon, relatively slow.

Sarah greeted Erica as she came in and handed her a few letters that were addressed to her. As soon as Erica sat down at her desk Frank came over.

"What is this Erica?" he asked. He waved the papers between their faces as if the motion would somehow help with her understanding.

"I don't know? What are you holding?"

"This article on the Old Home Day in Portsmouth."

"And?"

"And? What is this?

"It's what you asked for, right? New Hampshire feel, something local?"

"Erica," he said, his voice trailing off as he sat down on the edge of her desk. "You and Karen have been pushing out some fine articles. But this," he paused again to look down at the paper in his hands, "this is not what I asked for. Keep it light. Simple. It's fluff. What is this going on about the 'history of the strange,'" here he made the quotation marks with his free hand, "and the abduction story told by the Hills? How does this have anything to do with Old Home Days? You've got to focus."

When she didn't immediately respond, he continued, "I gave you some simple assignments to work. And yes, though I'm regretting it now, you were given permission to chase something a little more... esoteric. But now it seems that's all you want to write about."

"Frank, it's not like that, I just-"

"Maybe this isn't right for you." Frank shook his head and sighed. "I thought you had enough time off after your brother's passing. Was I wrong?" He looked down at her and shook his head slowly. Cathy at the next desk glanced over at Erica but looked away when Erica caught her eye.

"That's not fair Frank. When I left, I was reporting real stories, I was on crime. I haven't been back on it since. That's not right."

Here his voice, so often measured, rose in pitch and volume. "It's not your job to tell me what's right. It's your job to work the assignments. That's it. You understand?"

"Yeah. I got it Frank." She stared back at him.

"Then fix this. I don't expect anything more like this either."

"Got it," she said, short and clipped. She was angry, and she knew he could tell she was angry. She took some small amount of pleasure in knowing he knew it; if he was going to be an ass she wasn't going to indulge him.

"Weber's babysitting your other project, damned if I know why, but it's still my job to keep an eye on you day to day. And you've got to produce, same as anyone else here, OK?"

Erica nodded.

"Get me this revised tomorrow. It has to run soon. It's old home

254

days across the state. I don't have time for this shit."

Erica watched his back as he walked away. She could tell that her days at the **Gazette** might be numbered. Right or wrong, it hadn't been the same since she had returned. All the work she had put in fighting for a spot on crime was undone by a two week leave of absence. She had to work out this story on the Incident, get to the bottom of it one way or the other, and hope that whatever she found was enough to impress Weber and Frank and the owners of the paper and get her, at the very least, back on crime.

CHAPTER THIRTY-FIVE

The Derryfield PD was small and spartan, a free standing building that had been erected back in the 1960s beside the Town Hall. The lawn outside was well maintained, and green even through this summer's heat, but the blacktop of the parking lot was cracked like a pair of badly chapped lips. Will eased the truck into the lot, careful to slow over the particularly egregious bumps.

As expected, Lonnie greeted him inside the door where he manned the front desk and what functioned as dispatch, a headset clamped over his gray mane of hair.

"Hey Lonnie," Will asked, "is the Chief in?"

"Nah, sorry Boss," Lonnie replied. A long red Twizzler ran from the corner of his mouth. He always seemed to have one in his mouth or at the ready, poised to strike. "Hebert's in though, if you want to talk with him."

Will knew Chief Blake, but not well. He was a new Chief, brought in as a lateral transfer from one of the other towns in the area — Fremont or Kingston or Newton, Will couldn't remember. Blake was well liked, from what Will could tell, but still wasn't a part of Derryfield. He might be, eventually (he wasn't a flatlander at least), but he wasn't yet. Will figured it would be better to speak with Hebert anyways; he knew the man, and Hebert would understand and believe that something wasn't sitting right with Will.

Will walked over to Hebert's office, one of only two in the tiny department. The patrol officers and two sergeants had to man the desks in the open office space; the only other large spaces in the building were the holding area with a few cells and the large break/training room against the far wall of the building. Hebert didn't see Will enter the room, engrossed as he was with a sheaf of paper from some investigative file. His desk was covered in bounds of paper. The only decoration was a picture on the wall of the Statue of Liberty, an old picture from the looks of it, early twentieth century. Will remembered for the dozenth time that he meant to ask Hebert why that, and nothing else. Instead, he said, "Hey Tom."

Hebert didn't flinch at being called by his first name. He'd known Will long enough — and seen him often enough at Mark's Convenience, the local Shop 'n Stop, or Derryfield Hardware — that the first name basis, when not talking business, police talk, was fine.

"What can I help you with Will?" Hebert shuffled the papers together and placed them in the manila folder on his desk before turning back to Will and smiling. The act further hid his eyes behind his drooping eyelids, giving him the appearance of a happy sleeping man.

"You got a few minutes?"

"Of course. What is it?"

Will wasn't sure how best to share it, to tell Hebert what he had seen and what he had felt. So he started at the beginning. "I was out on a tow on 101 a few weeks back. Last time I was up there. Stanley Lewis's tow." Will nodded as he said this, as if the motion could calm him and reinforce what he was remembering and sharing. He continued, "And I saw something when I was out there."

Hebert clenched his mouth, pulling his lips into a tight thin line. "I heard you got spooked up there Will. I get it, trust me, I do. I heard you were at Stanley's tow. I know you knew him, maybe not close, but I get it. We should've called somebody else. I talked to Dougherty, he told me the whole thing. You get spooked, feeling... close to death. The Highway of fucking Death is right. Especially when it's someone you know. Happens to us too you know, getting a call in town for somebody you know."

"No, Tom, it wasn't that. It wasn't just a feeling." Will took a deep breath. "There was something out there. By the swamps, off the highway. Just... lurking out there. Trying to get at the accident scene. I saw it and then it ran off, back into the swamp. You ever hear of anything like that?"

Hebert shrugged. "I've heard lots of stories. People are always telling me about the things they've seen."

"I'm serious. I saw something out there." Will shook his head. "Something I can't explain."

Hebert stared at Will for a few moments. He squinted one eye, causing it to nearly disappear between the folds of his face. He sighed, leaned back in his chair. "You been hitting the drink, Billy?"

Will's anger was sudden, and surprised even him. It was an anger triggered not only because he was not being believed, but because Hebert would think — would even dare suggest — that the bottle, the very thing that took his father, would take him now. His father had been an excellent example; Will had learned better than that.

"Christ Tom, I wasn't fucking drinking!" Will yelled. He jumped out of the chair and stood for a moment, but the outburst released enough of the tension he felt that he sat down again.

"OK, OK. I'm sorry," Hebert said. He raised his hands to signal his acceptance of what Will was saying. Not believing, Will was certain, but at least accepting it, to hear him out. "So there's something out there, a hungry bear maybe, or a rabid moose let's say. You contact Fish & Game?" he asked.

"Uh, no." Will shook his head.

"Why not? They are the ones to deal with that kind of shit anyways."

"It wasn't a bear, or a moose, Tom," Will said. "If I saw a fucking bear or moose I wouldn't be here."

"Then what was it?" Hebert asked.

"I don't know."

"I told you, I hear this sort of shit all the time, Will. People telling me they've seen some big thing out there. You've got to understand me here, you know what I deal with, right? Drunks and old men and drug addicts stumble in here and tell me they've seen something in the swamps every other day. Invariably it turns out to be a heron, or a moose, or even a goddamn boater out there that someone too drunk or dumb to know better noticed and decided they needed to report it. Maybe the sun was in their eyes, who knows."

"I get that, I do. But it wasn't any of that. I wasn't drunk. It wasn't the sun in my eyes. I saw something out there. I'm not the only one who's seen it. I've heard a few others. We've got to do something, figure out whatever it is that is out there."

"OK," Hebert said, his tone making it clear it wasn't OK and that he didn't believe a word Will said. "Well what do you want me to do about it? You know I only have five officers on during the day, two at night until 3 AM most nights. You want me to get a few of us geared up and tromping around that swamp? What do you think we are going to find? Or do? We shoot the bears and moose out there until we're happy there's no more large animals out there?"

"Jesus, I don't know. I told you it wasn't a goddamn moose, or a bear. Something is fucked out there, I've seen it myself. We've got to do something."

"That's what I'm trying to tell you — even if I was convinced — and let me be clear, I'm not — that something like you said was out there, the Derryfield PD can't do shit about it." Hebert sighed again and waved at his desk and the pile of papers on it. "I'm under enough pressure as it is with this budget and the overtime we've got to pull with the Old Home Days coming up, as well as the 4th parade and fairgrounds from last month. The Chief is on my ass about this every week, cause the Board of Selectmen is on his ass about it. Do you get this? We've got selectmen giving me shit about coverage, residents giving me shit about taxes, and my wife's always bitching me out about getting home late. I don't have the man hours to have us exploring the swamp along the Pilwilla. I don't have much flexibility here, you picking up what I'm putting down?" he asked.

"I get it," Will responded.

"Good. You bring me something more, a safety concern, and I will see what I can do. Your thing out there kills someone, we'll be on it. Until then? Call Fish & Game. See if they can get out here and shed some light on whatever bear or moose or whatever the hell it is out there you saw. OK?"

Will sighed. "Fine, fine. I'll call Fish & Game."

"Let me know what you hear, what they find," Hebert said in a supportive tone. "I'm interested Will, I just can't do anything about this."

"Sure," Will said, and walked out the door, not bothering to look back or say goodbye.

CHAPTER THIRTY-SIX

The Hilltop was, as one would expect on a Tuesday night, rather quiet. A few familiar faces sat the counter nursing what looked to be now-flat beer, and the other fixture, Jerry Marchand, leaning on the bar in hunched conversation with one patron. Jerry raised a hand when Will entered and said, "Billy! Glad to see you back here again. Can I get you something?"

Will glanced up and down the bar, but Oscar wasn't here. He considered heading home but instead took a seat. He drank infrequently; his father's example had taught him early the dangers of frequent consumption. In high school and college Will had preferred a good blunt, and wished he had one now. He felt as though the anxiety and fear that had been birthed that night back on 101 continued to coil around his chest like a python constricting his breathing. He knew he needed to relax, and a drink was certainly the most easily accessible way to do so.

Will glanced at his father's mug, still hanging from the ceiling, and said, "Johnnie Walker Black on the rocks."

Jerry smiled. "Coming right up."

Will rolled his head around to try and ease the pain in his neck and shoulders. The two A/C units in the windows to his left rattled and blew cool air his way. The temperature inside was a only few degrees cooler than outside, but marginally drier and enough to make the bar a bit more comfortable.

Jerry came over with the whiskey and asked how Will was.

"Not right now, Jerry," Will said as he shook his head. "Give me a few minutes."

"Understood my boy." Jerry sauntered over to the other end of the bar and struck up a conversation with one of the patrons there.

It seemed both right and wrong to be in this bar drinking, the bar that took so many of his father's nights away. It felt like a mixture of transgression and fate; that this was where a Boucher should be when he needed a drink, though some part of him wanted to be any place but in this bar. He wondered how many nights his father had been here, thinking the same thoughts he was: what was that thing in the swamp?

A few minutes in and the whiskey helped. Not by making the memory in his mind any clearer or by helping him determine what, if anything, he should do, but simply by calming his nerves and slowing his thoughts. The anxiety in his head and the tension in his shoulders and the lump in his throat receded, if only a fraction. The whiskey went down easier as the minutes passed. Jerry circled around again but Will waved him off and sat brooding over his drink. He imagined his father sitting on the same stool thinking about the same thing, and almost laughed at the one difference: Winston wouldn't have been drinking, if what Oscar had said was true. What had finally sobered up Winston had driven Will to drink.

The bell hanging from the door behind him jangled and a blast of hot, humid air struck his back. Will turned slightly to glance over his shoulder and was surprised to see Erica. He nodded towards her but said nothing. She walked over and said, "Hey."

"Hey," Will responded.

"Can I sit?" Erica asked, motioning towards the empty stool to Will's right.

"Sure." He sipped from his whiskey.

Erica lowered herself on the stool and asked, "What are you drinking?"

"Johnnie Walker Black."

"Not my preference." Erica yelled over for Jerry and ordered a beer. In a few seconds he placed a bottle, head pouring over the top, onto a battered and stained coaster.

"Come here straight from work?" Erica asked as she pointed towards Wills' grease stained t-shirt and dirty jeans.

"Yep. You?" He nodded towards her pleated pants and blouse.

"Yep." They drank for a minute in silence. Will broke their silence by asking, "How'd you know I would be here?"

"I didn't. You think a little too highly of yourself." Erica grinned at him. Will chuckled and she added, "I wasn't looking for you. I'm here hoping to run into Oscar or Becki Corville. Wanted to chat with someone about that... thing out there."

The phrase hung in the air between them alongside the muted conversation, shitty music, and sticky air. Erica considered changing the topic of conversation, while Will thought about simply draining his whiskey and leaving. Instead, both sat there for a minute and studied their respective drinks.

"Listen," Will said breaking the silence. He took a deep breath and continued, "I want to apologize. For, well, giving you the brush off the other day. I, well, it's just that." Will was not certain what to say so he settled on the truth. "I don't know what to do."

"Shit, do any of us?" Erica asked. They laughed a mirthless laugh together.

"The... thing still on your mind?" Erica asked.

"Yeah."

"This might sound weird," Erica said, "but how have you been sleeping?"

Will took a sip of his whiskey. "Not well. I just... I can't get it out of my head. Whenever I close my eyes, I see that thing coming for me."

"Yeah, I know. Pretty much the same here." Erica tried to smile but it didn't come out right; instead of an expression of happiness or joy her face contorted, her lips pulled tight and cheeks up. Will looked away.

"How can just... seeing a thing like that fuck someone up so much?" Will asked. "I mean, I was scared, don't get me wrong but it's like that thing left an impression in my head that I just can't rub out."

"It's not natural," Erica offered. "Something about it isn't right, just doesn't, or can't, sit well I think."

Will took another sip and shrugged. "Why Becki Corville?"

"What?"

"Why Becki? Why would you want to talk to her about this... thing?"

"She says she's seen it."

"Shit." Will cleared his throat. "Well she's not the only one. Corey Barrington, a local kid who lives down the road, he saw it too."

"What? When? Did you talk to him about it?"

"Yeah. A few weeks back, sometime in July. He's pretty shaken up about the whole thing too. He's a good kid."

"I thought you weren't telling anyone about this. You went on and on about how-"

"I know what I said," Will interrupted. "The kid brought it up with me. Came by the shop and was chatty, I don't know why." Will described the conversation he had with Corey and what he had learned.

"I just thought you should know. It just seems like a relief. Two people, who knows, maybe we are both crazy, like lead poisoning or radon or something. But three? That kid Corey saw this thing too. Whatever is out there is real."

"I know it's real," Erica said as she shook her head. "I saw it for Christ's sake."

A new song started on the jukebox. Will could almost recognize it, like a memory just out of reach, more difficult to understand because of the alcohol and anxiety and fear in his blood.

"So, you still want to do something about this?" Will asked as he looked away from her.

"Yes." Erica nodded, took a gulp of the beer, swallowed, and repeated herself. "Yes."

Will turned back to her. "I'm in."

Erica raised her eyebrows and leaned towards him. "Why now?"

"It's still in my head, whatever the hell it is. But, well, you probably already know this, figuring what you were asking Oscar. But my dad saw this thing. And he was looking for it, before he well, passed. Was out there in the marshes, the swamps, multiple times, looking for it."

"Shit," Erica said slowly, drawing out the word.

"Yeah," Will responded. "He thought it worthwhile to try and find this thing. I think I'll do the same. Do him proud in some fucked up way I guess." Will laughed at the absurdity of it: his father, who he hadn't talked to in years prior to his death, now directing him from beyond the grave to search for a monster in the goddamn swamp in Derryfield while he talked about it in the bar his father had nearly drank his life away.

"Be careful if you head out there," Erica said.

"Why?" Will drained the rest of his whiskey while he awaited the answer.

"That thing obviously, but I was out there, off 101 last week on Tuesday morning. I bumped into some men who ran me off with the help of the PD. Told the PD at least they were from the EPA. I'm not sure I believe that, but I do believe they were Feds. I think they're looking for this thing too. I don't know why now all of a sudden, but they're out there too."

Will considered her words, then said, "I uh, went to the PD. Spoke to Hebert over there. He brushed me off, said there's nothing out there. I think he's heard a story or two about it, but seems to think its the ramblings of drunks and such. Doesn't sound like the police will be much of a help."

"Looks like it's just us then," Erica said.

They sat in silence for a minute again, each sipping on their drink and considering not only their next words but their next action. Finally, Will broke the silence. "So what's next for you?"

"We've got to find out more. Find out what this thing is," Erica said before tipping back her drink and draining the rest of it in a single gulp. "I've got some ideas of things to follow up on. Going to do some more research, look back at the archives, on Lexis and anything else I can get my hands on. Look into the highway and any other sightings of this thing."

Will nodded. "Then another round it is." He waved over to Jerry.

"What do we drink for?" Erica asked and smirked towards Will.

"For luck."

CHAPTER THIRTY-SEVEN

When Will closed the shop the last Saturday before his vacation, he felt a sense of anticipation and dread. His father had always closed the shop the second week of August and had chosen the week because his and Mildred's anniversary — August 10th — always fell on it. When Will was younger, they had taken the time together as vacation, traveling to the beach or camping in the mountains. When Will and Daisy grew older, his parents would take the week themselves, leaving him and his sister to fend for themselves. Due to the unfettered freedom Will had enjoyed that time nearly as much as the family vacations.

But this vacation week he was not planning much in the way of relaxation. This week would be the best opportunity he had to follow up on his father's search — now his search — for the thing in the marshes along 101 and out towards the coast. With the shop closed he would have no other pressing responsibilities and could spend each day on the hunt. He remembered that his father had stored at least one canoe up in the rafters of the garage along with a collection of mismatched paddles they had scavenged when Will was young. Will found it and had prepared the canoe and along with it some other gear to take to the rivers of Rockingham County and out to the coast.

Not wanting to waste the little time he had, Will loaded up the canoe, paddles, a life vest, some fishing gear, rope, a lunch and water, along with his father's .357. It had been a few years since he had ventured out to the range and fired it, but he felt more comfortable with it on his hip. He had considered just taking the .38 from the glove box of the F-350, as he had fired that more recently, but had instead ventured through the mess of the garage and retrieved the .357 from the gun safe. He remembered the recoil on the .357 was greater than the .38; he remembered as well the shape and size of the thing in the swamp, and that extra power seemed like a wise precaution. Though the Smith & Wesson had a long barrel, it fit snugly in the holster and lay tight against his hip.

Among the things his father had collected over the years, Will found a Geiger counter — a small yellow box with a handheld attachment and a needle and analog switch. He wondered how much his father had spent on it, along with all of the other survival and camping supplies he had purchased. Luckily, Will located the manual for the Geiger counter not far from the actual unit, and read through it in preparation for his search down the Pilwilla. If the thing was connected to Seabrook and irradiated, the Geiger counter might pick it up.

Lastly, but perhaps most importantly, Will attached a trailer to the F-350 that contained his old Yamaha dirt bike. He'd first drive east to someplace near Hampton Beach and drop the bike, so that after floating downriver and exploring some of the wetlands off the river he could run ashore, hop on the bike, retrieve the F-350, load up and repeat the process the next day.

With the gear all loaded in the back of the F-350 and the trailer hitched, Will first followed the Pilwilla southeast along Route 101 towards Exeter. After dropping the bike off near Hampton Beach, Will turned back west and drove towards the Derryfield Mills. He turned down Mechanic Street south of the mills and parked off the road in a patch of sand. A foot-worn path led down the river. Will knew the path well, having traveled it often as a kid to fish in the river. South of the dam, this spot was never as good, but in actuality no spot had been great; his father had told him it had something to do with all the shit the mill had dumped in the river over the years before the environmental protection laws took hold in the 1970s.

Will double checked his pack, making certain it contained food, water, a compass, and a map, cinched over the neck life vest, and man-handled the canoe down to the riverbank. He was only able to manage it by carrying it over head, and had to step carefully down the slope while he studiously watched his feet. In a final trip back he locked the truck, grabbed his pack and two paddles, and ventured down the slope.

Standing on the north bank, Will could see the four mill buildings to his right. The red-brown bricks of the three story buildings stood out against the blue of the sky and the green leaves of the surrounding trees. He could just spy the dam as a cascade of white water beyond the mill buildings. The falling water sent a fine spray into the air. It smelled of steel and rust and something else that Will could not identify; something unnatural, something man made.

The recent dry spell left the water level of the Pilwilla low: Will saw an assortment of smooth rocks on the far bank, those worked by the river during a wetter season. A few reeds meekly pushed out of the water and trees hemmed in both banks. A small cloud of mosquitoes and black flies hung near his face and he continued to wave them away.

He dropped the front of the canoe into the water, loaded his gear, and climbed in. He pushed off the bank and steadied the canoe with the paddle. It rocked side to side for a moment and Will was afraid it would tip and dump him into the knee deep water, but he crouched down, lowering his center of gravity, and the canoe settled.

His father had been certain the creature was related to Seabrook, but starting the search so close to the ocean would require Will to paddle against the current to search the upper bounds of the Taylor River and Ash Brook and into the Pilwilla, so instead, Will started at Derryfield in the Pilwilla just downstream from the mills and let the current carry him southeast. He would then try Ash Brook, then the Taylor, and finally then venture into the marshes along the Hampton River. Hopefully, somewhere along the way, he'd spy that thing or at least some sign of it, something to photograph and take and show to his mother, to Hebert, to everyone.

As soon as he was past downtown and the mills the insects dissipated. The Pilwilla was wide and shallow here and the current moved slowly. Will occasionally dipped a paddle into the water to keep the canoe towards the center of the river. He scanned both banks and the water, but saw nothing of interest. Besides the mill behind him, there were few structures along the river. A utility pole and power line occasionally poked above the line of trees. Every few minutes he waved the Geiger counter's lead around, but the needle in the display remained steady and the clicks the devices emitted were low and irregular.

The sun hung high overhead, a blinding white orb in an endless blue sky. Only a few wisps of clouds moved across it. The water underneath did not reflect the sky above; it instead was a brackish murky brown that obscured anything a few inches below the surface. Will wasn't sure if the mills upstream contributed to the opacity of the water, or if the heavy sediment and mud of the nearby marsh and bog affected the water quality. He scanned the riverbanks in hopes of finding some sign, some proof of the creature. All he saw were the trees, rocks, and occasional bird or squirrel on the shore. The air was a few degrees cooler on the river and Will did his best to enjoy the trip.

He hadn't been on the Pilwilla since sometime in college. After his second or third year he had returned home one summer and caught up with some friends from high school. They had spent the day on the water, fishing as they had so often in their youth. The trip had left him melancholic. The friends he had known since high school were unchanged, as though the two years working had only been a long weekend before the start of another semester of high school. But leaving Derryfield had altered Will in some way that he was just then beginning to perceive. It wasn't just that he was realizing the world was a bigger place or he knew even less than he had imagined or some other hackneyed cliche. The truth was the time away had served to clarify that these guys from high school weren't friends in the true sense. He didn't like most of them and instead realized they were just the best his small town had to offer.

But now he pushed those thoughts out of his mind and tried to enjoy the water. The twelve mile trip down the river from Derryfield to the coast took him most of the morning. When he neared the coast, Will cut the canoe to the south to venture into the marsh north of Seabrook. The ground was flat with tall grass throughout. The grass was not high enough to hide the buildings or trees far in the distance, but it did work to obscure anything nearby. The grasses swayed and whispered in the wind, a soft hush that came from every direction. The air was brackish with the scent of salt water.

As he floated south the industrial gray dome and boxy buildings of the Seabrook Nuclear Power Plant loomed large. A black sign bleached gray from the sun rose out of the water on a rusted metal spike. The text was difficult to read at a distance, and Will could not tell until he pulled alongside it read:

POSTED
NO TRESPASSING
KEEP OUT

Will glanced around and saw nothing but the sky, the marsh, innumerable blades of grass, and the tops of the power plant behind a stand of trees. He shrugged to himself and paddled forward. The bulky dome of Seabrook grew larger, the spherical top marred by the blocky outcropping along its one side. Will heard a noise ahead, a loud mechanical whirring that he couldn't place.

A rickety wooden dock extended a dozen feet out from the shore and floated on the water of the marsh. A man dressed in the blue slacks and shirt of a laborer's uniform stood on the deck, a cigarette in one hand. He was bald, and the sun was already reddening his white scalp.

"Hey!" the man shouted. He pointed at Will with his free hand and took another step farther out on the dock.

"Hey!" he said again. "You aren't supposed to be out here!"

"Shit," Will said to himself. He paddled more quickly and ducked his head to allow the brim of his hat to obscure his face.

"Hey! Where you going?" the man yelled. He moved briskly off the dock and onto the shore, in a loping haphazard gait that was not quite a run but beyond a walk. The man glanced over his shoulder at Will and pointed to him again, then turned and yelled something in the direction of the power plant.

Will paddled until he turned a slight bend in the waterway. A stand of trees hid all but the top of the buildings of the power plant from view. Will could no longer see the man but he could still hear him, yelling and stomping through the marsh. For a moment it sounded as though the guy was getting closer, but the slight current and Will's frantic paddling increased the distance between them.

Will paddled as quickly as he could away from the plant and out towards the ocean. Once he exited the marsh proper and was back into the mouth of the river the current helped pull him out towards shore. He spied his dirt bike parked by the marina. He directed the canoe over to the shore, careful to keep his distance from the larger boats moving out and into the harbor. After pulling the canoe up besides the rocks near the boat ramp, Will hopped onto the dirt bike and started up Ocean Boulevard to make the trip back to Derryfield to get the Ford.

Will's first trip down the Pilwilla in search of the beast had been unsuccessful. He knew during future trips he would have to keep more distance from Seabrook.

CHAPTER THIRTY-EIGHT

Her father's telephone call concerned Erica. It wasn't just the things he was saying — worrying about her mother again, about her inactivity, her general morosity — it was the way in which he said it. He had spoken quickly, but hushed, and his voice was pitched too high, unlike the slow syrupy drawl he normally voiced. She skipped out of work, nearly ran to her car, and tried not to let her anxiety grow any stronger on the drive over.

As soon as she was in the house Sam closed the door behind her and asked: "Where have you been? We didn't see you at dinner on Sunday."

"I'm sorry, sorry," Erica said and waved a hand in the air. "Work has been very stressful. It's just been tough lately. I've been busy with some-" and here she paused, considering what part of the truth to tell him, "work, a special assignment. It's taken up a lot of my time lately."

"That's fine. You just didn't call us beforehand, and I'm very worried about your mother." He nodded his head towards the rear of the house.

"What now?" Erica asked.

"She's still at home, hasn't returned to work. I know she's got leave time and all, but I don't think this is healthy. I don't know what to do at this point."

"Have you spoken to her doctor? Or called a shrink or something? She might need professional help. Some people do after things like this." It felt better somehow to refer to Nate's death in imprecise language, as though doing so allowed Sam and Erica to avoid thinking of it while they tried to help Judy.

"I tried. I called and they tried to set her up with an appointment with her PCP, but she didn't go. I don't think she's left the house once in the last month. I can't force her to."

Erica shrugged. "What do you think I can do?"

"I don't know? Talk to her some more?" Each sentence was a question. Erica did not know if this was because her father was uncertain she would do it or because he was uncertain it would help.

"And say what?" Erica replied.

"Just try to help. Convince her to get back on the horse so to speak. I don't think this is good for her."

"Fine, I'll try," Erica said. She took a deep breath and sighed. The living room was in the same state it had been since June: her mother reclined in a chair, a TV tray beside her, an ashtray and tumbler on top of the tray. The air smelled strongly of burnt cigarettes. Judy looked over to Erica as she walked in but said nothing.

"Hi Mom." Erica took a seat on the green couch along the back wall, the same couch she had sat and watched cartoons on with Nate for so many years. She did not immediately realize that she sat where she normally did as a child, left hand side, leaving the right hand side free for Nate. She glanced over at the empty space before turning her gaze back to her mother.

Judy said nothing. She continued to watch the TV screen, the images reflected in her eyes.

"Mom?" Erica asked. "Everything OK? Dad said you've been cooped up in here for a while now."

Judy tapped her cigarette on the ashtray before taking another drag.

"Mom, please, what's going on?"

Judy finally spoke: "I see that my only daughter can't even bother to come see me." She shifted in the chair — still reclining in it — to better face Erica. This, at least, was a change; she was engaging with Erica rather than doing her best to ignore her.

"Mom, please, don't do this." Erica shook her head and found it difficult to match her mother's gaze.

"Do what?" Judy snapped. "Expect the bare minimum from my daughter? Don't you think I've been dealing with enough as it is?"

"Jesus, Mom. I was just here the other week and you'd hardly talk to me."

"I think I've been through enough here. I don't need lip from you too."

Erica raised her voice. "When does this end Mom? When does whatever the hell this is... grieving? When does it end?"

The anger was unexpected and enough to quiet her mother's tongue. Judy looked away from Erica and back to the television set, her sudden silence enough a reaction to the outburst. Erica continued, "You don't think Dad and I aren't feeling what you are? You don't think we miss Nate too? We do, we just have to keep going Mom. What's the alternative? We can't just sit here in this house, waiting for our turn."

Judy turned back towards Erica slowly, as though the energy it would take to turn in an ordinary fashion was too much and had to be saved for something else. She saved it for her voice.

"He's dead Erica!" Judy yelled. "He's fucking dead! What the hell and I supposed to do? My baby boy, he's dead!" She cried then, a torrent of tears that erupted from her eyes and slipped down her cheeks in two streams. Erica moved to hug her mother. Judy continued to bawl but put one hand up to keep Erica at a distance, and between heavy sobs said, "No, no."

"What Mom?" Erica asked. "What is it you want from me?"

"Nothing! That's the point! There's nothing we can do. Nate is gone. There's just nothing." She cried even harder now, a heaving from deep in her lungs that caused her shoulders to rise and fall. Her sobs filled the room and seemed thick enough to impress themselves upon the walls, to mark the physical space with her emotion.

Erica shook her head and, fighting back tears of her own, left the room. Sam followed.

"I can't take this anymore Dad," Erica said as soon as they were in the kitchen. The sounds of Judy crying rose over the hubbub of the television and washed into the kitchen. "I can't do this. She's still just... angry at me."

"I don't know hun," Sam said. "I don't think it's anger at you, just at the way things are now. She's just, we've all taken it hard, it's just effecting her the most. She was always close with Nate, you know that."

"Yeah," Erica replied. She thought back to their time growing up together, all the football and baseball games their mother had attended for Nate, all the focus on his academics, how they had even hired tutors his sophomore and junior year to improve his grades in math. In contrast, Erica had done fine in school, had not needed that extra help or extra attention. And, to her credit, Judy had attended some of Erica's soccer games and field hockey games but, whenever there was a conflict, she was sure to be with Nate, cheering him on and helping him succeed.

Erica was disheartened — but not altogether surprised — at the pain and frustration she felt. It wasn't enough that Nate was gone. What compounded her anger was her mother's insistence on mourning him with seemingly no thought to the emotional needs of her daughter, to say nothing of the grief her father was feeling as well. It was as if Nate's death had cast them all adrift, and Judy had no perception of their collective ordeal and could only identify her own disorientation and despair.

"None of this makes any sense," Erica said, motioning with her hand over to the living room, but in her heart meaning everything she found herself in now: her mother's depression; the problems at work; the thing in the marsh.

"I know, I know. We just have to do our best to help her. All she has is us."

"I can't listen to this right now." Erica walked outside to the front porch. The sun was touching the tops of the trees across the road and the evening air was beginning to cool. Erica heard laughter from kids playing a few houses over and smelled steak cooking on a nearby grill. It all appeared too normal. A happy summer night. The Couture's world was in shambles, and the world at large didn't give a damn. Sam followed her out onto the porch and pulled the front door shut behind him.

"Nice night," he said.

"Yeah," Erica replied, not really meaning it. She wanted a cigarette or a drink or a hit of something, anything to put some distance between herself and what she was feeling and thinking and not understanding.

"I've got to go. I can't help her right now. I think we need to call the doctor again. We really need to get her seen. Would a doctor come to the house? There must be some that still make house calls, especially for situations like this."

"Yeah, maybe," Sam said. "I'll make some calls. Ask around work — discretely — if there's anyone people can recommend."

They stood on the porch and talked for a few minutes and watched the sun dip behind the trees. The shadows grew longer. After a few minutes Sam suggested he return inside to attend to Judy and make them both something to eat.

"Do you want to stay for dinner?" he asked.

Erica considered it and thought that it might help ease the tension between her and her mother, but instead said, "No, I can't. Work to do. But call me if anything changes. Love ya."

"Love you too," Sam said, raising a hand as she walked to her car.

Erica left. She rolled all the windows down and was again assaulted with the sounds of summer fun. She thumbed on the radio, tuned into a rock station, and turned the music up. She drove back towards the office.

She wondered if the thing she had seen had any connection to her brother's death. Had his accident been caused in some way by that creature? The despair she carried from his passing was slowly sloughing off, and Erica was surprised to find something new beneath it: equal parts fear and fury. She was afraid of that thing, but if it had something to do with Nate's accident, she was sure as hell going to kill it.

And if she couldn't find the thing by searching the marsh in person, she'd do it in the best way she knew how: by searching for it on paper, in the history of Derryfield and the Highway of Death.

CHAPTER THIRTY-NINE

Will was uncomfortable. Sweaty, muddy, and disappointed that yet another visit to the marshes and swamps and rivers of Derryfield and beyond had come to nothing. His father was certain that thing could be found out in the swamp, and Will was certain of it now too, notwithstanding the failures over the last week. Five days out there for nearly six hours each day had resulted in nothing of significance, aside from the close call with some of the staff from Seabrook and a few spikes from the Geiger counter, none of which Will could attribute to anything he had seen in the waters.

He didn't know what he would do next. The impact of his failure was lessened by the knowledge that his father had also failed despite trying for far longer. He would have to try again, to change something, maybe set some bait or even a wildlife camera to try and catch footage of it.

The air running through the truck cab helped but wasn't enough to entirely counter the heat and humidity. Will desperately wanted to change out of his clothes and enjoy a long cool shower and order a pizza from Derryfield Pizza. Will brushed his sweat sheened hair away from his forehead and thought again that he needed to get it cut. That — along with much else — had fallen to the wayside while he searched the swamps.

A Derryfield cruiser sat in the Will's driveway. The driver's side window was open and an arm stretched out with a lit cigarette held between the index and middle fingers. The end glowed like a firefly in the dying light. Will pulled up alongside the car and glanced inside. Tom Hebert.

The truck sat a few feet above the cruiser, so Will leaned over and greeted Hebert. Hebert raised his right hand in response, took a long drag off the cigarette with his left, and exited the cruiser. Will turned the truck off and slipped out of the cab.

"Thought you gave those up," Will said, nodding towards the lit cigarette.

"Thought I did too," Hebert said. "But the job is killing me, all this bickering over the budget and the union contract and all that. Gotta let out the stress somehow." He took another drag then tossed it to the ground and rubbed it out with the sole of his shoe.

"How's the shop?" Hebert asked.

"Closed this week, vacation. Could always be better, you know how it is."

"Yep. And your mother?"

"The same — wish she was better, but you know how those things go."

"I do. It's a fucked up thing, seeing someone go like that. Happened to my father same sort of way."

Will nodded, then said, "What's up, Tom? What are you doing here?"

"Just checking in."

"What about?"

"I'm worried about you," Hebert said. He glanced over at the canoe and dirt bike in the trailer behind the Ford. "I hear you've been out in the swamp, looking for your — what did you call it?" He shrugged. "Whatever it was."

"I'm fine, Lieutenant," Will said flatly.

"You been out there today?" When Will didn't respond, Hebert continued, "You certainly look the part." He pointed at Will's stained overalls and the pistol on his hip.

"What's with the weapon?"

"It's a free country, right?"

"Of course it is, but this seems like something new. I can't recall ever seeing you wearing a piece."

Will shrugged. "Seemed like a good idea. Still does."

Hebert pointed to the canoe. "You out in that? Are you paddling the whole way? You don't even have an outboard on it."

"Why do you care?" Will asked. "Well, ordinarily I wouldn't," Hebert said. "I'm all for enjoying the outdoors though, Christ its been a hot summer. But anyways, I got a visit from some Feds this morning. Came right down to the station, apparently making the rounds throughout the area, visiting Exeter and Hampton and Seabrook and everywhere else. They were here asking about some guy who's been up in the marsh. Over near Seabrook. By some of that protected wetlands. They said it was a slim guy, brown hair, wearing overalls, coasting by in a canoe. That sound familiar to you?"

"No," Will lied.

"See, the thing is Will, I don't believe you. You've told me as much you think there's something out there. I get it — well, maybe I don't, but the point is, you think you've got to do something about whatever it is you think you've seen."

"So you willing to hear me out about that thing out there?"

"Jesus Will, I already did. I don't know what you think you saw, but you can spend all your damn free time out in the swamps if you want, just stay away from the power plant for Christ's sake. I'm here as a friend. I told the Feds I hadn't heard anything about it nor seen anybody out there. I figured it was you but I didn't give 'em your name. But somebody has seen you out there, in places I guess you shouldn't be. You understand my concern now?"

"Who was it?" Will asked. "Who came to the office? The Feds, I mean."

"Some agents from the NRC — Nuclear Regulatory Council or something."

"Commission?" Will offered. He sought to conceal his surprise and interest. Will only knew the agency thanks to the piles of literature on nuclear power plants his father had amassed in the years before his death. Will had been leafing through it in the evenings after dinner, trying to make sense of his father's journal and all of the magazines and other articles on nuclear power he had collected. If it was something from Seabrook that created that thing in the swamp, someone from the NRC would know.

"Yeah, that's the one," Hebert said. "Two of their 'specialists' came by to speak with me. Like I said, guess they've been making the rounds near the Seacoast, inquiring with local officials. So I'll ask again: you been out in that area?"

"You going to arrest me?" Will ask and held his hands out as if to allow Hebert to cuff him.

"Christ Will. Would I be speaking to you if I was going to? It's me and not those two suits here."

Will sighed. "Not purposefully," he said. "I've been out in the swamps and the marsh, down the Pilwilla. I have just been doing some... recon I guess. I got a little close to Seabrook once."

"So you've got to cut that shit out." When Will remained silent, Hebert said, "I mean it. This is some serious shit."

"Or what?"

"I'll throw you in the goddamn drunk tank, that's what I'll do. For your own damn good."

"I haven't been fucking drinking, I've told you," Will snapped.

"It's getting to the point that I don't care," Hebert said, and cut Will's response off with a wave of his hand. "You're gonna be in worse shit if you don't start listening. I don't know why you've got this bug up your ass, and frankly, well I do care, but I don't care what's motivating your behavior right now. I need you to stop. Do you understand?"

"I hear what you're saying," Will said.

"Then will you stop for God's sake?"

"Will you help me find this damn thing?"

Hebert sighed. "Listen to me Will. There is nothing out there. *Nothing*," he said, stressing the word. "You know how long I've been on this police force?"

"Thirty-five years?"

"Thirty-eight. I've heard shit from all manner of people. Strange things they've seen. Scared people telling me scary stories about creatures in the dark and whatnot. Stories about killers and ghosts and God knows what else. And not once have I seen anything that matches what all these people have told me over the years. Or anything like what you've described. And I've been out in these streets, along the river and the marshes and all that for years. There's nothing there, Will."

"I don't mean there's nothing to this, to whatever it is you're going through. Stress can do things to people, make them see things. I've seen tweakers hallucinating about seeing angels and demons and all sorts of shit. Hell, I don't talk about it much, but my own son had some issues in high school twenty years back, had some well, mental issues, thought he was seeing things. But there was nothing to it. We got him some treatment and that was the end of it."

Will took a few more steps towards the house and said, "You didn't see it Tom. You didn't see what I fucking saw."

Hebert shook his head. "You're just as stubborn as your old man. He'd never listen to a damn thing I said to him about it either." He laughed and smirked at Will while he shook his head.

Will froze on the second step. Even in the humid air, under the wet heavy clothes he wore, a chill began at the base of his skull and worked its way down his spine. Will turned slowly and stared at Hebert, as if he looked hard enough he could discover some truth beyond the folds of the man's face.

"Did he talk to you about this?" Will asked. "Did he mention this thing to you?"

Hebert sighed again. "Yes, he did. Well at least something like what you're telling me. Some big thing out in the swamp, tromping around. As have a few others. I told you, ever year I hear about strange things all throughout Derryfield, including a monster in the marshes and the bog. Up and down the Pilwilla. And it never amounts to a hill of beans. Never found anything to support it. But the fine people of Derryfield call me and tell me they see something in the sky, they see something in the road, they hear something in their backyard. And what I find is a plane overhead, a deer in the road, and a fisher cat in their backyards. And Christ, like I just told you, probably half the time, they're drunk or high or stressed out of their mind for one reason or another."

"I wasn't drunk." Will repeated. "I don't know how many times I have to tell you that. I was stone cold sober. There's something unnatural out there. And I'm going to find it." Will shook his head and took a moment to choose his words carefully.

"You either help me Tom, or get out of my fucking way. I'm going to find that thing, with or without your help."

Hebert said nothing. He crossed his arms across his chest and nodded his head.

"If that's all, you can get the hell off my property." Will went inside without waiting for a response and closed the door behind him. Tom returned to the cruiser and before he left, lit another cigarette for the road.

CHAPTER FORTY

Erica's desk phone rang twice rapidly in succession, a tone she knew meant an interoffice call. She picked it up and was surprised to find Weber on the line.

"Good morning Ms. Couture."

"Good morning Mr. Weber."

"Please meet me in my office." He hung up before Erica could respond. Weber had made similarly cryptic calls for the past two weeks, choosing a different time of the day for each call. Each summons had resulted in Erica appearing in his office to deliver a verbal or written update to Weber concerning her research on the Route 101 story and how it was — or rather, might be — connected to the Exeter Incident. She was now bemused by his interest, but tolerated it because that interest seemed to be the only thing keeping the story alive. She needed to chase this, and as long as she was getting paid to do so, well that was just a bonus.

This time when she arrived at the office a man she didn't recognize sat in a chair before Weber's desk. He was tall and thin and his hair was cut close, nearly making his scalp entirely visible. He wore a military uniform that Erica recognized as Air Force, the pants and shirt starched and pressed. The man turned slightly as Erica entered and glanced at her with an upturned eyebrow. He said nothing and then turned back to Weber.

"Ms. Couture," Weber said, then cleared his throat. He made no effort to introduce the stranger. "I've reviewed what you provided to me last week." He waved a sheaf of paper. "I see now that the concerns voiced by Mr. Harris were not exaggerated."

"Excuse me?"

"You don't recall? He was concerned about your focus here."

"Who is this?" Erica asked motioning towards the uniformed man.

"This is Captain Billings. He's from the US Air Force," he said smugly.

"Why is a Captain from the Air Force here about my draft article?"

Billings raised his hand to stop Weber from responding and fielded the question. "I understand, Ms. Couture, that you have been speaking with witnesses of the incident of September 3, 1965."

"Yes? So? What of it?"

"I'm simply interested in what you have learned," Billings said in an even tone. "You know, of course, that the Air Force was involved all those years ago. We took statements and investigated the claims. We still have a lingering interest in this matter," he said this last bit with a sigh, clearly bored of the assignment and annoyed at the time it took away from whatever an Air Force captain did on a Wednesday morning in August.

"What do you want?" Erica asked. The words came out too quickly, her tone too sharp. She took a deep breath and tried to calm herself.

"I want to know what you've heard. What you've learned. Our presence here in the area — I mean the Air Force's presence here of course — has been somewhat reduced since the closure of the base in 1991."

"You've read what I wrote?"

"Yes, Mr. Weber here was gracious enough to provide me an opportunity to review the copy he has there," Billings responded.

"Then you know what I know."

"Well," Billings said, and turned more in his chair to better face Erica, "I've heard that you have been speaking to some persons retired from the Air Force, asking about what they knew."

"Yes, and?" Erica said and shrugged her shoulders. She knew her discussions with Hutchinson were above the board. She had identified herself and backed off when he resisted her questioning. He certainly hadn't offered anything of substance, and now she knew why. He had kept his lips shut and then communicated with someone at the Air Force to inform them of her inquiry. Which was troubling, but interesting. Why did the Air Force care what she asked about a 30 year old UFO sighting?

"And I've heard that you had something of a close encounter yourself." Billings smirked at this statement, amused at his own humor.

Erica frowned.

"So you've heard of that, thing out there," Erica said. "You know there is something out there. Something in the swamps near the Pilwilla River."

Billings chuckled. He adjusted his tie. "I know people claim to see things everyday, and most everything they claim to see is — pardon the term — horse shit. Still, I'm interested to know what you believe you saw, if for no other reason than to close out this damned file so I can get back to D.C."

Erica paused to consider what she would say. She could lie, but reasoned that it wouldn't do any good: she had said enough to Frank and Mr. Weber, and all that had likely been shared with Billings already.

"Yes, I was out there. Off Route 101. It was late. I was tired and.... I thought I saw something. I'm not sure, but I thought I saw something out in the marsh."

Billings leaned forward, eyes a bit wider, following Erica closely. She could sense that he was carefully listening to every word despite his proffered disinterest. This manufactured indifference bothered her; he clearly was more interested in what she had to say than he wanted her to realize.

"What was it?" he asked.

"I don't know."

"A bear?" he offered. "Perhaps a moose?"

"No, it wasn't a bear, it wasn't a moose," Erica said. "You don't think I stopped to consider that?" She shook her head and her eyes became unfocused, her gaze inward rather that at either of the men in the room with her.

"I didn't get a great look at it. It was dark, remember. But it was like nothing I've ever seen. Large and fast. More than four limbs I think. And a big mouth."

When Billings raised his eyebrows in disbelief, Erica repeated herself. "I don't know. It was late. It was dark. I saw something but I don't know what it was."

"Then let me ask it this way: what do you think it was?"

"What does this matter anyways?'

"I'm just following orders ma'am," Billings said. He smiled again, a half grin that showed the teeth on the right side of his face. He meant it to be endearing, an "oh shucks" mannerism to communicate a shared frustration over their respective bosses' expectations. Again, Erica found it off-putting. He was suave — and attractive, with a strong jaw and clear blue eyes — but even though his mannerisms seemed well practiced they carried a hint of inauthenticity.

"What are you going to do about it? Are you going to get some men out there and find it? That thing could be dangerous. It's huge. We've got to figure out what it is, track it, study it or maybe capture it or something, understand it at least."

Billings shook his head and smirked again. "It's just me here Ms. Couture. Even if I believed what you are telling me, that there is some large creature out there along the Pilwilla, I certainly wouldn't be out there myself in this uniform."

"But you could call in more men, right?" Erica realized her voice was rising again and she fought to control the urgency and anxiety rising through her chest and tightening her throat.

"You could get the military here to find it. The area itself isn't that large, the river and the marshes and all, it can't be more than 20 square miles or so."

"Ma'am," Billings began and sighed, "if there was something out there like you think there was, don't you think we would have already found it? This is New Hampshire, not the Amazon."

"Fine," Erica replied, "But what about those EPA agents out there off 101? They are looking for this thing too, right? You talk to-"

Billings interrupted her. "I think I've heard enough." He stood and nodded to Weber. "I want to thank you for your time Mr. Weber," the nodded to Erica, "and you Ms. Couture." He turned back to Weber and said, "Please be in touch should you learn anything else of note."

Erica watched him closely as he passed by her on his way out the doorway. He walked out without catching her eye or turning towards her.

Mr. Weber and Erica waited a few moments until Billings had traversed the hall and was on his way down the stairs.

"What's this all about? When did he get in touch with you?" Erica asked.

"It's not important," Weber said dismissively.

"It's not important? Why the hell is an Air Force captain coming into the Derry-fucking-field *Gazette* about a retread of a story that's nearly 30 years old?"

"Watch your language."

Erica shook her head. "That doesn't answer my question."

"I don't know the answer to your question," Weber said. "Captain Billings was not very forthright with his answers to my questions."

Erica could sense something different about Weber. Previously, all conversations with him were punctuated by Weber's smug self pleasure in speaking and commanding the conversation. His attitude was consistent, so much so that it became obvious on some level that the way in which he approached a conversation was a pretense. But that air was not present now. Weber did not meet her eye.

"Back to this draft, Ms. Couture. I am not looking for an opinion piece here, nor your subjective feelings on the matter. I need objective reporting. Stick to what was originally assigned: the highway and yes, its significant fatality rate, and the factors that contribute to it, such as the undivided aspect of the highway and the kind of traffic it sees. Please excise anything related to this so called 'sighting' of a creature."

"You're just trying to bury this," Erica said. "You want this to go away. Or he does. Billings doesn't want the story published as is. Why?" She nodded towards Weber, waiting for a response, then said again quickly, "Why?"

Weber crossed his arms against his chest and rested them on his ample stomach.

"Excuse me Ms. Couture, but you will watch your tone — and your accusations — when speaking to me. If you value your job in the slightest that is."

Erica wasn't certain what to say. She shook her head and stared at him. Weber sat unmoved in his chair and held her gaze.

"Again, you didn't answer my question."

"And you are not here to ask questions of me, nor to receive answers. You are here to listen to criticism, accept it, and change this story as the editors and owners of this paper direct you."

"So you've handed this over to him?" Erica asked to Weber.

"Excuse me?"

"You already have me coming here, rather than to Frank. Should I be going to Billings for this now?"

"Enough!" he yelled. He lurched to his feet. It was a slow, awkward movement. He first slipped his hands far back on the rests on the side of the chair in order to push with his legs and arms at the same time. "I've had enough of your poor behavior. Another word and you'll be suspended without pay for a week. Get back to work."

Erica said nothing and left, though there was plenty she wanted to say.

CHAPTER FORTY-ONE

Corey had called Alex's house several times in the last two weeks and had only spoken with Mrs. Marino. Each time she had told him that Alex was there, but didn't want to speak with him. Each time she didn't ask Corey to elaborate, or explain why Alex didn't want to speak with him. Her apparent disinterest in the rift between them bothered Corey — not as much as his friend refusing to take his call — but bothered him still the same. He thought she should do something, try in some way to get their friendship back on track.

This new loneliness reinforced his wish that he had been friendlier with more of the other kids in his classes. Corey got along well enough with most of them but never managed to form the same kind of connection with them as he had with Alex. Corey had invited a few of them over during the school year, after school or on a weekend. But each visit had ended in awkward goodbyes and the boys had never asked to come over again and Corey had never extended the invitation again on his own.

The long summer days grew even longer now without his friend to share them with. Alex's absence wasn't like before, when he was traveling and visiting family, a known temporary separation that Corey longed to end. Now, Corey wasn't sure when — of even if — they would start hanging out again. The prospect of the rest of the summer without Alex seemed unbearable.

It was Saturday, which again meant chores. Corey finished mowing the lawn just before noon and reported back to his father. Their conversation was short and terse; Ted was distracted with the chainsaw he was tinkering with. Corey managed to get his allowance for completing his assigned chores, and then meandered down to Mark's Convenience for a snack and a Coke. The cap from his last Coke was tight against leg in his front pocket. It was his fourth free winner; his luck here at least remained strong. He purchased a can of Pringles and a Coke and enjoyed the salty chips with the sweet soda.

After a handful of chips and a few sips of soda, Corey walked down to Derryfield Auto. As he neared the circle he could hear the sound of impact wrenches and the solo from Zeppelin's *Stairway to Heaven*. The bell over the door rang when he pulled it open and stepped inside. No one was in the office. Corey noticed the nose of a green car and a cardboard box just outside the door to the garage.

"I'll be right with you!" Will yelled from the garage. A minute later he came out from the back. The front of his blue shirt was black with grime. He wiped his hands and forearms with a rough red rag.

"Hey kid, what are you doing here?" Will asked.

"Hey Will, I just..." Corey started. He stood there, a soda in one hand and can of Pringles in the other, his brow furrowed, uncertain what to say. He had thought many times about coming down to talk with Will about the thing out there, about what they should do. But he had not given thought to exactly what he would say, nor how he would broach the subject. Facing Will now, a man he knew little more than a stranger, Corey searched for the right words.

"Everything OK?" Will asked. He took a step forward and leaned against the counter on his left elbow.

"Yeah. Can we talk about the monster in the marsh? I think we should do something. Like, mount an expedition. Find it, or evidence of it, you know?"

Corey could see that Will was surprised by his words. Will crossed his arms over his chest and let out a long breath. He glanced over his shoulder back into the garage.

"Does he know? The other guy that works here?" Corey asked. He knew the shop had at least one other employee; he'd seen the man working as well as riding his motorcycle to and from the shop. Will shook his head.

"Robert. No, he doesn't. But it's not just us who does. Do you know Erica Couture? She's a reporter at the *Gazette*, the local paper. She knows. We've talked about it. She wants to go out and search for it some more. I've already been out there myself, kid. The shop was closed earlier in the month, and I was out there nearly every day. I didn't see anything, not a trace of it."

Corey took a sip of his soda and considered this. "Maybe you aren't looking in the right place."

The phone rang. Will held up his hand to Corey. "One minute."

Will answered the call and Corey took a seat in one of the three stained chairs. He glanced through the stack of magazines on the small coffee table but found nothing that interested him. When Will finished the call he stepped back beside the counter and called to Corey.

"I think it's important that we like, find this thing," Corey said.

"I get it, I do. I tried talking to the police but they didn't believe me. I tried looking for it myself. But what did you mean about looking in the right place?"

"Well I've been talking to Mimi — Ms. Gagnon — and she's heard stories about this thing. Going back years she says. Has something to do with the mill, like all the pollution that comes out of it. I think the monster lives in the bog near the mill. I asked around at the mill too. My dad works there, so I went in with him one day. Talked to an old guy there, he had heard stories about it in the swamp too. I think it's near the mill. Have you been looking there?"

"Well, not really," Will said, surprised and slightly amused with himself that he was taking Corey's criticism seriously and responding. He was impressed with the kid. "I mean, I traveled down the Pilwilla, but I don't think it's as much up here in the bog as it is down by Seabrook, down in the marshes by the Hampton River."

"Why do you think it's down there?"

"I don't think it's the mills, but the power plant. Maybe its drawn to the plant cause of the radioactivity. But I've been searching the whole Basin, from Derryfield down to Seabrook."

"We need to find it," Corey said in a low voice.

Will felt a pang of sympathy for the kid. Whatever the hell this thing was, it had shaken Will up. He hadn't even stopped to consider how it might be affecting Corey.

"How you holding up?" Will asked. "Is it on your mind a lot?"

"Yes," Corey said in the same low voice. He was scared of it, whatever it was, but intrigued, and wasn't sure how to communicate this to Will. "I need to do something about it. I don't know why. I've walked the marsh as much as I can all around the highway, looking for it. I need proof. I need to show my dad and Alex."

"I get it, trust me I get it," Will said. He grimaced and cracked the knuckles on his right hand.

"So what are we going to do?"

"Nothing right now. I've got to get back to work. I can't do anything right now." Will shrugged.

"Then when?" Corey asked.

"I don't know. I'll let you know." Will took a few steps towards the door back into the garage and kept an eye on Corey, expecting him to do the same by moving towards the doorway to the circle. When he didn't move, Will asked: "Anything else right now? I really do have to get back to work."

Corey was angry. He felt Will was brushing him off, downplaying whatever it was they had seen. He scowled. When Corey didn't move or say anything, after a moment Will walked to him.

"Corey. I'll let you know what's next, OK? Whatever that is, it's just not right now."

"OK," Corey said.

He left the shop feeling no better than when he had walked in. He hoped that at least the two of them would do something about it. As he considered Will's words, Corey ate more of the Pringles and finished off the Coke while he walked over to Fort Barren. He stayed busy by working on the fort. He hoped to have the roof completely finished, and maybe even another ladder along a limb and down the other side of the trunk as another way, an emergency exit, to leave the tree house. But though the work helped the sun along its axis, it brought little joy to Corey. He had always meant for the Fort to be a project to complete with Alex.

As he worked, Corey continuously checked the woods surrounding the Fort. He had only seen the thing that one night; he reasoned that if it was out during the day, many more people would have seen it by now and it would be known, cataloged, like another coelacanth or other Jurassic fossil still alive despite the rigors of time. Even still, Corey wasn't completely comfortable without checking around every few minutes, listening carefully to the forest for any signs of that creature approaching.

After an hour or so of working on the fort, Corey grew bored and walked the surrounding forest. He again explored the edges of the marsh where the Pilwilla fed into the low lying swamp in hopes of finding some evidence of the creature. He stayed on the North side of Route 101. The cars on the highway whizzed by, the distance between them only feet. The two lane highway looked treacherous, especially so from the angle above and behind it Corey viewed it from. It looked as if the passing cars would collide, but they drove on, the driver's ignorant to the near death experience they barely avoided.

Corey's searches however, again proved fruitless. He wasn't sure what exactly he was looking for, but figured he would know when he saw it. Perhaps a footprint, or an egg, or droppings from the creature. After an afternoon of unsuccessful searching, Corey emerged from the forest dirty and sweaty and hungry. A meal and shower later, Corey had *MonsterVision* to look forward to. This Saturday was a special monster marathon, four movies from 8 PM to 4 AM. Corey doubted he would be able to stay awake for all four, but Ted was always more lenient on Saturdays and would let him stay awake until at least midnight, and, if Corey was lucky and Ted fell asleep before him, as long as he could manage.

The first movie that night was *The Thing*. Corey watched with interest the story of the Air Force officers in the Arctic fighting against the plant-like alien from a crashed saucer. He took careful note of the way in which the men dispatched the Thing with electricity. It had a weakness, and once understood, the service men were able to kill it.

The Blob was next. Corey hadn't seen this film, but recognized the title. He remembered his mother talking about it, and her love of the lead actor, Steve McQueen. His mother and father had talked about seeing it at a drive-in theater one summer in the late seventies when they were first dating. Sandra had talked about her love of the movie; Ted had talked about how he liked when Sandra had moved in closer during the frightening scenes when the blob was enveloping someone. As with *The Thing*, Corey studied *The Blob's* climax. Here it was not electricity but cold that killed the beast.

The next was *The Monster that Challenged the World*, but by then Corey was starting to drift off. He had the foresight to lower the volume and fell asleep before the blueish hum of the television set. He slept uneasily that night, his dreams full of creatures both imagined and real.

CHAPTER FORTY-TWO

They considered meeting back at the Hilltop, but after Erica explained that she had a number of things to show Will that might not be best to discuss in public, they decided to meet at the shop after close. Will was tidying up the desk when Erica pulled up outside.

"You're not going to fucking believe this," were the first words out of Erica's mouth. She smiled, but it was forced and little more than a small lift of the corner of her lips.

"Believe what?" Will asked as he shut and locked the door behind her.

"The Air Force are back on this. I've been questioning some of the men who served at Pease back in the '60s. None of them talked to me, but I think they sent it back up the chain of command. Had a captain on my ass at the paper, came right in and sat down with my boss's boss with me."

"Shit..." Will said. Erica described to him the conversation with Weber and Captain Billings. Will sat quietly, listening to her words without interruption. When she finished, Will shared his interaction with Hebert at the Derryfield PD and how Hebert had brushed off Will's concerns.

Will sighed heavily. "Listen, I've been out there a few times, looking for it. Hebert tried to talk me out of doing that as well."

"When were you out there!" Erica yelled. "Why didn't you tell me?"

"I just wanted to get out there, get a feel for the area, see if I could find signs of it."

"I could have been there with you! You shouldn't go alone!"

"Why?" Will shrugged.

"Because Will, I know where that thing is, or at least, where it spends some of its time."

"Where?" Will asked, his face contorted to express his skepticism in Erica's pronouncement.

"It's out by the Overpass to Nowhere."

He laughed, but like Erica's smile earlier, the laughter held no mirth. "Apt. But how do you figure that?"

"Well," Erica said as she opened her satchel and rifled through it, "I pulled all the records I could find on accidents along Route 101. I focused on all the fatals I could find." She flipped through the pages in a manila folder before brandishing one and centering it on the table before them. It was a map of the southern tier of the State, and she set it down oriented for Will, north facing up. Approximately three dozen blue dots peppered the map, all along a thin line identified as Route 101.

"Fuck," Will said. "I've pulled I don't know, eight or nine fatals out of Route 101. I was called to fucking Stanley Lewis's just last month. I wonder if this thing had something to do with it."

Only moments before he said it the connection struck Will. "Erica, do you think this thing could have caused your brother's accident?"

Erica glared at him but Will didn't think her anger was directed at him.

"Maybe," she said. "Could be. I haven't figured that for sure, but I think it's possible. Some of the accidents must be natural, as in, no influence from this fucking thing. But certainly some must have been caused by it."

"Jesus, I'm sorry. So its causing at least some accidents on 101. We can be certain of that."

Erica nodded, her face still hard. "But that's not it. See here," she said, pointing to Derryfield, "The worst of it is here, right around Derryfield. More fatals here. And not just fatals on the highway. I thought to myself, what other weird shit could be going on? So I looked to see what I could find in the archives. Asked some of the other reporters who've been here a while, to see what they could recall. Checked through some of the microfiche. It's not just fatals on the highways, there's been more suicides along 101 than elsewhere in the state, per capita."

"See," she continued, hands now before her like a conductor preparing to lead an orchestra, "I thought maybe it wasn't just on the road. That it would be elsewhere; something else could be affected. It must be hungry, right? What if it's going after people out there alone? I figured there'd be other deaths, lost pets or something, but it's not that. It's also suicides, and I can't figure out why."

In his mind, Will pictured it again: a grotesque beast hunched to the ground and edging towards the puddle of blood at the scene. A reflection of the fear he felt then returned, like some long lost echo rebounding off a distant shore and carrying with it a shade of the original.

"Maybe," Will began, already disliking the idea forming in his mind, "it's people that have seen it? People who just can't, uh, shake it? Puts them over the edge?"

For the first time, Will focused on Erica's face and not the map before them and recognized what he felt in her. Erica worked her jaw back and forth as she ground her teeth together and her eyes were pinched tight, as if she was leaning into a dusty wind.

"I... I don't know," Erica said. "Maybe. Maybe it's something else."

"You suggesting it can sense someone's suicidal tendencies? Like smelling their emotion or something?"

"I don't know. How am I supposed to even guess at this?" Erica raised her voice and shoulders in unison.

"Jesus Christ," Will said. "What the fuck is it?"

"Again, I don't know. I don't think anybody does. But I think it's drawn to this place. Causes all these deaths in some way, pushes the needle in that direction. Enough to make a statistical difference. Maybe it means to, but maybe not. It's just an effect it has on its environment."

"Like it's some fucking ghost or something."

"Not a fucking ghost Will. We've both seen this thing, heard it. It's flesh and blood."

"I know, I know. But what?"

"I don't know!" Erica said. She threw her hands up and shook her head at Will. "Maybe some undiscovered creature. Like the that thing out in Scotland-"

"The Loch Ness Monster," Will added.

"Yeah that, or Bigfoot. Maybe it's something from the Exeter Incident, something left behind. Maybe something from Pease, something they captured, something that got loose once the base closed. I don't fucking know. But it's here. We've both seen it."

"Like something out of the fucking *Weekly World News*," Will said. "Jesus. I don't think I'll be reading that again." He rubbed his forehead and added, "I think it's something from Seabrook. Something that got irradiated. Like a... I don't know, a mutant seal or something. It lives in the bogs and crawls out to feed."

"Maybe," Erica said. "But I think it's been here longer than Seabrook — the increase in fatalities and suicides goes back further than the completion of the plant."

Will rubbed his head again. He stared at the map. "Whatever it is, it definitely likes the water."

"Why?" Erica asked.

"Well look at what you plotted here," Will said as he pointed to the map before them. "Every single one of these dots is pretty close to some body of water. Most of them next to one of the swamps along Route 101 here. Look at this cluster here," Will continued as he moved his finger across her map towards a blue cluster of dots in Derryfield, "I don't think it's the Overpass to Nowhere it's drawn to. Look at that cluster you identified near the overpass — that's right near the Brown Stump Bog past the mill. Just so happened the Overpass is right along the rise beyond the Bog."

"And these others here," Erica said, picking up on Will's suggestion, "These are all around rivers or swamps and such." She traced her finger on a line up to the Great Bay Estuary. "And some along the bay too."

"Almost all of it along Route 101," Will said.

"Yep," Erica replied. Will stood with his hands on his hips; Erica with her arms crossed. Both looked down and pursed their lips, comfortable with the momentary silence as each processed this new information.

"Who have you told about this?" Will asked.

"About the deaths and the suicides? The location of it?" When Will nodded, Erica added, "Just you."

"Clearly the Air Force knows something. Like I told you, the PD are at least aware that the Feds are out there looking into something in the swamps. If I believe your theory, if I believe that this thing is somehow causing those deaths out along 101 — what makes you think we can do anything that the Air Force won't? Let's just let them have at it. They'll send somebody out there, take care of it, right?" He shrugged and ran both hands slowly through his hair.

"No, because they aren't interested, not really. I pushed this Billings character on it, asked him if the military was going to send anyone out there. But he just wants to sink my story. Somebody is here in New Hampshire on it, but I think they're here to sweep it under the rug, just like they did 30 years ago."

"Who cares? If they get rid of that thing out there, who cares if they sweep it under the rug?"

"Aren't you interested in it in the slightest?" Erica said. "Look what I just showed you. What happened to the whole, finishing off what your father started? They don't want us out there because they don't want us to know what it is."

Will tried to ignore an initial burst of anger which followed her mention of his father and instead considered her words.

"What the hell can we do that they can't?"

"Dammit Will, we have to do something. I just showed you that this thing somehow kills people, or drives them to suicide or something. It's been fucking with this area of New Hampshire for years. We need to fucking stop it."

When Will didn't respond, Erica said, "You still having those dreams?"

Will looked down at his feet. "Yes," he answered.

"Me too. I can't get it out of my head. So let's stop it, get it out of our heads."

"Even if I agree, and we don't leave this to the Air Force or the EPA or whatever, what do we do? Try to kill it? Capture it? What's the endgame here?"

"We fucking kill it," Erica said. "We end it. It's doing something. Hunting or eating or driving people mad. It's not... natural. You and I know that much at least."

"What are you suggesting?"

Erica sat down on one of the stained chairs. "We get back out there. We know it's out by the Overpass. We figure out some way to track it maybe. It's got to be doing something out there. When did you go out to the marsh?"

"During the day. Closed the shop for a week like we always have, took a few of the days to go out and canoe down the Pilwilla and through the swamps and marshes."

Erica rubbed her chin and stared at the floor between them as though that section of tile might have some of the answers she was looking for.

"That must be why?" she said absentmindedly.

"That must be why what?" Will asked.

"Why you didn't see it when you were in the swamps. When did you first see it, on the tow?"

"Just after dusk. Just like you-" Will started, seeing the connection.

"Just like when I saw it. An hour or so after sundown. What about the boy, Corey? When did he see it?"

"The same, I think. I talked to him the other day; he thinks it has something to do with the mill, is downstream from the Washington Mill."

"We have to go out at sundown, or right around it. Or maybe dawn. Whatever this thing is, I think its active during dusk or at night."

"If it's nocturnal, it could be hiding or resting someplace during the day. Maybe it's even underwater," Will proposed. He realized he would likely have to go out to the river or Bog during the night. Besides making the travel more dangerous, the thought of being out there in the dark again, even armed with the .357, only magnified the fear that had not left him since that night in July.

"So we should go out then, at night." Erica spoke in more hurried tones and nodded her head in an effort to psyche Will — and herself — up.

"And then?" Will asked.

"Once we find it, we stop it, and if we can't, we at least get someone else to stop it once we have proof. We've got to at least try. It's fucking up Derryfield. It's killing people. I can't just walk away from this. Can you?"

Her words were a challenge, and Will could tell she was afraid, same as he was.

"No, I guess I can't," he said, not pleased with the challenge or his response.

CHAPTER FORTY-THREE

Corey was certain of two things: Will and Erica would need his help, and they wouldn't ask him for it. With no way to be certain when Will and Erica might go out and look for the creature, Corey kept an eye on the shop. It wasn't too difficult to do so. He was no longer grounded and it was only a few minutes walk from his house to the circle. One afternoon, while watching the shop from where Pine street emptied into it, Corey saw a young woman park her car in front of Derryfield Auto a few minutes after five PM. When she didn't come out after a five minutes, Corey set off.

He walked quietly up to the shop door and could see Will and a young woman inside he assumed to be Erica, the reporter Will had mentioned. He watched as she brushed some of her brown hair away from her face while she talked with Will. He couldn't make out their conversation, but could tell they were both agitated by the intensity of their voices and the way they gestured as they spoke.

His knock on the door startled them both. Erica nearly dropped the paper in her hands. Will fumbled for a set of keys in his pocket, walked over to the door, unlocked it, and let Corey in. Corey wore a pair of jeans, his hiking boots, a t-shirt with long-sleeved shirt tied around his waist, and a black backpack slung over one shoulder.

"Hey Corey, what are you doing here?" Will asked.

"Is that her?" Corey said in a stage whisper.

"Yeah, that's Erica." Will turned to her. "Erica, meet Corey; Corey, Erica. This is the kid who saw it too."

Erica came over and shook his hand.

"Nice to meet you, Corey," Erica said.

"Nice to meet you too. When did you see it?" Corey asked.

Erica took a deep breath and told him about seeing the creature off 101, but left the part out about being there to visit her brother's cross. Corey listened with interest and, once she had told her story, shared his of falling asleep in Fort Barren and waking to find it in the forest nearby. Will sat and listened.

"What'd you come by for?" Will asked.

"I'm ready to go with you."

"No," Will said. "You can't come with us."

"What do you mean? Why not? I've seen it too. I know you guys are going out to... well, stop it. And I know the bog and the forest like the back of my hand. You said the cops didn't believe you. You need more people to help you out, right? Not less people."

"No, it's too dangerous. We can't be responsible for you while we're looking for this thing," Will said.

"I've already been out looking for it, during the day. I figure we have to go at night, when it's out. I'm going to search for it, with or without you." Corey crossed his arms on his chest and cocked his head to one side.

"Well he's right about that," Erica said. She was impressed. "We do need to go out at night, Will."

"Corey, listen," Will said. "We don't know what we are going to do. We don't have any plan. We don't know how to stop this thing, or even if we can. Do you understand that?"

"Yeah, I get it. It's dangerous. But you still need help."

"I can get a map Corey. It's better you stay safe."

"Come on!" Corey yelled and raised his hands in protest. "I can help!"

"Corey, I don't know," Erica interrupted. "Will makes a good point. Plus, what if something happens to us? You could get help. Call the police or the national guard or something."

Corey could sense that the conversation was nearly at an end. Will tapped one foot in a sign of impatience; Erica clasped her hands together and pursed her lips. If he didn't convince them shortly, the argument would be lost. He knew he could go out there alone, but he wouldn't cover as much ground without them. They could do this together.

"You guys have to let me come. You don't even know how to stop it," he said. "And I do."

Will and Erica froze. Will's foot ceased its incessant tapping and

Erica turned on her heel to face Corey.

"What do you mean?" Erica asked. She took a step forward and blinked rapidly as if doing so would help her better process his words.

"Every monster has a weakness, right? Everything does, something that hurts it no matter what. Like, something that is its opposite. The Thing was weak to electricity; the Blob was weak to cold. We just have to figure out what its weakness is, what thing is its opposite. Like fire maybe, or acid."

Will nearly laughed; not because he thought the kid stupid, but because the earnestness of it, the honesty of his statement reminded him of himself as a child, of that certainty one can have about things completely beyond understanding.

"That's a great idea Corey, but this isn't a movie. We aren't even sure what this thing is," Erica said.

"We've got to figure out what it is to track it, to know what to do to fight it," Corey replied.

Will threw his hands up and decided to humor Corey. "Well, we've got some ideas. Whatever is happening really started once Seabrook came in. I'm sure it has something more to do with the radiation out there rather than anything else. My old man was on this then, it's got to be related to that. Some sort of mutant seal or octopus or something."

"But those things don't even spread radiation Will," Erica exclaimed.

"What do you mean? Haven't you heard about Chernobyl, or Three Mile Island?"

"Yes, of course I have," Erica responded, "and those were accidents. Mistakes when things went wrong and allowed radiation out. But nothing has gone wrong with Seabrook. There hasn't been any kind of leak. It just cycles water though to get electricity, no radiation gets out."

"Well that's what they tell you," Will said. "But what if they have had leaks but it hasn't been disclosed? You expect me to believe that if they had we would know, that the Feds would have told us? You've already said they're trying to bury this story."

"They couldn't keep a thing like that secret." Erica shook her head. "There's too many ways people could find out. They could test the soil or the water to find any kind of leak."

"But it could have been a small leak, or in a single location. Enough to create... this thing." Will shrugged.

"Would some leak even do that though? Mutate something that far?" Erica asked the question but didn't really want an answer, or to spend any longer imagining what a radiation leak might do to the natural fauna or flora of the Estuary and nearby waters.

"Besides, you've seen what I've pulled. Something has been going on in this area for decades, long before Seabrook was built. I think it has something to do with the Exeter Incident. I know this sounds crazy, but it's I think, something from another world. Something that got left behind."

"Like some fucked up E.T.?" Will asked. He glanced over at Corey. "Sorry about the language." Corey laughed and smiled.

"That's just... unbelievable." Will rubbed the sides of his head. "An alien?"

"Is that any more friggen' unbelievable than some radioactive mutant like you're suggesting? Like a goddamn Godzilla in the swamps of New Hampshire?" Erica smirked to add some levity to her comment, but Corey could tell she was angry.

Corey, who had been quiet for this exchange, finally chimed in. "I think you're both wrong. I talked to Mimi — Ms. Gagnon, my neighbor," he added, recognizing that they wouldn't know her by Mimi alone, "and she said she's heard stories for years. She thought it might have something to do with like the waste and stuff coming out of the mills, getting washed downstream and some of it ending up in the bog. And I talked to some guys from the mills, they said they heard stories like this going back a long time. Something to do with the chemicals in the water."

"Everyone I talked to said it goes back to the '60s. I swear its connected to the Exeter Incident," Erica replied.

"Nah, like I told you," Corey added, "it's been here longer than that. Mimi said the stories go back since at least since she was a kid. That's like," and here he paused and looked up towards the ceiling as he did the mental math, "at least the 1940s, maybe even older."

"Does it even matter?" Will said and sat down on the stool behind the counter.

"It could," Erica said. "If we know how it came to be, maybe we can figure how to end it. We've got three options: a radioactive monster, an alien, or a toxic creature."

"I guess," Corey said.

"This is fucking ridiculous," Will muttered under his breath as he shook his head.

"We need to know how to fight it," Corey continued. "We've got to figure out its weakness."

"So we're going to kill it? For sure? That's the plan?" Will asked.

"What else are we supposed to do?" Erica responded. "I thought we had established that this thing is killing people out on 101. Doing something out there, right? We need to be prepared for whatever may hurt it, whatever we can do to drive it off or kill it, to stop it. At the very least, we need proof of it, undeniable proof. A photograph, a sample of it, like a footprint or something. If the three of us can't stop it, we at least need proof to convince other people, to get the military here to do something about it."

"Yeah, we need proof," Corey chimed in.

"Then let's get what we need." Will told them about his canoe and trailer.

"But what do we bring to stop it? To kill it or drive it off? We might need to protect ourselves out there," Erica said.

"I've got a pistol," Will offered. "At the very least we can shoot it."

"But that might not be enough," Corey said. "We need to figure out its weakness and have things with us to use those weaknesses against it."

"Like what?" Erica asked.

"I don't know. Fire. Ice. Electricity. Like the elements, right, the basic things which might hurt it."

"Sure," Erica said. Will rolled his eyes. Sensing his annoyance, Erica added, "He's got a point Will. We don't know what might spook it. We've all seen it, we know its size. We need to have someway to stop it should it come for us. It's got to be predatory."

Erica's vocalization of the threat it might pose caused all three to pause. They knew now that the experience they had each had separately, of simply seeing the thing, had left an impression that remained, a fear that seemed rooted in their minds. Standing together, talking through its implications helped — to a degree — but each realized that until they had done something, or someone else had, the fear would remain.

"I'll bring a camera," Erica offered. "I dabble in a little photography for work and have a decent camera I can bring. We need to try and get a picture of it."

"We should bring some plastic baggies, like sandwich bags, to collect any evidence we find," Corey said. "Like scat — that's poop — or any feathers or anything it might drop."

"You think its feathered?" Will asked.

"I don't know, it just looked like it was shedding something when I saw it. I thought it was feathers. But I think we should try to collect anything we can of it, for proof."

"Right," Will said. "My old man bought a Geiger counter — a device that can pick up radiation — when he was out looking for this thing the last few years. I'll bring that." Will held up his hand to stop the argument he believed was about to ensue. "I know, we don't agree on what this thing is. But bringing the Geiger counter isn't going to hurt."

"But what about defense? Will, I know you said you'd bring a pistol, but what else?" Erica asked.

"I don't know. Some fireworks maybe? An air horn? Other things that could spook it?"

"Yeah, that makes sense," Corey said.

"So we in agreement? We'll go out tomorrow at dusk, search for it, try to find proof. If we can, we'll stop it ourselves," Will said.

Erica and Corey nodded.

"Then get a good night's rest, gather what you have that you think might help, and if the weather holds, meet me here at 6 tomorrow. We'll drop my truck off downriver first so we can canoe to it and ride it back here when we're done." Will said.

Corey left first, waving briefly to both. Once he was out of earshot, Will turned to Erica and said, "So we really bringing him along?"

Erica shrugged. "What choice do we have? I get the feeling that he's going to be out there, with or without us. Stands to reason it will be safer with us than without, right?"

Will sighed and and nodded his head. "Guess you're right. We'll have to keep a close eye on him though."

"He's a good kid. Smart enough to drop in on us here, and he has some ideas about this whole thing."

"Yeah," Will said. He paused and considered his next words, considered arguing further with Erica but thought better of it, and instead said, "Well, see you tomorrow."

Once out of the circle and onto Pine Street, Corey turned back once to watch Erica climb into her car and Will turn off the lights in the garage then lock the front door. Even though the thing out there still scared him, Corey thought it felt good to have someone to talk to about it. He liked Will and Erica; they had listened and they would work together to find evidence of the creature's existence.

His mind full of thoughts of the task before them, the short walk home for Corey seemed very long.

CHAPTER FORTY-FOUR

Brown Stump Bog stank. The smell was instantly recognizable to those that lived nearby, but most found it difficult to describe. A mixture of rotting vegetation, methane, and putrefying flesh that was only matched by the odor that occasionally rose from the mill during high production days. The sun hung high in the western sky, its rays illuminating the fumes rising from the fetid water, causing the air to shimmer.

Will, Erica, and Corey stood off of Route 101, down the embankment along the shore of the Pilwilla. Will's small canoe sat between them. Will wore jeans and fishing boots, Erica khakis and hiking boots, Corey jeans and sneakers.

"So where do we go?" Corey asked.

Erica glanced at the map in her hands. The panels gently flapped in the breeze and the creases in the map made it difficult to read.

"Will pointed it out: we think this thing uses the waterways to get around," Erica said, "like it's some giant amphibian or something. So we travel the Bog and the streams running into and out of it. It stays near the water, as best as we can tell. Centered right around the Overpass to Nowhere."

"I'm still not clear on what we do when we find it," Will said. He glanced at the net bundled across Corey's left shoulder, the backpack over his right shoulder, and the slingshot sticking out of his pants pocket. Will also checked the can of mace hanging off of Erica's belt, the camera around her neck, and the fire extinguisher in the bottom of the canoe along with a pack of rat poison. A collection of other items lay in the boat as well, including plastic baggies, flashlights in a sealed plastic bag, a gallon of freshwater, some granola bars, and the Geiger counter.

"We stop it," Erica said.

"Not with that stuff we don't," Will replied. "Maybe with this," he added, pointing to the pistol at his hip. "Put enough lead in anything and it will die."

"If it comes to that," Erica said.

"Better to be prepared, right Corey?" Will replied.

"Yep," Corey responded.

"I've got this too," Corey said as he pawed through his backpack. He held up a soda bottle filled with a clear liquid. "It's gasoline. A Malotan cocktail."

"Molotov," Will corrected.

"Yeah."

"Jesus, be careful with that, please," Erica said.

"I will," Corey said. "I sealed it up. If we need to use it I can open it and stuff a rag in the top, then you light rag on fire. I've got a lighter too."

"Yeah, we know how it works," Will said and laughed.

"All right," Erica started, "I say we head down the Pilwilla, towards the the Overpass and Brown Stump Bog, and see what we can find."

The canoe was just large enough for the three of them and their gear. Any quick movement rocked the canoe, threatening to tip and dump the three and their gear into the water. The water was not deep; every twenty feet or so Will pushed the oar down into the water, and each time he continued to feel the squelch of mud underneath the tip of the oar.

After a few minutes the smell began to fade in their minds. The scent was too strong to completely forget though, and with an occasional breath the moldering stink multiplied like a crescendo of rot and sulfur. At one point Corey gagged and was concerned he might vomit; the gurgling in his stomach did not stop until the smell receded again. The breeze they had felt up on Route 101 disappeared once they descended to the water. Every so often a wisp of it would appear and ruffle their hair, but the relief was only momentary and worked to further aggravate the three as it teased the better environment that lay within sight of the shoreline receding behind them.

They only had two paddles, so Erica and Will paddled while Corey occasionally glanced at the map. The current carried them down the

Pilwilla and as they approached Brown Stump Bog, Will and Erica maneuvered the canoe out of the river and down a small tributary. Corey peered through a pair of binoculars across the fetid waters and towards the far shorelines. The tributary narrowed quickly and fed into a small channel lying east. The banks were populated by crowds of small scrubby trees. Though standing only twelve to fifteen feet tall, these trees provided some cover from the sun, particularly this late in the day, and helped to lower the temperature a few degrees and offer a respite from the open waters behind them. Corey reviewed the map and confirmed that this channel would bring them along to another significant body of the bog and towards the Overpass to Nowhere.

They traveled in this fashion for a quarter of an hour, weaving down the channels connecting the bog. Will set down his paddle every few minutes, picked up the Geiger counter, and waved the device around. The ticking noise it emitted remained low and steady, which Will explained to Erica and Corey meant low background radiation, the kind one expects to be present everywhere.

As they rounded one bend of the channels near the bog Erica saw a tan mound along the the the shoreline. "Hey, guys, you see that?"

Corey and Will followed her outstretched finger. Will pushed the canoe with his oar towards the mound while Corey tried to get a better look with the binoculars. As they drew closer the stench of the swamps grew stronger. The bow of the canoe made a scratching, scraping noise as it lifted out of the water and onto the damp bank. The trees a few feet beyond the bank stood close together; their leaves thick enough to hide anything beyond. The trees could continue for miles, or might hide another part of the bog just beyond the copse. *We will have to make sure we follow that map closely,* Will thought to himself.

Corey stepped out first. "It's a dead deer. Well, another dead deer. I saw one a while back, earlier this summer, kind of like this."

"Don't touch it," Will said.

What little remained of the deer lay scattered across of patch of muddy soil about six feet across. Enough fur lay around it to give the appearance of a beat up rug that had washed up on the shore. Its eyes were gone and the flesh from much of its face was missing revealing bone, an off white cream centered in a pink mass. Large chunks of flesh were missing from its legs. Dessicated pink muscle was obscured by the black flies and wriggling maggots. A coil of intestines spilled out from the deer's burst underside.

"Yeah, just like what like I saw a few weeks ago," Corey said and poked at what remained of one of the front legs with the toe of his sneaker. As he did so a cloud of flies erupted from the corpse like a swirl of buzzing smoke arising from a fire. A moment later they settled back down onto the rotting flesh.

"Don't do that," Will said and waved his hand in front of his face in an effort to reduce the stench. He stepped out of the canoe carefully and reached back to try the Geiger counter. He stepped closer to the carcass of the deer while trying to avoid the viscera spread along the shore, the bits of gray and pink and red visible among the brown sand. Will waved the black lead over the carcass. The device emitted a soft crackling and the needle on the display jumped a few times.

"That thing giving off radiation?" Erica asked and took half a step back towards the water.

Will shook his head. "Maybe? I mean, I think so. Hard to tell if it's anything more significant than the background radiation this thing's been picking up."

Corey turned to Erica and Will. "You guys think it did this?"

"Maybe," Erica said. She glanced around them. "Could have been something else too. A bear, or coyote maybe, right? There are other things out here that can take down a deer. We don't even know what it is, can't say for certain what it eats."

Will gripped the handle .357 at his hip and glanced up and down the narrow bank. He squinted as he scanned the wall of trees before him.

"All the same," Will said, "let's mark it on the map. If it's connected, we need to plot it out, keep track of where we see things like this. OK?"

Erica nodded, took the map from Corey, and folded it on her thigh while she scribbled an x on it in pen.

Corey held up the bag of plastic baggies he had brought along and asked, "Should we bag some of it? To test I mean."

Will looked at Erica. Erica shook her head.

"No, I don't think it would help Corey," Erica said. "It's been decomposing for a while. I don't think-"

"Just a little," Corey said, ignoring Erica's words. He selected a nearby piece of driftwood to spear one of the slivers of deer flesh and deposited it in a baggie. The flies protested again in an eruption into the air. Erica turned away and gagged at the smell.

"Careful Corey," Will said.

Once Corey had sealed the bag Erica said, "You can carry that Corey. Don't put it near me please."

"Sure," Corey said. He held the bag up to his face to examine it in the fading light.

"Why don't we keep moving," Will said. They carefully climbed back into the canoe, and Corey pushed them off the bank and into the still waters of the channel. They floated deeper into the bog for the next hour as the sun disappeared beyond the horizon. Eventually the Overpass came into view, a hulking piece of concrete rising to their left beyond the shore of the bog.

"If I'm right," Erica whispered, "it's probably close. I think this stretch of the bog might be it's nest or lair. The most activity — the accidents, the suicides, all center near the bog."

"Keep your eyes open," Will whispered back. He didn't know if this thing was near, and if it was, it could hear them, but it made more sense to be cautious and whisper all the same. Corey leaned forward slightly and stared into the water. Will removed the Geiger counter's lead again and pointed towards the water. The machine crackled slightly and the needle jumped. Both Corey and Erica looked back to Will and he shrugged.

The bog here was relatively narrow, only a hundred or so yards wide at most, and ran parallel to the highway for a few hundred yards. Will thought he could hear the cars from Route 101 but wasn't certain if what he heard was an illusion or even just the buzzing of insects and the slow trickle of water filtered through his anxiety. Will continued testing the depth of the bog and was surprised to find in a few sections he could no longer reach the bottom with the tip of the oar.

"You think this is the spot?" Corey asked. "It... feels right."

"Could be," Will said. "The stuff Erica found out, makes it seem like it's centered in this area. I'm not expert with the Geiger counter, but I think it's picking up something."

They drifted slowly. They each waved away at the bugs that

clustered around their faces, but otherwise were still, instead watching and listening carefully to their surroundings. The few trees standing in the water were gray sticks devoid of any foliage. In some spots, weak sloping grasses pushed up through the murk.

When the sun had nearly hidden itself behind the horizon, Will suggested they push forward and get the boat down to where the truck was parked. They all found leaving the bog was even worse than entering it. As frightened as they all were, at least beginning the evening's expedition brought with it a hope for resolution to the thing that plagued them. But an evening that only brought bug bites and exhaustion and heightened anxiety with no release left them all even more disheartened.

After loading the canoe and all their gear in the truck they drove back to the center of Derryfield in silence. As they neared the shop Corey broke the silence.

"Let's go out again. Soon. OK?" he said.

Will nodded. Erica said, "We will."

CHAPTER FORTY-FIVE

Will, Erica, and Corey didn't find the thing until the second week of their search, on the fourth evening they were out in Brown Stump Bog, by the Overpass to Nowhere. By then, each began to believe that they might never find the creature or any other sign of it.

Corey was concerned that with each venture his father would discover his whereabouts and forbid him from being out in the bog with these two adults. The luck evident in Corey's streak of free sodas went further still: his father had been working second shift for a few weeks, meaning Corey had considerable freedom from 3 to 11 every evening. Corey hoped his father wouldn't discover the clandestine hunts, as he was beginning to enjoy Will's and Erica's company. Will could be a bit short with him, but had let Corey paddle the canoe a few times and told him more about how Will's father had been searching for the thing a few years back, and, when the search stretched on and none of them wanted to talk about the creature, he dispensed tales about busted cars which were towed into the shop. Erica shared her water and snacks and identified for Corey some of the birds and plants they saw. It didn't match the friendship he had with Alex, but Corey was beginning to appreciate their time together nonetheless.

The fourth time out in the swamp seemed no different than the others, save for the thick gray clouds overhead. The weather was warm and muggy, the bugs plentiful, the stink ever present. They paddled down the Pilwilla and then traversed the marsh and bog. Again, as they neared the part of Brown Stump Bog closest to the highway and the Overpass to Nowhere, Erica, Will, and Corey grew quiet and carefully examined the dark waters. They each had fallen into familiar roles now: Erica poked the water with her oar to test the depth of the water, while Corey scanned the area with binoculars and Will manned the Geiger counter.

"These goddamn mosquitoes," Corey said, waving his hand in front of his face, pleased that he could curse in front of these adults and they wouldn't look at him twice.

Will waved the Geiger counter, watching the needle quivering in the box.

Suddenly, the creature was upon them, a quivering gray mass with a gaping black maw in the center of its body. It rose up from the depths of the bog as it drew its appendages under itself. Its form was alien, a confusion of limbs and speckled skin.

Multiple appendages twisted away. Some were as thick as a barrel of oil, others as thin as Corey's arm. Large sections of skin, as wide as three feet across, peeled back from its bulk and ended in wisps of translucent tissue. Smaller pieces flaked away as it moved and floated in the air around it. The creature looked sickly, but moved quickly despite its bulk and — at least to the eye — awkwardness. It looked like a creation God had forgotten, or perhaps one he had only finished after a few too many beers, a conflagration of snakes and sinewy muscle with too many appendages, lacking any semblance of symmetry.

Its sudden appearance startled them all.

Will whispered under his breath to the others, "Jesus Christ."

Corey stood up and pointed and Erica leaned away from it, an instinctive reaction to distance herself from the horror that arose from the depths of the bog. The canoe rocked back and all three fell into the bog. The water was cold — colder than they expected — but shallow, only two feet deep. The bog floor was muddy and their hands sunk into the muck. They each scrambled for a moment to get their feet below them. Erica rolled towards Corey and grabbed him. As they struggled to climb to their feet, each was alarmed to find the mud beneath them giving way to their weight. Will and Erica's boots began to fill with muck. Corey, weighing considerably less, only sank into the mud a few inches. The water still nearly rose to his waist, but rose to Erica and Will's thighs.

"Shoot it!" Erica yelled.

Will fired the pistol. Erica and Corey winced at the loud retort. The shot, however, went wide, the creature already upon Will, its multiple appendages unfurling in a gray blur to strike him. It knocked him backwards and into the murky water of the bog. Corey and Erica watched in horror as he disappeared underneath the surface with a splash.

The thing turned towards Corey and Erica, the central appendage rotating and twitching methodically until the dark maw at its core faced them.

Erica wanted to scream. She wanted to yell, to argue, to plead, to channel her emotion through her voice and hurl it at this thing before her in some effort to stave it off, to stop it. But she remained silent. Her thoughts blew away like wisps of this thing's skin, leaving only her fear and disgust, which seemed to know no end, like the black maw at the center of its body.

Corey started towards where Will had hit the water. His movement provided the stimulus Erica's mind needed to break its singular focus on the thing before her. She glanced over to Corey, then back to the creature, uncertain what she should do. She yanked the can of bear mace off her belt, pointed it towards the monstrosity, and pulled the trigger. A plume of red mist burst forth and billowed out towards the creature, enveloping it for a moment. The creature froze, but as the red cloud dissipated it appeared no different, still twitching, its appendages arcing in unnatural positions. Erica turned and sloshed as best she could through the muck and water towards where Will had disappeared. The creature's central mass rotated with her movement and it scurried towards her, small wakes of brown water emanating from its appendages as it propelled itself forward.

Will broke the surface and gasped in a huge breath. His hands were empty, the .357 lost in his fall into the water. He wiped the murky water from his face and faltered in the muck of the bog bed. Will moved through the water as quickly as he could towards the up-ended canoe. All he could think about was the other weapons they had: the Molotov, the mace, the fire extinguisher.

The central mass of the creature rotated again, this time turning towards Will. It sloshed in the water towards him. Erica froze again, indecision once again flooding her mind. Will stood in the muck over her right shoulder, behind her. The creature moved past her. She could tell it was not focused on her, but was afraid it would bowl her over all the same. Instead, its bulk flowed past her, its appendages rippling around her like a curtain waving in the wind.

When the thing was nearly upon Will again, Corey yelled.

"Stop!"

Then the rain came. The clouds overhead, invisible in the twilight, opened up and dropped their payload of moisture. A cool rain that swept through turned the bog into an assortment of rippling grays that erased all detail and distorted distance in the low light. The creature, already indistinct in its form, merged with the weather and become even more formless. Will stopped, trying focus on it, but with the rain in his eyes, the moisture in the air, the pounding in his skull, and the fear in his heart, he found it nearly impossible.

As quickly as it had appeared the creature disappeared beneath the bog. The water was only knee deep, so it splayed its appendages out in a circle around it and flattened its body. In one fluid motion it sank into the murky water and disappeared into the rippling waves.

"Where did it go?" Will yelled above the sound of the rain.

Each of them watched the water and the ever expanding concentrics as the water from above met the water below.

"Where is it?" Will yelled.

"I don't know?" Erica yelled back.

"It looks like its fucking dying!" Will shouted. "Did you see its skin? It was disintegrating or something!"

"What the fuck is it?" Erica replied.

"I don't know! Watch the water!" Will shouted back.

"Stop!" Corey yelled. "We have to stop running from it!"

"What the hell do you mean?" Will yelled back.

"It only chased you when you ran! It was just standing there, and it didn't chase you until you ran! Then it moved towards Erica when she ran! It only came after us when we ran!"

Erica nodded. "It's just going for him cause he's running. Like a lion or something, chasing prey."

"Like the T-Rex in *Jurassic Park*!" Corey yelled. "Don't run from it!"

The thing appeared again, this time further from them, thirty or forty yards distant.

"Where's the fucking camera!" Will yelled above the sound of the storm.

"I don't know!" Erica replied. "It must have fallen off my neck when we were dumped into the water. It's got to be somewhere in the water!" She dropped to her knees and began to feel around the mud near the canoe in hopes of finding the camera.

The creature shook all over, a quivering that began in its central mass and rippled outward through its appendages, like a dog coming in from the rain. A sheen of water erupted off its form, along with a cloud of skin and tissue. As it did this more of its skin flaked off and flitted about in the air, making it appear as though a squall had dropped a cloud of dirty snow about it. The rain falling from overhead immediately dropped the cloud of skin and debris into the bog. Will could see no hesitation in the movements, no indication that it was in pain.

In the same moment, each became aware of what was happening. It wasn't dying. It was molting. It was changing. Whatever it was now, it would soon become something different. The realization was difficult to process, as none could fully grasp its current form, and had no way of imagining what it would become next.

For the first time it made noise. It wasn't a roar or some deep bellow like Corey had expected. Instead the thing clicked and chattered, a sound like a thousand crickets echoing from its maw. Whether by some nature of the noise itself or some primordial response in an ancient part of their brains, each was suddenly stricken with an ache in their head and a renewed feeling of fear. The chittering reverberated and layered over itself, becoming ever more oppressive. They instinctively covered their ears to block out the sound. But this did little. The chittering noise instead worked its way past their fingers, past their palms, and burrowed deep through their ears and into their minds.

The creature continued to chitter and shake itself. The shaking grew more violent until it became a vibration, which sloughed off increasingly larger flakes of skin. They watched in horror as the flesh expelled from its body grew larger in mass. Underlying flesh — visible by its oily sheen — began to flake off. At first one, then two, then three of its appendages dropped into the marsh and sank below the water line.

Something in its central mass changed as well. It twisted and hunched over, increasing in size. A ridge erupted along its central mass, and the creature dropped into the water. Unidentifiable parts of its body bobbed in the water and floated away before sinking under the waves. The creature threw itself forward and started to swim, part of its central mass now working as a tail, thrusting side-to-side to propel it through the water.

"Come on, let's go," Will cried. "We can't lose it!" He hustled over to the drifting canoe and rolled over the side into it. Corey joined him and leaned in, nearly tipping the canoe. Erica waded through the water and joined them.

"What are we going to do?" Erica asked.

"Follow it. We need to see what it's doing!"

As Erica and Will righted the canoe, Corey waded over near where the thing had shed its skin. Thin layers of tissue floated on the surface of the bog, bobbing in the ripples made by the rain. Corey reached out and picked one up; it felt oily but crinkled in his hand. He pulled a plastic baggie out of his pocket and placed the skin inside before zip-locking it shut.

"Corey, get over here!" Will yelled. Corey looked back to see Erica and Will inside the canoe paddling towards him. As they came up alongside Will reached out and in one fluid motion Corey jumped and Will lifted the boy into the canoe.

Corey kept his eyes on the creature as Erica and Will furiously paddled in an attempt to keep it in their sights. The rain continued, the new deluge of water strengthening the current and pushing them downstream. Thankfully, the thing was also moving with the current and they were able to follow it. At times it disappeared around a bend for a moment, but each time they followed its wake and spotted it again once they came to more open waters. The rain lessened and the sky overhead began to clear; the sun was already hidden behind the trees on the horizon, but still provided enough illumination for the three of them to sight the creature and follow its wake. They continued to follow it down river, its broad back thrusting above the water as it pushed along the river bottom.

They followed it downstream, further and further away from Derryfield and closer to the coast. It was not keeping an even pace. At times in nearly swam out of sight but after a minute or two of furious paddling they would catch up and see it moving through the water before them.

"What is it doing?" Corey hissed.

"I don't know," Will said.

"Me neither," added Erica.

"You didn't find the camera, did you?" Will asked.

"No, I wish," Erica replied.

There, at the river mouth of the Hampton River, in the brackish water where the river met the sea, with the dome of Seabrook to their right, the creature increased its speed. It became harder to see in the low light. The only way they could track it was the disturbance of water that trailed behind it.

Will expected that the change in the water or the surf might alter the creature's direction or its speed. But it plowed forward, and out under the bridge over the inlet. It crested the water a final time before the waves of the Atlantic, and they all saw its new form in the growing moonlight: it was sleek, the many appendages now fewer in number and trailing behind it like a squid, the prominent ridge rising from its center mass. It did not appear to the eye like a creature of the bog any longer, but something instead of the sea, a creature that could survive among the depths.

They watched it crest once more, then disappear beneath the incoming surf. Will and Erica stopped paddling and allowed the current to continue to push them towards the ocean. No one said anything, but each felt a abatement of the ache in their head, as though the memories of this thing contracted in their minds with its passage to the sea. After a few more moments of watching the surf and the moon glittering on the dark waters, they pushed the canoe towards shore.

CHAPTER FORTY-SIX

They traveled back to Derryfield in silence. Will drove; Erica sat in the passenger seat and stared out the window. Corey sat between them and tugged absentmindedly on his seatbelt.

Will gripped the steering wheel with both hands until his knuckles were white. It stopped the shaking in his hands. The sound the thing had made continued to reverberate in his mind. He could hear it still, even over the rumbling of the diesel and the whip of the wind coming through the open windows. Driving was appreciated, a distraction from the uneasiness he continued to feel.

Erica stared out into the blackness of the night. She avoided looking over at Corey or Will. She didn't know what to say, and was afraid that if she looked at them, she would lose her edge and yell or cry. It felt like an end, watching that thing swim out into the sea, but it didn't feel like one. It felt like they had failed. They had no proof and they had no way to ensure that whatever it had done was now over.

Corey fidgeted. He tugged on the seatbelt across his lap, shifted in his seat, and reached out to fiddle with the radio but reconsidered and dropped his hand back to his lap. It didn't seem real, he thought. Not the search, nor the what they found, nor the drive back to Derryfield along Route 101. It was dreamlike: some details were so sharp, like the feel of the water on his legs and the sight of the creature. But the setting was insubstantial, the swamp stretching into a indistinct expanse. None of it sat well with him, and he still could not believe he was here, now, sitting in a truck with two adults who were unknown to him a few months back.

Corey broke the silence. "Is it, is it gone?" He looked to Will; Will kept his eyes on the road. Corey glanced over to Erica. When he did so, she looked down at her clasped hands.

Will cleared his throat. "I think so. I hope so."

"How do we know it won't be back?" Corey asked.

"Maybe it will."

Erica sighed loudly. Will and Corey looked to her.

"I think it's gone. It finished whatever it was doing up here, in the marsh, in the bogs. It... molted, and it's gone now. Out into the ocean." Erica said.

"Like a salmon or something?" Will said. "Coming up river to lay eggs?"

"You think there are eggs out there?" Corey asked. His voice was high, even for a twelve year old. He hadn't considered this idea and the prospect of it, of more of those things hatching, scared him.

"Did you see any eggs?" Erica asked and shrugged.

"No, but I wasn't really looking for eggs, I mean there was a lot of shit going on out there. Are there more of those things out there do you think?" Corey asked.

"No," Will said. "I don't think there are more. I still think it's something from the plant. Something from the nuclear energy getting into the waters."

"That doesn't explain how sightings of this thing go back so many years, or all of the deaths in the area. It started after the Exeter Incident. I'm sure of it," Erica said.

"How would the radiation get up the stream anyways," Corey said. "It was downstream from the mills, something got into the water there and went downstream. But it's even older than that, I told you, there's been something out there for over fifty years."

"It doesn't matter," Will said. "It doesn't matter where it came from. It's gone. It has to be."

"Should we go back to Brown Stump Bog? Try to find some piece of it, that well, molted off?" Erica asked.

"We don't need to," Corey said, pulling the small plastic baggie out of his pocket, "I already got a piece of its skin." Corey held up the baggie and Will flipped on the overhead light. Will glanced over at the baggie then back to the road; Erica and Corey studied it more closely. The flaky, off-white translucent piece of flesh was about as wide as Erica's palm and only a few millimeters thick. Its oily sheen reflected some of the yellowed light from the cab's interior. Looking at it caused some small part of their prior fear to resurface from the depths of their memory, as though the impact the thing had on them might never entirely disappear. Will flicked off the light and kept the Ford going West on 101.

"What should we do with it?" Corey asked.

"Get it tested. Send it to someone who can run a DNA test on it, find out more about what that thing is," Will said.

"I can ask around, I know some people who have worked on DNA testing from my time working crime at the *Gazette*. Corey, can I take that."

"Sure,"Corey said. He handed the baggie to her gently, as if its contents might escape and do them further harm. Erica carefully placed it in her shirt pocket.

They rode in silence for a few more minutes. Will turned to Corey and asked, "What will you tell your father? What have you been telling him? Out this late at night, I mean."

"I don't know." Corey shrugged. "That I was playing out at the fort. That I fell asleep. Who cares?"

Erica glanced sidelong at them. Will did not argue the point; whatever excuse Corey told his father didn't matter at this point, not after what they had seen this night.

Will slowed the Ford about a mile from the exit for Derryfield and pulled over. Traffic was light. The hazard lights of the Ford blinked and clicked in the darkness. Will immediately felt anxious, and realized that the clicking of the hazards reminded him of the sound the thing had made. He flipped the switch to disable the hazards and turned to Corey.

"You sure, here is good?" Will asked.

"Yeah," Corey said. "It's just up the hill. I've got my flashlight," he patted his backpack, salvaged from the canoe, "and my dad will expect me to come through the backyard. Won't work if you guys drop me out front."

"Be careful," Erica said as she stepped out of the cab.

"I will, thanks," Corey said. He waved once to them, then turned and walked towards the tree line. After a few steps all that Will and Erica could see was the small beam of Corey's flashlight. It flickered for a moment and they heard, over the noise of the summer night, the unmistakable sound of Corey smacking the flashlight against his hand. The flashlight flickered back on, and Corey walked away from the highway. He circled by the Overpass to Nowhere and began walking home.

Will and Erica drove the rest of the way into Derryfield. Will offered to drive her to get her car tomorrow. They both knew, without needing to vocalize it, that they wouldn't get it tonight. Too much had happened, and they both needed time to decompress, to consider what they had experienced.

Two cars were parked at the end of Will's driveway: a marked Derryfield cruiser and an unmarked dark sedan.

"What do we say?" Will asked when they saw the vehicles.

The next moment was perhaps only two seconds — long enough to Erica to consider her response, to consider their response to the police and whoever else was in Will's driveway. But those seconds stretched on as Will slowed the truck as they approached the turn off. She knew her response would direct them down one of two paths, and that it could make all the difference.

"I'm not saying a damn thing to them until we've got this all sorted."

When Will pulled in, the blue lights atop the cruiser sparked to life for a few seconds. Will stopped the Ford alongside the two vehicles and stepped out of the vehicle. Erica followed.

Lt. Hebert stepped out of the cruiser with a flashlight in one hand. He frowned at Will and stood there with his arms across his chest. A man in a suit and tie that Will did not recognize stepped out of the sedan, also holding a flashlight. Erica rounded the corner of the truck and saw that it was Billings.

"Jesus, where you been Will?" Hebert asked, eying Will's damp clothes and dirtied face. "Out at Seabrook?"

"Maybe. Why you asking? Who's this?" Will said and nodded towards Billings.

"He's with the Air Force. Captain Billings."

"Over here with me please, Ms. Couture," Billings said. He motioned for her to follow him to the other side of his sedan.

"What did I tell you Will?" Hebert asked. He didn't wait for a response. "I told you to stay out of those goddamn swamps." He shook his head. "I told you there were Feds looking around into this."

"Why? What does it matter if I was out there? And why the hell does the Air Force care?"

"You think I know why?"

"What about the NRC? They here too?"

"No, but I expect I'll have to speak with them about this. They left a card you know, asked me to let them know if I heard of anything fishy going on."

"Why are you here?" Will asked.

"This Billings character came by the station. Said he heard there were some people in the wetlands by Seabrook, someplace they shouldn't be. Asked me if I knew who it might be. Said he'd get all of us at the Derryfield PD out trawling through the marsh if I didn't let him know who, said it was a matter for the Feds."

Meanwhile, Erica had followed Billings and stood where he directed, her back against the rear passenger door of the car.

"What were you doing out there Ms. Couture?"

"Out where?"

Billings placed his hands on his hip and stared at her. "In the wetlands by Seabrook. I can smell it on you."

"I like to fish. Been doing it since I was little."

"What did you see out there?"

"A lot of water. Some birds. A turtle too I think. Fish weren't biting though, damn shame."

"Don't get smart with me. Turn around and put your hands on the roof of the vehicle," Billings said.

"What?"

"You heard me. Now." His tone was harsh

"What right do you have to search me!" Erica asked. Billings swept back his suit jacket to reveal a badge and gun.

"Are you even an Air Force Captain?"

"I'm with the Federal Government. That's all you need to know. Do it. Now."

Erica begrudgingly turned around while Billings patted her down. "What's this?" he asked as he grabbed the plastic baggie in her shirt pocket.

"What's this?" Billings asked again. He shone his flashlight into the baggie and peered at the contents within.

Erica turned to him. "Nothing. It's mine, give it back to me."

On the other side of the cruiser, Will and Hebert could hear the voices of Erica and Billings arguing, but couldn't make out the specifics words of their conversation.

"You going to arrest me?" Will asked.

When Hebert didn't respond, Will added: "What are you going to arrest me for?"

"Listen Will. I don't understand what all the hubbub's about. But something you or she did," he said, nodding over towards where Erica stood with Billings, "got the interest of somebody. Really riled them up. More than just trespassing from what I can tell. I don't understand why. Maybe that shit you were telling me wasn't all bullshit."

"So now you believe me?"

"I don't know what to believe. I hear shit stories every day. You got anything? Proof I mean," Hebert growled.

"We saw it, Tom. I mean we saw it again, tonight. It fucking touched me, pushed me like, into the water. We got a piece of it, like a piece of its skin. It was molting or something."

Hebert raised one eyebrow, the heavily lidded eye below becoming a bit more visible.

"My old man was right. It was out there."

"Was?" Hebert asked.

"It's out to sea now. I... I can't explain," Will said, recognizing the impossibility of describing to Hebert all he had seen. Hebert shrugged one shoulder, stuck the flashlight under one arm, and reached for his pocket to retrieve a pack of cigarettes. He lit one up and took a long drag. Will waited.

"That all?" Will asked.

"That's all from me for now," Hebert said between drags. "I need to get home and have a beer. It's been a long week."

Both turned towards Erica and Billings. Billings voice was raised.

"You realize it's a crime to lie to a federal official?"

Erica wasn't backing down. She stepped up to Billings, a full head shorter than him, and spoke just as sternly back to him. "I know you've been lying to me from the beginning. I know something more has been going on, you know there's something out there. I don't have shit to say to you." She spat the last words at him, daring a response.

"You search him?" Billings barked at Hebert.

"Ah, yep," Hebert said before taking another drag on his cigarette.

"Anything?" Billings asked.

"Nope," Hebert replied.

"I've just about had enough of you," Billings yelled to Erica. "You've been told before to stay out of that marsh. It's protected. I don't care what you think you saw. I hear that you're out there again and I'll have you arrested and charged with federal crimes."

Hebert gently elbowed Will in the ribs and nodded at him. Will took the hint.

"Listen fellas," he said as he stepped away from Hebert, before Erica could respond. "I've really enjoyed all this, but as you can see, I'm dirty, wet, and tired. I'm heading into my house now to take a shower, and I don't expect to see either of you when I'm out of that shower. I expect Erica's going to do the same." Will caught Erica's eye and smiled. It felt forced, but she returned it.

Will turned on his heel and walked towards his house and didn't look back. After a moment, Erica followed.

"Anything else?" Hebert asked of Billings as they watched Will and Erica enter the house. Billings did not reply. When Hebert turned back Billings was already getting into his car.

"Anything else Billings?" Hebert yelled over the engine.

Billings shook his head and drove away. The sedan lurched forward out of the driveway as he pressed the accelerator to the floor.

As they approached the doorway, Erica stepped up beside Will. She reflected for a moment, realizing they had found themselves in this moment many times over a decade ago while dating, walking side-by-side into Will's house. The memory disappeared as quickly as it had come, instead replace by her anger at Billings and losing the one piece of proof they had of the creature from the bog.

"Will, he took it!" Erica hissed. "He took the bag with the skin in it!"

"Fuck," Will muttered under his breath. He rubbed his head with the palms of his hand.

"We'll have to go out tomorrow." Will glanced up at the night sky and the moon overhead. "When it's daylight. Try to find something to prove it was there."

"Do you really think it's gone?" Erica asked while Will opened the front door.

"Yes," Will said. "You?"

"Yeah," Erica said as they stepped inside.

"It's changed, whatever happened out there tonight," Will added as he closed the door. "I think we have to accept that it's moved on, and for what it's worth, maybe try to do so ourselves now."

PART IV
SEPTEMBER

CHAPTER FORTY-SEVEN

Summer was over. The sun was setting earlier in the evening and the clouds of mosquitoes had dissipated after the new season's first cold nights. The leaves hadn't yet begun to change, but the chill in the air in the morning signaled that they would soon.

Corey hadn't spoken with Alex in nearly a month — an unheard of amount of time in the boys' lives. The last Saturday before school would start, Corey ventured out to Fort Barren to install an old window he had salvaged from a neighbor's remodel, and was surprised to find Alex there.

Alex stood before the fort, arms crossed over his chest. The wolf pine rose high behind him, the shadows partially obscuring his face.

Corey set down the window and raised a hand. "Hey Alex."

Corey took a step forward and Alex frowned.

"I'm sorry man." Corey glanced at his feet and back to Alex.

"I'm sorry," Corey said again. "I shouldn't have hit you. I was angry but I shouldn't have hit you. It was a bad thing to do. I wish I had never done it."

Alex considered these words. The silence, though only a few seconds, seemed interminable to Corey. He listened to the rustling of the leaves and the songs of the birds.

Alex adjusted his glasses, dropped his arms, and cleared his throat. "It's OK. You didn't mess up my face too bad." He rubbed his jaw, grinned and laughed. Corey laughed with him and smiled.

"Honestly, it was a pretty shitty punch," Alex said. "You're lucky I didn't want to fight you back because I would kick your ass." Alex's tone was playful and he smiled again as he needled Corey.

Corey stepped up to Alex and said, "I'll give you a free shot now." He dropped his hands to his side and jutted out his chin. "Fair is fair. You should get to punch me. To make it even."

"Nah," Alex said. "Maybe later."

"You sure? I mean it. I wouldn't tell on you."

"Nah, it's OK."

"Friends?" Corey said and held out his hand. Alex smiled, took his hand, and shook it.

"Friends," he said.

They climbed into the fort and spoke for a few minutes there, catching each other up on all they had seen and done in the last few weeks. Both avoided any talk of the creature from the bog; Corey didn't mention it and Alex didn't inquire. They knew that they would have to talk about this eventually. Finally, Corey couldn't avoid it any longer. He had to tell someone, and he knew that the first person he had to tell was Alex. He dropped his voice, glanced out the fort windows to be certain nothing was out there, and turned to Alex.

"We saw it you know, right?"

"Saw what? Who is we?" Alex asked.

"I went out to Brown Stump Bog with Will, the guy who owns the auto place down on the circle, and Erica, a lady that works for the newspaper."

"You went out to the bog with them?" Alex said, incredulous.

"Yeah."

"How did you meet them?"

"Well you know Will, I just ran into him and the monster came up somehow. And he knew Erica. Went to school with her or something. So we went out there. They had both seen it too. We found it."

Alex raised his eyebrows behind his glasses but said nothing more.

"I even got a piece of it, like a piece of its skin in a bag!"

"Eww," Alex said and scrunched up his nose.

"Erica is going to get it tested, check to see what else we can learn."

"Wow," Alex added. He raised his eyebrows and pursed his lips.

"But it's gone now," Corey said. "It, well, didn't die. But it's gone. It went out to sea. I don't think it will be back."

Alex said, "OK. That's good, right?"

"Yeah, definitely." Corey nodded and hugged his knees tighter. "It wasn't good — like it wasn't having a good effect on things in Derryfield I don't think. It's good that it's gone."

When Alex didn't respond, Corey added, "And really, I don't care if you believe me, I just had to tell you. We did it. It's real."

Alex nodded. "I'm sorry I said I didn't believe you," he said. "I just, I don't know." Alex shrugged.

"It's OK," Corey said. He nodded and threw an arm around Alex's shoulder. He did this without second thought, a friendly gesture of one boy to another, the kind that seems to vanish as boys age. They sat that way for a minute, each enjoying the moment, their friendship tested and now both certain stronger for it.

The sun was already setting when they set off for home, the window Corey had salvaged installed in the rear wall. Corey accompanied Alex home first, the two planning on the walk home the next addition to Fort Barren. After dropping Alex off, Corey set out for his house. He passed Mimi's along the way. She sat on her porch, bundled in a thick purple sweater. She smiled, a knowing smile and waved but said nothing. Corey returned the wave and approached.

"Mimi," he said.

"Yes dear?"

Corey worked up the courage to tell her; sharing it with Alex made it easier somehow. "I saw it again. The Bog Monster. I saw it out by Brown Stump Bog."

"Really?" Mimi said and leaned forward in her rocking chair.

"Yeah. It's real Mimi. Whatever you heard when you were little, what the people said was in the mill. It was out there."

"Was?" she asked and cocked her head.

"I think it's gone now. It's hard to explain, but I think it left. Please don't tell my dad, OK? He doesn't believe me, and if he knew I was out there looking for it I think it would just piss him off."

"Watch your language Corey," Mimi retorted, "but I'll keep this between us. A boy needs some secrets. You sure it's gone?"

"Yeah," Corey said. He couldn't explain to Mimi all he had seen and done; that would be too much even for her to keep secret. He also couldn't explain — not for lack of trying — how he knew it was gone. The thing's travel out to the ocean seemed final in a way that Corey could feel in his bones.

"I'll be seeing you around," Corey said and waved goodbye.

"Mind the traffic," Mimi said as Corey crossed the road, though no car could be seen in either direction for hundreds of feet.

When he arrived at the house his father was preparing dinner. Corey had said little to his father the last few weeks, and mentioned nothing of what they had found in the swamp. By some stroke of luck Ted had not asked about Corey's whereabouts those evenings he had traveled into the Bog with Will and Erica. The alibi of spending time with Alex was, for now at least, still effective.

"Where you been?" Ted growled. He looked sidelong at Corey as he dropped a heap of macaroni and cheese on a plate.

"Out in the woods playing with Alex," Corey said.

Ted grunted and continued to scoop macaroni and cheese out of the pot and onto his plate.

"Why did you make macaroni and cheese?" Corey asked. "It was Mom's favorite."

His mother had always been a picky eater, and, when for a few years in elementary school when Corey had been particularly picky as well, the two had eaten macaroni and cheese many nights while Ted grumbled about the meal to himself.

Thinking of his mother made him angry, and Corey realized that he had not been thinking about her as often the past month. The fight with Alex, the search for the monster in the marsh, his new friendship with Erica and Will; it had all been enough to completely consume his attention and divert it away from thoughts of his mother. Now they came crashing back, as though his month long reprieve had only been a dam that was now burst, the feelings washing over him in a flood.

"Huh?" Ted responded. He raised an eyebrow but his eyes remained fixated on the meal on the table before him. Corey knew he heard him, knew that he had just ignored the question.

"Why did you make mac and cheese? It was Mom's favorite!"

"It's all we had in the house Corey," Ted responded as he lifted his spoon to his mouth.

"But, but, Mom's not here. We should have it with her."

"I know she's not here. It's all we had Corey," Ted said again.

Something about the exchange was too much for Corey. The wave of memory, combined with anxiety released from the past month's events eroded away the last measure of his control.

"Why did she leave!" Corey yelled. With that outburst he was unable to hold back the tears and they spilled forth and tumbled down his face. He cried out once, his shoulders rising and falling with the sound.

"Corey," Ted said. His voice weakened as he spoke, like a boom box losing its battery charge.

"Why did she leave? Why won't you tell me?"

Ted sighed. "It's complicated."

"No, don't say that. Don't say that. Tell me why!"

Ted shook his head. "I love — well loved — your mom very much. But sometimes, sometimes people just grow apart. They change a little every day and then... just wake up and it doesn't seem well, right anymore. I don't know how to explain it." He raised his hands in the air and then shrugged his shoulders. "It's like their life went down a path they didn't expect, you hear?"

Corey heard but didn't respond.

"I didn't want her to leave, same as you. Wasn't my choice, you understand? I couldn't make her stay. Neither could you."

"But, but, but, I miss her," Corey said.

Ted nodded and said, "And I do too sometimes. I do too. But we can't... we've got to make do with what we got, right? We've just got to press on. Complaining about it doesn't change the fact that she's gone."

Corey's sobs had softened and he drew his right forearm across his face in an effort to remove the tears and snot clinging to his face. Then he lurched forward and clung tightly to Ted.

"I'm sorry Dad," Corey said.

"I'm sorry too," Ted said and hugged him back. His thick arms crossed Corey's back and pulled him in tightly. He smelled like sweat and grease and the dark stubble on his lower chin tickled the side of Corey's face. They held each other for a few moments before Corey stepped back. Ted kept his right hand on Corey's left shoulder and squeezed gently.

"Listen," Ted began, "I know things will remind us of her and it might be hard. It's never going to be quite the same around here. I don't do everything the same as Mom. I'm not going to get everything right. But I'm doing the best I can Corey. We just have to keep moving forward. One day at a time. We got this. OK?" He smiled and squeezed Corey's shoulder again. "We'll be OK. We'll get through this."

"Yeah," Corey said, reluctantly at first. "Yeah, we got this."

CHAPTER FORTY-EIGHT

Peter Rath walked into the shop, all swagger and smiles in a suit. He pulled on his cuffs and nodded to Will.

"Mr. Boucher, it's good to see you again," he said.

It took Will a moment to place the man before he remembered that he had been in the shop last month, droning on about how he wanted to purchase the place and the land it stood on.

"Afraid I can't say the feeling is mutual," Will growled.

"Ah, I don't want to get off on the wrong foot here, Mr. Boucher. I'm just here again for my client, looking to see if you have considered the offer to sell this place."

"I haven't heard an offer, just your interest. And who exactly is your client? You didn't say."

Rath clucked his tongue once, as if Will was a student who had just disappointed his teacher.

"I can't say, unfortunately. Client confidences. Suffice to say, my client is a developer in New England that is looking to expand in Derryfield." Rath raised his right eyebrow. The right corner of his mouth rose in the same direction in a smirk.

"Plenty of property downtown," Will responded. "You drive by? Quite a few mill buildings are empty, or at least mostly empty. Plenty down there."

"I understand that, but I'm, well, my client's," he stressed, "not interested in that property. This land here at the circle is much better suited for his interests, you understand."

Will set down the report in his hand and stared at Rath. "What do they want to put in?" Will asked.

"Again, you're asking me questions I can't answer. I just want to know if you want to sell."

Will said nothing.

"Just think," Rath continued, "a man your age has many years in front of him. You could sell this place, take the proceeds and go far. Buy a new truck, a new house. Put some aside for retirement. Your call."

Will considered the man's words. He spoke a truth; selling the shop, paying off any debts, and cutting ties with it might be the best. The shop had never had banner years. It generally plugged along, and as Will was experiencing, the lean years were a balance on a knife's edge of debt and income. If he sold, he'd have the house free and clear, could maybe head back to school, finish his degree. He could liquidate this life he inherited and start back on his own. He could forget that shit he saw in the swamp and ignore the mystery he had uncovered but would likely never solve.

Will considered all this, and rejected it. He had seen his father's goals through in the bog; he could see them through with the shop, here in Derryfield.

"My father started this business," Will said. "Bought the land in the '50s, when most of this was still the sticks. I'm not interested," Will said.

"I think that's a mistake. My buyer could make something more of this location. You've got to understand," Rath said, folding his hands together in front of his chest and moving them in time with his words, "the land itself is worth quite a bit, located here on the circle. Projections show this area is likely going to grow, situated as it is close to Manchester and the coast."

"I've heard you out," Will said.

"I appreciate that-" Rath began.

Will interrupted, "I've told you no twice now, and you don't seem to be getting the message." Will stepped around the desk and motioned towards the door. "So let me make myself very clear. Get the fuck out."

Rath's cheeks reddened. Will could see him clench his jaw and narrow his eyes, but, to his credit, the man said nothing more and walked out the door. Will crossed his arms and watched him climb into his Mercedes and peel out of the lot.

Robert, having heard the commotion, walked up to the office and asked Will, "Who was that guy?"

"Just some asshole," Will answered.

"Trying to sell some shit?"

"Nope," Will said, "trying to buy. Wants to buy the shop and the land and all, says he's a buyer or agent or something for some business man, wouldn't tell me who."

"What'd ya say to him?"

"Told him to fuck off."

Robert laughed. It was a loud laugh that came from deep in his belly and was enough to cause him to reach to a the desk to steady himself.

"Yep," Robert added, "if anyone had any doubt, you're definitely a Boucher. I can see your old man saying just that. He'd never have sold this place either. Put too much of himself into it."

"I'm probably a dumb ass," Will said. He shook his head and continued, "You know it seems we're barely above water here. It's week to week Robert, not like it was when I was in high school. Things just slowed down, cars taking too long in here, not enough moving in and out. Maybe I should sell, get something out of this. You'd have no trouble working up at Patrick's Auto or one of the shops in Manchester or Epping."

Robert grunted dismissively. "I don't wanna work any of those places. I've been here long enough to know this is the place for me. When someplace feels right, you know, know what I mean? You feel it in your bones."

"You've got plenty of that to feel it," Will said and cracked a smile.

"Hey now!" Robert said but smiled as well. He slapped his belly and said, "Why go for a six pack when you can have the keg." They both laughed.

"I'm glad you said no," Robert continued. "Your pops would be real proud of you, taking on the family business and keeping it going."

"Yeah, I guess."

"You guess? You're doing him proud Billy. He was always really proud of you and all. Going away to college, gonna be a big architect, he never would shut up about that."

Will was unable to stop the surprise he felt from showing on his face: his eyes opened wide and his eyebrows rose to accommodate the change. He had never spoken at any length with his father about college or the choices he had made as a young adult. It wasn't as if he had disfavored his son's choices, so much as he seemed agnostic to the whole thing.

After a few moments of silence Will said, "I didn't even finish the degree…"

"You think he cared about that?"

"If he did, well, he wasn't one to say much to me."

Robert nodded his head. "Yeah, wasn't his way, Billy. He was never gonna say much to you or your sister about it. But he told me plenty of times. Ask any of the regulars that came in here. He wouldn't shut the hell up about his kids — you out in New York learning to be an architect, Daisy out in California working on movie sets. But family's first, and you did the right thing, coming back when he passed. It's good a Boucher's here, steering this ship."

"Thanks Robert," Will said. He rubbed the inside of his left eye to remove the growing moisture.

"Why you thanking me? Just the truth."

"Well thanks anyways."

Robert started back towards the shop.

"Since I guess I'm here to stay, been mulling over another change," Will said. "I know money's tight, but I'd thought we could bring on that kid from up the street, Corey Barrington. What do you think?"

Robert turned and shrugged. "Your shop boss."

"Think it might help. He could give a hand with minor stuff, cleaning, stocking, get me free to help more out back, push more cars through when it does get busy, so we don't have to turn them away."

"It's how I got started, helping out as a kid. When's he start?"

Will laughed. "Haven't figured that out yet. I'll let you know."

Robert nodded, entered the garage, and starting tinkering with the Buick in the first bay.

Will called out, "Robert. Drinks on me after shift. Let's work on that keg."

Robert laughed again. "Won't say no to that. My call though right? You buying, I pick the place?"

"Sure," Will said.

"Derryfield Pizza. You need to meet this girl Jessica. I'm telling you, you'd like her. Smart as a whip, funny too — and not bad on the eyes."

"All right, all right, you've convinced me!" Will said. "Derryfield Pizza it is. Now back to work, these cars ain't gonna fix themselves."

Will checked the schedule, then called back to Robert that he was going to pick up some parts.

The air outside was warm and dry. Will took a deep breath, enjoying the early September weather. He checked his watch: only one-thirty. Plenty of time to visit his mother and pick up parts before customers starting coming in after work to pick up a completed repair or drop of for a needed one. He followed the two miles of River Road towards the nursing home.

The Pilwilla was, as always, beautiful this time of year. The vegetation along its banks had flourished all summer and stood tall. The river was full and coursed through the bed downstream to the mill buildings. The memories of what he had encountered in the bog was not enough to tarnish his appreciation of the beauty now.

Still, he tried not to think back on that misadventure and the thing they had seen. It was gone, whatever it was, but he knew that some piece of it would not leave. The creature had left an imprint upon something inside him. Had he been a more religious man he might have used the word soul. Whatever it was, whatever it had done, he knew some vestige of it would continue to mark him. This didn't bother him — at least not to a significant degree — not any longer. He knew he would carry it with him, but he welcomed it in a way. Will had finished what his father had started.

Will stopped by on the way to Riverview to pick up a bouquet of sunflowers and lilies for his mother. His anticipation to give them to his mother was tempered by a small sense of shame: he knew his mother would appreciate the flowers, but he infrequently brought her anything like that, and realized he should do things like this more. It would take so little effort to provide her this measure of happiness. The flowers today were a good start.

Will managed to avoid Ms. Mitchell on his way into the nursing home.

"Hi Mom," Will said when he walked into her room. Mildred looked over at him and smiled the same smile he had always known. She must have showered recently, as her gray and black hair was not yet ruffled and sat orderly on her head.

"Billy!" she exclaimed, "it's so good to see you! How are you?"

"I'm... I'm good."

"I'm so glad to hear that," she said. "What are those?"

"Some flowers for you." Will set the vase down on her vanity and took a moment to rotate it to make certain the most colorful section of yellows and pinks faced towards her.

"They're beautiful." Mildred smiled again and clapped her hands together. "Come here and give me a hug." Will leaned in and wrapped his arms around her. He felt her shoulder blades when he embraced her. She was so thin now, so much smaller than he remember from his youth, when her hugs would encircle him and shut away everything else.

"I'm glad you like them," he said. Will pulled up a chair next to his mother and glanced at the empty bed behind them.

"You feeling OK?" he asked.

"Yes honey, I am. How are things at the shop?"

Will thought of lying, telling her the same predictable story. Instead, he said, "Honestly, it's tough Mom. Still seeing the regulars, but getting new business in the door is hard, as is getting the work done when we have with so little help. Seems like prices go up every year on all the equipment and parts and such, just tough to get everything in the green." Will sighed. He didn't want to unload on his mother like this, to cause her to bear some of his burdens. She had enough on her plate fighting her illness. Still, she had worked in the shop for years, and if that part of her was still present, she could commiserate and understand.

"It's like that from time to time," Mildred said. "Ups and downs, like all things in life. You'll be fine. Your father and I always were."

They spoke for a few minutes about the topics Mildred always wanted to discuss: the food in Riverview; the weather; and family, primarily Winston and how she missed him. When the conversation inevitably turned to Winston, Will knew he had to tell her something about the thing in the swamp.

"Mom, do you remember how we were talking about Dad a while back? About how he saw something, or was looking for something, out in the swamps? Out by Brown Stump Bog?"

Mildred furrowed her brow — her gray eyebrows pulling in towards her eyes — then shook her head.

"Can you remember? He told you about it. Something he said he saw out there, he wasn't sure what it was, but he was looking for it. Looking for proof."

"No," Mildred answered. "I'm sorry honey, I don't remember. You know my memory is not what it used to be. When were we talking about this? What were we talking about?"

Will considered telling her everything: what he saw, what she had told him, what he did and what he knew now. If she remembered it, which was a big if in and of itself, she likely wouldn't tell anyone. And if she did, any listener would likely brush it off as the ramblings of an elderly and ill woman living out the rest of her days in an assisted living facility. He could tell her and it wouldn't even matter. But instead, he just waved his hand. "It's nothing Mom. Don't worry about it. I just wanted you to know, well, Dad was right."

Mildred smiled again. "Good. He often was, as much as I hated to tell him that." She laughed warmly and looked over Will's shoulder, into the past, into her memories of Winston and their life together.

"He passed too young," she added. "I miss him you know, every day. He had his faults, Lord knows we all do, but he did us well. He did the best he could, and that's all we can ask."

"Yeah," Will said, "I guess he did." They sat together for a few minutes. Neither spoke. It was a comfortable silence, both simply enjoying the presence of the other. Mildred looked out her window at the trees beyond the parking lot, their greens already tinged with warm oranges and reds of autumn.

"It's good to see you Billy," Mildred said. She patted his hand with hers and smiled. "Do you like my flowers?" Mildred asked.

Mildred smiled again and pointed at the bouquet Will had just delivered. Will thought of trying to correct her, to tell her that he was the one who had brought them in. It made him sad, knowing that his mother was having difficulty recalling something from just a few moments ago. All that was clear to her now were events which had happened long ago, as though proximity to the present was anathema to her memory.

"They're beautiful, Mom," Will said.

CHAPTER FORTY-NINE

"Andrew," Erica said, realizing mid word that she was calling him by his first name for the first time. "It's gone. Whatever it is — well was — it's gone."

She heard him inhale over the telephone line and expected an immediate response, but the line stayed quiet for a moment.

"Gone how, Erica. Where did it go?"

"Out to sea. I can't really explain it... it changed. Like a metamorphosis. Became something different, more like a manta ray almost."

"So you saw it again," Stewart said in hushed tones.

"Yes. It was... terrible." Erica thought back on the evening in Brown Stump Bog. Only days distant, the memory was already calcifying; instead of losing details, it seemed the entire ordeal was seared into her mind. Recollection brought with it anxiety, but the fear she had felt for so long was lessened by her belief that it had left the bog and would no longer be out prowling along 101.

"And you are certain it is gone?" Stewart asked.

"Yes, I don't know how to tell you how I know. I could feel it though. It was final. Whatever it was is gone now, out to the Atlantic. At the very least, it's not New Hampshire's problem anymore."

"Do you have anything to show of it? A photograph per chance?"

"No," Erica said glumly. "We were in the bog, Brown Stump Bog, that's where it seems to have nested, and the canoe tipped and I lost my camera. We had a piece of it, some skin it had shed, but afterward, a captain from the Air Force took the baggie with the piece in it. We went back out the next afternoon and looked for it, well remains of it, but we couldn't find shit in the swamp."

"That is a shame you do not have any proof, but I am not surprised your search the next day did not uncover anything," Stewart said between a short spell of coughing. "It stayed hidden for years. I would not expect it to serve up all of its secrets now."

"I guess," Erica replied. Her disappointment was already overcoming any lingering fear or anxiety. She had finally had a good night's sleep — her dreams undisturbed by the creature from the bog — but her disappointment upon awakening was like a pain in her chest.

"The thing is," Erica began, "it wasn't just motor vehicle accidents out on 101. It was doing something else, either intentional or not. I pulled the figures on all sorts of reportable events in Rockingham County. For example, suicides have been higher in the area for decades. There was something more at work there too."

The line was silent for a few moments. Then Stewart said, "I did not know that. It surprises me, but I believe you. That only seems to deepen the mystery. What do you think it was doing out there?"

"I wish I knew. Feeding maybe? Maybe just existing, and its presence alone caused all that... discord? Whatever the reason, mark my words: the rate of fatals on the highway is going to plummet. So will the suicides. Whatever that thing was doing, whatever force it was exerting on the area, it's gone now."

"Though perhaps not the closure we both wanted, I thank you for letting me know. You should know it gives an old man like me no small amount of relief to know it has ended."

"I wrote a story on it too," Erica added. "The whole ordeal, from the '60s to the present. The paper wouldn't publish it. Had everything: what I found by looking through the archives about fatals and suicides, what people claim they've been seeing for years out there, what I saw. Editor rejected it. Said it was 'too personal.' Bunch of bullshit if you ask me."

"I am not surprised it was rejected," Stewart said. "Though perhaps not as comprehensive, I chased this tale and had a number of articles rejected as well. It is a story that some seem to feel is best left untold."

Erica glanced around the office to make certain no one was near, listening in on her call. She lowered her voice and said, "I'm done at the *Gazette*. Weber's all over me, giving me shit from on high."

"Weber is an ass," Stewart said and chuckled.

"I applied to a position at the *Globe*. Boston would be a change from Derryfield, but I think it's what I need."

"And I wish you all the best should it come to pass," Stewart said.

"Thanks," Erica replied. "I'll let you know. If I hear anything else about the other thing, I'll let you know on that as well."

They said their goodbyes, and when Erica hung up the phone, she had the distinct feeling that she would not be talking to Stewart again. Their connection was only really through the thing off 101; with it gone, they had no reason to converse, nothing to share, no other event or relationship that connected them together. It seemed to Erica an odd way to end, and she felt sullen and — as if her motivation was not already diminished — unable to focus on her work.

Erica sat at her desk and listened to the buzz of the office around her. It all seemed so mundane to her right now. She felt as though confirmation of the creature in the bog had energized her, given her a look behind the curtain of what others believed reality to be. But that knowledge provided nothing more. When she awoke that morning in her apartment, she still did the same morning routine, still showed up to the same office, was still working the same job. It seemed to her that more should have changed. Her internal world had — the world around her should respond in kind.

She gathered a few personal items into her satchel, shut off her computer, and walked for the door.

"I'm done," Erica said to Katie, the second floor receptionist.

"You're done?" Katie asked. "What do you mean?"

Erica ignored the question and was out the door, down the stairs, and in her car in less than two minutes. She wasn't sure where she would go. She just wanted to be away from the Franklin Building. She drove around Derryfield for a few minutes before heading towards her parents house, figuring they would both be home on a Saturday afternoon. She was surprised to find the front door uncharacteristically locked. Erica searched her purse for her old house key and, when she couldn't find it, rang the doorbell. She continued to search and after a few seconds heard footsteps approaching the door. Judy opened it and nodded to Erica.

"Hi Mom," Erica said. Her mother nodded in reply but said nothing. "I heard you are back at work now."

"Yep," Judy said. "Those assholes said I got 12 weeks leave time from that new law, but had to come back or I'd be fired. And I didn't feel like getting fired."

"Glad to hear you're back, that's good Mom." Judy stepped aside and let Erica in the house. She glanced at the hallway wall and noticed that all the pictures were hanging back on the wall. In many of them Nate stood smiling with Erica and their parents. Erica felt another pang of grief, it's depth and immediacy surprising her. She only hesitated for a moment and then walked down to the kitchen while her mother closed the door behind her.

"Where's Dad?"

"He'll be here soon. He just ran off to get some take out."

"Did you come by for dinner?" Judy asked. "Finally coming by to see your poor mother?" Erica ignored the bait and sat down at the table. The small television set was on the table, but turned off. Judy pulled out a pack of cigarettes. "Do you mind?"

Erica thought of saying something, arguing with her mother and telling her she needed to give up the smoking. Instead she just waved her hand and said, "It's fine."

Judy lit up the cigarette, took a long drag, then blew the smoke out of the corner of her mouth away from Erica.

"How's work for you? As bad as it is for me?"

"Fine," Erica said and shrugged. "Well, actually, not great. I'm done at the *Gazette*. I applied for a job at the *Globe*. Think I'll head to Boston."

At first Judy said nothing in reply. She nodded her head slowly while she stared at her feet and took another drag on the cigarette.

"I see how it is," Judy finally said, "one child leaves me, and then the next."

"What, no Mom-"

"I get it, you can't stand me. You see me grieving my only son's death and you hate me because of it. You can't stand that I loved him so much and he loved me so much. You don't understand what it's like, a mother losing her child!"

"What?" Erica asked, incredulous. "Mom, what do you mean? I fucking miss Nate too — I do every day."

"It doesn't show. Enjoy Boston," Judy said and stomped away, a faint wisp of smoke trailing behind the cigarette in her hand.

Erica sat stunned, silent, and still. She considered her words and wondered if she could have broached the subject differently. Tears formed in her eyes, but she brushed them away and waited for her father to return. Sam came back with a paper takeout bag stapled shut at the top. Erica could smell the beefy scent of the local Chinese food restaurant.

"Hey honey, good to see you!" he said when he saw her.

He set the bag down on the table and pulled up a chair next to her. "What are you doing here? Where's your mother?" He began to unpack the bag of food, setting out the white cartons on the table in a line as Erica answered.

"I'm done at the *Gazette*. I applied for a job at the *Globe*. I want to move to Boston."

"Wow!" Sam said and stopped arranging food on the table. "Wow!" he said again. "Really? When are you thinking of moving?"

"In a few weeks," Erica said.

Sam, never an emotional man, wiped at his eyes and looked away for a moment. Erica was shocked. She didn't remember him crying at any point during Nate's wake or funeral. She reached out and grasped his shoulder and squeezed. She had not expected him to be the one to take the news so emotionally.

"It'll be OK Dad. I won't be far."

"I know, I know," he said. "I'm gonna miss you is all. You'll understand someday if you have kids. At least you've always been close, here or in Durham. I could keep an eye on you. I know, I know," he said again and waved his hands when Erica started to make a face, "You're an adult. You can take care of yourself."

"I'll miss you guys too, Dad. I'll be close though. Boston's only an hour away."

Sam rubbed his eyes again. "Where's Mom?" He asked. "Have you told her?"

"She uh, didn't take the news so well," Erica said. She looked away from her father, not wanting to make eye contact with him in that moment.

"Let me go talk to her," Sam mumbled and left the table.

Erica could hear their voices in the sun room out back. The distance from the kitchen and the closed door between her and her parents muffled the words but Erica could make out the tones. Her mother was yelling and her father, though initially calm, was beginning to shout back. Erica sat and listened to their voices. She could only remember them fighting like this a few times when she was growing up. It scared her then, and did so now. After ten minutes that felt much longer, a door slammed and footsteps approached the kitchen.

When he returned, Sam only said, "Sorry about that. Your mother needs some more time."

"OK," Erica said, unsure of what else she should say.

"She's trying, she really is," Sam said, in an effort to convince either Erica or himself. "She's back at work." He shrugged.

"You hungry?" he asked. Erica nodded.

They each grabbed a plate and dished out servings of now cold Chinese food. Erica wanted to tell her father more. Not only about her work, but about what she had seen in the past few months, what she had learned and what she now believed to be true about this world. She thought of the skepticism of her father weeks ago and the immediacy of this moment. It didn't seem right to tell him now about that thing in the bog, to twist this conversation into something different and unbelievable. He had enough to worry about as things were.

Sam's attitude was happy, but subdued, a reflection of the news Erica had shared and her mother's response to it. They sat and ate and talked together about O.J.'s trial, the IRA ceasefire, and the Patriots new season. The enjoyment Erica felt with her father in the moment was bittersweet for two reasons: she wished her mother would join them, and she knew this type of time together would occur much less frequently should she move to Boston.

Sam raised his glass and offered a toast: "Congratulations honey, you've earned it. To new experiences. But don't forget us old farts." She laughed with her father, but sensed the seriousness in his voice.

She left after dinner, Judy still holed away in the far end of the house. Traffic was light on 101. With Labor Day come and gone, the vacation season had officially ended. Some of the businesses along the coast would remain open through leaf-peeping season, but many had already closed, their best days behind them for the year. Erica drove mindlessly, the trip itself more instinct than conscious thought. The sun was setting behind her. She pulled over when she neared Nate's cross.

Erica stared at the marshland to her right, the placid waters interrupted by bursts of grass and long dead trees. The sun glimmered a muddied reflection in the opaque waters. Her fear still lay within her, like a thorn embedded deep in her flesh, but it no longer sent out tendrils of pain throughout every waking moment. It returned here, like pressure on a wound, but it felt as though it was healing.

Her pager buzzed; a call from the office. Erica took it off her belt and threw it into the car.

She walked up to Nate's cross. Cars whizzed by on the highway only twelve feet away but Erica ignored them.

"Love you Nate," Erica said to the cross. She placed her hand on it gingerly. Part of her expected the sensation to be different, to feel charged with energy, but all she felt was warm painted wood. She rubbed the wood with her fingers for a moment then dropped her hand to her side.

"Miss you, buddy. I found the thing out there," Erica said, glancing again at the marshland to her right. "At this point, it probably doesn't even matter. I don't think we — I was out there with some friends — I don't think we made any bit of difference. All that running around, all that work, for nothing. The paper won't publish the story, our proof was taken, we don't even have a fucking photograph of it." She wiped at the tears forming in her eyes.

"Seems like a big waste. But it's gone. Whatever was happening here should end. I guess it won't be the Highway of Death any longer."

Erica stared at the cross.

"I hope that it wasn't the last thing you saw, Nate. If it was, at least it's gone now. But I hope you were thinking of something better when you left us."

CHAPTER FIFTY

When Will rose the third Saturday of September, the prior night's chill still lingered. As he sipped on a cup of coffee in the kitchen, he noted with surprise that a few dozen leaves littered the back lawn and the trees were tinged with bright reds and oranges. A slight breeze lifted a few leaves into the air where they danced for a moment, suspended a foot above the ground, like figure skaters in bright leotards twirling above the ice. Autumn always reminded Will of the seasons more sharply than any other time of year. Though each brought a change, it was only the burst of colors in the trees giving way to the gray shades of winter that made unmistakable the shift from one season to the next.

The back of his neck was sore from poor sleep and Will rubbed in with his left hand. Though he was sleeping better than at any time since he had seen the creature out by 101, questions remained, and those questions continued to interrupt his sleep. Whatever they had encountered in the swamp had changed him in some way. The world seemed a much larger place; if the swamp five miles from his shop could contain that creature, what else might the rest of it hold?

He still wasn't certain what exactly it was they had found, or if it was truly gone. But no matter the ultimate resolution, the uneasiness that had wormed inside of him weeks ago had disappeared. Though his sleep was still interrupted, he was now again rested after a long night in bed. The thing off the highway still emerged in his mind's eye, but it no longer devoured his other thoughts. The fear his father had described in his journal — a fear Will had never seen displayed but something Will had come to feel himself — was gone.

So, like most other Saturdays, he ate breakfast, dressed, and prepared for a morning of work at the shop. It should be easy, just few oil changes and tire rotations, simple stuff squeezed in for those customers who couldn't or didn't want to take time off during the week for routine maintenance.

Will enjoyed the ride into the shop. The leaves were changing all across town. The peak of Mount Majassic to the west was likewise splashed with oranges, reds, and yellows. Will knew the colors would spread and ferment through the fall season into a vibrant canvas before the last winds of fall would strip the trees bare.

When he arrived at the shop, a red Ford Taurus and a blue Chevrolet S-10 sat out front, two drop offs over the weekend. Perhaps not enough to justify the costs of opening on a Saturday. A gamble Will had taken and lost this week, though the Saturday before had resulted in more than a day's work and confirmed Will's hunch that having Corey around some days would be a big help.

He opened the bay doors and turned on the air compressor before looking at the two drop off envelopes for the Taurus and S-10. Corey and Robert arrived a few minutes later, Corey by foot, Robert by motorcycle. Robert would continue to ride so as long as the weather held.

Traffic was light that morning, and Will heard Erica's car rounding the circle before he saw it. He wasn't sure if he could tell by the sound of the engine, or if there was something he could sense, but he knew it was her. Will set down the pen in his hand, grabbed the nearest rag, wiped his hands in a few quick motions, and exited the office.

He found her already out of her car, walking towards the shop, her hair pulled back in a ponytail and tattered gray t-shirt tucked into her jeans.

"Hi, Will," Erica said.

"Hey," he responded, wanting to say more, but unsure what the right words would be.

Will saw that the back of Erica's Taurus was filled with tan cardboard boxes and unruly splashes of reds, blues, and greens he identified as clothing. "You moving?" he asked.

The moments it took Erica to decide what to say next only took a few seconds but felt much longer to her. It was like she neither heard nor saw anything while she considered the question, though she already knew the answer. Instead, she felt her pulse in her ears and a weight in her stomach, as if all her organs were pulling together and reaching a critical mass.

"Yes, down to Boston. I've got a great offer to work at the *Globe*."

"Good, good for you," Will said.

"What about..." Will began.

"I'll keep an eye on the news. I know what to look for. I'm sure it's gone. But if it comes back, I'll know it."

"OK." Will stood there, hands on his hips, simply enjoying their closeness.

"Well, I wanted to say goodbye, but not goodbye, I'm sure I will see you again soon. I just wanted to let you know that I'm leaving."

"Thanks," Will said. "I mean, thanks for coming by. Not for leaving. I..." he was not sure what to say. The time they had spent together over the last few months had rekindled some of what they had shared a decade ago. But it was tenuous, not fully formed, the boundaries and meaning unclear to both. He felt strongly towards her, and she towards him, but all of the words he could think of didn't seem right. They had seen things he had never expected, had relied upon each other for much, but as well as they knew each other, in so many ways they were both strangers.

Will settled on, "I'll miss you."

"Me too," she answered. Her smile only half-appeared. She caught his eyes for a moment but neither held the other's gaze. Both looked away and clasped their hands.

"Be sure to stay in touch," Will said.

"I will," she answered. She said it again to emphasize the point, "I will."

Will said, "Good. Let me get Corey. You should say goodbye to him too."

Erica raised her eyebrows. "He's here?"

"Yeah, he's giving me a hand. Picking up quite a bit from Robert."

"Good, that's good," Erica said. "I'm not sure what to tell him."

"Tell him what you told me," Will began as he walked back towards the office, "He'll understand."

Erica waited a few feet from the door to the office. Part of her wanted to walk inside, but she didn't. It didn't feel right. She wasn't here for service. Entering the office would have been another commitment here, would have felt like delaying; she was on the road to Boston and needed to stick to her schedule, even if she did indulge in this short detour.

The bell above the door jingled and Corey burst forth from the shop. "Erica!" he yelled. He bore the mark of the mechanic: a fat strip of grease ran across his forehead where he had rubbed it with the back of his hand. He ran towards Erica with his arms wide open. She glanced at his hands and saw those too were dark with dirt or oil, and hesitated for just a moment before opening her arms and wrapping them around Corey.

"Hi," she said, unable to hold back a smile. "How are you, kid?"

Corey gave her one more squeeze then stepped back. "Great! Will and Robert are teaching me all about cars. I'm helping them work on a Chevy right now. We have to change the brakes and look at the suspension."

The doorbell jingled and Will walked out to join them. He stood a few feet back from them, to allow Erica and Corey time to say their goodbyes.

Corey looked over his shoulder, and finding only Will behind him said, "Did your friend test the stuff we found? You know, the skin."

"Did you tell him?" Erica asked Will.

Will grimaced, looked down, and shook his head.

"Tell me what?" Corey glanced at Will and Erica. "Tell me what?"

Erica sighed. "Well, when we returned to Will's house, a police officer and an Air Force officer were waiting for us there. They took it, Corey. They took the piece of the thing you grabbed."

"What? Did you guys do anything?"

"We couldn't," Erica said and shrugged. "There was nothing we could do. Will searched the bog next day with me. We couldn't find any trace of it."

"Wow. That means we don't have anything! We don't have any proof!" Corey yelled.

"We do," Erica said. "We do. We all saw it. That's the proof we have. We know it's out there. You, me, and Will."

"Some others too," Will added. "Some other people in town have seen it too."

Corey nodded. "I guess. Just sucks, you know?"

Erica and Will laughed. "Yes, it sucks," Erica said.

"Well, are we going to get to work on your car?" Corey asked.

"No," Erica said. "Well, not right now at least." She pointed back over her shoulder towards her Taurus. "I'm all packed up actually. I'm moving down to Boston, I've got a new job down there."

"Oh," Corey said. "Really?" He took one step backwards and the warmth that had appeared in his chest at the sight of Erica dissipated into a hollow, throat tightening and his stomach dropping into his gut. He pushed thoughts of his mother out of his head. Erica was leaving, and whatever bond the three had forged over the last month would not continue. Perhaps it never could, even if she had stayed. They had come together, faced whatever it was that was in the bog, and could move on now.

"What if it comes back?" Corey asked.

"I don't think it will. Do you?"

"No," Corey said.

"But if it does, I'll know," Erica added. "You'll know. We'll keep an eye out, both of us, Will too, OK?" Will nodded.

"OK," Corey said. Speaking was difficult; the words seemed to struggle to squeeze out his clenched throat.

He looked back to Erica. "What is it? Your new job?"

"I'll be working for a paper down there. *The Boston Globe*. It's a great opportunity. Bigger circulation, more exposure. It will be a good change."

"But you won't be far, right? You'll come to visit?"

"Of course," she said. "I'll be up often. I've still got family up here you know, my parents."

"Will I get to read your stories in the newspaper?" Corey asked.

"Yes," Erica said, and looked up to Will. He nodded to her and smiled. "I think Will might buy that paper, and you two could read my stories together. I'd like that, knowing that you two were reading what I wrote."

"Please be careful," Corey said. The syllables seemed too small, too short to contain all that he wished to convey and the friendship he felt with her.

Erica stepped forward, hugged him again, and squeezed shut her eyes to force back the tears forming, surprised at her own vulnerability in this moment and the feelings she had for Corey.

"I'll be careful. I promise," she whispered into his ear.

As Corey stepped back Erica wiped at the corners of her eyes quickly, then rubbed her hands on her jeans.

"I'll see you around," she said.

"Yep," said Will.

Will and Corey watched as Erica pulled her vehicle out of the parking lot and into the circle. She slowed briefly, looked back to them and waved. Will raised his hand and Corey smiled and waved back. They stood like this for a few seconds, transfixed, as if by their stillness they could lengthen the moment and forestall the goodbye, the feeling of loss that would approach in her wake. Both knew they would see her again. Erica had family here, and she would only be an hour or so away. But the distance would be a wedge that would drive them further apart. The summer was over, and with it the events that drew them all together would only move further away in time.

As Erica's Taurus exited the circle on the far side and disappeared from sight, both Corey and Alex dropped their arms and began walking back towards the office, heads slightly bowed.

Corey turned to Will, looked up at him and asked, "What's next?"

Will thought for a moment, shrugged his shoulders, then answered.

"Whatever rolls into the shop."

ACKNOWLEDGMENTS

As with any venture, a novel takes the efforts of many.

Thanks goes out to the Weare Area Writers Group, who read initial drafts and made many solid recommendations for revisions. In particular, thanks to Ellen Reed, Kevin Lane, and Sharon Czarnecki, This book is without question stronger and better for the time you spent reading and providing criticism.

Thank you to David Ross and Lindsey Hilliard for your assistance with the cover. I think it looks fantastic, and I'm betting others do too.

Special thanks to my family, both by blood and marriage, all those who read the drafts and provided feedback. Lastly, and most importantly, thanks to my wife, for putting up the drafts and re-writes and questions and pleas for help across the many months this took.

ABOUT THE AUTHOR

JS MacEachern is a writer and attorney living in southern New Hampshire. He loves to read as much as he loves to write, especially in the genres of horror, speculative fiction, and science fiction. When he's not reading or writing or working, you'll usually find him fishing, practicing archery, and building LEGOs with his wife and children. You can find out more about JS and his upcoming releases at *www.jsmaceachern.com*.

Made in USA - North Chelmsford, MA
13132_9781737811510
10.04.2023 1437